GUARDIAN I
THE SURRENDER

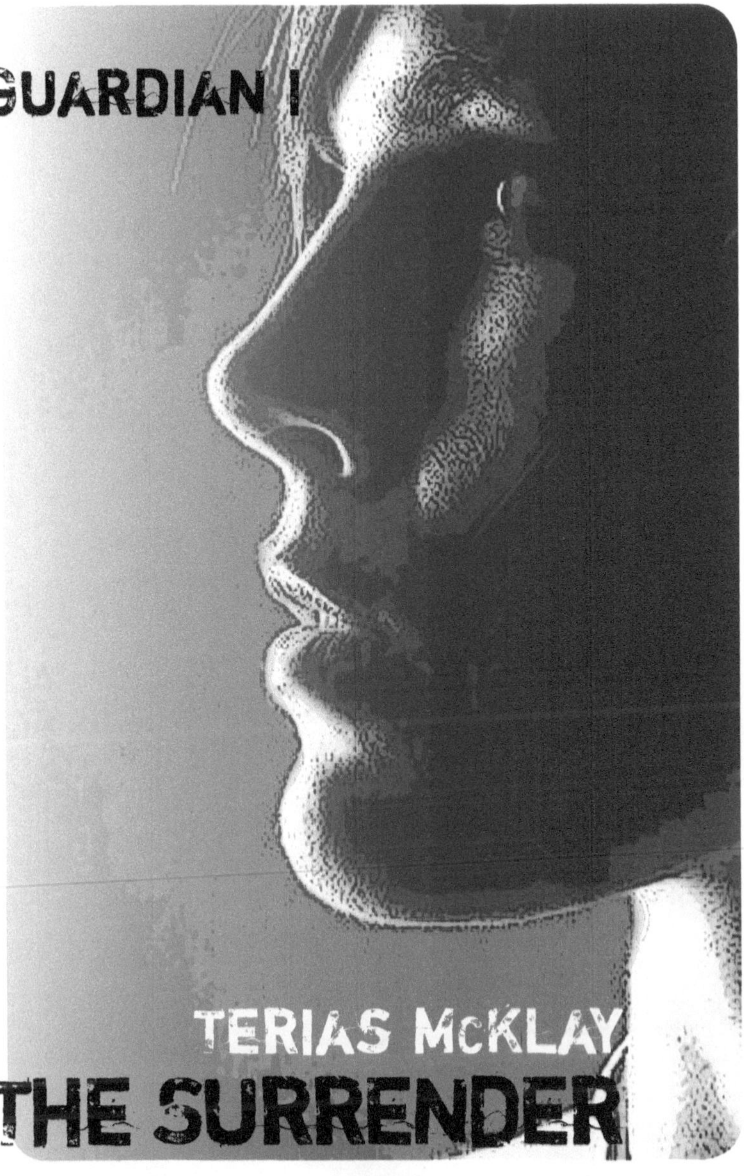

GUARDIAN I

TERIAS McKLAY

THE SURRENDER

Bink Books
Bedazzled Ink Publishing Company • Fairfield, California

978-1-939562-64-7 paperback
978-1-939562-65-4 ebook

Cover Design
by

TreeHouseStudio

BInk
a division of
Bedazzled Ink Publishing Company
Fairfield, California
http://mindancerpress.bedazzledink.com

J.G. Who didn't take the first rough hewn, dung covered copy of this manuscript and fling it back at me.
and
A.M. Who hasn't buried me under the pile of dirty laundry that goes undone while I write until the wee hours.
and
C.P. Who has pulled, prodded and nagged me over many a finish line.

CHAPTER 1

ALL HER NIGHTMARES were the same. Different scenarios. Different characters. But when she tore the meat away and got to the bones, they were all the same.

Blood.

There was always blood.

Sometimes the rivers ran red with it, pouring into oceans of dark crimson. Other times there was no sight of blood, only the gagging stench wafting into her nostrils. Tonight, her mind was kind enough to allow her to taste it. Fat drops of thick liquid chased one another, warming tanned skin as they trailed towards the corner of her mouth. She wiped the offending drips away, her mind recoiling at the tang of liquid copper as it hit her tongue.

She hated the taste of blood.

It wasn't a demure hate. It was a strong, virulent hatred. It was the type of hatred that put her teeth on edge.

Running.

There was always running.

Tonight she didn't know what she was running from. It was almost a nice break from the usual monotony of never-ending bad guys, guilt trips from dead loved ones, and the occasional failed final exam.

Fear.

There most certainly was always fear.

Fear for her friends and family, for herself. It wasn't a vague fear. It wasn't a fear comprised of what-ifs. It was a fear built upon a foundation of terrible experience. A fear born from losing the one thing she had thought meant the most, only to discover she still had so much more to lose.

No. Tonight's nightmare was no different than any other night. The flesh of it had altered a little, but the skeleton was the same. There was blood. There was running. And there was Mariska, scared shitless.

Rivulets of sweat mixed with blood as it trailed down her

temple, along the sculpted line of her ear, across the crevices of a strong jaw, inching towards full lips. She brushed it away. Pumping her arms, she ran as fast as her long legs allowed. Her boots beat a quick, steady cadence as she pelted across an open playground.

She couldn't slow down. She wasn't sure why. Nothing made sense. Not the who. Not the why. Not the where. Especially not the where. The buildings, the people around her, were achingly familiar and yet wholly alien at the same time. The sole, undeniable truth amidst the confusion of her thoughts was that she couldn't stop.

The fog that had clouded her perception lifted, clearing the vision in her mind's eye.

Tall buildings. Dark shadows.

The stench of garbage and human filth was almost comforting in its familiarity. Rather, it would be, if it didn't make her want to heave the remnants of her last meal onto the cement.

An alley. Of course.

"Where else would I be?" Nothing quite like spending your every waking, and apparently sleeping, moment in the company of the dregs of society.

The quiet snap of a silenced bullet broke her from her thoughts as she ran. The hiss of lead was nearly simultaneous with the projectile's impact, sending white hot shards of pain streaking through her shoulder. She cried out, stumbling, one blue leather-clad knee smashing against the rough cement before she made her way back to her feet.

She had to keep running.

"Why am I the only moron in this city without a gun?" She didn't even know where the shot had come from. Was she running towards the gunmen or away? She was in a dark stairwell now. "How?"

She couldn't stop.

Up was the only way. She ran blindly up the stairs, cradling her damaged arm to her chest.

A door.

A way out.

She drove her foot into the metal latch, launching the door open. She sucked in a breath as every muscle in her body protested. She couldn't fight. She had to keep going.

The wind on the rooftop whipped mercilessly at her, knifing through the Lycra of her outfit with ease. The chill gusts did nothing to ease the pain of her wounds. If anything, it whipped her into further frenzy as she investigated the roof. Where the hell was she?

"Mariska!"

She turned at the sound of her name. Panic gripped her chest as her mind registered the voice, one as familiar as her own.

Lisa.

Lisa on a ledge.

"Lisa!" Her lover stood at the precipice. The wind blew, harsh and cold, driving rain into her eyes, obscuring her vision. It tore at the tattered remnants of Lisa's clothing, blue leather whipping in the wind, threatening to pull Lisa into the abyss. She held out a hand, deep trust shining in her blue eyes.

Mariska put on what little speed she had left and sprinted for the ledge, arm outstretched.

Running, there was always running.

She was almost there.

She couldn't stop running. Could. Not. Stop.

Fingers brushed, light enough to be more imagination than actual contact. She didn't care, just a little more. She could stop all this. Stop the nightmares. Fix the reality. Get her life back.

Mariska's fingers, slick with her own life blood slid along Lisa's, unable to find purchase.

Blood, there was always blood.

Mariska watched as Lisa slipped from her. Gray eyes locked onto terrified blue, in a moment that seemed without end, as Lisa's body went over the edge.

Fear, there was always fear.

"No!" She could make it right, she could fix it. Ignoring all—the panic, the gagging taste of blood, the wind rushing in her ears—she dove into oblivion.

Mariska landed with an undignified thud, head and hip slamming on the cold hardwood floor. She groaned low in her throat and opened her eyes to stare up at the yellowing ceiling of her apartment. In her sleep-induced fugue, the wail of noise in her ears sent her mood spiraling downward as she searched for its source. She was somewhat relieved when her brain identified the ear-piercing sound—not unlike that of a Klaxon horn—was her alarm clock rather than the ringing of a concussion.

"Christ, I'm up already," she muttered as she groggily reached along the floor for the cord and tugged.

She winced as the clock bounced off her forehead, still shrieking loudly. Somewhere in her sleep-addled brain pulling on the cord had seemed like a good idea. She hit the snooze button and tossed the alarm to the side, then inspected the damage to her forehead with her fingers. Nothing bleeding. That was a plus at least.

She lay back on the floor, the hardwood cool against her head, and tried to recapture the dream. She was too far awake for that now. She had lost the dream, whatever it was, and was left with was a vague sense of unease and frustration. Not that that was anything new.

Mariska pushed herself to her feet and ran her hands through her shoulder-length chestnut hair. Her body operated on auto-pilot as she stumbled towards the kitchen to make her coffee. She opened the cupboard with a yawn and reached blindly for the jar of insta-coffee, only to come up empty handed. Narrowing her eyes, she looked at her recycling bin where the empty jar mocked her. She took a deep breath. Mornings weren't her thing on the best of days.

She closed the cupboard with a little more force than was necessary and made her way to the washroom. She turned the shower tap on to warm the water. She stripped out of her pj's, hopped in the shower, and shrieked at the icy daggers that pelted her bare skin.

"Motherfu—" She twisted the tap violently and grabbed a towel from the rod. She took a deep breath, looked in the mirror, and saw the post-it note taped to it. She peeled it off and crumpled it in her soggy hands. *August 17th, water tank servicing, no hot water*. Of course. "Oh ho, it's going to be a beautiful day."

She gazed at her five-foot-nine reflection, trying to determine the best way to tame her hair, which was now standing up every which way, exposing a lean neck and clean jaw. Steel gray eyes were red-rimmed. Another consequence of too many late nights with too little recovery time. Her nose, once straight, now had the charming trait of looking like it had been broken and never set properly. Which was exactly what had happened. Numerous times. At twenty-two, her face had lost the soft look that her mother and aunts had been so fond of. She'd worked on creating a lean body over the years, bringing her weight down to help increase her agility. Small scars littered tanned skin, remnants of fights both won and lost. They were easily concealable under a thin layer of foundation but when she went natural the imperfections gave her face a distinctly more . . . rugged look.

Mariska didn't find herself unattractive by any stretch. The changes gave her body character, if nothing else. She still cleaned up well enough to keep her family from worrying, and it wasn't as though she had a girlfriend to impress. Her throat tightened at the thought, a snippet from her nightmare coming to the surface.

Lisa. Again.

"Christ, Cooper, it's been over a year." She looked at her haunted reflection and shook her head, shrugging off the morose thoughts. She needed to get moving. She decided on the ever-trusty ponytail to quell the dark mass atop her head and pulled her hair back.

Mariska nodded at her reflection in the mirror, then headed into her bedroom. She tossed her towel to the side and pulled an outfit for the day from the closet. She needed to be in Scarborough at eight for her doctor's appointment, then back down at the University of Toronto campus for her midterm by ten. Not exactly the ideal way to spend her morning—especially given the way the morning started.

She was dressed and on her way with time to spare, her textbook-laden backpack slung over her shoulders. The early morning sun glinted off the cars as she walked towards the subway. It looked to be another beautiful day in the city. Her cell phone rang as she walked and she flipped it open, unsurprised to find Lucas's number on the call display.

"Morning," she greeted, pausing at a magazine rack to pick up a copy of the daily newspaper.

"Morning, Sunshine," Lucas said, his voice full of forced cheer. His loathing for mornings paralleled her own. "Wake up call."

"Thanks. I'm already up and on my way."

"You? Up early? I think the world just reversed its rotation."

"Hardy har, your faith in me is overwhelming," she said as she stopped at the subway entrance.

"I'm just saying—"

"Yeah, yeah. Need I remind you which of us slept through their English diploma exam?" There was dead air on the line. "That's what I thought." She thought she heard a disgruntled "whatever."

"Anyway, say hi to Dr. Acco for me and good luck on your midterm."

"Thanks. Try not to be late for work, for once. I'll talk to you later." She snapped the phone closed and flashed her Metropass at the toll booth operator before heading down the steps to track level. It was rush hour, so the subway train was quick to arrive. It was also packed to the brim. She took a deep breath. She didn't do cramped quarters well.

She squished in with the rest of the commuters and flipped open her newspaper, searching for one article in particular. She found it at the back of the local news section and squinted to read the small article in even smaller print.

"Guardian Thwarts Deli Store Robbery."

It wasn't exactly a front page headline but it was always nice to be acknowledged for her work.

She spent the rest of her commute to Scarborough nose deep in her crossword. The train emptied considerably as they hit the North/South interchanges. As she stepped out at Victoria Park station, she no longer felt she was in danger of being trampled.

She walked ten minutes to the clinic and waited inside for Dr. Acco to come fetch her. She had moved out of this section of the Greater Toronto Area when she had started university, abandoning her childhood haunts for the trendiness of the west end. Her parents still lived in the area and, with the current difficulties of finding a decent family doctor, she'd elected to stay with her old one.

"Miss Cooper?"

Mariska looked up to see Dr. Acco smiling at her with a file in his hands.

"Morning, Dr. Acco."

They walked into his examination room, and Mariska closed the door behind them.

"And how's my favourite superhero this morning?" Dr. Acco asked.

Mariska rolled her eyes, dropping her backpack onto the

floor. That was another reason, perhaps the main one, she hadn't changed doctors. He had known her since childhood and was one of the few people who knew the face behind Guardian.

Early into her career, she had shown up at his home one night with her shoulder dislocated, unable to seek care from the hospital for fear of her identity being discovered. Given how many times he'd patched her up since then, he now had a more intimate knowledge of her body than she'd ever intended a sixty-year-old man to have.

"Mariska?"

"Hmm, sorry, spaced out." She hopped up on the medical bed. "I've been pretty good. My economics class is murder."

"Have you ever thought of doing the Police and Security course at one of the colleges? Humber or Sheridan maybe?" he asked as he put the blood pressure cuff on her arm.

He was always trying to nudge her towards a more legitimate crime-fighting career. It wasn't that Mariska didn't respect the police, but their hands were tied with bureaucracy that seemed to be geared more to protecting the criminal than helping the victim. She just couldn't abide by that.

"You want to throw a vigilante in with a bunch of overzealous kids who want to be cops? Surely you jest, Doc."

He didn't respond, his attention occupied by the ticking of Mariska's heart. "Blood pressure is good. How have your headaches been?" he asked as he pulled the stethoscope from his ears.

"Good, only get them once in a while. I lost a little bit of time awareness though. I mix up the order stuff happens in."

"Multiple concussions will do that to you."

"Well, next time I'll make sure and ask the bad guys to come quietly before I throw myself into a brawl."

"I'm serious, Mariska. There's a limit to how much a body can take, and you just keep trying to test yours. Whether you're twenty-two or my age, you keep getting hit like that, you could end up with—"

"Memory loss, retinal detachment, permanent ringing in my ears. I know, Doc. You've been reading me the same riot act for the last four years."

"Maybe one of these days you'll actually hear me," he said,

staring into her eyes to convey the gravity of his words. "You're not invincible. Just look at what happened to Lisa, she—"

"Isn't up for discussion," Mariska said. "Please," she added in a gentler tone.

Seeming to sense he was at the limit of her good graces, he nodded and quietly continued with his examination. "You seem to be in good health, all things considered. I wish you hadn't taken those stitches out yourself." He pointed to the faint scar on her arm, courtesy of a broken beer bottle and its drunken wielder.

Mariska shrugged and slid off the medical bed. "I didn't, Lucas did."

He shook his head and produced a purple lollipop from his lab coat pocket. "Be careful out there." He handed her the candy.

She smiled, gave him a quick kiss on the cheek, then picked up her backpack and headed out of the office.

She paused at the bus stop, her gaze falling on the graffiti tags littering the glass shelter. She looked up from her inspection of the eyesore on the bench as the bus pulled up in front of her. The bus was crammed with passengers already. After allowing the others waiting at the stop to get on first, she decided it would be less hassle to just walk the ten minutes to the subway station. Her cell rang as she walked, and she fished it out of her pocket as she zoned in on the fresh fruit stand across the alley.

"Hey, what's up?" she asked Lucas as she stepped across the side street. She flipped the bird to a disgruntled driver who had been trying to make an illegal turn off Main Street, his speeding car missing her by inches. "Where'd you learn to drive? Asshole!"

"You're such a classy lady," Lucas said.

Mariska traded a dollar for a mango at the fruit stand and headed for the Victoria Park subway. "Don't make me kung fu you." She tucked the mango into her bag for later. She brushed some hair back from her face. Even at nine a.m. the humidity of a Toronto summer morning was near unbearable. The spandex vest under her t-shirt didn't help either.

"Pssh, like you could. Anyway, we have a problem."

Mariska checked her watch. "How big a problem? My midterm is in forty-five minutes." She turned off Main Street and walked north towards the subway station.

"Bomb threat on a subway train," Lucas said. "Police got an

anonymous tip that the good detective Perkins was kind enough to pass on to us."

"How kind of her," Mariska said. "Where's the train now?"

"Coming down your way. You've got maybe a minute and a half."

"Damn." Mariska closed the phone, shoved it into her pocket, and sprinted for the subway. She maneuvered between two pedestrians, calling out "sorry" as she spun around the steps, taking them two and three at a time. She flipped her Metropass to the toll booth guy then vaulted over the gate, only to realize for a heart-stopping moment that she didn't know which train the bomb was on. Lucas, ever the picture of preparedness, was already ringing her phone again.

"Westbound, car 1519."

Mariska bounded up the steps of the escalator and reached the top just as she glimpsed the train heading towards her in the tunnel. "One of these days I'm going to ask how you get all this crap done before you go to work in the morning. It's not slowing down."

"There's a virus in the subway control system. I'm trying to get in but the train control program is locked down. It's not going to stop!" Lucas said. Furious typing was audible in the background. "I'm trying to hack in and give control back to the transit system, but you're going to have to get yourself on that train."

Mariska closed the phone and tucked it into her pocket. She looked around the platform, noticing the dozen or so people scattered around. Everyone was focused on the oncoming trains. Perfect. She unslung her backpack and pulled her mask out, a spandex face mask that concealed her from the bridge of her nose down. She tugged the mask into place and grabbed three shurikans from the front pouch of her bag. Hopefully the small throwing stars would be enough to get the job done. They had done well enough for the samurai of old.

"This is such a bad idea," she muttered as she watched the front of the train rush by. It wasn't going full speed but it was fast enough to mess up her day if she miscalculated.

She threw the first star. It skipped harmlessly off the rearmost car. She let loose the other two. They lodged solidly in the metal plating but not shattering the window as she hoped.

"Damn damn damn."

The car was nearly at her now and picking up speed. She picked up her backpack, at least twenty pounds of textbook goodness.

She launched her backpack at the window of the last car, shattering the weakened glass to give herself a way in. She sprinted after the departing train, long legs eating up the distance. She took hold of the edge of the window and hauled herself into the car just as the train cleared the platform. She landed shoulder first on the metal seats, then rolled to the floor. Wincing, she stood and looked at the bewildered occupants.

"Um . . . I hate taking the bus?" She shrugged at an older man who was staring at her. She cleared her throat, picked up her backpack, and headed for the front of the car.

Mariska stepped in between the cars, ripping her shirt from her body and letting it fly in the wind as the train picked up speed. She had on her blue spandex vest—one of the earliest incarnations of her Guardian gear. Unlike her new Kevlar and leather suit, it was easily concealable beneath her clothes for the occasional daytime crisis. She tugged on the snaps at the base of her neck, unfurled a large hood, and pulled over her head. The top half of her face was concealed beneath the shadows of the hood as she opened the door to the next subway car and walked in. All eyes turned to her, some in recognition, others discarding her as simply one of the numerous oddly dressed people in the city.

Mariska pulled her sunglasses from the side of her backpack and put them on—the yellow tint of the lenses bringing a certain crispness to her vision. She placed the ear bud in her ear as she walked and turned on the video feed, nodding at passengers who cleared the way for her.

"I'm online," she said, the video transmitter also acting as an audio transmitter, giving Lucas a real time account of what was going on around her.

"Yeah, I've got you," Lucas said. "Are you in 1519?"

"Calm yourself, I'm nearly there." She opened a second door and crossed over into the next car. "Any information on who we're dealing with?"

She lightly shook the hand of a little girl who reached out to her as she passed. The toddler gave a shrill giggle at the contact, and Mariska smiled. She liked kids.

"No clue, the tip came in anonymously to the PD," Lucas

said. "Sorry about the short notice. We're just lucky you had your appointment with the Doc this morning."

"I'm trapped on a train with a bomb," Mariska said in a low voice so she wouldn't alarm the other passengers. "What kind of mental definition of 'lucky' is that?"

Lucas snorted.

"Yeah, 'cause that was mature."

"Whoever is doing this is going for maximum effect," Lucas said. "The viral program has the train scheduled to stop at Bloor and Yonge. If the bomb goes off in that station . . ."

"I know." The casualties would be catastrophic. The station was one of the busiest interchanges on the line, and it was peak operating period. Someone definitely wanted some attention. "We need to minimize damage. If this goes bad, you can't let the train make it that far along the line."

"I know. I'm working on stopping the train. The police are evacuating the stations as quickly as possible. You just worry about the bomb."

"Well, jeez, don't you have something hard for me to do?"

"Focus."

Mariska blew out a breath, looked into car 1519, and saw two armed men flanking what she presumed was the bomb.

"Two men?" Lucas sounded incredulous. "Amateurs."

Mariska scanned the other occupants of the car and focused on a man with a hand concealed beneath a newspaper and another who was much too calm. He was either an emotional dunce or a co-conspirator.

"Focus. Besides, I count four." Mariska pulled out two shurikans from her vest pocket. "Ah, jeez," she muttered as she caught sight of the wrist leashes that held a string of kids together.

"What?"

"I've got a lot of preschoolers on this train, Big Brother. I think it's some kind of field trip or something." She shifted to get a better view. "There's got to be at least twenty-five kids in car 1519."

"Dammit."

"They're not handling our resident villains very well."

One boy, nearly purple in the face, was screaming at one of his caretakers. The woman was busily trying to hush him, fear written across her face. One of the gunmen moved towards the boy.

"Be careful," Lucas said.

"Copy that." Mariska opened the doors to car 1519.

The men turned and aimed their guns at her.

She let loose the shurikans. One knocked a gun to the ground and the other sank deep in the other gunman's hand. She ran for the pistol and kicked it away as the man reached for it. In one fluid motion, she grabbed him by the back of his collar and drove her knee up into his chin, snapping his head back. He landed in a boneless heap.

Mariska dropped her heavily booted heel onto the other man's wrist, forcing the gun muzzle down and away from the passengers. She let her momentum carry her forward, her elbow driving into his temple and putting him down for the count.

"Guardian, look out!"

Mariska turned. The man with a newspaper was raising a pistol. He fired, and Mariska grunted as the bullet skimmed her bicep, shattering the glass of a nearby window. Growling, she grabbed the bar overhead, picked up her legs, and drove her feet into his head. He landed with a hollow thud on the floor.

Mariska landed and winced at a solid punch to her kidney. She dropped into a near-split and drove her fist upward into the man's groin. He howled and doubled over. Mariska swung her legs around and drove the toe of her boot into his temple. He landed with a thud, and Mariska pushed herself to her feet.

"Fun part's over." She stared at the large device at her feet. "What the fuck do I do with this?"

An LCD screen came to life and the timer on the bomb began to count down.

"I have to get these people out of here. Tell me you've got a way to stop this train." She turned to the kids.

Many were screaming and calling out for their mothers as their caregivers tried to comfort them.

"I'm trying," Lucas said. "The damn TTC servers keep kicking me out."

Mariska didn't like the frustration in his voice. "If you can't stop the train, stop the bomb."

"I can't." His voice cracked. "The station you passed must have had some sort of trigger. I can't access the bomb remotely. You're going to have to do it manually."

Mariska touched her finger to the auto adjust on the camera, hoping to clear up the view for Lucas. "And I suppose you're going to be able to tell me which of this rats' nest of wires I should cut?"

"Uhh, I suppose eenie meenie minie moe isn't what you're looking for?"

Mariska looked at the LCD, the angry red numbers ticking downward much too quickly for her liking. "Not really, no."

She walked around the bomb to give Lucas a full view of it. They had dealt with bombs before, but each one was different and every psycho had his quirks.

"I'm looking for similar bomb schematics but I can't seem to get a fix on any. It looks like a hodgepodge of designs. Touching the damn thing could set it off."

"Thanks, that's exactly what I need to hear." She wiped the sweat from her brow. She looked around the car, then closed her eyes for a moment and put her hand to her head. This was bad. Very bad.

The kids were fussing, not understanding the commotion as their teachers tried to keep them in control. She could see the terror in the eyes of everyone in the car. Between the gunshots and the threat of an imminent *kaboom*, she could certainly understand why. Hell, she was used to this and she could feel the panic edging at her mind. If Lucas didn't move his ass, they were just over a minute away from becoming a tragic headline.

"I'm trying to locate the manual override."

"Try harder." Mariska scanned the outside of the car for a way to get the bomb off the train without splattering them all over the tunnel. "One minute." She approached a door. She pulled her knife from her boot, slid it between the doors, and wedged them open. She pulled the doors apart, willing herself not to look down or consider how very fast they were going, or how quickly her life would end if she miscalculated her balance and fell. Satisfied the doors would remain open, she returned to the ticking bomb.

"Can you at least tell me if this thing will blow if I try to move it?" Mariska asked.

"Wait one."

"I don't have 'one'!" She dropped to the ground and felt around it. Not bolted to the floor. No trip wires, no bolts, and no time to second guess. "Fuck it, I'm moving it."

She stood and took hold of the handles on either side and

heaved. Every muscle in her body screamed. She didn't have enough strength to move it on her own.

"You." She pointed at the closest, burliest man. "Come here." He blinked at her startled and rushed to her.

"Help me." Mariska looked down at the timer.

Thirty-five seconds.

They grabbed a handle and muscled the bomb to the door.

Twenty-five seconds.

She could make out the light at the end of the tunnel. They weren't far from the bridge that would take them over the nature reserve. The first car of the train cleared the tunnel. She nodded and they picked up their ends of the bomb and held it as high as her over-taxed muscles allowed.

Fifteen seconds.

Car 1519 cleared the tunnel. Mariska poked her head out the door and prayed they were moving fast enough to clear the bridge's railings.

Ten seconds.

"On three." She swung the bomb back. "One." Forward. "Two." Backwards. "Three!"

The bomb sailed between a set of posts and cleared the main girder. It clipped the edge of a support beam and spun wildly as it fell.

"Get down!" Mariska pushed the man to the floor and covered him with her body as a thunderous boom echoed through the car.

Shattered glass pelted her and the train rocked and hung to one side for a single heart-in-throat moment then settled back into its track. Even at a distance, Mariska could feel the scorching heat through her jeans.

She pushed herself to her feet and brushed the glass pellets from her shoulders. The other occupants seemed bruised and shaken but all right overall. She breathed a sigh of relief.

"Well, that's one way to do it," Lucas said. His tone was sarcastic, but she knew he was as relieved as she was.

"I didn't see you coming up with anything better," Mariska said as she helped a little boy to his feet. She knelt beside him and brushed the tears from his dark cheeks. "You're okay, buddy."

He wrapped small arms around her neck and squeezed. Mariska smiled as he nestled his head into her shoulder. She rubbed his back gently and nodded at the woman who held her arms out for him. She released him to his caretaker who took his hand and led him back to his class. He looked back at her, cherubic face beaming, and she gave him a wave.

"Cute kid, you're good with them," Lucas said.

"Don't tell my family that. I'll end up knee deep in babysitting jobs."

"I'm into the control program now. I'm going to stop the train."

"Wonderful," she said as she checked on the unconscious culprits of the debacle and then handcuffed three of them to the subway poles.

The last man managed to get up and hauled ass to the back of the train car.

"He's getting away," Lucas said.

"Thank you. Your powers of observation are overwhelming." Mariska sprinted after the would-be bomber, dodging the stunned passengers of the crowded train as they rushed from car to car. She put out a hand to grasp the back of his collar. He swung a woman around in front of Mariska, knocking them both to the ground. Mariska twisted to land on the bottom and cushioned the woman's fall with her body.

"You okay?" Mariska asked.

The woman stared at her stunned, but gave a quick nod.

Mariska pulled out from beneath her and kept running. The man wasn't in the next car. Mariska felt the train slow as they pulled into a station. She would lose him in the rush hour crowd if he made it out of the doors.

"I need you to keep those doors closed!"

"Can't. The security system threw me out again. It'll take thirty seconds to get back in."

"Shit."

She ran into the next car and saw the man. Mariska ducked to the side and pulled hard on the emergency stop. The train wheels screamed against the track as they halted. She gazed out the window. Looked like the train was half in the tunnel and half in the station.

The man crashed into the side and slowly picked himself up as Mariska approached. Disoriented, he blinked at her as she smirked at the large gash across his forehead. She grabbed his wrists and cuffed them around a pole.

"You know, it's unlawful for anyone but transit personnel to move between cars when the train is in motion. I'm afraid you'll have to be taken into custody."

He sneered at her, and Mariska gave him a small salute, went to the back of the train, and slid out of the car into the tunnel.

"I need a way out," she said, scanning the darkness for an easy way to get topside.

"G . . . S . . . indi . . . tunn . . ."

Mariska frowned. Some sections of the tunnel were better than others for getting a signal. Figures they would pull in to where she couldn't get a read. She grabbed the flashlight from her backpack, clicked it on, and searched for a maintenance door to get out of the tunnel before the transit workers or worse, the Toronto police, figured out she'd been on the train.

It wasn't that her relationship with local law enforcement was adversarial, just that bringing in the outlaw vigilante Guardian was a quick route to a promotion.

Mariska continued down the tunnel, her bright light sweeping across the area. She let out a sigh of relief at a maintenance ladder that looked like it would take her to the surface. She tucked her flashlight into her vest and climbed the ladder. Behind her, she heard the transit Special Constables as they pushed their way to the back of the train. She turned off her flashlight, then climbed to the manhole cover. She hunched over and used her shoulder to push the cover up and off.

Mariska did a quick check around the dark alley for witnesses before pulling herself out and dusting off her pants. Even in the bright sunshine of a summer morning, the alley was cast in shadow. Such was the consequence of too tall buildings put too closely together she supposed. Life in the big city.

"Got me?" she asked over the radio as she tugged the manhole cover back into place.

"I read you," Lucas said, his voice loud and clear.

"Time check, please," Mariska said as she pulled the backpack from her shoulders and tugged the hood back from her face. She rolled the hood under the snaps and took an extra shirt out of her bag.

For her usual night patrols, she wore more durable leather gear over her Kevlar vest. The spandex outfit was for the impromptu daily events that seemed to be popping up more frequently. It had been dicey when the men pulled their guns on the train. Her reputation and bravado did little to shield her against bullets. Thankfully, her quick reflexes and bad aim on the perp's part had saved her from anything beyond the small nick on her arm.

"Time is 0923," Lucas said.

"Shit! Midterm's in half an hour." Mariska slung her backpack onto her shoulders. She gave herself a once-over—a mess, as usual. Her boots had survived the encounter but her favourite pair of jeans were toast. Between the blood, scorch marks, and grease from the ladder, they had officially become unwearable. Even by her low standards.

"Can't win them all," she said as she headed towards the nearest bus stop. She had a feeling the subway service would be a little slower than usual.

MARISKA SLID TO a stop in front of her classroom, quickly tucked a loose strand of hair behind her ear, and tried to quietly enter the room. The door refused to cooperate and squeaked.

"Miss Cooper, how nice of you to join us."

Mariska felt a blush creep up her neck as her professor pinned her with icy eyes. He hadn't liked her since she'd come late to the first class. It hadn't been her fault. There had been a holdup at her bank and damned if she was going to let some gun-toting amateur get his paws on her hard-earned cash.

"Sorry, Professor Lockden," she said.

"Sit," he said coolly before tossing a test booklet onto the desk nearest his own.

She sighed and obeyed, despite her desire to lash out at being ordered around. She bet no one ever ordered the mafia dons around. Served her right for having scruples. The bad guys got to have all the fun.

CHAPTER 2
A Day In The Life Of A Vigilante

TWO STRESSFUL HOURS later, Mariska walked from the classroom, flipped open her cell phone, and dialed Lucas's work number. He picked up on the third ring, the sound of his swift typing audible over the line.

"Hey, how'd the test go?" he asked, his typing continuing without pause. Despite knowing him for nearly their entire lives, she was still amazed he was able to do his computer programming for Virtuos Technology while holding a decent conversation. Most of Lucas's coworkers just grunted at her when she greeted them.

"Not bad," she hedged as she walked across the large campus towards the subway.

"Failed it then?"

"I think I pulled a gentlemen's C," she said. "I haven't exactly had time to study lately. A hero's got to have priorities you know. Trying to track down those illegal fight clubs is seriously eating into my curricular activities."

She heard the fizz of a pop can lid being opened. She rolled her eyes, knowing it was Lucas's coworker Crash breaking into a fresh can of energy drink. Freaking computer geeks.

"Tell Crash Master back there to stop drinking that crap before his heart explodes."

"Crash, dude," Lucas yelled, slightly muffled from probably trying to cover the receiver, "Rish says she loves you too much to let you die of a caffeine-induced heart attack, so get rid of the fuel."

Mariska heard a muffled reply.

"He says he loves you too."

Mariska raised an eyebrow. Crash's shyness was legendary. In the two years Lucas had worked at the programming company, the most she had gotten out of him was "uh," "um," and, when he was feeling particularly brave, a red faced "hello."

She stepped to the side as a cyclist passed her from behind on the narrow sidewalk. "Some warning would be nice," she yelled at his departing back. He lifted a finger at her. "Screw you too. Ride on the road, jackass!" She ignored the curious stares of the couple who passed her going the other way.

"Beautiful day in the neighborhood, eh?" Lucas asked. "Oh, speaking of the reason for flunking your exam—"

"I didn't flunk."

"Right, anyway, looks like we've got a lead," Lucas said. "Meet me later?"

"Roger that."

"Boss is on the way, gotta go."

"Later then." Mariska disconnected and tucked the phone into her pocket. She winced as a pedestrian clipped her injured arm, reminding her that she hadn't done more than a haphazard attempt at first aid. She switched directions and walked south through the sprawling downtown campus, heading towards Lake Ontario.

Lucas's family, well-to-do WASPs, owned some of the derelict warehouses along the lakeshore. Lucas had asked for possession of one of the warehouses, and his parents, rarely denying their son anything, had given it up without question. She, Lucas, and the now absent Lisa had spent six months quietly converting various levels of the warehouse into an apartment, several storage areas for their weaponry and computer gear, and a mechanic bay for their vehicles.

Mariska was currently most interested in the medical room and its supplies as she hopped aboard a streetcar to cut across the city more quickly.

"Or not," she muttered as the streetcar came to a stop behind a long trail of traffic. "Now what?" She rang the bell to signal she wanted off, waited for the doors to open, and slipped off the streetcar and onto the gridlocked street.

It didn't take her long to find the source of the disruption. Police cars had blocked off the streets leading towards one of the large downtown banks.

"That can't be good." She sighed, trying to push her way to the front of the crowd to see what was going on.

Three ass grabs, two elbows, and a slew of glares later, Mariska was at the front line of the chaos. Several forensic vans were parked along the side street. Even from a distance, she could see the bullet casings that littered the street.

She momentary debated slipping under the tape but quickly nixed the idea. There were too many prying eyes, and anything she could learn here she could get from their police contact later. She did stay long enough to see them load a body into an ambulance. She shook her head, trying to shake off a moment of guilt. She couldn't be everywhere at once. She knew that. It was still hard to see that while she'd been trying to save a train load of people, someone else had gone without help.

Deciding she'd seen enough, Mariska continued towards the lakeshore. She hoped to get to the warehouse before her arm bled through the gauze and ruined yet another shirt. She reached it in decent time and looked up at the three-story former factory. It still didn't look like much on the outside—crumbling brick, barred windows, and overgrown dirt parking lot.

Mariska unlocked the sturdy security box and placed her hand against the scanner. It beeped its acceptance of her handprint, and she heard the lock on the steel door disengage. She gave it a tug, slipped in, and closed the door behind her.

The lights flickered to life as she entered, revealing the first floor of the warehouse: the vehicle maintenance bay. Two ATV's and a Kawasaki motorcycle sat clustered in a corner, unused but well cared for. A rugged Jeep was in the center of the bay, the engine lifted from it and hanging slightly to the side. A dented black Mustang, Lucas's first car, was parked in front of the garage door beside Mariska's motorcycle.

Mariska passed by the vehicles and the large freight elevator and took the stairs to the second level, the training area. Hardwood floors, eight-foot mirrors, punching bags, rope obstacle course, and weapons rack. They had it all, including a large stash of medical supplies in their first aid room.

Mariska occasionally wondered how Lucas explained the considerable sum of money he had spent on equipping their operation. The Guardian team had been small scale at first, one car between them and gear that was repaired again and again until it threatened to fall off their backs.

Things had changed when Lucas had come into part of his trust fund three years ago. Though his parents didn't have much say in where the money went, she was certain they were curious about how it was spent. She had expressed her concern to Lucas, who had waved it off, as had his sister, Lisa. Their parents were apparently happy to ignore any odd expenditures so long as the family name remained untarnished.

Lucas had even suggested that he pay her tuition for her. He had reasoned that she wouldn't have to spread herself so thin with school, working to pay her bills, and being on the streets. She'd been tempted, if only for a moment. But she was nothing if not stubborn and proud. She had declined. Now, swimming in student debt, she sometimes wondered if she'd made the right decision.

"*Que sera sera*," she said as she walked to the first aid station. She tossed her bag to the floor and pulled her shirt and her spandex vest from her body, and grimaced at the bruise that was developing near her kidney. If she ended up peeing blood, she was going to break into the Toronto lock-up just to hit that guy from the train again.

She pulled a fresh roll of gauze from the cabinet and snipped the bloody bandage from her arm with medical scissors. The wound leaked sluggishly down her arm. She watched, oddly transfixed, the red liquid follow the creases of her muscles. She dropped a bucket onto the ground, grabbed a bottle of saline solution, and leaned over the bucket.

Mariska gritted her teeth as the salt water hit her damaged flesh and cleared it of leftover debris that splattered into the bucket. She wrapped the gauze around her arm and taped it in place. Thank God it had only been a glancing shot. It no doubt required stitches, but she'd be damned if she'd go back to Dr. Acco today. Not after they'd just finished the conversation about the possible consequences of her vigilantism.

She knew what could happen, better than most. She'd been dealing with the consequences for fourteen months now. Her mind strayed to Lisa. She shut her eyes and braced herself against the counter as she tried to bring her welling emotions under control. The events of the subway had shaken her more than she realized. It had been the night she had lost Lisa all over again. Not the same situation of course, not even close, but the same feeling of being out of control and unable to help the people who needed her most.

"Stop it, Mariska. Breathe." She inhaled deeply and exhaled slowly. Inhale. Exhale. Inhale. Exhale.

In the days following Lisa's death, this was what her life had amounted to. Calculated breathing, moment by moment, forcing herself to keep her head above water, for Lucas's sake if nothing else. It was . . . better now, if that was really the word for it. Her guilt no longer consumed her life. It just occasionally reared up and gave her slowly recovering ego a solid sucker punch.

"Rish?" A hand landed on her shoulder.

She turned with fists up.

"Whoa, easy."

She let out a breath. "Lucas, Christ, you scared the hell out of me." She hadn't even heard the elevator. How deep in her thoughts had she been?

"Yeah, sorry about that. You okay?" he asked, worried blue eyes searching hers.

"Fine, just a scrape," she said with a wave.

"Not what I meant," he said gently.

Mariska rubbed her temple. She couldn't do this right now. They both harboured guilt over Lisa's death, but she wasn't about to drag him down into her pity party. "I'm okay. Really." She touched his arm in assurance and turned away to clean up the mess she'd made.

"You know," he said, "it's been over a year. Maybe you should try and go out a little, meet some people, move—"

"If the words 'move on' come out of your mouth, Lucas, I'll slap you."

"Lisa loved you. She'd want you to be happy. It isn't a betrayal of her to try and get that piece of your life back."

"I can't have this conversation right now. Please, just not right now, okay?" Her voice threatened to crack, and she gripped the table, hard, swallowing her emotions.

"Okay," he said, and she felt strong arms wrap around her from behind. "You're as much my sister as Lisa is . . . was. I want what's best for you."

"I know, Luke, I know." She patted his arm. "I just need a minute."

"All right. I'm gonna go downstairs. Meet me down there?" he asked, already heading for the elevator that would take him to the basement level where they housed their computers and patrol gear.

"Yeah, just let me get this stuff put away." The elevator closed, leaving Mariska to finish cleaning up in silence.

She headed for the stairwell to the basement. As she stepped onto the bottom stair, she was tempted to shield her eyes. Lucas generally had so many screens going it was like looking at a solar flare.

Three thirty-inch screens were suspended from the ceiling by high tensile wire. Two slightly smaller monitors were mounted on the desk, and Lucas manipulated them all like a pro, busily switching from one keyboard to another, one program to another, with little pause.

Beyond his desk lay their weapons racks, various incarnations of their old gear, prototypes for grappling guns, new camera mounts for sunglasses and the like. To the right, a large sewer entrance had been sealed with a steel door. After years of practice, Mariska could navigate most of the sewer tunnels with ease. To the left, encased in glass, was Lisa's gear, a tribute to their fallen teammate and a reminder that their duties could carry deadly consequences.

"What's our lead? A drop?" she asked, sidling up next to him.

Lucas nodded. "Yeah, somewhere in the west end. Still waiting on the exact location."

"Guess that phone tap finally got us somewhere."

"Actually, the tip came from Detective Perkins," Lucas said. "She contacted me this afternoon. Seems she was approached by someone from IAB. Apparently, one of her squad isn't as clean as he ought to be, and IAB had her quietly tailing him."

Mariska looked at him with mild disbelief. "Nina agreed to work with the rat squad? She doesn't strike me as the type to get cozy with Internal Affairs."

Lucas shrugged. "She's a cop who hates dirty cops. Anyway, it's a lucky break for us. They're investigating him for money laundering, but turns out Perkins overheard him talking about the fight clubs."

"So he's a diverse scumbag, wonderful." Mariska sighed as she headed to her gear to get ready.

Various modifications of her patrol gear were hung up in the kit room. Some were meant to be hidden under her street clothes. Others, more durable ones, were to be worn when she went out looking for trouble. She only wore a half mask, having found early on that a full mask was too constricting. Instead, she relied on the shadow of the hood to hide her upper face. To keep Lucas in the loop, she also wore the pair of sunglasses that were equipped with sound and video.

He'd been out of the field for over a year now. Mariska knew he was still trying to come to terms with the fact that, while he was still in the war to protect their city, he couldn't be on the front lines. Hardest of all, they were both still adjusting from being a trio to a two-person team.

"Speaking of our favourite detective, has she heard anything about the subway yet? Who was involved? Or the bank robbery?"

"Funny you should ask. She's got some preliminary autopsy photos for you to pick up. They killed one of the bank robbers in the firefight while he was trying to make his getaway." So the body wasn't an innocent bystander after all. Any death was still unfortunate, but the death of one of the instigators was definitely more palatable than the alternative.

"Can't you just hack into the morgue servers and grab them?"

"No," he said with a shake of blond hair. "They've upgraded their firewall. I'll crack it but why waste time when Perkins has the files?"

"I could have gone in and nicked them if I'd known they were putting a rush on it. We shouldn't be using Perkins as our personal go-to. The less contact we have with her, the better it is for us."

"I'm aware of that, but one, she volunteered, and two, the last time you went into the morgue to get files, you nearly hospitalized the coroner's assistant."

"He was a perv," she said. "He thought I was an intern and that it gave him permission to put the moves on me. I was just disagreeing with him."

"You broke his nose."

"He grabbed my ass. Bet he thinks twice about putting his hands where they don't belong."

Lucas put a hand to his forehead. "Would you please just get dressed and get out there?"

Mariska pulled on her Kevlar vest, the protective armour fitting snugly around a trim midsection. Her utility belt sat low on her hips with straps that clipped around her legs to prevent too much motion. Within the belt was a built-in flashlight for a belt buckle, first aid material, a few smoke bombs, shurikans, and a small police scanner that transmitted through the ear bud on her glasses.

"You need to get a move on. You have to meet Perkins in twenty." Lucas handed her the newly modified grappling gun.

He had increased the tensile hold of the wire and upped the carrying capacity of the gears after a close call involving her, a damsel in distress, and a very high rise.

"Be careful with this. The new trigger is pretty touchy, make sure the safety is on."

Mariska nodded and tucked the gun in the holster on her leg. She tried not to be too reliant on the tool. If she shot the grapple into anything questionable, from a weak brick to a slightly rusted piece of metal, the grapple could fail, and she would plunge to her death before the retractor pulled in the cable and let her fire again. Lucas had broken his ankle a couple of years back, using their first modification of the gun. He had misjudged his weight, the grapple had pulled free, the retractor had jammed, and he had hit the ground from two stories up.

There had been a couple of those kind of incidents in the beginning—failing grapples, sparking ear transmitters, and the like. They'd gotten better over the years as they upgraded their gear and honed their skills. Their current equipment had been put through the rigors of patrol, and all of it seemed to be holding up, more or less.

Mariska and Lucas were another matter.

She had all but lost feeling in a part of her right calf when an errant knife had slit her leg open from knee to ankle. Her left eardrum had been blown out twice. Once with a concussion grenade that had detonated prematurely, and again when she'd been struggling for a gun that had gone off next to her head.

Lucas hadn't done so well either. One night of organized chaos had ended his field career when he had taken a shotgun blast to his knees. He walked with a cane now, after nearly eight months in a wheelchair, but the incident had officially ended his old crime-fighting persona.

And Lisa. Well, she tried not to think about Lisa. If she dwelt too long on the subject, she wouldn't be able to put her gear back on. Her death had nearly ended them as it was.

Mariska shrugged off the thoughts and pulled her head back into the game where it belonged. They had a job to do. She tucked her snap-out baton into its place on her leg and pulled her hood up to hide her face.

"Here." Lucas reached around her neck, put a throat mic in place, and attached it to the earpiece in her sunglasses. "I've upped the signal strength. There's going to be a lot of interference if you're in the bottom set of tunnels." She gave him a thumbs-up and headed for the door that would lead into the sewers. It wasn't her preferred method of travel. She'd gotten a taste for the skies with their new base jumping gear. But sometimes the old ways were the best ways.

"You sure you don't want to do the meet while I patrol? I know you've been looking for an excuse to see Perkins again."

He looked at her crossways. "I have not."

"Whatever, brother. You've had the hots for the good detective ever since we saved her ass in that gang shootout."

"I have . . . would . . . would you just go, please?" His ears tinged pink. It was cute.

She often forgot that he was a good-looking man. She'd been hanging out with him so long she no longer saw him for his individual features. He was just Lucas. On the occasions she took the time to look at him objectively, it wasn't hard to see why he never had trouble with women. Even as a gay woman, she could appreciate that he was easy on the eyes.

His six-foot, two-inch frame had evolved over the years from that of a gawky kid to a densely muscled young man. His arms, while never puny, had become particularly toned after months of physiotherapy and wheeling himself around in the chair. Short-cropped, blond hair did little to hide the slightly oversized ears that gave him his boyish appearance, even after four hard years on the streets. Azure blue eyes were accented by a broad jaw and straight nose. His nose had been broken over the years, but his parents had the money to spend on plastic surgeons to set it properly.

Lucky bastard.

Even with Lucas's chiseled features, Mariska still thought Lisa had gotten the lion's share of their family's good looks. Lisa hadn't been as tall as Lucas. At five-foot-six, she was the shortest on the team by a solid three inches. But her lean body had belied the strength of the muscle underneath. Blue eyes, a shade icier than Lucas's, were the centerpieces of a delicate face. Blond tresses had felt like silk when Mariska ran her hands through them.

"Rish?"

"Huh?" She turned to Lucas, frustrated that she'd been caught taking a walk down memory lane.

"You're going to be late."

"Right. Okay. Let's get this show on the road. Same meeting place as last time?" Mariska walked into the sewer access, threw her leg over the sleek metallic blue ATV, then turned on the engine.

"Yep."

Mariska roared out of the warehouse and into the sewers, easily navigating the tunnels by memory. The drop off wasn't far from their Lakeshore warehouse and with the small vehicle, she made it to the alley with time to spare.

She climbed the access ladder to the surface, shouldered the manhole cover out of place, and hauled herself out of the tunnel.

Perkins was already there, leaning against a dumpster, sharp eyes scanning the alley for trouble. She wasn't in uniform but Mariska could see the flash of her badge under her coat and the bulky shadow of a pistol at her hip. At six feet, she was an amazon of a woman, an image only compounded by the midnight hair that hung past her shoulders.

Perkins had been in uniform on the few occasions Mariska had met her in person. It was odd to see her in civilian dress. This was an altogether different type of imposing look for her than the gun belt, tactical boots, and long hair tightly wrapped in a no-nonsense bun. In jeans and a leather jacket, with hair free, Mariska understood the crush Lucas had on her.

"Detective," Mariska called out.

Perkins looked her way, pushed off the dumpster, and walked deeper into the alley to meet Mariska. "I always forget how short you are." She handed the folder to her.

"I'm only short to you because you're a giant," Mariska said as she flipped open the file. "Anything useful?"

"Few tattoos. He's not local so far as we can tell. His prints haven't come up in our system yet."

"Anything on the subway?"

Perkins shook her head. "Nothing so far. No one's talking."

"All right. How about our buddy Beregic? Did you find the meet?"

"Alley near Queen and Lansdowne, north side. IA wants him picked up tonight. I can hold them off for a couple of hours but not much more."

"That's all right." Mariska walked towards the sewer. "I only need him to show me where they're holding the street kids they keep picking up. After that, he's all yours."

"Watch yourself. Beregic's got a nasty temper."

"Aww, Detective, you almost sound like you care."

Perkins merely watched as Mariska climbed back down the ladder and into the sewer.

Mariska called out a thanks as Perkins pulled the manhole cover back into place. She hopped aboard her ATV and gunned the engine.

"So, did you drool all over your keyboard?" Mariska asked as she drove, adjusting her sunglasses. "I mean, I know you like a woman in uniform but she's not bad in her civvies. You should totally go for it."

"You know what? Not cool, okay? I don't have the hots for Nina."

"Oh, so it's Nina now is it?" Mariska pulled to a stop and headed to the access to get topside. She made her way out of the sewer and climbed the fire escape of the nearest building to get a vantage point.

"Shut up, dude, just shut up. She plays for your team anyway, ass."

"Perkins? Are you sure?"

"You want me to print you a list of her movie rentals?"

"Why—?"

"I investigated her when we agreed to bring her in," he said.

"Of course you did. I'm sure it was all very professional and work related. I'm on site," Mariska said as she lay down on a rooftop and waited for the arrival of the police officer who would be trading innocent street kids for hard cash.

"Copy that," Lucas said, his voice business like once more. "Keep your eyes peeled. He may not be alone."

Mariska nodded and settled into position to wait. She was glad summer still kept its grip on the city. Stakeouts in winter sucked.

"Looks like the party's starting," Mariska said as she turned her head and focused the mini-cam on an approaching van.

"No sign of Beregic?"

Mariska wasn't sure why Lucas asked. With the camera, he had as good a view of the proceedings as she did. "Negative." She shifted in place and watched as two men, each looking like Donnie Brasco rejects, stepped from the dark van. One lit a cigarette while the other scanned the alley, probably for potential witnesses. Evidently satisfied, he motioned with his head to the back of the van, then the pair lumbered to it and pulled open the door.

The man with the cigarette reached in and tugged two disheveled teenage boys out on to the pavement. The pair were blindfolded and handcuffed and were trying to get themselves to their feet. The man with the cigarette pulled a pistol from his belt and dealt each boy a swift strike to the back of the head.

Mariska let out an angry curse as the other thug looked down nonchalantly at the now unconscious teens. She could take them down. A couple of well-placed shurikans and a dropkick from three stories up would sort the immediate problem out.

"We need Beregic," Lucas chimed in her ear. "These are low-level wise guys. Beregic is the one with the actual connections to the fight club. You pounce on them, he'll disappear. IAB will grab him, and we lose everything."

She said nothing and simply settled back into position. *We need the trade to go through so we can track the cop to the underground arena,* she reminded herself. She would get a crack at them sooner or later. Chances were the guys would pop up on her radar again.

"Got anything yet?" she asked.

"Not yet. Facial recognition bots are still working. Still no sign of Beregic?"

Mariska opened her mouth to say no, then shut it. A black sedan pulled into the alley. She could see the ghost image of the police emblem on the side door. He was buying kids and transporting them on the taxpayers' dime. Classy.

"Looks like he just showed up. Going stealth," she said.

They would have no further audio contact on her end until the meet-up was over. She climbed down the fire escape on the opposite side of the building with light steps. She hit the pavement and dashed into the alley where she could see Beregic and the wise guys conversing. She pulled a tracer from her belt and snuck to the back of Beregic's car, secured the device in place, then pressed the button to activate it.

"Can you get into his car?" Lucas asked.

Mariska ducked low and slid along the driver's side, ever mindful of the position of the others. She gently pulled on the door handle. Locked. She cursed under her breath and shook her head. She didn't have time to pick the lock.

"So much for downloading his GPS history," Lucas said. "All right. Can you get a tracker on the other vehicle?"

Mariska nodded and scurried to a dumpster and tucked herself behind a set of garbage cans. She watched as one wise guy shook hands with Beregic while the one with the cigarette hoisted one of the unconscious teens over his shoulder and took him to the back of the cop car. While they kept themselves occupied with their exchange, Mariska crept along the wall, in the shadows, and headed for the back of the van. She tucked a tracer onto the undercarriage, pulled out her grappling gun, and went around the corner. She activated the trigger and it pulled her to the roof.

"Tracers on both vehicles are up and running. How's it look from up there?" Lucas asked.

Mariska crawled to the edge of the roof and looked over. "Wrapping up. They must have shoved that other kid in the trunk too."

The men entered their respective vehicles, and Mariska dismissed the thugs. The cop and his cargo were her concern now. She watched as the cop car turned the corner of the alley and headed into the city streets.

"He's going south."

"So I see."

South was the direction towards the highway. This wasn't going to be fun. She took off along the front edge of the building and trailed behind the car. Frequent stops at the traffic lights allowed her to keep the car within sight as she jumped from building to building. The car turned a corner, and she was forced to abandon the rooftops.

Mariska jumped forward, wrapped her arms around a lamp pole as she fell, and slid to the ground. Unable to keep pace with the car as the lights turned green, she abandoned the road and ducked into High Park. She could cut diagonally across the park and head him off at the pass.

"You don't even know if he's going to go west," Lucas said, as her heavy boots pounded the dirt path.

"Traffic on the QEW at this time is insane. He has to go west if he doesn't want to sit in downtown traffic for forty-five minutes with two hostages in his trunk." Mariska grunted as her boot slid in the soft dirt while she cut across the center of the large park.

A city maintenance truck passed her at a crossway. She grabbed onto his bumper and tucked herself behind the tailgate.

"He's going to beat you to Lakeshore," Lucas said.

"No, he's not." She jumped off near the large duck pond, her feet hitting the pavement at full stride and carrying her towards Lakeshore Boulevard. Pumping her arms with her breath coming in a deep steady rhythm, she put on what was left of her speed to run up the concrete slope that separated High Park from the busy traffic of the highway.

"His speed is constant. He's not stopping anywhere near St. Joe's," Lucas said.

"Shit."

The cop car passed her, and she sprinted across the highway and unhooked her grappling gun. She aimed at the shelter of the streetcar platform that was high overhead and pulled the trigger. The grappling hook hit its mark and pulled her level with the platform. The streetcar sped past her. She jumped for the back step and dug her hands between the cracks of the door to hold on to the streetcar as it moved.

"I'm going to lose visual on Beregic." She watched the car pick up speed on the highway and pull away from the streetcar.

"I've lost your video signal, and you've got about two clicks before you lose audio with me as well. You're moving beyond our short-range capability."

"Damn it." Mariska climbed to the top of the streetcar, her leather gloves slipping on the smooth metal surface. She braced her boot on a window ledge, pulled herself onto the top, and ran low on the roof towards the front of the car. She tugged her binoculars out and searched for the undercover police car.

Mariska saw him in the distance, making a left turn into an apartment complex. "There you are." She tucked the binoculars into her vest and took aim at an approaching street lamp with her grappling gun. She fired, let out a small grunt as it caught, and swung towards the building.

She hit the ground at a run, dodged a passing car, then sprinted across a large field and slipped into the underground parking lot.

"Anything?" Lucas asked, his transmission fuzzy over the distance.

Mariska sighed as she caught sight of the police car. The empty police car. Shaking her head, she popped the lock on the trunk, unsurprised to find it empty.

"Um . . . you're not going to like this."

MARISKA THREW HERSELF onto her bed, grabbed her pillow, and held it against her face before letting out a deep yell. She'd not only lost the cop and the kids, she had spent another hour backtracking and chasing down the van involved, only to find out those creeps had switched cars as well. She hadn't seen the swap, and despite two tracking devices and hours of work, they were still empty handed.

Lucas wasn't impressed and neither was she. At least they had visuals of the thugs who were nabbing the kids. They could hopefully get an ID from the police files and trace them back to a particular organization. Beregic had been nabbed by IAB and, according to Perkins, had lawyered up faster than Mariska could say arraignment. They wouldn't be getting anything out of him.

To make matters worse, she had to work the late shift tomorrow at the restaurant. She wouldn't have a chance to patrol or try to pick up the trail of the missing street kids. She was beginning to get frustrated.

"STOP GETTING SO worked up, they're just kids," her coworker said, rubbing Mariska's arm.

Mariska looked across the restaurant where she waitressed and narrowed her gaze at her section of the patio. "They're not just kids. They're demonic hell spawn." She watched the large birthday party that had her swimming in teenagers.

The popular waterfront area was a hot spot for the older teenage set. The ones who were all attitude. Mariska hadn't felt such a strong need to hit something since a rather embarrassing incident where she had been run down by two henchmen on a moped. And now, the brats were making all kinds of noise, disturbing the other customers and aggravating her headache to the point that it was threatening to turn into a full-blown migraine. It was time to start laying down some smack.

"I'm going to try one more time to get their order and then I'm gonna start bouncing people." She tucked her notepad into the waistband of her jeans, then walked towards the rowdy group.

She stood at the table and waited for one of them to shut the hell up before finally crossing her arms and staring at the boardwalk. She could see a young couple walking hand in hand and felt a dull ache in her chest. She missed that, missed the holding hands, the doe-eyed looks. All of it.

Mariska had tried to date again after Lisa, once, at Lucas's insistence. It hadn't worked. Her mind had compared the woman to Lisa and had come up lacking.

Mariska sighed and pulled herself out of her morose thoughts. What was done was done. They had all known the risks when they had taken on the job.

"Hey!" Mariska grabbed wandering fingers before they could reach their target. "Your hands touch my ass, you better make it good 'cause it's the last thing they'll ever have the privilege to feel." She pushed the errant hand to the side. The teen looked at her wide-eyed before sitting back in his chair and placing his hands in his lap.

"Are you ordering or am I tossing you all out of here?" she asked, pinning them with her coldest stare.

She had almost made a Mafioso cry with that stare. These kids didn't stand a chance. They finally quieted down and picked up their previously ignored menus.

"You have sixty seconds." She couldn't believe she wasn't much older than these kids. Four years made a difference sure, but the gap between them seemed to span light years.

Though, if she were honest with herself, she was beginning to feel that way with people in her own age group as well. On the rare occasions she found herself with enough free time to hang out with her classmates, she was hard pressed to find anything in common to talk about. Most of them spent their free time boozing and cottaging. She spent hers training, tuning the ATV, and working on her gear.

Her more intellectual peers often waxed about how classism and social politics created crime, thus the criminals should be given some leeway. While they debated the *whys* of criminality in class, Mariska was in the trenches dealing first hand with gun-toting gangbangers who were robbing convenience stores and holding up people in alleys. It often put her at odds with those who didn't care about crime unless it was in their laps, and the ones who felt it was society's fault and not the criminal's. She felt a huge disconnect and, coupled with missed study dates, parties, and the like while Guardian dispatched criminals, she found it hard to be friends with anyone these days.

Mariska loved her work. She knew dedication and vigilance were keys to survival, but sometimes she wished she hadn't jumped headlong into her vigilante career. Sighing at her own thoughts, she turned to the table. The boy who had made a grab for her seemed to have taken her sigh as further impatience and nodded to tell her he was ready to order. She tucked a strand of hair behind an ear, the hot afternoon sun making her wish she'd gone through with her attempt to cut it.

"What do you want?" She wrote down his order and moved on to his friend, only half listening as her ears perked up at the blare of police sirens. No sound of fire trucks though, if she concentrated, she could hear the helicopters. The sirens came closer, and then the crash of glass and metal meeting concrete, as though someone had hit the murals in the parking lot.

Mariska turned to the lot and watched as two dazed and skeevy-looking men made their way out of their vehicle as police cars careened around the corner into the lot. The men retrieved pistols from their waistbands, sprinted past the patio, and headed for the bridge that linked Mariska's side of the marina with the walking paths on the other side. She had no idea where the idiots thought they were going.

The bridge dead-ended on the opposite side. The pedestrian paths were under construction, which meant they were about to trap themselves, and she didn't have her gear, what a shame. She continued to watch as four uniformed officers pelted after the men, hot on their heels, keeping up well enough.

"Miss?" one of the teens at the table asked, her tone more question than anything else.

"Shut up," Mariska said, watching as the thugs shouldered past a young family. The father pitched forward at the hit and attempted to find his balance. She could swear time slowed as the toddler on the lanky man's shoulders fell forward and over the edge of the railing into the water below.

"Shit." Mariska dropped her notepad and hopped onto the long table, ran the length of it, and vaulted the railing that separated the diners from the pier. She headed for the bridge at a flat-out sprint, boots resounding loudly on the wooden pier.

The couple was frantically trying to figure a way into the water where the boy had gone in, a good thirty feet down. The father was climbing onto the railing to jump as Mariska shot past him and used a bench to get up and over the barrier. She put her body into a dive, hands slicing through the water as she hit, and cleared the path for the rest of her body. She opened her eyes in the murky water and caught sight of a frantically moving boy who couldn't seem to fight his way up. Baggy denim overalls, now soaked with water, were too heavy for him to get any kind of lift. Mariska kicked down to him and took a small hand in her larger one.

She pulled him to her chest and kicked upwards, the lack of oxygen already making her lungs burn. Her own clothing wasn't swim friendly either. The sheer top and the slip underneath weren't a problem, but the heavy leather boots were like anchors on her feet, making every kick a trial as she swam towards daylight.

She surfaced with a sputter, treading water as she brushed the wet hair out of the boy's eyes. "It's okay, buddy. I've got you."

She paddled towards the nearest shore, holding tightly to the back of the boy's coveralls. He wrapped his little arms around her neck and his legs around her waist as she continued to swim, his small head tucked into her shoulder.

"You're all right, your mom's coming," Mariska repeated quietly, as she swam.

As she neared the shore, she could see the standoff between the police and the criminals through the slats of the wooden boardwalk. The men were against the edge of the railing, trapped by construction equipment at their back and police officers ahead of them. No way she could just throw the kid onto the paths. Stray bullets could be flying everywhere shortly. It seemed most everyone else had cleared the bridge, which made things a little easier. At least she wouldn't have to fight her way through a panicked crowd.

"Hmm."

The safest way to get the boy across to the other side was to use the bridge itself. They would be sheltered from any but the most awkward angle of bullets.

"All right, buddy, we're going to be okay." Mariska rested the boy against her chest, grabbed one of the support beams under the bridge, and wrapped her legs around them for extra support. She found a comfortable spot on her hips for the boy to rest. She dropped her legs and climbed through the crisscross of support beams back to the side where the boy's parents were.

She could hear the police attempting to negotiate with the men as she passed under their feet. It didn't seem to be going well. She paused, and spared a look at the support struts beneath her and, still further down, the water. That would be a nasty fall. The boy let out a quiet sniffle, and she shushed him gently. The last thing they needed was cracked-out junkies with guns taking potshots at them. It was also the last thing the police needed.

She sighed and swung her legs up once more to support herself. "Hey buddy, what's your name?"

"Aaron," the boy said, his voice muffled against Mariska's neck.

"Aaron, I need you to be a brave boy for me. I'm going to put you right there." She pointed to a 'y' of the crossbeams. "I want you to sit and hold tight, okay?" He gave out a soft mew of protest, but held tight to the beam as she settled him in place and made sure he was stable. "I'll be right back."

She wrapped her legs tightly around the beam, let go of it, and unbuckled her belt. Sue tugged it from her waist, put it in her mouth, then climbed back to the opposite end of the bridge. She grabbed the bottom edge of the bridge, and, her abs protesting, she pulled herself level. The backs of the criminals legs were visible and, ten metres further away, the knees of the officers.

She had only one chance and she hoped to hell it worked out.

She let go of the bridge with one hand and threw her belt at an angle with the heavy buckle going first. The buckle flew back towards her as the belt wrapped around the ankle of one of the men. She grabbed the buckle with both hands and pulled the criminal off his feet as she fell. She heard the dull thud as he landed almost simultaneously with the crack of two gunshots.

Mariska dropped her belt and grabbed the support beams high above the water below.

She could see the second criminal's downed body through the spaces on the walkway and the blood trickling through the cracks between the boards. Satisfied no further help was needed, she climbed back to Aaron then swung them to the shore. Keeping her head low, her sopping wet hair obscuring her face, she walked the boy to his frantic parents and pushed into the crowd.

CHAPTER 3
Old Memories, New Beginnings

"THAT WAS STUPID," Lucas said some hours later as they watched the footage on the six o'clock news.

"I know," Mariska said, watching for the third time as the first criminal did a face plant on the bridge. Whoever had been filming was too busy with the police to notice her underneath. It was pure dumb luck she wasn't on YouTube yet.

"Anyone could've seen you."

"I know."

"You put everything at risk. If someone figures out who we are—"

"I know, goddamn it." Mariska tossed the remote control down in disgust. "What was I supposed to do, let the kid drown? Let some cops get shot up in the middle of the street? There were bystanders everywhere. People would've gotten killed."

"You don't think someone you worked with noticed you? Saw what you did?" Lucas asked in a raised voice.

"What does it matter? Everything they have on me is fake anyway, my name, my address."

"They know your face. That's more than enough to start with."

"Assuming anyone even links me to the whole thing."

"Someone will, that's the point. There's always someone out there trying to take us down."

"I don't need your goddamn lectures. I've been in this game just as long as you have."

"Then start acting like it."

She narrowed her eyes at him before throwing up her hands and stomping out of the den of his one bedroom condo. "I'm going home." She pulled her purse from the counter.

"There are sacrifices that have to be made to protect who we are," Lucas said. "We can't help anyone if we're dead or in jail."

"And when that sacrifice is something like losing a shoplifter or waiting a day to grab some pissant drug dealer you can come and talk to me. When it's the life of a child and the men and women who put themselves on the line to protect this city, you don't get to make that call." She pulled the door open. "I think you need to revisit why we do what we do, Lucas. It's not just about catching the criminals, it's about the people we help. If you've lost that, you shouldn't be in this game anymore."

WANTING TO BLOW off steam before she made her way home, Mariska walked with no destination in mind. She was still certain she'd made the right choice. When it came to someone's life or revealing her identity, there was no choice. The safety of innocents was paramount above all else. Hell, it had been Lucas who had nudged her into the crime-fighting life. All the brawls, all the scars, all the pain had started out as an innocent day of tobogganing. How one cold afternoon could alter their lives so completely, she still wasn't sure . . .

"Dude, I'm freezing my rear end off. Why am I out here instead of wrapped around a mug of hot chocolate?"

Lucas looked at her, holding his saucer-shaped toboggan in gloved hands. "Because it's fun. You know, that thing you have when you're not nose deep in a book."

Mariska glared at him. "You know, rich boy, some of us actually have to pay for university next year. I need to keep my marks up for my scholarship."

"Come on, one more run won't kill you. I'll drive you home after and even buy you your damn hot chocolate." He gave her a charming grin, white teeth a stark contrast to the black balaclava he wore to ward off the cold. "Scout's honour."

"You were kicked out of the Scouts. Why isn't Lisa out here freezing with us?" she asked as she watched Lucas settle himself on his toboggan.

He made a displeased sound. "She's hanging out with that ass Parker."

"He is her boyfriend," Mariska said, sitting down behind him and holding on to the edge of the saucer.

"He's an ass."

"Luke, you've hated every one of her boyfriends. Sooner or

later, one of them is going to stick around longer than it takes for you to death stare him."

He shook his head. *"No way, there isn't a guy out there good enough for her. Why can't she date women? At least then I'd know she could hold her own if they tried something."* He looked over his shoulder to check if she was ready. *"And don't act like you're not just as protective of her as I am. You were right there beside me when we pulled her out of that jerk's car at the football game."*

"That was different. He was too old for her, and his hands were going places they had no business being. Now would you just shut up and push so we can get this over with? I think my ass might actually be numb."

"Whine, whine, whine." He pushed off with his hands, and they sped down the hill at a clip that was far beyond sensible.

"You know this is really going to hurt if . . ."

They hit an unseen ramp and were suddenly airborne. They landed hard, bounced out of the saucer, and slid along on their sides down the icy hill, their toboggan continuing on past them.

"Ow." Mariska pushed herself to her feet and adjusted her balaclava. Damn it was cold. *"You think you could have found a bigger ice hill to launch us down?"*

"I think I broke my ass," Lucas said as they picked their way down the remainder of the icy slope.

"Like you have an ass to break," Mariska said. *"Your legs move straight into your back."*

"Shut up. I have a nice ass." Lucas bent over, illustrating his point as he picked up the toboggan.

"Dude, your ass is flatter than Calista Flockhart," Mariska said, trudging up the small hill to get to the sidewalk. Lucas made his way up behind her, and they walked towards his car. *"Hey, what's going on up there?"*

Lucas followed her gaze up the street where an older woman was flanked by two young men who were trying to take the grocery bags in her arms. He handed Mariska the toboggan and walked towards the trio, his back straight and face stern.

Mariska sighed. Whoever said chivalry was dead had never met Lucas Forsythe. She followed after him, toboggan still in hand, readjusting her balaclava as she went.

"This isn't your business," one of the teens said.

He looked familiar. Mariska was fairly certain the boys went to her school.

"I'm just asking you to leave the lady alone," Lucas said, his shoulders squared as he faced off against the younger boys. The woman, now trapped by the three teens, looked at Mariska for help with frightened eyes.

"I said it wasn't your business, punk." The one nearest Lucas shoved him, hard, sending him into a parked car.

Lucas lunged forward and cracked his fist against the punk's jaw.

Mariska pulled the woman out of the path of the flying fists. The second boy moved forward, and Mariska brought the toboggan up to shield Lucas's unprotected back. The boy's fist cracked hard on the metal saucer, and he cried out, cradling his hand as he stepped back.

Mariska thrust the blunted edge of the saucer into his stomach. He doubled over. Lucas's struggle with his opponent behind her sounded like the scuffle had gone to the ground.

The boy she'd been fighting dove towards her, hit her in the stomach, and pushed her into the car behind her. The toboggan fell from her hands, and she grabbed his shoulders and drove her knee into his chest. He backed off, and she turned from his grasp, took him by the back of his coat, and slammed his head against the hood of the car. He slid to the cement with barely a sound.

"Rish, on your three!"

Mariska turned to see the second boy rushing her. She dropped low, kicked out, and took him out at the shins. He sprawled forward onto the cement and didn't move.

For one heart-stopping moment, Mariska thought the worst. She let out a deep breath as she saw his chest rise and fall, a little puff of breath visible in the cold air. She'd scared herself for a second.

"I freaking told you tobogganing was a bad idea," Mariska said, bending down to check on the boy she'd knocked into the car.

He was breathing as well and seemed to be coming around, albeit slowly. She looked at Lucas and saw a split lip. The knees of his jeans were also shredded.

"You okay?" he asked from the cold cement.

She rubbed her side. It was tender but nothing worse than

she'd gotten in kickboxing. She turned her attention to the woman who was leaning against the car with a look of shock on her face.

"Uh, ma'am, are you all right?" Mariska asked.

The woman nodded weakly and bent over to retrieve her groceries, which were spread out over the sidewalk. Lucas helped her and even ran down the hill to catch an errant orange.

"How about we walk you home?" Mariska said.

"Thank you," the woman said.

Mariska took the grocery bags in hand as Lucas walked on the other side of the woman and helped her across an icy patch of sidewalk. They reached her house, a small two story, and walked her to her door.

"God bless you," the woman said.

They waved to the woman and headed back to the scene of the crime. The boys were gone and the only evidence of what had occurred were a few blood spots splattered on the sidewalk.

"They took my toboggan," Lucas said, his tone bordering on disbelief. "Those little shits."

"C'mon," she pulled him towards his car, "it's not like you can't afford another one."

He "hmmphed" at her as they got into the car and started the engine. He pulled off his balaclava, blond hair going every which way from the static. Between the Einstein-esque hair and the odd glint in his eyes, he looked positively insane.

"That was kind of cool," he said, putting the car into drive and pulling out onto the quiet street.

"Nearly getting our asses kicked was kind of cool?"

"We totally had them."

Mariska stared at him like he was insane.

"Okay, you totally had them. We helped that lady." His eyes were wild with . . . something. "We saved her, isn't it an amazing feeling? All the training we've done, we're always learning to protect ourselves, but that? Protecting someone else? It was different. It was a total rush."

"You're nuts," she said, pulling off her own balaclava and tucking it into her pocket. "And I know that look, Lucas Forsythe. You want a rush? Take up skydiving. Whatever crazy idea you're cooking up, you'd better just forget it."

"Is it crazy to want to help people?"

"You want to help people? Become a doctor, a cop, volunteer for Habitat For Humanity. Don't go getting some fool idea about throwing yourself into every brawl you happen by. We don't know what those kids were capable of, what weapons they might have had. We were damn lucky they were just stupid punks. We could have gotten ourselves killed."

"But we didn't," he said, turning his attention from the road to Mariska. "Look me in the eye and tell me you didn't feel an adrenaline rush when you were in the middle of the scrap."

She looked at him. It had been kind of cool to finally test her mettle outside the dojo. If she had to get into a fight, doing it to help someone who couldn't help themselves was a better reason than most. That didn't mean she wanted to run around half-cocked, playing superhero. But Lucas was right; it had been pretty cool.

"Yeah, that's what I thought." Lucas grinned, then winced as his split lip protested.

It would be the first of many injuries to come.

"CAN I GET another?" Mariska asked, holding up her bottle for the bartender to see.

He nodded and turned to get her drink while she looked over the bar. Calling the bar seedy would be a compliment. The felt of the lone pool table had been burned with cigarettes and the stools surrounding the table looked barely stable enough to support a child let alone the weight of a grown man. Served her right for drinking in her own crap-ass neighborhood.

She wasn't certain how she had found herself here. Fighting with Lucas always left her unsettled. She got tired of walking and stepped into the blue-collar bar at the edge of the lake for a few minutes to take the edge off. Given the day she'd had, a drink seemed like a good idea. Two beers later, her thoughts weren't any clearer.

"Here ya go."

Mariska handed the bartender the money and waved off the change as she sat deeper on her stool and leaned against the bar, surveying the patrons.

She focused mainly on a lone woman reading at a table across the bar.

Her eyes seemed to move of their own accord as they continually settled on the woman. Deep auburn hair was pulled loosely back in a ponytail revealing a slender neck. Emerald eyes moved along the page of the book as the dull light above her illuminated a dusting of freckles across pale skin.

In pressed slacks and a silk shirt, she was quite out of place among the regulars. Even Mariska, in her jeans and collared shirt, felt overdressed compared to the paint-stained cutoff sweatpants and tank tops of the local crew.

The woman seemed to have no interest in the patrons as she kept her head down in her book. The others had certainly noticed her. One group of young men seemed to be particularly interested and were cajoling one of their group to go to her table.

"I've got a feeling that's a bad idea," Mariska said quietly, before taking another pull from her beer.

One of the men finally stood up and walked over to "Red," his thumbs hitched in the back pockets of his jeans. He invited himself to sit down and leaned forward into the woman's space to converse with her.

His quarry sat back and levelled a cool glare at him that very nearly made Mariska wince in sympathy. She had seen some nasty looks in her day, but this woman definitely had the don't-fuck-with-me one down pat.

The young man seemed to be feeling no pain, though, and leaned further forward. Red said something to him that finally made him rethink his idea. He stood on wobbly legs and staggered from the table, looking ego bruised and a little angry. Couple that with booze, and Mariska bet something stupid was bound to happen.

The woman stood, closed her book, and finished the last of her drink with a zealous gulp. She collected her light coat from the chair and walked away from the table. The woman, perhaps in her early thirties, gave a slight nod to the bartender and her eyes briefly met Mariska's.

Mariska was startled by the current that seemed to pass through her from the stranger's gaze. She shrugged off the odd feeling to get her head back in the game as two of the men left after the woman, each holding cigarettes. She eyed them suspiciously. They hadn't gone out to smoke all night, and she didn't see a lighter between them.

She put her beer bottle on the counter and followed, hand going to her shirt. She had her spandex vest underneath. She scanned the area for Red and the two young men and saw them all not far off. The woman was headed for the parking lot overlooking the pier, the men close enough on her heels to be awkward but not outright threatening. Yet.

Mariska surveyed the area for any prying eyes before ducking into an alley, pulling her street clothes off as she went. She tucked them behind a dumpster and released the snaps around her neck that held her folded hood. She tugged the hood up to cover her face and pulled the mask over her nose. The men were getting dangerously close, and she busted ass to close the distance between herself and the trio.

By the time she got to them, the men were blocking the woman from her car.

"Excuse me, gentlemen, I don't believe the lady is interested," Mariska said coolly, her hand on a shurikan. Before the first clod could move, she let the shurikan fly and easily knocked the knife from his hand. The shurikan neatly clipped him in the back of the head on its return trip, knocking him to the ground. Mariska calmly stepped over his unconscious body, eyes focused on his partner as she knelt to pick up her shurikan.

"Who the hell are you?" he asked nervously as he backed away with his hands up.

"Oh, c'mon now. I think you already know the answer to that." Mariska flashed her shurikan, the turquoise Guardian symbol stark against the dark blue metal, her personal calling card. Not that there were any other masked crime fighters running around the city. Her reputation really did precede her. She kept close watch on his hands as they returned to his sides, some of his drunken bravado returning.

"We didn't mean nothin', just trying to scare her a bit is all. She shouldna been so rude."

Mariska rolled her eyes, took a step forward, and put the bulk of her body between the man and his intended victim.

"Bad manners or not, you don't get the right to scare anyone, least of all with knives." She flicked her wrist and released the shurikan. It knocked the knife from his hand and landed on the cement with a soft clang. He looked at her in shock. Idiots. It was hard to actually teach them a lesson when they were thick as bricks. Disarmed, the man did all he could think to do.

He ran. Smart move.

Mariska pulled her weights on a rope from her pocket. She swung it twice over her head and let it fly at his legs. The momentum of the weights wrapped the rope tightly around his legs. He fell hard against the cement and didn't get up.

Satisfied he wouldn't be going anywhere for the moment, Mariska turned to the would-be victim. "Red" still wore the same cool, self-assured look, as though she hadn't just been threatened by two overzealous punks. If only they could all be so centered.

"You okay?" Mariska asked, picking up the woman's book, which had fallen to the ground in the fray. "Nietzche? Interesting choice for a Friday night."

"We all have our quirks," the woman said. "Some of us read in seedy bars, others dress up like trick or treaters and indulge in their hero complexes."

Mariska stared in surprise as the woman brushed past her and settled calmly into the driver seat of her car.

"Huh," she said, looking down at the unconscious men. "How do you like that?"

MARISKA YAWNED AS she waited for the coffee shop line to move forward. The one downside, okay not the only one, but currently the most notable, to being a masked vigilante was the double-duty workday. She had waitressed until nearly midnight, then patrolled until four in the morning. All before an eight-thirty class, of course. She was going to need a caffeine IV if she pulled many more of those kind of days.

"Hey, lady, let's go, you mind?"

Mariska turned to glare at the man behind her before taking a deliberately slow step forward. It wasn't smart to start shit with her before she was properly caffeinated. People could get hurt.

"What can I get for you?"

Mariska gave her order, far more caffeine than was likely healthy, then searched her purse for her wallet. Pen, cover-up, loose change, shurikan . . . She heard a deep sigh behind her and faced the man full on, one hand on the shurikan in her bag.

"I've got it," a female voice said.

Mariska turned in surprise.

"Put a latte on there as well."

"I, uh, thank you," Mariska said.

Her rescuer was an attractive redhead in a business suit. By the perfect way it hung on the woman's athletic form, Mariska was willing to bet it wasn't off the rack.

"No need," she said, waving it off. "I was shamelessly using you to jump line. It's worth a couple extra bucks."

Mariska smiled while her mind worked in overdrive to identify how she knew the woman. She was certain she'd seen her before.

"I think our order's ready."

"Huh? Oh, right." Mariska turned away to grab her drink, an Americano with a triple shot of espresso, and handed the latte to the woman. "I'm Mariska by the way."

"Alana," the woman said over her shoulder as she weaved through the crowded cafe to the sole unoccupied table.

Mariska spotted a yuppie-looking couple eyeing it before suddenly veering off. Alana was levelling a deadly stare at the couple.

Mariska knew that stare. The woman from the bar. "Son of a—"

Alana gave her a curious look.

"Spilled some." Mariska sat at the table as Alana motioned her down.

She certainly looked different in the business suit with her hair down. The curly locks made her jaw less severe, though the crisp line of the suit didn't leave her without any sharp edges.

"Thanks again," Mariska said, raising her coffee in thanks, reminding herself that this woman had been rude to Guardian, not to her. Not everyone appreciated the job she did, and she accepted the line she straddled between justice and her own criminality was a fine one. If she didn't know how to classify herself, how could anyone else?

"No problem, always willing to help out a woman in need," Alana said with a confident smirk.

Mariska consciously fought not to suck in a mouthful of hot cappuccino. The irony of that statement could have killed her. "Really? You make a habit of swooping in to save college students from their lack of change?"

"When the occasion calls for it, though, I'll admit I had an ulterior motive."

Mariska looked over the brim of her coffee cup at Alana.

"I was hoping to get your phone number, the coffee was my convenient segue. My next tactic was bumping into you on the way out the door."

"You want my phone number?" Mariska let out an uneasy laugh.

Alana nodded. Her expression was calm as she sat back in her chair and looked at Mariska as though getting her number were a foregone conclusion. Mariska quirked her lips slightly at Alana's bluntness. It had irked her last Friday but now, in the light of day, it was strangely appealing. Women with confidence were a turn on. But that was beside the point.

"Listen, Alana, I appreciate the offer but I'm not—"

"Gay?"

"Available."

"Married?"

"No."

"Partnered?"

"No."

"Dating someone?"

"Not as such, no." Not unless you counted meeting Perkins in a back alley as a date.

"Then you're available," Alana said, the corners of her lips curling upward.

Mariska took a breath and held it as she waited for an appropriate response to come to mind.

Evidently reading her silence as acceptance, Alana smiled.

Mariska was surprised by the transformation. Alana's stern face went from slightly intimidating to undeniably attractive in a split second. She stopped that thought in its tracks. She wasn't in the market and giving Alana any ideas to the contrary was just bad form.

"I'm not really dating at the moment," Mariska said. "Anyone."

"All right then, we don't have to call it a date, how about we call it drinks?"

Mariska fidgeted with her cup. "No, isn't in your vocabulary, is it?" She took a sip from her coffee.

"What do you think?"

"I think I'm going to be late for class." Mariska stood up. She was almost tempted to give in but the last thing she needed was to deal with the emotional fallout of a failed relationship.

"Let me give you my number," Alana said. "C'mon, now you get to be in control. Believe me, that's not a privilege I give out to just anyone."

Mariska sighed and nodded somewhat reluctantly. There was something to be said for tenacity.

Alana reached into her purse. "Of all the days not to have a pen."

"I've got one," Mariska said, put her hand into her bag and felt the soft leather of her wallet. "Huh, weird."

She shook her head, she really was useless before her coffee. She pulled out a pen and a little notebook. Alana quickly scribbled her number down on a blank page and handed the notebook back, their hands keeping contact longer than was necessary.

"I'll be honest, I don't—"

"You'll call," Alana said, her lightly freckled face breaking into a confident grin. "Don't worry, I won't hold your hesitation against you."

Mariska watched Alana leave the coffee shop, a swish in her hips was too pronounced to be unintentional. Despite herself, she found her eyes following Alana's hips as she walked. Alana pushed open the door, met Mariska's eyes for a moment, gave a quick wink, and strolled away. Shaking her head, Mariska headed for class.

Three hours and a mid-class nap later, Mariska walked up the steps to the small computer programming company Lucas worked for. They hadn't spoken all weekend. Their pigheadedness was legendary and their friendship had come close to ending on more than one occasion because neither wanted to be the first to give in.

Mariska signed herself in at the front desk and took the elevator to the third floor where the resident geeks kept their cubicles. She stepped out into the large expanse of offices, always surprised by the homage to all things nerdy. She headed for Lucas's cubicle, among the ones closest to the wall of windows that faced the busy downtown street.

The bright early afternoon sun glinting off dozens of computer screens did little to break up the unnatural light of the fluorescents that flickered overhead. Nor did it do any justice to the puke green color of the walls. The various geek accoutrements were the sole bits of character in the otherwise blasé space. She passed a Star Wars poster, a bobble-headed Jean Luc Picard, and a particularly over-endowed statuette of Power Girl.

"And Lucas says I need a life," she muttered.

He wasn't at his cubicle, likely at lunch given the hour. She had hoped to catch him. She heard the telltale pop and fizz of an energy drink being opened and circled Lucas's cubicle to see the geek dubbed Crash Master nose deep in his screen, with a fresh can in his hand. She leaned against the cubicle wall, waiting for any sign that he had noticed her.

Mariska leaned over and waved her hand in front of his face. He gave a violent start, threatening to shower her in his Ginseng, Taurene, Super Duper Energy Booster. His gaze hit the floor before traveling up her boots, denim clad legs, pausing on her form-fitting tank top, and finally up to her eyes.

"Oh, uh . . . Did I get you? I didn't . . ." He turned nervously in his chair. "I have a napkin, I can—"

"Easy, boy, you missed me," Mariska said, wondering how many shades of red the poor guy would work through before his skin settled on one colour. "How are you?"

"Oh . . . I'm good, thanks."

Mariska raised her eyebrows in surprise. She had never gotten a full, coherent sentence out of him before. She plucked the energy drink from his hand and substituted it with the orange juice she had brought for Lucas.

"This stuff isn't good for you." She dropped the drink into his trash can. He looked at her as though she were from another planet. "Have you eaten?"

"Eaten?" he asked, pushing his square-rimmed glasses up his nose.

"Unbelieveable. You geeks only come in two types. Overly skinny 'cause you don't eat at the computer, or supersized 'cause you eat all the time at the computer. Obviously you're the former." Mariska threw him the sub sandwich she had prepared. "God knows you need the calories." She looked at his short, skinny frame and was convinced he had been hooked into caffeine while playing his video games as a kid and it had stunted his growth. "Is Luke around?"

He was focused on finding a way into the plastic-wrapped sub. "Crash?"

"Huh? Oh, ummm . . ." His colour, almost returned to normal, reddened again.

"Don't stroke out on me. I don't want to have to give you CPR," she said. His colour went nearly purple, and she couldn't help but let out a quiet chuckle. "You really need to relax."

"Lucas went home." Mariska turned at the unfamiliar voice, and blinked at what she could only describe as a female version of Crash. "He got a phone call and told the boss he had to cut out early."

"Oh, huh, thanks."

The woman nodded and disappeared into one of the cubicles.

"Nice talking to you, Crash. I'll see you later." She heard a muted "bye" as she walked down the hall and couldn't help but smile to herself.

Mariska headed for the warehouse, having a feeling Lucas didn't leave work to deal with a simple issue at home. She pulled open the door of the warehouse to see the lights already on in the vehicle bay. She wandered down the steps to the operations room, unsurprised to find Lucas immersed in three different computer screens.

"You're going to go blind if you keep sitting that close," she said.

He turned to her. "Hey," he said in a subdued tone.

"You don't have to do that kicked puppy routine, Luke. You're an ass, but I love you anyway. Tell me you're sorry—that it was my call. It was risky but I was right."

He ducked his head. "I'm sorry. You made a good call. It was risky but you were right."

"Something I never get tired of hearing," she said with a laugh. "So, what's so important that you cut out of work early?"

"Perkins called, she needed a hand. Seems Detective Beregic is in the wind. She was hoping we could help track him down."

"I thought IAB had him."

"They did but he posted bail."

"How did he manage the cash to do that? His accounts were

frozen. He doesn't own a house. Wasn't his bail set at like half a million?"

Lucas shrugged. "I have no idea where the money came from. An account IAB missed, or maybe whoever was paying him to get the kids footed the bill. I'm hoping, if I can track the money, I can find him."

"My bets are whoever was running those fight clubs probably popped him out of jail to make sure he didn't roll over," she said.

Lucas's expression showed he had reached a similar conclusion.

"I give it a couple of days before he shows up in the lake, sans life preserver."

"Think so too, eh?"

She nodded. "Whoever's running these things didn't think much of dumping dead street kids in the gutter. I doubt they'll be squeamish about knocking off a cop. I can take a look at his apartment if you think it'll help."

"Would you mind? Perkins comes through for us a lot. I'd like to give her this one. It'll look good for her if she brings him in."

"Aw, that's so sweet," she said.

"For the last time, I don't have the hots for Detective Perkins."

"Whatever you say, partner." Mariska went to the gear to grab her grappling gun.

"Do you have your glasses? I want to tweak the audio feed. I had a lot of static last time."

"It's in my purse," Mariska said as she pulled her hard shell backpack from its rack and stowed her grappling gun as well as a set of shurikans inside.

"What's this?"

"What's what?" Mariska turned to see Lucas with her purse in one hand and a piece of paper in the other. "It's nothing." She waved it off.

"Really?" He looked at the paper. "'Cause it looks like a phone number."

"Very astute, Captain Obvious." She pulled her motorcycle jacket on and shrugged into the backpack, her helmet under one arm.

"How'd you get someone's number?"

"I didn't have a choice. She wasn't the type to take no for an answer. You going to fix the glasses or not?"

He held up his hands in surrender and picked up the glasses to fiddle with them. "She hot?"

"What?" Mariska looked up from her online search of Beregic's address. "Yeah, I guess." She clicked *print*.

"You gonna call her?"

"Nope." Mariska tucked the map into her pocket and plucked the sunglasses from his hand and headed for the stairs.

"Yes, you are," Lucas said as she tucked the audio transmitter into her ear.

"I am not." She kicked the engine of her motorcycle into life, pulled out of the warehouse, and gunned it through the gravel parking lot, then onto the road.

"I'm dialing you through right now," Lucas said.

"You most certainly are not."

"It's my call. It's risky but it's the right thing to do."

Mariska winced at hearing her words thrown back at her. "Don't you dare."

"You won't step off this ledge yourself, so I'm going to push you. One date, for me, please."

Her ear was full of dial beeps and a ringing phone.

"You motherf—" She hadn't even known he could do that. It was still ringing, she had no way to disconnect, maybe Alana wouldn't pick up. What good would that do? Maybe Lucas was right. Maybe Alana had shown up for a reason. Fate had seen fit to throw them together twice, perhaps it was a sign. "All right already." The machine picked up and Mariska waited for the beep.

"Um, hi, Alana, it's Mariska. I'm just calling to, uh . . . say it would be okay to call me." She shook her head, thinking it was possibly the lamest voicemail ever as she listed off her phone number. "Anyway, I guess that's it, bye." She heard the phone disconnect. Lucas had been listening in.

"I may have to kill you," she said into her mic as she gunned it through a yellow light, narrowly avoiding a turning car.

"I'm an ass, but you love me," he said.

She snorted loudly into the mic and turned off onto Beregic's street, pulled into the back alley, and killed the engine. She left her helmet on, tugged her grappling gun from her bag, and took aim at the bottom level of the fire escape. The retractor lifted her up and on to the platform, and she searched the wall for the right window.

"It's the next one over," Lucas said.

Mariska knelt down and tried to open the window. Locked. She shrugged, put her boot through the thin glass, and reached inside to undo the lock.

"Very stealthy."

"If he's dead, he won't mind. I thought the point of being a dirty cop was to live beyond your means." Mariska looked around the ramshackle apartment.

"And . . ."

"And I've been in crack houses cleaner than this." She used her boot to overturn a stack of pizza boxes. "What should I be hoping to find? The cops have already been through here." She wiped off a layer of fingerprint powder and held it up to the camera to illustrate her point.

"His accounts here are all frozen, and I haven't seen anything to indicate he has accounts offshore. If he's gone underground, he had to get the money from somewhere."

"Translation?"

"He has a safe, and the police haven't found it."

"Why didn't you just say that?"

"You didn't ask?"

Mariska sighed and looked around the small living room, trying to figure out the best place to hide a safe.

The lock on the front door disengaged, and she froze. Too far from the window, too big to hide behind the lone recliner, she dove for the door and tucked herself behind it, flat against the wall.

"He can't be stupid enough to come back," Lucas said.

Mariska tightened her hand on a shurikan, just in case. She breathed a silent sigh of relief as she recognized the tall, dark-haired woman that walked through the doorway.

"Detective."

Nina Perkins whirled, her pistol drawn and at the ready.

Mariska put her hands up. "I come in peace."

"What are you doing here?"

"Selling cookies for charity. What's it look like? I'm trying to find out where our friend Beregic may have run off to."

"CSU went over this place with a fine-tooth comb."

"If you actually believed that, you wouldn't be here," Mariska said.

"You can do better?"

"I think we can do better," Mariska said, having no interest in getting into a territorial pissing contest with Perkins. "Now, if I were a crooked cop, where would I hide my ill-gotten gains?"

Perkins looked around and her gaze fell on the bookcase tucked tightly against the wall by an old TV. "Beregic never struck me as the literary type."

They walked to the shelf, and Mariska pulled the bookcase away from the wall. Nothing.

"Well, that was anti-climactic."

Perkins brushed past her and pushed on the wall and floor, trying to find something. Anything.

Mariska looked over the bookcase. It seemed normal enough. She tipped it onto its face and drove her boot through the back with a crash.

"What the hell are you doing?" Perkins asked.

Mariska knelt down, shoved her gloved hand into the hole, and pulled out an envelope. She tipped out a sheaf of papers, handed part of the stack to Perkins, and read through the others.

"Bonds," Perkins said.

"Lots of bonds," Mariska said.

"How did you know?"

Mariska looked up, way up, at the tall detective. "Used to have one of these shelves when I was a kid. I guess it's a design flaw but it comes in pretty handy for stashing stuff you don't want your parents getting a hold of. What do you think the chances are of Beregic making a run for it without his cash?"

"Nil," Perkins said with a sigh. "Shit. So much for him leading us to his bosses."

"Sorry, Detective." Mariska stood and handed the rest of the bonds to Perkins.

"Guess I'll just go back to the station and wait for a body to show up," Perkins said tiredly.

"Perkins . . . Nina," Mariska said. "This isn't your fault. These people obviously have friends in high places. If they wanted him, they would have got to him anywhere."

Perkins let out a deep breath.

"Let us know if there's anything else we can do," Mariska said.

"Just find the fight clubs. Innocent kids are dying. At this point,

I couldn't care less about Beregic or where his body shows up. He got what was coming to him." Perkins made her way to the door.

"Wait!" Lucas yelled.

"What?" Mariska asked.

"I said Beregic—"

"No, not you, detective. What's up, big brother?"

"The symbol on the envelope, at the corner. Focus on it." Mariska complied. "I've seen that symbol before. It was tattooed on the bank robber."

"Are you sure?"

"Positive. I'm cross referencing the images now."

"What's going on?" Perkins asked.

Mariska pointed to the envelope in her hands. "Sounds like we've got a connection. Your bank robber had this on him." She tapped the symbol.

Perkins looked at the envelope. "One of the subway perps had this on his wrist."

"Looks like we've got a new player in town," Lucas said.

Mariska sighed. Another crime syndicate in Toronto. Wonderful. Just what she needed.

CHAPTER 4
STELLA

"LOOK, I DON'T care if you have to hire a hooker to take him to bed. I need leverage on him to push the sale through." Alana listened impatiently to a steady stream of excuses. "Hey! I want those wetlands. The site survey says they'll be top producing oil wells. Just get it done, dammit. That's what I pay you for."

What a shitty day.

Things had started out well enough. She'd met the woman from the bar in the coffee shop. Mariska had eyed her all night on Friday and Alana decided it was time to approach when those idiots sent one of their friends over to harass her. After that debacle, she was in no mood to play the game, even with someone as attractive as Mariska.

And afterwards . . .

She sighed and looked out over the Toronto skyline towards the lake. The morons had followed her out of the bar with ill deeds on their minds. By that time, she had been itching for a fight and had baited them in close enough to start doing damage when that damned hero had shown up.

Guardian.

Alana snorted aloud. The little crime fighter had dispatched the delinquents easily enough. Not that they'd been much more than annoying children but she was willing to give credit where credit was due. Guardian had been around for some time and one didn't survive long in that line of work without being either extremely good or extremely lucky. Perhaps both.

At any rate, the vigilante had looked at Alana like a dog begging for a treat. A thank you. An acknowledgment of a job well done. Alana hated beggars. Couple that with her irritation at being denied a good round of fisticuffs and her reaction to Guardian had been less than friendly.

No matter.

Her mood had been much improved when she had seen

Mariska that morning, but she didn't have the luxury of a bar line as a cover to introduce herself. Unwilling to let the opportunity to talk to her slip by again, she resorted to something she'd given up years ago. Pick pocketing.

She had slipped Mariska's wallet from her purse while she was in her early morning haze. It had been easy, as though she'd never given it up as a teen. After paying for the coffee, she dropped the wallet back into the open bag and led Mariska to an empty table. She had to use the glare she usually reserved for legal opponents and underlings but had gotten them a seat.

Given how interested Mariska had seemed on Friday, Alana had been surprised at her resistance to giving up her phone number. She seemed genuinely apprehensive about it, for whatever reason. That made her all the more intriguing.

Alana was used to getting what she wanted with minimal effort. Mariska presented her with a challenge, albeit a small one. She liked challenges.

It had been a pleasant surprise, amid the maelstrom of crap that was her day, to find Mariska's message on her phone. Again, the apprehension had been evident, as though Mariska was no more sure of calling than she had been of accepting Alana's number in the first place.

The timid phone call had been the highlight of her day. Protesters in the wetlands acquisition project had stalled her company from buying the land. The judge had issued an injunction to stop the sale so now she had to deal with the VPs and shareholders breathing down her neck while she tried to find a way to finesse the local-yokel legal system.

She sighed and leaned back in her chair. She massaged her temples, trying to ward off the headache she felt coming on. Honestly, why she chose corporate life, in an oil company no less, over any other day job she could have had, she really didn't know.

She was smart enough to do anything, really. Medical school, research, business, it wasn't about the money—more about the air of respectability, the appearance of it. She supposed she could never truly be respectable. She didn't have the breeding or background for that type of thing. But appearances meant a lot and so, when she needed a front to hide her more dubious business practices, she had chosen to go corporate.

It meant long hours in the beginning, but now she mostly dealt with entertaining high-level clients and presentations for shareholders. It had put her in contact with a lot of people over the years. People she had been able to use to help further her own enterprises because they had the pull to get things done. And there were few people with as skewed a moral compass as oil executives.

It was usually an ideal situation. Except today.

Sighing, she stood up from the dark cherry desk, ignoring the suit jacket on her chair as she headed out of her sixteenth-floor corner office to grab a cup of coffee. She had sent her assistant home hours ago. Unlike most of her colleagues, she actually treated her staff like humans. It kept them happy and productive while doing their jobs, more or less. Her peers couldn't say the same.

Her cell beeped as she poured coffee, and she flipped open the small mobile.

"Yes?" she asked, returning the coffee pot and picking up the sugar. The coffee wasn't great but she had drunk worse. Regularly. The coffee from the shipyard tasted like someone had run oil from a ship engine through a filter and called it potable.

"The shipment's arrived," the voice on the other end said in greeting.

"Good. Start unloading. I'll be there shortly." She snapped the phone closed and took a deep sip of her coffee. It was going to be a long night.

ALANA TUGGED HER red leather coat tighter around her body as she surveyed the docks. The lake air tended to be chilly even in summer. The men were quickly unloading the drug shipment. She demanded efficiency.

Alana wasn't a dealer. Point of fact, she hated drugs. They were just an excuse for fuck-ups. A reason and a way to run from the not so niceties of life. They were a weakness. If they weren't worth so much money, she would have nothing to do with them.

But, she was nothing if not a realistic capitalist. The drugs would find their way into the country one way or another. Better the money was in her pocket than someone else's. Her company transported the goods from point A to point B, eliminating some of the risk on the supplier's end. The risk paid well.

Her moneyman informed her that the payment had been transferred to her account. Now she could concentrate on her end of things. The money would be moved shortly to an offshore account in payment for a shipment of guns. One of the Central American governments had massacred a few rebel settlements and needed to get the guns out of the country. She was getting the weapons at a rock-bottom price.

Alana shook her head. The rebels paid her to transport the cocaine, which they sold to buy weaponry to fight the government. The government, in conjunction with their international comrades, fought the rebels to get hold of the drugs. In turn, they sold them to their own distributors, covering up their actions by farming out the evidence to gunrunners to get it out of the country. She sold the guns back to the rebels at just under market value with the agreement that they use her as their mode of transporting the drugs across international waters. Central America was a goddamn gold mine. The War on Drugs was the best thing to happen to Alana and her company.

On a less global scale, the shipment in front of her meant she was able to pay her people. Nothing extravagant. For most of them this was secondary income. A way to buy an extra toy at Christmas or be just a little ahead on rent next month. She was sometimes curious how they justified their actions to themselves. Presumably, some of them felt some sort of guilt for their illegal actions.

She didn't.

She had long ago accepted who and what she was. Society's ideas of justice and law had never been her own. She had never attached herself to the plebian, moralistic code. Her concern was ultimately herself and getting what she wanted. Whatever the means.

Speaking of what she wanted—Mariska.

Alana pulled out her phone and punched in Mariska's number.

"Lucas, I told you I have to finish this paper. If you're not in danger of bodily harm—" a distracted-sounding Mariska said after the second ring.

"Mariska?" Alana heard a pause in the typing on the other side of the line.

"Yes?"

"It's Alana."

"Alana?" Mariska confused. "Oh! Sh . . . Alana, hi, sorry."

"Bad time?"

"No, it's . . . look, I'm . . ."

Alana sensed whatever resolve Mariska had mustered earlier in the afternoon was faltering. "You're going to go out for drinks with me on Thursday."

"I am, am I?" Mariska asked after a pause.

"Yes," Alana said. "I'm guessing by the sound of a keyboard that I didn't wake you."

"Ha. University students don't sleep, or don't you remember?" Mariska asked, yawning.

Alana let out a quiet laugh. "I dimly recall."

She watched her men swiftly removed the drugs from beneath an order of bananas. She winced as a crate came loose of a crane and began to tip. Men shouted, and she covered the mouthpiece with a red-gloved hand to muffle the sound.

"What about you, don't you sleep?" Mariska asked.

"Corporate executives never sleep," Alana said.

"Corporate exec, eh? Is that how you can afford to save damsels in distress?"

Alana smirked. At least Mariska had a sense of humour to match her good looks. She was getting tired of the typical, vapid pretty girls.

"Something like that," Alana said, motioning sharply with her hand to an approaching dock worker. He stopped in his tracks, mouth shut as he waited for her. "Listen, I've got to go, I'm waist deep in work." She looked at the crates surrounding her. "Drinks on Thursday." She left no room for argument.

"All right. Around sevenish?"

"Seven on Thursday it is. I'll make reservations and give you a call on Wednesday to confirm."

"Okay. Goodnight, Alana."

"G'night, Mariska." Alana closed the phone and adjusted her mask before signaling the dockworker forward.

"Stella." He held out the manifest. "We're missing two crates."

Alana sighed. She took the clipboard from him, then scanned the documents. The cargo had been accounted for at the initial pickup. Somewhere between Columbia and Toronto, it went missing. Likely at one of the transfers. Cuba probably.

"Get the men working in Cargo B."

"Yes, Stella."

Alana rolled her eyes as he turned on his heel and headed towards the ship. She had never taken on the name Stella. It was the name of the front company she'd created. Special Tactics Extraction and Location of Lost Artifacts. STELLA. Somehow, she had become the embodiment of the name. If she had known that was going to happen, she would have come up with a better name. Honestly. Stella? It was horrible.

"Oh vice thy name is vanity," Alana muttered as her men approach. Her hand rested comfortably on the silver-plated Glock strapped to her leg as the men came within shouting range. Her battle gear was, oddly enough, nearly a red parody of Guardian's.

She hadn't planned it that way. She'd used this incarnation of her gear for years before she had come to Toronto the spring before last. It was her way of ensuring her anonymity—a front company, a mask. Her shields between herself and a world, specifically a woman, that wanted to bring her down.

She doubted word of her arrival had actually spread through the city. She was always careful about how hands on she was with the day-to-day operations. It was much easier to maneuver around people who didn't know you were there. By the time the police forces knew STELLA was in the city, the operations had vanished.

"Gentlemen, it's come to my attention that we're missing some cargo. Explain."

One man shrugged. Actually shrugged. As though he had misplaced a crayon and not three million dollars worth of cocaine. Evidently, they had forgotten whom they worked for. She had been too hands off.

"This," she mimicked his shrug, "is not an appropriate answer."

She pulled her pistol from her holster, calmly released the safety, and pulled the trigger. The silencer made a quiet whisper as the round fired and landed in his knee, sending up a quick spray of blood.

"You," she turned to the second man, "explain."

"It wasn't us, boss. Damn Cubans, pulled two crates for taxes," he said, looking down shakily at his moaning partner.

She cursed under her breath. This was going to be a problem. "Get him and go." She pointed with her pistol to the bleeding man. She watched in silence as the man was dragged back to the docks. The manifest worker gave her a curious look. "I thought the Cubans had been paid."

Alana growled low in her throat, put the safety on, and holstered her pistol before she gave in to her urge to go postal on her men. The Cubans had been paid. Either they had raised the prices without warning or some meathead had decided to get stupid and skim off the top. She pulled out her untraceable phone and punched in numbers.

"Get me Ferrero," she said to the young woman who had picked up the phone. She heard soft words and a disgruntled groan before the phone exchanged hands.

"What?" Ferrero asked in heavily accented English.

"If you don't get me those crates, and I mean now, I'm going to fly down there and personally put a shotgun against your nuts. No arguments, no excuses. I don't see them north of the forty-ninth by sundown tomorrow, I will end your pissant operation." She snapped the phone closed and tucked it into her vest.

"Is Ferrero the one who took them?" the man asked.

"I have no idea but my guess is, if he's not he'll find out who is. It's all about providing the proper motivation."

"I HAVE NO motivation for grad school at this point." Mariska sipped from her martini. "My undergrad is more than enough for now."

"And what do you plan to do with your degree?" Alana took a drink from her glass of wine.

"I'm not certain yet. With a business degree, I can do any number of things. Work in an office or start up a store or a bar. I can do most of the accounting myself and I have a friend who's a whiz with computers."

"A bar?"

Mariska nodded. "I like the atmosphere of bars. There's something alluring about dark rooms and heavy beats."

Alana looked intrigued.

"So how about you? How did you get into business?" Mariska asked.

Alana waved her hand dismissively. "Oh, you know, too many John Grisham novels, not enough episodes of *ER*. Can't forget my ego. It was high-level corporate or surgery, and I don't have the taste for digging around in someone's chest cavity."

Mariska laughed lightly before taking another sip of her martini.

"You certain you're old enough to drink that?" Alana teased.

"Yes, thank you. Are you certain you can handle being up this late?"

Alana flashed an almost predatory grin. "Believe me, I can handle being up a lot later than this."

Mariska smiled shyly as she looked around the high-class bar. She hadn't quite expected to be drinking a twenty-dollar martini when Alana suggested drinks. She supposed she shouldn't be surprised. Nothing about Alana said cheap date.

"Are you enjoying yourself?" Alana asked, her head resting against her hand as she looked in Mariska's eyes.

"I am."

"Don't sound so surprised."

"No, it's not that I . . ." Mariska paused. "I've been out of the dating pool for a while and I was being honest when I said I wasn't up to really getting involved."

"Well, you know what they say about recovery, one day at a time."

Mariska gave her a curious look. "Why are you doing this?"

"What do you mean?"

"You're gorgeous," Mariska said, earning a smile from Alana. "You're well read, obviously well off, you could go after any woman you want. Why bother with me?"

Alana straightened. She ran her fingers along the rim of her glass. "You intrigue me."

Mariska looked at her expectantly. "That's it?"

"There needs to be more?"

"No, I suppose not."

"Since we're playing *quid pro quo*, why did you say yes?"

"Well, to be honest, my friend Lucas pushed me into it. He worries about me. I was hoping it would help him relax a little."

"What's the real reason?" Alana asked, her gaze questioning as she stared into Mariska's eyes.

Mariska admitted the answer had sounded a touch lame to her own ears, even if there was some truth in it. She knew the real reason but she pushed it down to contemplate later. She had said yes because she wanted to. She was lonely and wanted to try to fill part of the void Lisa's death had caused.

The realization was quickly overrun by a wave of guilt. To think that she could ever replace Lisa was unconscionable. Following on the heels of her guilt was anger, a deep rage that, at twenty-two, she had already been cheated out of the life she truly wanted.

"Mariska?"

"Hmm? I'm sorry." Mariska wiped at the corners of her eyes.

"Are you all right?"

Mariska nodded, taking another drink to give herself a moment to recover. "I'm fine, I'm sorry I—"

"—can stop apologizing," Alana said. "I think you're vibrating."

Mariska's eyes widened as she watched her purse dance across the bar top.

"Oh, um sor . . . Do you mind?"

"Please."

Mariska looked at the text message on her cell phone.

"Aw, crap," she muttered. 911 from Lucas. "I know this is going to sound contrived but—"

"You have to go?" Alana asked, sounding unsurprised.

Mariska nodded and, taking a breath, decided to act against her better sense. "But, maybe I can make it up to you. Say, dinner?"

CHAPTER 5
Fight Night

"SO THEORETICALLY, GIVEN Beregic's GPS records and our tracker, you can isolate the areas that they might be using as fight clubs?" Mariska asked, her butt parked on the edge of the desk as she faced Lucas.

He massaged ointment into his knee as he nodded. "Yeah, from the historical information Nina gave me on his squad car's GPS, I've pared it down to three possibilities. There was also another abduction reported this morning."

"You think it's fight night." No wonder he had 911'ed her away from her date.

Alana hadn't seemed to mind, saying she had mountains of work to do at any rate. They had set another date, and Mariska smiled at the memory of the nearly shy kiss Alana had given her. If Alana had projected anything, it had certainly never been bashfulness. It had been quite endearing, and the small thrill it had caused did nothing to quell Mariska's confusion. It would have been so much better if Alana had been a bitch.

"Hello?"

Mariska started from her daydream and looked down at Lucas, who seemed on the verge of waving his hand in front of her face to get her attention.

"Sorry, you were saying?" she asked, slightly embarrassed to have been caught with her head in the clouds.

"How much did you have to drink? I'm not sending you in the field if—"

"I'm fine," she said, holding up a hand. "And for the record, you're not the one who gets to make that call. I know my limits, thank you." She pushed off the desk to gear up.

Once she was suited up in her usual turquoise leather vest, she headed over to her ATV. The vehicle was just the right size for maneuvering in the sewer tunnels. The small amplifier on the back would further bolster her radio signal and enable Lucas to piggyback on any computer system within range and siphon the contents into a private server.

"Ready?" Lucas asked, his voice loud and clear over the radio.

"Five-by-five, Big Brother. On the move." She gunned the engine, the small all-terrain vehicle jumped forward and tore into the tunnels.

"THIS SITE'S A dud," Mariska said twenty minutes later as she walked around the makeshift arena in a dilapidated warehouse. The fighting ring itself had been taken down. Not long ago though, judging by the thin layer of dust. Probably after the last round of fights.

"Looks like they were here recently." She bent down and crumbled a piece of brick in her gloved hands. "They just pulled out all the posts for the ring." She could see the rough outline of an octagon built by the post holes, the cement rubbed down where the bottom of the fence had scratched along the ground.

"All right, the next location is two kilometres northeast."

"Roger that." She hopped on the ATV then turned towards the appropriate tunnel and opened up the throttle.

"There's an increase in electrical output, I think you've got a live site," Lucas said.

Mariska put on the brakes, killed the engine then stepped off the four-wheeler. She made easy work of the maintenance ladder and shouldered the manhole cover out of place to find herself outside of a warehouse not unlike the other. A flick of her lock pick, and she was in the back door.

She ping-ponged a shurikan between the first pair of guards and knocked them out. She quickly found herself in the holding pen, a large group of costumed fighters milling about as a smaller group of street kids tugged on the bars of the cages that held them prisoner.

"You!"

Mariska turned around.

"You're new."

She looked around and took a step closer to the costumed fighters before shrugging nonchalantly. "Yeah, just in."

"First round," the little man said, pushing her to the front of the line.

"Shit," she muttered as a group of four men muscled past her on the way out to the ring.

Mariska looked around the arena, taking in as much information as possible. The place was considerably more ornate than the other one. Catwalks had been built in three tiers, presumably with the VIPs closest to the carnage.

The old stonework of the warehouse had been scrubbed free of years of detritus and filth. The glass panes that she would have expected to be broken or missing had all been blacked out

The cemented cinder block walls of the pit itself were the better part of twelve feet high, ensuring no fighter was able to escape to the seats above. The gray stone was splashed with red in some places. Mariska had a fairly good idea of what had been used as paint. This arena was far more developed than the others they'd discovered, the host appeared to be pulling out all the stops. Even with the blood, it was pretty swanky. As far as death pits went anyway.

"Are you getting all of this?" Mariska asked, turning her head to capture the images of the fight club and the observers. They were almost exclusively well-dressed types, save for a choice few, who wore more casual clothing but were sporting nasty pieces of hardware.

"Hey," she said, focusing one man's weapon. "Isn't that—?"

"The newest mod of the AK? Yeah," Lucas said. "Whoever is running these fights has connections and serious bank."

Mariska could hear him typing furiously in the background. "Great. That makes me feel infinitely better." She grunted as one of the costumed beefcakes shouldered her from behind. "Am I supposed to fight these guys? 'Cause it could get all kinds of messy up in here." She looked around the sand-covered ring. This arena was considerably larger than the last fight site. Lucky her.

She took an instinctive step back as a spear pierced the ground at her feet. Her peers also had spears. She had seen something like this once, but it involved Russell Crowe and a small army.

"Big Brother?"

"Hold them off, I'm going to route police to your location. Try to pin down a leader and get some footage." Mariska widened her eyes as the beefiest of the men stalked towards her.

"Would you like me to do this before or after this steroid

monkey turns me into applesauce?" Mariska said, keeping a close watch as the man picked up a spear and headed for her.

"Huh, that can't be good."

He charged Mariska, waving his spear forward and back and taking aim at her.

"Oh, Christ!"

He released it, and Mariska waited for the last possible moment, then threw herself to the side. She rolled, grabbed her own spear, and swept it in a wide arc at ground level at the man's ankles.

The crowd around her cheered as the man landed face first in the sand. She brought her spear high overhead and twisted it to bring the blunt end down across the back of his shoulders, disabling but not killing him. The crowd recognized her mercy and the thunderous boo nearly caused her to jump.

"Jesus, and you call me trigger happy," she muttered to Lucas.

She turned her attention to the other three combatants who seemed content to slug it out with one another for the moment. She took her chance to scan the area once more and saw a discrete logo painted on the wall behind the VIP box. She pressed the auto zoom and focused the mini video camera on the symbol—the same one from the bank and the subway. The new guys in town were heavy hitters.

"Got it?" she asked.

"Affirmative, police are ten minutes out."

"From the building or from securing this place?" Lucas remained silent. "Damn it." Who knew how long it would take for the boys and girls in blue to get to her and disperse the crowd.

"Just hold them off, you're doing fine."

"Yeah, until the beefcakes remember they've got a chick half their size in the ring with them." She jammed her spear into the ground, then grabbed a shurikan. She could disarm at least one of them. The other two would pounce on their downed fellow, which would buy her a couple of minutes. She raised her arm, ready to toss. A screech echoed through the arena.

She fought the urge to cover her ears and turned to the source of the sound. A rusted metal door was being opened and the freshly scrubbed and poorly costumed street kids were being manhandled into the ring.

One small girl clung to the side of a fierce-looking brunette whose keen eyes were scanning the arena. There were six of them in all, two girls and four boys—they couldn't have been out of their teens. Mariska recognized two of the boys from the alley two weeks ago.

It was as though a dinner bell had been rung. The remaining warriors turned on the kids, feral expressions in place.

"You've got to be kidding me." This wasn't going to be a fight, it was going to be a slaughter.

Mariska raised her shurikan, let it fly at the nearest warrior, and knocked his weapon from his grasp as she sprinted to front line the kids.

"What are you doing?" one of the men shouted. "We're supposed to fight them, you idiot."

"Change of plans, boys." Mariska turned to the hostages. "Fan out, keep moving, stay in pairs." She settled herself to meet the next man head on. "C'mon, beefy, looks like it's our turn to dance."

He shrugged as he walked, cracking the knuckles of large hands. "Your funeral." He swung for her head, and she threw up both hands to deflect the punch, catching the brunt of it on her forearms. She dropped to one knee and drove her fist into his groin. He dropped like a stone and tucked himself into a well-muscled ball.

"I don't care how big you are, that always hurts," she said with a smirk as she stood. She thought she could hear Lucas moan in sympathy. She drove her boot heel into his face, putting him down for the count.

She sensed a spear swinging towards the back of her shoulders and dropped to avoid the blow. With startling speed, the wielder switched directions and swung over her head. He brought the weapon under her guard and up into her gut and lifted her off her feet. She grunted as she landed hard on her back.

Mariska coughed, trying to suck breath back into her lungs as she used her legs to push herself backwards and out of range. She rolled to the side as he swung downward, the metal tip of the blade coming dangerously close to her hooded head. She kicked upward and landed her boot on his hand, hoping to get him to drop the weapon.

He merely adjusted his grip and stabbed downward. She

opened her legs and let out a yelp as the spear tip landed mere centimeters from her pelvis.

"Hey, just 'cause I don't think with that area doesn't mean I don't need it." Mariska kicked up, wrapped her legs around the spear, and took a better hold with her hands. He picked the spear up, Mariska still attached, and swung it like a baseball bat. He released his grip at the high point of the arc and sent her into a brick wall with a dull thud.

Mariska dropped to all fours and spit out a mouthful of blood as she felt her ribs. Definitely broken. The man retrieved his weapon and turned his attention to the kids who were dashing around the ring trying to avoid the other warrior.

They were doing a good job of it until Mariska's first adversary, looking tired of the hunt and getting jeered by the onlookers, raised his spear and heaved it at one of the kids. Mariska turned her head as the teen dropped to the ground, the weapon protruding from his chest. The cheer was disgusting in its intensity.

She grabbed a shurikan and tried to raise her arm for the throw. Her ribs screamed in protest as she let it fly, and the shurikan skipped across his bicep, leaving a thin streak of blood along his arm.

"Big Brother?" she asked, coughing slightly to clear her mouth of blood.

"Police are making their way into the sewer. Five minutes."

The gladiators had turned on the young women now and Mariska marveled at the bravery of one stern teen. She stood her ground, tall body blocking the men from the younger girl behind her.

"Not this time, asshole." Mariska moved as fast as she was able, taking a spear from the ground as she went.

She lobbed it at the man just as he put a meaty hand on a Bowie knife on his belt. His eyes widened in surprise as he looked down at his side to see the spear sticking out of his body. He fell without a sound, sending up a puff of sand. Mariska hated to kill but she wasn't above doing what was necessary to keep innocents safe.

"I don't believe," she coughed painfully, spitting out blood, "I said I was finished with you yet." She took a step towards the man who had thrown her into the wall.

He narrowed his eyes and stepped towards her. An alarm blared through the arena.

"Breach!" one of the guards yelled.

Mariska heard the cocking weapons. She looked up to see them taking aim at everyone in the ring, warriors and kids alike.

"Shit, get down!" she yelled, diving for the two girls and tackling them to the side.

The first spray of bullets missed them and her last opponent. He looked at her for a moment, eyes blazing hatred before he ran for the exit.

"Guardian?" Lucas called, his voice nearly drowned out by the sound of automatic gunfire.

The gunmen were ushering the patrons out the exits. Only one man remained. He stood directly above them, scanning the arena for survivors. It seemed she and the two girls were the last.

"Go for the walls. Run!" She pushed the girls forward as she followed. She needed to be out in the open to get a good angle to knock the gun from his hands. She tossed a shurikan, focused on his finger on the trigger with her dead in his sights.

The bullets slammed into her vest just as her shurikan knocked the gun from his grip, sending it tumbling to the sandy floor. She dropped to the sand, groaning in pain. It felt like three solid hits to her sternum. He really hadn't been fucking around.

"Guardian? Guardian do you read?"

Mariska closed her eyes, trying to focus her mind through the chaos around her. There was so much noise.

"Guardian! Mariska, answer me!"

She had enough consciousness left to register that Lucas had broken code. He was worried. That couldn't be good.

She felt bony hands wrap around each of her arms, and her body moved across the sand. She opened her eyes and stared at the parallel trails her boots left as she was dragged across the arena. Her head lolled back, and she could see the elder girl with a determined set of her jaw, tugging her backwards, her companion wrapped around Mariska's other arm. She groaned as they jostled her, not expecting the quiet "sorry" from the more demure of the two.

"S'okay," she managed to say. They got to the edge of the arena, the sand turning to stone beneath them. "Police, coming," she sputtered. "You're safe."

"What about you?" the girl asked as they stopped and propped her up against the wall. What about her indeed. If the police caught her, that would be the end of things. "You have to get out of here."

"Just gotta get t'my ATV." She had enough in her to drive for a bit. Far enough to be out of the search area anyway. Lucas could come get her.

"Where is it?"

"Not far, corner," Mariska said, trying to push herself to her feet. She could barely get her butt off the ground and began to sink back down before hands wrapped around her biceps. She could hear the police screaming orders at the top of their lungs.

"Come on, there isn't much time."

Mariska leaned heavily on the girls as they made their way to the ATV. She slumped herself in the seat and leaned forward on the handlebars. She couldn't straighten up without her ribs screaming bloody murder. She was fooling herself if she thought she could drive out under her own steam.

"You have to go," the taller girl said. "The cops are coming this way."

Mariska sat back, put her hands on the handlebars, and sucked in a deep breath as the pain threatened to make her black out.

"Can't." She shook her head. Maybe Perkins would be the one to find her. Not likely, but she was her only hope at the moment.

"Alexis, get in the back."

Mariska felt someone slide in behind her. Thin arms reached past her to grab the handlebars. "How do I do this?"

"Right handle," Mariska said. "Pull back gently or you'll throw your friend off the back."

They moved forward, jerkily at first, until the young woman behind her got the hang of the controls. The bright lights of the ATV illuminated the dark tunnels, and Mariska directed them back towards the warehouse.

"Big Brother, get decent, I'm bringing home company."

"What? Why? How badly are you hurt?"

"A call to the doctor might be in order," Mariska said as they reached the turnoff to the warehouse tunnel.

"Are you sure about the civilians?"

She knew that Lucas knew she wouldn't expose people to the danger of their secret unnecessarily. Every person who knew their identity or anything about them became a potential target. But there hadn't been much choice. She needed help. And, considering how the kids had likely ended up in the fight club, she wasn't certain leaving them with police was a good idea. Not some nameless patrolman anyway. She would get them into Perkin's hands. Then they'd be safe.

"I'm sure, open the doors," Mariska said, waiting to see the light as the steel doors gave way to reveal the computer lab.

Lucas was standing in the doorway, a dark silhouette amidst the glow of computer screens and fluorescent lights.

Mariska nearly gave a start as they pulled up and Lucas came into better view. He was wearing his mask, a royal blue spandex balaclava, blue tinted goggles tucked over his eyes. He hadn't worn that since . . . Well, it had been a while. Muscular arms were crossed over a broad chest, his powerful upper body an odd contrast to the weakness in his legs as he walked towards them. He wasn't using his cane.

"Can you get up?" he asked as the ATV jolted to a stop.

Mariska nodded, somewhat weakly and tried to swing her leg around. She held her damaged ribs to minimize the pain.

"Damn." She got both feet onto the ground, her legs threatening to collapse beneath her as the edges of her vision tunnelled.

"Come on." He took her arm and did his best to support her as she walked gingerly towards the freight elevator.

She felt him stumble with her weight. His knees weren't going to be happy.

"Hey, kid, one of you gimme a hand would ya? Get that elevator gate open," Lucas said.

The smaller of the two rushed by and pulled open the gate. Small hands wrapped around her unsupported bicep, and Mariska turned to see the other girl.

They made it to the elevator, up to the second floor, and into the medical room.

Lucas helped her walk up the step stool and onto the bed. "I'm going to call the doc and see how far away he is. Don't touch anything." He eyed the two young women.

The small girl ducked back behind her taller companion. The command had come out harshly, even to Mariska's ears. Lucas was nervous about having strangers in the inner sanctum. She could understand but that didn't mean the poor kids needed to be barked at.

"Don't worry about him," she said, watching as he limped away to use the phone. She winced as she unbuckled her utility belt. Even breathing was going to be hell for the next few days. "Thanks for the hand . . ."

"Brooke," the taller girl said. "Alexis." She looked at her companion.

"Brooke and Alexis." Mariska pulled her gloves off and put them next to her belt. "If you check in that closet," she pointed with one hand tightly tucked to her ribs, "there should be some sweats that'll fit you."

Alexis and Brooke looked down at themselves as if noticing for the first time that they were clad in little more than a leather bra and skirt. Indeed, Mariska had been so busy, she'd barely noticed herself, but she bet a clean set of clothes would go a long way towards making the pair more comfortable.

Alexis wandered to the closet while Brooke remained near Mariska, thin arms crossed as she stared at her.

"I thought you were some kind of urban myth."

Mariska snorted, immediately regretting it as her ribs screamed in protest. "Well, hopefully, if this particular myth gets rewritten, I'll knock the bad guy out before I take three in the chest."

"Yeah, well, not many people would put themselves out like that to help street trash, so thanks."

Mariska looked into the girl's stern face. The girl was younger than her but her eyes spoke of things Mariska couldn't even guess at.

"You're not street trash and you certainly didn't have what those guys planned coming to you. You can change in the bathroom, Alexis." She raised her voice so the girl would hear.

Alexis nodded shyly and then went into the small room.

"Cute kid. She your sister?"

"No."

Mariska hoped for more, and they sat in uneasy silence.

Alexis reappeared in sweats that were far too big for her small frame. Gray cotton fabric pooled at her feet as she walked back to Brooke and Mariska. She held her leather costume in one hand and a second set of sweats in the other.

"They're comfy."

Mariska smiled and pulled her hood back. It was too warm to wear it in the warehouse.

"You're a chick?"

Marisha pulled her chestnut hair from its elastic confines and raised an eyebrow. "You were expecting what?"

"Your voice . . ."

Mariska narrowed her eyes, then realization dawned. She tugged the neck of her vest down to reveal the throat mic that also acted as a mild synthesizer and deepened her voice.

"Prevents voice recognition," Mariska said.

Brooke's stern face seemed to soften, if only a fraction. So the kid was nervous around men. Mariska filed that away for later reference.

"Get changed," she said. "You'll feel better."

Brooke cast a wary glance at Lucas, who was walking back towards them. "Don't worry, you're safe here." She nodded and disappeared into the bathroom.

"Doc'll be here in ten. He says he owes you for saving him from listening to his son-in-law talking about the Maple Leafs' preseason prep."

"Wonder if that means he won't lay on the 'I told you so' quite so thickly."

"I wouldn't count on it," Lucas said, his attention split between Mariska and Alexis, who had mustered enough courage to wander around the training floor.

"Relax, she can't hurt anything," Mariska said.

"How old do you think she is?"

"I'd bet sixteen, the other one's maybe eighteen." Mariska unclipped the straps from her legs and Lucas pushed her hands away. He loosened the straps, then pulled them from her before bending down to work on her boots.

"What do we do with them?" Mariska asked, adjusting her sunglasses. She looked at Lucas.

It was so disconcerting to see him back in his Guardian gear. When he stood there, back straight, looking every bit the hero he had once been, it was easy to forget that Lisa wasn't somewhere behind him, prepping the medical bay or working on their gear.

If only it could be that easy. Just hit the rewind button, redo that one night over again.

"You okay?"

"Yeah, just . . . thinking. Blindfold them, send 'em to Perkins.

They might know something about who was running this freak show. If not, Perkins should at least be able to get them into a shelter or the foster system, get them off the streets. She's the only cop I trust right now. I don't want to hand those girls over to the department just to find them in a dumpster two days later."

He nodded. It would be naive to think that Beregic was the only cop on the new syndicate's payroll.

"Feed them something too, would you? The little one'll shatter if she ever takes a spill," Mariska said, looking at a frail Alexis.

"You bring them here and now you want to subject them to my cooking? I thought you wanted to save them."

"There're leftovers in the fridge from a couple of days ago. I know you can work the microwave."

Brooke stepped out of the small bathroom, bare feet padding quietly across the hardwood as she walked towards them.

"Go on, I'll wait for the Doc," Mariska said.

Lucas limped off without a word to Brooke and headed for the elevator.

"He's going to get you guys a bite to eat. He'll behave."

Brooke followed Lucas with her eyes.

"I promise."

Brooke nodded and followed Lucas, Alexis quickly fell into step behind her.

Mariska leaned her head against the wall, closing her eyes and doing her best to ignore the painful throbbing of her entire body. She remembered the feeling vividly. It was one of the physical reminders of the night Lisa had died. The pain had been her penance, a well-deserved punishment for failing to protect Lisa. As much as it had hurt, she had treasured the pain. It had been one of the few tangible proofs that the life she had shared with Lisa had been real. That she hadn't always been alone and broken.

The sound of the elevator broke through her thoughts. Mariska heard the approaching footsteps of Doctor Acco.

"If you were going to ruin my dinner, you could have at least had the decency to get shot before Thomas started talking to me about his stock options," he said.

Mariska opened her eyes and pulled her mask down from her face. "Sorry, I'll try harder next time."

"Hmmph." He gave her a cursory once over to make sure she wasn't in danger of bleeding out from anywhere.

"Ow," Mariska said as Acco unzipped her vest and tried to wrestle it from her body.

Two slugs fell from the Kevlar, landing with twin clinks on the floor.

"Fucker had good aim," she said, wincing as she wrangled herself out of her leather and Kevlar vests. The final bullet was embedded tightly in the armour.

Close one.

Acco took the suture scissors from the tray and cut open her undershirt, then sucked in a breath. "You're going to be in rough shape," he said, as he gently ran his hands along her side to check for broken ribs.

Mariska could tell she had broken two floaters, and the bullets had left fist-sized bruises along her sternum.

"Lie down, I'll dope you up while I take care of this."

Mariska nodded, allowing Acco to lift her legs onto the exam table as she leaned back. "I couldn't save them all," she said as she felt the quick pinch of the needle piercing her skin.

"I know," he said quietly as he took her hand. "Better some, than none."

Mariska closed her eyes, willing the tears not to come. She felt a wet trail make its way down her cheeks. They were barely more than children. This was the worst part of the job. The simple truth was, no matter how fast she was or how hard she worked, she couldn't save everyone. It didn't seem so simple now.

"Get some sleep. Things will look better in the morning," Acco said.

Mariska nodded slightly, allowing the sedative to work its magic. "I have to find them," she murmured sleepily, not certain who she meant by "them." Things were getting murky. Anesthesia was kicking in.

"You will. Sleep now."

Reassured by the voice of a man she had known and trusted for years, Mariska slipped into unconsciousness.

MARISKA WOKE THE next morning, at least she thought it was morning. It was hard to tell with the blackout curtains. Feeling groggy and achy, she tried to swing her legs off the medical table nearly sending herself into apoplexy. She decided to remain still until she could move without killing herself.

She turned her head to the side. Lucas was slumped in his computer chair, his blond head resting against his fist as he slept. She blinked as she tried to speak to wake him up. Sleeping sitting up wasn't a luxury he could afford anymore. His knees would make him suffer for it. He was going to be cramped as hell.

"Lu . . ." She coughed and groaned as her broken ribs made themselves known.

Lucas woke and stood quickly. He was even less fluid than usual, limping heavily as he favoured his left knee, the more damaged of the two. Poor guy.

"How you holding up?" he asked, checking the bandages Acco had somehow managed to wrap around her midsection.

"Hurts," she said honestly. She remembered broken ribs.

Last summer she had dealt with four of them. They were notoriously bad to heal. Any jarring or strikes to her midsection during the bone knitting process usually meant starting at square one. It had taken nearly three months to recover from the last time and even now, over a year later, they weren't back up to standard.

"You're off patrol for the next couple of weeks at least," he said firmly, leaving no room for Mariska to argue. Not that she had good reason to, he was right. That didn't stop her from giving in to her need to counter him, just for the sake of appearances.

"I'll be fine in a week," she said.

"Not a chance," Lucas said with an indignant snort. "You're grounded until these finish knitting. Your ribs are your Achilles' heel and you know it."

She nodded, grudgingly accepting the truth. They had never been the same since last year. She could take a shot to the jaw that was unheard of for most women, but a well-placed strike to her lower ribs would have her nursing her midsection for days on end.

"Where are the girls?"

"Sent them off with Acco. I dropped a little tranquilizer into their food, knocked 'em out."

"You drugged them?"

"Did you want to be the one to tell Brooke that she was going to have to get into a car, blindfolded, with a man she didn't know?" Mariska had a vague idea of how well that particular conversation would have gone over. "Anyway, no harm done. Perkins has them now."

"Good." At least they were safe and she could move on to the next problem.

"Let's get you moved upstairs." Lucas put one arm under Mariska's and helped to slide her off the table.

Mariska did her best not to pass out, knowing Lucas's knees couldn't take both of their weights.

"Any idea who's setting up these fight clubs yet?" she asked as they walked slowly to the freight elevator.

"Nothing so far. I'm still running the symbol through the police database but I'm not getting any hits. Perkins doesn't recognize it either."

"I've seen it before," Mariska said. "Before the subway. I thought it was just a graffiti tag. It's all over the city."

"Going by what we've seen so far, whoever these people are, they've got a pretty diverse criminal portfolio."

"Marvelous."

Lucas closed the elevator gate and pushed the up button. "I don't suppose you remember when you first started seeing them?"

Mariska searched her memory for the first time the symbol had registered. "Last January is the first time I consciously remember it. I saw it at one of those skate parks." She grunted as Lucas walked them out of the elevator to the apartment on the top floor of the warehouse. "But I'm sure I saw it before then. I just can't put my finger on it."

"Don't stress about it. We'll know soon enough." He sat her on the couch, walked over to the blinds, and pulled them open, letting in the early morning sun. "Hungry?"

Mariska shook her head. The very idea of food at the moment made her nauseated. "No thanks. Can I have some water though?"

Lucas grabbed the crutches leaning against the side table, then used them to swing his way into the kitchen.

Mariska sighed sadly. Lucas didn't resort to using his crutches unless the pain was getting intense. They were both in rough shape.

"Here you go," he said, handing her a large water bottle.

"Thanks. Come sit down, get the pressure off your knees," Mariska said, shifting over slightly to give him room to sit.

"Thanks." He groaned as he picked up the remote. "Can you believe we're only twenty-two?" he asked quietly, as he rubbed his knees.

"Certainly hasn't felt that way for a while." Mariska put her head on his shoulder. He turned the channel, finally landing on something they would both enjoy, though she figured it would only be minutes before she drifted back to sleep.

This used to be their early morning ritual when they had been a trio. They would make breakfast and watch a movie to decompress. Lisa would invariably end up in the middle, used as a pillow for Lucas and Mariska. They had been so insanely protective of her. It was a cruel irony that Lisa had been the first to go down. One night, one mistake, had changed everything.

Mariska sighed, trying to shake off the melancholic thoughts. She knew they had been brought on by the girls the night before. Brooke had been damn determined to keep her companion out of harm's way. Mariska saw a bit of herself in the girl. She had put herself in harm's way, more than once, to keep Lisa safe, though admittedly, Lisa had never had trouble holding her own. God, she missed her.

"I miss her too," Lucas said, as if reading her thoughts.

"I know, Luke, I know."

They watched the TV in silence.

CHAPTER SIX
Healing

MARISKA YAWNED WIDELY as she clicked on the next image, threw it out, and clicked on the one after it. The computer had identified over three hundred near hits from her photos at the fight club, and she'd been wading through them, one by one, trying to find the tag that would identify their new friends.

"Huh," she said as the next image popped up. "Gotcha." She fidgeted in her chair to lessen the aggravation on her ribs.

"What do you have?" Lucas asked, looking up from where he was repacking her parachute. It had been due for its six month check.

He went to the computer and clicked on the appropriate spots to enhance the image. He motioned for her to move away from the computer and let him in. He could be so territorial.

Mariska stood, hip leaning against the desk, arms crossed, as Lucas searched through the database to identify where the picture had come from.

"Damn it," he said as the appropriate file came up on screen. It was from the F.B.I.

"What?" Mariska asked, leaning down to see. "Stella?"

"STELLA."

"That's what I said. What the hell kind of a name is Stella for a criminal?" She scanned the file.

"It's an organization, not a person," Lucas said with a shrug.

"Honestly, that's a horrible name for a crime organization. It doesn't exactly strike fear into the hearts of innocent Torontonians everywhere," Mariska said. The organization obviously meant business, but Stella? Really? They weren't even trying.

"I'm aware of that," Lucas said before his eyes took on a mischievous gleam. "Didn't we know a Stella? She was married to a detective or something?"

Mariska frowned. Leave it to him to bring that up. "His name was Kowalski. It was a TV show. Can we move on?"

She couldn't believe he was going to harp on her now about her childhood crush. Ass. It had been exponentially worse when she had tried to date a Stella in her freshman year. Frasier Benson jokes had run free.

"Uh huh, TV," Lucas said, nodding his head sagely.

"Yes, TV. Let's stay focused in reality. Big bad super criminal invading the city," she said, trying to divert Lucas's attention away from embarrassing childhood memories. Though, to be honest, it was nice to see him in a playful mood again. He'd been dark and withdrawn for so long now. Neither of them smiled the way they used to.

"What show was that exactly?"

"*Due South.*" She tried to push his hand out of the way so she could use the mouse to scroll down the page. "Evil-doings organization hell bent on destruction."

"Weren't you convinced the crazy little Polack and the Mountie were shacking up?"

"They were." She looked away from the screen. "They kissed." She hit her fist on the desk.

"I think he termed it, buddy breathing," Lucas said, looking up at Mariska.

"It was a front." She paused. "I don't know what's sadder. The fact that I'm arguing over a ten-year-old show or the fact that, of all those episodes we watched as kids, your memory is somehow locked onto the buddy breathing moment. Are you trying to tell me something?"

A wave of realization passed over his face and turned back to the computer screen with a cough. "Evil-doings organization hell bent on destruction." He pointed at the computer screen.

"Yeah, that's what I thought," she said in a wry tone as they perused the file.

Stella.

Fucking honestly.

MARISKA RUBBED HER eyes, trying to get the grit from them as she read over the dossier Lucas had given her. It seemed Stella was actually STELLA. Special Tactics Extraction and Location of Lost Artifacts. Lost artifacts her well-shaped ass. The only lost thing they ever seemed to find were federal witnesses who, having been found, were promptly lost again.

Gun running, drug smuggling, money laundering, the occasional hit. Seemed they had a finger in every pie. Of course, to give the company some degree of credibility, they seemed to actually employ a couple of explorer teams. Probably just some well-dressed meatheads with undergrads in archeology who ran around robbing graves.

The organization moved from city to city, a small core group of underlings who employed locals once they set up shop. The group was supposedly headed by a woman named Anna Jones. That was obviously a fake. The woman existed only on paper, and it seemed the FBI, and others, had taken to just calling her Stella. There were no visuals, not even vague descriptions. Seemed she kept herself a pretty low profile. Smart. Unfortunately.

Made sense though, all things considered. You didn't build an international crime organization from the ground up without having something of substance between your ears. Mariska flipped the file closed, nudged it off to the side, then pulled out her economics textbook.

With all the hubbub trying to track down the fight clubs, she'd been falling behind. With only a week until the final, she couldn't afford to let things slide much longer if she had any desire to pass the course.

She blew out a frustrated breath as her phone rang. She clicked it on. She'd told Luke she needed to study. If this was him calling about some over-the-top all-encompassing criminal conspiracy thing, she was going to brain him. And make him take her test.

"Hello?"

"Mariska?"

Mariska tried to fight her smile as Alana's voice registered. Part of her was still balking at the thought of dating again. Her logical mind was telling her Lucas was right, Lisa would want her to be happy. Maybe Alana wasn't the one to bring that happiness to her, but she had to start somewhere.

"Alana, hey." Perhaps Economics could wait a little longer. "I was beginning to think you'd blown me off." She hadn't heard from Alana since their non-date the week before.

"Hardly," Alana said. "Just had a bit of a crisis at work."

"Oh, that's too bad. Get it all sorted out?" Mariska asked, leaning back in her recliner. She winced at the twinge in her ribs. A week later and she still wasn't up for anything more zealous than a rousing game of checkers.

"Not yet, but I will," Alana said. "I was hoping I could interest you in a quick supper. I have to come back to the office tonight, so I can't spare much more than a couple of hours, but I thought maybe we could hit a takeout."

Mariska checked her watch. Couldn't study on an empty stomach, right? Right. "Sure. Where did you want to meet?"

"I HOPE I didn't pull you away from anything too important," Alana said, before maneuvering chopsticks full of chow mein into her mouth.

"Nah," Mariska said with a wave of her own chopsticks. "Just an economics chapter I wasn't too keen on reading."

"So tell me some more about yourself. We really only had time for pleasantries last time."

"What would you like to know?" Mariska asked. It was easier to remember any lies she had to tell if specific questions were asked. *Where did the bruises come from? How many concussions have you had? Where were you at two-thirty this morning? Et cetera, et cetera.*

"What do you do for fun?"

Mariska had to think on that one. Between school, work, and her ass kicking, she wasn't exactly awash in free time.

"I, uh, dabble in the martial arts, hit the gym a couple of times a week. Read nontextbooks when I can find a minute."

Alana canted her head, lips quirked. "Martial arts, huh? You don't look like the fighting type."

Mariska returned the smile. "In this city, everyone's the fighting type." She pushed the spent box of egg rolls to the side. "How about you?"

"Oh, nothing quite so exciting as martial arts. In my line of work, I can't really afford to show up with a black eye. I run most mornings. My job doesn't leave me with much free time."

"And what time you do have, you spend eating mediocre Chinese food with a university student," Mariska said.

"Yes, well, we all have quirks. I think I like it that way,"

Alana said, reaching into Mariska's takeout box and pulling out a chicken ball.

"Me too," Mariska said, surprised to find she meant it.

"I DON'T LIKE it," Lucas said as he watched Mariska tug on her freshly repaired costume.

She had become fairly adept at sewing up bullet holes over the years. Three new sets of stitches marked where the slugs had hit her chest. They weren't the only sets of stitches. It wouldn't be long before the vest wouldn't be fit for polite company.

"Would you relax? It's been a month. I'm fine," she said, buckling up the straps over her vest and setting the throat mic in place. "Look, I need to do something. I've gained five pounds from sitting on my ass for the past four weeks."

"Mariska—"

She held up a hand as her cell phone rang and let a small smile cross her lips as she recognized the number on the caller ID.

"Hey you," she said in greeting. She tucked the phone into the crook of her shoulder as she pulled her gloves from her pocket and tugged them on.

"Hey, got a second?" Alana asked.

"For you, I've got two." Mariska double-checked she had a full load of shurikans in her belt.

"Do you own a dress?"

"Um, sure. I haven't worn it since I was ten, but I'm sure it's in my closet somewhere."

Alana laughed quietly. "I was going for something a little more mature."

"In that case, no. Why? What's up?"

"I have to go to that gala next Friday, and my escort backed out on me this afternoon."

"Oh, well, I'd be happy to go with you, but I'm not sure how well I clean up. I haven't done anything classy since prom," Mariska said. She had a lot of scars to cover up.

"Nonsense, everyone there will be jealous that I've got you on my arm," Alana said.

Her tone was so matter-of-fact that Mariska couldn't help but believe her. Alana had that effect a lot. She didn't offer compliments as freely as other women Mariska had dated, but when she did, she was so direct and firm about it that Mariska couldn't help but be flattered.

"Okay, well, did you want to go shopping sometime this week? I'm not really sure what I should be looking for."

Alana had mentioned the gala in passing the week before. It was supposed to be filled with the who's who of Alana's company and some high-class officials. Mariska read about those types of people in the papers, she didn't socialize with them.

"Of course, how's Wednesday for you?"

"Sounds great." Now that the damnable Economics class was finished, Mariska had more free time. It would be a nice break.

"Fantastic, I've got to finish up some stuff here at the office, are you at work now?"

"Um, more or less, just getting changed," Mariska said as she looked at the equipment spread out at her feet.

"Long shift, short shift?"

"Not sure yet, depends on how busy we get," Mariska said, shaking her head. It never failed that she ended up having to lie about her whereabouts.

"If you get finished at a decent time, give me a call. I have the day off tomorrow. Perhaps we could open a bottle of wine, watch a movie?"

"You mean actually spend some time together like regular dating people do?"

"Yes. I thought it might be nice to try it on for size," Alana said.

"You're on. I'll call you when I'm done."

ALANA CLOSED THE phone, tucked it into her vest, and walked back to where the men had hung one of their peers from a meat hook. Not actually on the meat hook. Not yet anyway.

She shook her head at him. He seemed so out of place, well dressed, short, neat hair, trimmed fingernails, all blindfolded and bound by rough rope, hanging in a meat locker. His wrists were chafed and bled from the pressure of his weight. Some of the droplets had frozen as they trailed down his arm. He really should have known better than to cross her path.

It had taken her over a month to ferret out the little traitor. He'd been quietly siphoning off product for nearly a year, usually covering his tracks. Well enough that she hadn't noticed at any rate. But Ferrero's search for the missing coke had led him to her own backyard where she had taken over. The last thing she needed was for some half-rate wannabe guerilla knowing she had leaks in her operation.

"Who've you been selling to?" she asked.

He didn't answer.

She wasn't certain if that was from spite or unconsciousness. She nodded at the man next to him who delivered a swift punch to his kidney. The man groaned, muscles twitching as he swung on the hook.

"Come on, Lance. You already know how this is going to end. Make it easy on yourself."

Her mind was only half on the task at hand. She already knew who he'd been dealing the coke to, she just wanted to hear him say it. She was actually more concerned about the state of her apartment. She'd been in a rush this morning, she was fairly certain she had at least made her bed. Her coffee cup was definitely still in the sink.

Mariska had been to her apartment once before for only a few minutes when Alana had to run up to grab her forgotten purse. More extended stays hadn't been possible and whether that was bad luck or Mariska's own hesitance, Alana wasn't certain. Their schedules seemed to conflict regularly, and Alana had a feeling it was more by Mariska's design than random coincidence.

It was frustrating, but the circumstances kept her interest in Mariska piqued. Alana had a habit of tiring quickly of her partners, but Mariska proved to be somewhat of an enigma.

Mariska seemed driven and intelligent yet hadn't developed any plans beyond her graduation in April. She could easily work within her field while going to school but had chosen instead to wait tables and do other menial jobs. She spoke often about her family and friends. One man specifically, Lucas, but rarely about past lovers. Mention of past relationships left her with a haunted look that made Alana unusually uncomfortable. It was sad to see a look like that in someone so young.

"Stella?"

Alana looked tiredly at Lucky, her number one muscle man. "Kill him," she said with an absent wave. "Use the incinerator this time. I don't want him washing up on shore like the last one."

The last one being the loose lipped Beregic. He'd been careless enough to be caught by Internal Affairs, and she had no doubt that the police raid on her last fight club had been in part because of his lax behaviour.

When she had bailed him out of jail, she'd toyed with the idea of putting him in the ring with the other competitors. Give him a taste of the misery he'd helped visit on others. It would have been a rather glowing example of poetic justice. If she believed in such tripe.

In the end, common sense had gotten the best of her. No matter how much people liked a good blood bath, watching a cop get skewered as opposed to some nameless street rat would have raised a few eyebrows.

She had taken matters into her own hands but had foolishly left the body dump to someone else, ergo the need for a cover-up. The problem had been solved, and now she had to deal with the here and now. Forced to kill yet another employee who had come up lacking.

It really was a shame to have to kill Lance. He knew his end of the business inside and out and had been her contact in Toronto for a number of years. He also made good arm candy for the insipid events she had to attend to keep herself abreast of her social peers. No matter. Mariska would be a far more entertaining date.

"HEY, C'MON UP," Alana said into the speaker and pressed the button to unlock the door downstairs.

She finished wiping her hands on the dish towel and placed it back on the oven door, just so. The wine was open and breathing on the counter, the lights of the large two-bedroom apartment were dimmed with candles at strategic points providing extra illumination.

She wasn't sure what had possessed her to go through such a grand gesture. Perhaps it was a need to see if she could remove the haunted look from Mariska's eyes. A challenge of sorts. Yes, a challenge. And she hated to lose. Mariska would enjoy herself, if it killed them both.

Not literally of course. There had been quite enough of that for one night. Lance was only the beginning. Alana had needed to rip through three more underlings who had been working with him, by either doctoring the manifests or hiding cargo. She had taken a more hands-on approach with the others. The first rule of leadership. Never order your people to do what you weren't willing to do yourself. She might be a criminal but she did take a certain bit of pride at being good at what she did.

She heard a soft tap and headed for the front door. She opened it to find a disheveled Mariska clad in a university sweatshirt and sporting a worn-looking backpack.

"You look exhausted." Alana pulled the backpack from Mariska's shoulders and waved her inside.

Mariska began to yawn before stifling it behind her hand and gave Alana an apologetic look. "Sorry, long day."

Alana smiled, put the bag on the floor, then approached Mariska and buried her hands in the front pocket of her shirt. She leaned forward and dropped a kiss "hello" on soft lips. "Don't worry about it. Go have a seat. I'll grab us some glasses."

Mariska nodded, stole another quick kiss, and headed to the leather couches that were in front of a large screen TV.

Alana walked into the kitchen and opened the fridge to grab the fruit she'd bought at the market. One thing she'd managed to learn over the last few weeks was that Mariska tended to be a bit of a health nut and went for fresh berries before junk food any day of the week. It was one of the many quirks that made her all the more appealing.

Alana found it odd that she had any interest in Mariska at all. Her usual types were the sleeker businesswomen or lawyers who drank expensive wines and bought three-hundred-dollar handbags. People who walked in her world. Not students who took her out for bad Chinese and showed up on her doorstep in faded jeans and a loose ponytail. But she couldn't have talked for hours on end with any of those women, and certainly never would have thought to cater any portion of her life to them, not even as small an allowance as going to the market to buy fruit. It was disconcerting but not altogether unpleasant.

"Do you need a hand in there?" Mariska asked.

"No, I'm good. I'll be right out," Alana said, balancing the bowl of fruit and the glasses of wine easily in her hands. "Here you are." She handed one glass to Mariska and put the bowl on the coffee table.

Mariska's eyes immediately went to the fruit, her stomach rumbling in appreciation.

"I thought you worked at a restaurant, don't they feed you there?" Alana teased, tucking her feet under her and looking at Mariska.

"They would, but my choices are deep fried, broiled to a crisp, or going hungry," Mariska said, taking a sip of her wine. "That's delicious."

Alana smiled. She certainly hoped so. She had broken into the best of poor Lance's supply.

"How was your day?"

"Shit. But my night is looking up," Alana said, settling herself against the arm of the couch.

"Glad to be of service."

"Well, I was actually talking about the wine," Alana said dramatically, unable to keep a straight face at Mariska's pout.

"Aww, that's not nice," Mariska said, taking another sip of her wine.

"I'm not nice," Alana said, her voice coming out more serious than she had intended. She'd meant it to be a joke, no matter how true the statement was.

Mariska shook her head. "You invited me over, opened a bottle of wine that probably costs more than my paycheck, set up all these candles, and bought me fruit, which I know you hate since you practically threw the cherry from the sundae at me the last time we went to the ice cream shop." She leaned forward, her lips close enough to Alana's that she could feel the heat from her mouth. "That seems pretty nice to me."

Alana closed the distance between them, all thought of fruit and niceties forgotten.

Their lips touched, not the usual quick kiss, but one of intent. Smiling into the unexpected intimacy, Alana tugged gently to bring their bodies together.

Mariska stiffened and pulled away.

Damn it.

"What's wrong? Too fast?" Alana tucked a stray strand of dark hair behind Mariska's ear, the soft touch meant to reassure.

Mariska jumped to her feet and backed out of range. "I'm sorry."

"For what?" Confused, Alana stood to block Mariska from walking away. "Mariska?"

"I . . . I can't do this," Mariska said, in a pleading voice. "I want to, I want to be ready for this but . . . I'm not."

Alana tipped her chin upward to look into her eyes. "Who did this? What did she do to you?"

Mariska looked Alana's eyes and let out a shaky breath. "She died." She pulled away from Alana. "I'm sorry, I've got to go."

"Mariska . . ."

Mariska threw her backpack onto her shoulders and headed for the door. She paused, her hand on the doorknob. "Alana, you're great. Really great. This isn't fair to you. Maybe we shouldn't. I think you could find someone better." She slipped quietly out the door.

Alana stood in the center of her living room, staring at the door in confusion. What the hell just happened? Everything had been going well. Mariska had even seemed less skittish than normal. She had even taken the lead in what had been their most heated kiss to date and seemed like she had finally conquered whatever reservations she still held from her last relationship. Victory had seemed at hand and then . . . nothing.

"I can't believe she broke up with me." No one broke up with her. If anyone was going to be doing the leaving, it should have been her. "Yeah, and if anything with Mariska actually made sense so far I wouldn't have bothered with her longer than the first few dates." She shook her head. This was ridiculous.

What was even more ridiculous was that she had felt . . . something when Mariska had walked out the door. It wasn't the usual relief that came to her at the end of a relationship, but a vague sense of loss. She was going to miss Mariska. How odd.

Mariska brought a brightness to her day that she hadn't really known before. Even their rushed encounters left her feeling somehow lighter. She stared at her couch where only minutes before she and Mariska had been comfortably sitting. It had been so mundane, talking about their day and she hadn't felt so peaceful, so willing to just sit, ever.

Alana walked over to the window and looked down at the busy street below. She saw Mariska leave the building and cross the street. Her first thought was that Mariska wasn't wearing enough to ward off the chill of the cool night air. Her second was that her steps were less graceful than usual. Mariska was visibly upset, even from eleven stories up.

"Damn." There was a limit to how far she was willing to chase Mariska. At some point, the prize wouldn't be worth the expense. The real question was, had she reached her limit?

MARISKA DIDN'T KNOW where she was going, only that she needed to walk. To think. Organize her feelings. She found herself on a park bench, her hoodie wrapped tightly around her body to ward off the late October chill. She hung her head in her hands, not bothering to hold back the sobs that wracked her body.

She was so confused. Alana was a great woman. Attentive, considerate, way too easy to fall in love with.

She'd felt the emotions tinging at the periphery of her mind, waiting for the right moment to break down the walls she'd built after Lisa's death. Every time they seemed to surface, they brought a guilt that pulled her back down into the abyss. It didn't matter how she tried to reason with herself, or how much Lucas tried to reason with her. As much as her head told her she should be getting over Lisa, her heart was still holding on and her relationship with Alana felt like an affair.

Mariska exhaled. She had grieved Lisa, mourned her loss, but she knew she had yet to move into completely accepting her death. Even though she'd felt Lisa die in her arms, the tiniest, most irrational part of her brain hoped that Lisa would somehow find a way back to her.

It had been easier at first with Alana. Their dates were more friendly than anything else—drinks after work or rushed dinners between boardroom meetings and night patrol. Nothing that overtly screamed romance, which had helped keep Mariska on an even keel. The lack of traditional dating rituals had allowed her willing mind to keep control of her recalcitrant heart.

But tonight . . . the wine, the candles, it was pretty romantic as far as Alana went, and Mariska wasn't certain she was ready for what that implied. A good time, a kiss here and there, was one thing but now they seemed to be steering dangerously close to relationship territory. And that prospect terrified her.

"You'll catch your death out here."

Mariska looked up, her vision blurred by the tears in her eyes. Alana, holding the throw from her couch, sat on the bench next to her. She wrapped the blanket around Mariska's shoulders and pulled her to her.

"How did it happen?"

Mariska sniffed, burrowing her head into Alana's shoulder. "She was murdered, she . . . she went out one night. The police said it was a robbery that went wrong." She hated that lie. Hated having to drag Lisa's lifeless body to an alley to create a fake crime scene for the police to investigate. Hated foisting the guilt of Lisa's death on some nameless entity instead of setting it firmly on her own shoulders where it belonged.

"I'm sorry that happened to you," Alana said, her strong hand massaging at the back of Mariska's neck. "She must have been someone very special to still be so close to your heart. Survivor's guilt is normal. But you did survive, Mariska. Don't you think it's time to get back into the world? If this woman—"

"Lisa."

"Lisa," Alana said, "was as good as you think she was, I don't think she'd want you to spend the rest of your life alone."

Mariska shook her head.

"What?"

"You sound like Lucas," Mariska said. "And you're right, my head knows that. I just, I don't know how to move forward."

"Like I told you when we met. One day at a time."

"It's not fair to you."

"Why don't you let me decide that," Alana said as she tightened her arm around Mariska's shoulders. "I'm not in a rush, and I certainly don't have any better offers on the table."

Mariska felt a kiss dropped on the top of her head. "All right, but don't say I didn't warn you."

"Fair enough," Alana said, before being overcome by a sneeze.

Mariska sat up and looked at her. "You can't be getting sick? We've been out here for two minutes."

"Yeah, well, what can I say? I hate Canadian winters."

"WHATCHA MAKING? SMELLS good," Lucas said, two days later. "I'm hungry."

Mariska snorted as she stirred the soup and dropped in a handful of basil. "This isn't for you, you Home Ec reject. It's for Alana. She caught that bug that's been running around." She raised her voice so it would carry out of her small kitchen and into her equally small living room where Lucas was lounging.

"Spreading your cooties to her?" Lucas asked.

Mariska could practically hear the wiggle of his eyebrows.

"Hardy har." Mariska ladled some soup into a bowl and carried it to him. "Taste it. It needs something."

He tasted the soup and made all manner of faces before nodding sagely. "Needs salt."

"I don't cook with salt. Mom wouldn't even let it in the house after Dad's blood pressure scare."

"I know you don't cook with salt. I'm guessing that's why the soup needs it."

"You're an ass."

"You love me." He turned back to his tech geek magazine. "And why do you insist on feeding everyone?"

"Eh?" She spooned some of the soup into her mouth. He was right, it needed salt. Ass.

"Alana, those girls from the arena, you've even been bringing meals to Crash at least once a week."

She shrugged. "Food is comforting. I'm Ukranian. What do you want from me? It's what we do. Just because you blue bloods are afraid of eating doesn't mean the rest of the world doesn't enjoy a good meal."

"Touché."

CHAPTER 7
Two Nights At A Museum

"WHEN YOU SAID, 'Do the CN tower,' I thought you meant ride the elevator up and take a look around. Not haul myself up a million stairs," Alana said the next weekend as she followed Mariska up the countless steps towards the top of the building. She had to admit Mariska's shapely rear in front of her was a good view but still, walk the whole way up? Who the hell did that?

"Hey, you said whatever I wanted to do." Mariska looked back at Alana. "You can't live in Toronto for a year and a half and not do at least some of the tourist crap there is to do around here." She continued upward.

"You're lucky you're pretty, woman," Alana said, grabbing onto Mariska's belt, then giving a slight tug to get her attention.

Mariska looked down, her lips immediately captured by Alana's. She felt Mariska smile into the kiss and returned it before pulling back.

"We could always quit if you're too winded," Mariska said.

"Ha! I didn't get this far to leave without getting to be a tourist and going 'ooh, ahh' at the pretty view." She walked past Mariska and headed up the stairs. "You coming?"

"Yeah, just enjoying my own pretty view," Mariska said.

Alana looked down in confusion and saw the smirk on Mariska's face. She didn't usually get compliments, particularly overt ones like that. She never allowed anyone close enough to give them the liberty of making them. Given her pleasant rush, maybe she'd been remiss.

She took Mariska's hand and admired the contrast between her own pale skin and Mariska's tan. She tugged Mariska even with her and trudged up the steps.

Things had been better since the night on the bench. Mariska's apprehension certainly hadn't disappeared but she didn't seem to be constantly on guard or in danger of bolting for the door. With the change came a pleasant shift in their physical interaction as well. Alana was no longer concerned that an unannounced kiss would send Mariska running. Indeed, Mariska had even been initiating physical contact more often in the past week.

It was a nice change and gave Alana hope that she wouldn't forever be battling the ghost of Mariska's dead lover.

"C'mon, the sooner we hit the top of this, the sooner we can hit the ice cream shack." Mariska grinned.

"Race you to the top?"

THEY DIDN'T RACE. They walked the rest of the way up at a leisurely pace, chatting about whatever topic happened to come across their minds. Nothing much of substance, random facts they had heard in their travels or stories from school or work. It was nice and relaxed, as was the lunch they shared at the revolving restaurant. The food was mediocre but the company more than made up for it, and Alana found herself smiling. It had been years since she'd been in such a pleasant state of mind.

She and Mariska shopped for most of that afternoon, trying to locate a dress for the gala. They hadn't found anything and parted company in the late afternoon so Mariska could get ready for work.

That was three days ago. Their schedules, particularly Alana's, hadn't allowed for more than a few brief conversations. There was a new shipment of weapons arriving and someone had tipped the Coast Guard so she had been busy trying to pay off the proper people and, failing that, finding alternate routes to transport the weapons along.

If worse came to worst, she would stop the crates in New York and farm them out to a middleman she knew in Alphabet City. It would mean taking a hit in profit but better that than lose the entire shipment. Sighing, Alana looked out her window and over the lake, her work forgotten on her desk. She and Mariska were set to meet up this afternoon, but she had no desire to waste an entire afternoon with her shopping for clothes. As pleasant as it was to watch Mariska fit her athletic form into various dresses, she could think of other things she'd rather be doing.

She picked up her phone and dialed her assistant.

"Cindy, I need a fitting appointment with Stephen today, around two if possible." She hung up the phone, knowing it was good as done. The woman could sell a steak to a vegan. If Stephen had previously booked a two o'clock, it would no doubt be rescheduled shortly.

"I DON'T KNOW, this seems a little . . . much," Mariska said later that afternoon as Stephen pinned the dress to be taken in.

Alana tried to keep her eyes from wandering towards Mariska's plunging neckline, which was being presented to her in mirror reflection. The dark blue satin was a perfect complement to tanned skin, as were the straps that hung just at the edge of her shoulders, giving a perfect view of Mariska's toned back.

"How so?" Alana asked.

"I can't afford this. You know that, so I'm assuming you intend to buy it for me."

"That would be a correct assumption, yes," Alana said.

"That's where it seems a little much. It's only one night. Wouldn't it just be better for me to look for something a little more off the rack?"

Alana ignored Stephen's insulted snort. "Stephen, could you give us a moment?"

He nodded and retreated into the small office beyond the fitting room.

"Okay, what's up? You don't like the dress?" Alana asked, running her fingers across Mariska's silk-covered abdomen.

"No, I mean yes." Mariska seemed at a loss. "I love the dress, but it's expensive."

"I fail to see your point," Alana said, honestly confused. She was paying for it, why was Mariska worried about it?

"You really do," Mariska said, sounding slightly surprised. "Is it really nothing for you to spend this kind of money?"

Alana smiled, put a hand on the vast expanse of skin that the dress left exposed along Mariska's back, and looked at her in the mirror. Her eyes moved lazily over the crisscross of scars that littered tanned skin, remnants of a car accident Mariska had been involved in. Given how nervous she was in talking about the incident, Alana assumed there was more to the story than a simple collision. But seeing Mariska's troubled expression during the conversation, she'd refrained from pushing any further.

"It's not nothing. In terms of dollars and cents, it's ultimately a drop in the bucket," Alana said. "I'm not concerned about the money. What's important is that you're coming to this event for me. You need this dress specifically because of me. It only makes sense to buy the dress for you."

"Okay, but it doesn't need to be so expensive."

"You don't even know what the price is," Alana said, smiling at Mariska's reflection in the mirror.

"If it doesn't have a price tag, it's way out of my tax bracket," Marisksa said.

Alana merely grinned, Mariska certainly did have a good sense of humour. "Look, you've already told me you feel a little intimidated about hanging around with the people who are going to be there. I think you'll feel even more so if you show up dressed for your tax bracket instead of theirs. I want you to have a good time and feel comfortable," Alana said, only slightly surprised to find she actually meant it.

She was concerned about how Mariska would feel being amongst the higher-ups of the political strata. And God help anyone who made her feel like she was less. Her feelings of protectiveness over Mariska had been unexpected at first. She rarely helped anyone but herself. It took a little time to get used to them and now she merely accepted them for what they were. It was getting too hard to lie to herself anyway.

She was slowly coming to realize what had started as a personal challenge, had mutated into genuine affection for Mariska.

"So, this is all about making me feel good?" Mariska asked, as though the idea was somewhat foreign to her.

"Yes," Alana said simply, earning herself a quick kiss. She took Mariska's chin in a light hold and looked down at her. "Well, that and I can't have my arm candy looking off the rack."

Mariska chuckled, touched her forehead to Alana's, and brought their noses together for an Eskimo kiss. "So, does your arm candy at least get to buy you supper?"

"I was thinking more of ordering in."

MARISKA TOOK IN the rich decorations around her and her gaze fell on Alana about ten metres away and speaking with one of the partners of her firm. Alana was a vision in the emerald green sheath that hugged her slim form. Curly hair was left to roam free, falling seductively over bare shoulders. It had taken some considerable will power to actually get themselves out the door and to the party.

Alana shook the partner's hand and turned to walk towards Mariska. She deftly swept two fresh glasses of champagne from the waiter's tray as she passed.

"Sorry about that," she said as she handed one glass to Mariska, took the empty one from her hand, and put it on the table.

"No worries, I'm just admiring this place, I love it here," Mariska said, scanning the crowded room. "It's gorgeous."

The museum had required little altering to tailor itself to the high-class patrons of the night. Limestone brickwork towered towards the high ceilings, which were decorated in rich mosaics of reds, browns, and yellows. The floor was cool gray marble, as was the main staircase, all of it polished to a mirrored shine for the gala.

The people around them were similarly well polished. The men were in black tuxedos and the women were dressed in rich gowns of satin and silk. Mariska's own dress, created from crisp midnight blue fabric, rivalled the beauty of any of the women on the floor. Alana had pulled out all the stops to accommodate her for the night. The thought made her happy.

"How about we go check out the exhibits?" Alana asked, linking their arms and leading them towards the art displays.

They spent the better part of an hour milling around. Mariska focused on the artifacts that had been shipped from the amphitheatre in Rome. She wasn't usually so taken with Roman history. Perhaps it was her experience in the arena last month that piqued her interest.

"You like weaponry?" Alana asked, laying a gentle hand on Mariska's exposed back.

Mariska was gazing at a short blade, more a dagger than a sword, the ivory handle surprisingly well kept for being over two thousand years old. The metal, while dull, seemed to be in good condition as well.

"It's amazing," she said, barely restraining herself from touching the glass case that surrounded the weapon. Something about it seemed to call to her. Societies had been built and toppled at the tip of swords like that. If only her own troubles could be solved so easily.

"Alana," a male voice called out.

Mariska turned and straightened from her slight crouch to stand next to Alana as a man approached.

"You haven't introduced me to your plus one."

Mariska tilted her head slightly to look at Alana, curious at the flash of irritation that crossed her face.

"Alexander, this is Mariska," Alana said. "Mariska, Alexander, a . . . colleague of mine."

Mariska didn't miss the way Alana stumbled over the word colleague and immediately prepped for defense.

"Pleased to meet you, Mariska, it's so rare to see Lana here in good company," he said, toothily smiling at her as he took her hand in a limp grip. She did her best to smile back and reclaimed her hand as quickly as she thought was polite.

"I happen to think the company she keeps is just fine," Mariska said, taking a side step to bring herself nearer and slightly ahead of Alana, her ever-present protective instincts rearing up at the covert insult.

Alexander's smile dimmed a little and he turned his attention back to Alana. "I hear you lost the Milton account. Looks like you're slipping a little, Lana."

Mariska spared a glance at Alana who had adopted the steely glare that had been Mariska's first impression of her. She hadn't seen that look since the coffee shop nearly two months ago.

"Hope that promotion isn't going to your head."

Whatever retort Alana had in store for him, died on her lips as the emcee for the night took the stage. Hoping to defuse the situation, Mariska took Alana's hand and pulled her away from her rival and towards the crowd that gathered around the speaker.

"I'm sorry about that," Alana said, looking at Mariska. She squeezed her hand lightly.

"Don't worry about it, I'm a big girl. 'Sides, why else did you bring me here except to run defense?"

"Because when I'm with you, everything is more fun," Alana said absently as she looked over the crowd.

Mariska smiled happily then turned her attention to the speaker.

ALANA SIPPED SLOWLY at her champagne, watching as Mariska wove her way through the crowd towards the restroom.

The speaker finally finished up and the crowd dispersed to go back to their drinking and gossip.

The night had gone relatively well so far. There hadn't been any major run-ins with her peers from work. Even the little scuffle with Alexander had barely registered. What did stand out in her mind was Mariska's immediate defense of her. It seemed almost automatic the way Mariska stepped slightly in front of her, as if to shield her from the verbal barbs being tossed her way. She'd been scowling on the outside but inwardly . . . inwardly, she felt a part of her touched that she thought had been long dead and buried.

As far as her own comment afterward, she hadn't meant to say it out loud. Her surprise at herself almost made her miss the pleased smile Mariska had thrown her way. Seemed they both had surprises tonight.

Sighing and wishing she could just enjoy the night for what it was but knowing that she couldn't, Alana wandered over to the displays. In two weeks' time, the current exhibition would be moved out and another, involving some priceless pieces of Egyptian history, would be moved in. STELLA didn't usually make a habit of heisting museums but on occasion, when the price was right and she was feeling the need to get back to her roots, she would take on a job.

It was unlikely the security setup would be altered between now and then. She could see the discrete flashes of the security cameras, some well hidden at the corners of the ceiling, others not so covertly placed on the marble pillars.

Alana made a mental note of each one, planning her angle of attack. Taking out the cameras would be first priority before an entrance could even be attempted. A number of ground crews patrolled the area. It seemed entry and exit from above was her best bet.

She took calculated steps between each podium, conversing with the socialites along the way, all the while keeping careful count of how far it was between pillars. Once she was beneath one of the decorative skylights, she surveyed the various angles to the displays. She wouldn't know which area the actual artifact would be in until just before the heist so she would have to plan for all possibilities.

She didn't want to carry more rope than necessary. The extra weight would be a hindrance but she also wanted to limit her time on the ground. There tended to be nasty surprises once she actually set foot on the floor: laser grids, pressure plates, motion sensors. The idea of such heightened security seemed a little much for the ROM but she wasn't one to be caught flat-footed.

"Perfecto," she said quietly, her gaze sweeping across the room.

"What's perfect?" Mariska asked.

Alana turned to Mariska. "You, in that dress." She took the tanned hand that had come to rest on her hip and dropped a kiss onto the palm. "How are you enjoying yourself?"

"It's great, although I've never really cared for art like this. Some of it is a bit abstract for me. And the people are nice, but I guess they're just a little rich for my blood," Mariska said with a self-deprecating shrug.

"Hey." Alana tugged on Mariska's hand. "You know enough to know that money doesn't make the man. I'd choose your company over any other in this room." She didn't like that Mariska felt inferior to these people. She'd been told the same throughout her childhood. That she would never be worthy of sitting in company like theirs.

She had proved everyone wrong; she sat in the company of men who thought themselves kings and found it lacking. While the people she had grown up with had been passionate about life, their jobs, their loves, these people seemed apathetic to nearly everything. Fake smiles and shallow friendships. Their golden world shimmered brightly, but in the end it was all pyrite, fool's gold.

"Really?" Mariska asked, still looking uncertain. Alana shook her head, Mariska was generally so confident. It seemed odd that she would let a situation like this trouble her.

"Really," Alana said. She took one last look around, satisfied that she had gleaned all she would need to make a respectable plan of attack. "Come on." She tugged Mariska towards the coat check. "I believe there's some wine and blueberries calling our name."

MARISKA SHRUGGED OUT of the dress and laid it carefully over the bed in Alana's spare room. It had been an interesting night—going to a high-class gala dressed in a gown that would have cost her at least a month's pay. She'd felt like a princess, particularly when Alana had turned admiring forest green eyes on her.

As Mariska talked to more people, heard how they spoke, she couldn't help but feel somewhat out of place. Sure, she had a degree, or nearly so, from a reputable university, but these people had an inbred education that would never allow her to walk in their world. Mannerisms and subtleties that left her feeling as though she were some sort of country bumpkin trying to address the queen.

She had never felt particularly rough. She'd grown up lower middle class, went to a decent high school, taken out loans for college like all of her friends, with the exclusion of Lucas and Lisa. The people at the gala had driven past her soccer fields in their Lexuses, slept their way through college because they hadn't paid for their classes, and could look forward to a job in the family business, regardless of their performance.

Next to them, Mariska had felt like the blue collar raised woman she was. Superhero or not. When she was out of Guardian gear, she was a twenty-two-year-old college kid. One who happened to be dating a rather prominent, well-off corporate executive. What did Alana even see in her? It wasn't as though she knew about her night job. The dozens or maybe hundreds of people Mariska had helped over the years were yesterday's ghosts. All she saw was the kid in jeans and a sweatshirt.

"I just don't know," she muttered, running a hand along the satiny fabric of the dress.

"Don't know what?" Alana asked.

Mariska turned, surprised that Alana had managed to sneak up on her. Her senses were usually better attuned than that.

"Why I'm here, why you're with me," Mariska said honestly. "It's not like I have a lot to offer you. I mean, in the beginning, I figured it was, I don't know, something fun. But, now I'm . . . and you're . . ." She gestured helplessly. University graduate indeed, she was certain most of the people who had been at that party could string together a sentence. Even in emotionally charged terrain. Hell, those people probably didn't even wander into emotionally charged terrain. Maybe they were onto something there.

"Hey." Alana pulled her forward and rested warm hands on

Mariska's bare biceps. She rubbed gentle patterns across Mariska's skin with her thumbs.

Mariska shivered as goose bumps lined her arms. She tucked her head into the crook of Alana's neck as strong arms wrapped around her.

"I'm with you because you're not like them, because you mean it when you smile," Alana said. "Because no one else has brought me soup when I was sick."

Mariska laughed and rested her hands on Alana's hips.

"Honestly, I don't know what it is," Alana said, her lips close to Mariska's ear. "I just know that whatever this is, whatever we are, I want it. I want you." She rubbed her hands up and down Mariska's back, and Mariska sighed into the light touch. "I don't care what they think, Mariska, never have." She tilted Mariska's chin up with her forefinger. "Your opinion of me matters, not theirs."

Mariska sighed breathily and turned to kiss the palm of the hand that was now gently cupping her face.

"I happen to have a pretty good opinion of you," Mariska said, returning to her resting spot at Alana's shoulder. "Sorry about the bout of insecurity. I'm not usually like this." She tried to recall when she'd last felt quite this unsure of herself. It had been the first time, after Lisa's death, that she'd put on her gear and reclaimed her Guardian persona. She'd looked down on the city she had chosen to protect and wondered if she had any right to make such a decision.

The wind was strong that night, high above the city. It threatened to take her off the roof if she made a misstep. Part of her hoped it would. Her depression had nearly drowned her in those first few weeks after Lisa's death. And Lucas . . . poor Lucas. He'd been too injured, physically and emotionally, to even act as radio backup. Mariska was, for the first time, well and truly on her own. She would live or die by her own abilities and she worried that she would come up lacking.

She felt a few moments of utter terror when an unexpected gust of wind caught her off guard and carried her off the rooftop. Reacting purely on instinct, she calmly pulled her grappling gun from its holster, sighted a holding point, took aim, and fired. She knew the shot was good the moment it left the gun and merely

*waited for the line to catch her and swing her forward, parallel to
the flow of traffic below.*

*If someone had watched from the streets, she would have
appeared as if she'd planned the entire motion. As she swung
herself to the next ledge, hundreds of feet above the unknowing
populace, her fears and doubts disappeared. No matter her
emotions, her instincts and her body knew the routine, knew the
job too well to let her fail.*

Mariska wished she could find that ledge now; find that gust
of wind that would send her over the edge to prove that she could
catch herself on the way down.

"Why don't you stay over?"

Mariska looked at Alana. "I'm not read—"

"Just to sleep. It's late, and I don't want you going home in the
middle of the night."

Mariska waged a silent war with herself before deciding a cold
bed in a lonely apartment couldn't hold a candle to Alana. "Okay,"
she said, allowing Alana to pull her from the room and the dark
thoughts that seemed a constant threat to consume her.

MARISKA SURVEYED THE rooftops, debating which would
be the easiest to jump onto from her current position. She was high
atop one of the downtown office towers, searching for any signs of
trouble with her binoculars. The city had been quiet tonight, too
quiet for her liking given the day she'd had. Crime had seemed to
slow to barely a trickle these last couple of weeks. She didn't mind
most of the time. It meant being able to devote more time to Alana
and their slowly blossoming relationship. Tonight, however, she
hoped for the opportunity to kick some ass.

She'd been on edge all day, nearly snapping poor Lucas's head
off when she had entered the basement to gear up for patrol. The
weekend had started out well enough. She spent Friday night
hanging out at Alana's, watching bad Kung Fu movies.

Saturday she patrolled, and the night quickly bled into Sunday
morning. She'd promised to meet Alana at her apartment for
breakfast.

Alana was drying her hair when she showed up with a bag of
groceries to cook the meal.

Considering she'd managed to wake up on time, do groceries at the twenty-four-hour store, and make it to the apartment before nine a.m., she figured her day was shaping up pretty well. Never a good sign.

"Morning," she said, dropping a quick kiss at the base of Alana's neck. "Want me to get coffee started?"

"No. I'm sorry. I have to cancel. I've got a brunch meeting that completely slipped my mind." Alana turned slightly to give Mariska a proper kiss.

"On a Sunday?"

"Clients are in from L.A. I'll make it up to you, I promise. Are you working tonight?"

"When am I not?" Mariska said, a little miffed that Alana hadn't called her before she rushed to get everything done. She hated mornings—hated with a capital H.

"You know, if you found something in your field, I'm certain you could make more money with quite a few less hours."

Mariska shrugged, knowing it was true. But that wouldn't allow her the freedom to move shifts, call in sick, or quit on command so she could go do her other job. The one that mattered. A straight nine to five would mean giving up aspects of her life that she just wasn't ready to part with.

"I like what I'm doing."

"I'm just saying, the longer you sit without using your degree, the harder it is to get a job." Alana turned back to the mirror to finish her hair. "I'm certain you don't want to be a waitress forever."

Mariska dropped her hands from Alana's hips and took a small step back. "What if I did?"

Alana raised an eyebrow. "Come on, Mariska. You're too smart to just wait tables all day. Think of what else you could be doing, owning a business like you said. No bank will give a loan out to a college graduate swimming in debt, who's working minimum wage at a pub or chip house."

Mariska knew Alana was right. She did have goals beyond Guardian. She wouldn't be able to be on the streets forever. Her vocation definitely had a shelf life. She also didn't want to wait until her body started to fail her before starting up her life. But, for now, she was happy with where she was.

"I like doing what I'm doing. When I stop liking it, I'll change."

Alana shrugged. "That's fine for now, Mariska, but how long do you think it's going to be fun for? You need to start thinking about the future and not be so caught up in the now."

Mariska hadn't had an answer for that. She couldn't give one without revealing her other self. She also felt put out because she didn't feel she had to justify the way she lived. Nothing overtly offensive had been said, but the conversation just rubbed her the wrong way. Maybe she'd been PMSing.

At any rate, to avoid snapping at Alana and potentially blowing things out of proportion, she dropped a kiss on Alana's cheek and told her she'd get going.

Her day went downhill from there.

Her car had been stolen, her own goddamn car. Well, Lucas's car that she'd borrowed to go grocery shopping. Same difference.

She'd gotten it back, of course, Lucas easily located the GPS and she'd gone into the chop shop thinking bloody murder. It had been quick work to get the car back—minus a hubcap—and she had neatly tied up one of the smaller rings of car thieves. She wasn't surprised when she saw STELLA'S logo emblazoned in a graffiti tag along the shop's wall. Figured. Goddamn STELLA was going to try and ruin her day.

She returned the car, promising a replacement hubcap to her disgruntled partner and had gone to get some lunch. After nearly being run down by a careening Audi followed by three black and whites, Mariska groaned, realizing her protesting stomach would have to wait. She followed the cars, keeping up easily enough on foot when thickening traffic forced everyone to slow down. To escape the traffic jam, the chased car decided to pull onto the sidewalk. Luckily, she managed to catch the ass end of the bumper with her grappling gun.

She wasn't sure why, but it had seemed like a good idea at the time.

The car accelerated and plowed into the pedestrian-filled walkway, nearly tugging Mariska off her feet. Balanced on her heels, she was tugged along for nearly fifty feet before the car pulled sharply back onto the road, leaving her the choice of letting go or being swung into oncoming traffic. As it was, she nearly had her head taken off by one of those damn bike messengers. She was going to be writing the messenger company a very stern letter. It had all been for naught at any rate.

The police ran down the fleeing car, and Mariska ruined a perfectly good pair of boots along with her spandex costume. She switched back into civvies to watch the arrest and snapped quick photos of the men to identify later. When the cop muscled one of them into the car, the criminal's collar pulled down and she saw STELLA's emblem tattooed on the side of his neck.

Fucking STELLA.

Letting out a sigh, Mariska stepped down from her perch on the building and walked to the opposite ledge.

"You can't tell me after a day like today that you have no one for me to take it out on," Mariska said.

"Sorry," Lucas said. "All's quiet on the western front, and the eastern, southern, and northern."

Mariska sighed, put her binoculars to her eyes, and swept her gaze across the lakefront and back to the buildings closest to her.

"Hey, now, what have we here?" She focused her view on a red leather clad . . . someone. She brought it into crisper view. Aside from the outfit, which was unusual enough in itself, the person on top of a building was looking down through a skylight. "Huh, that can't be right, Big Brother can you identify that building?"

"Trajectory from your position indicates it's the ROM."

"Yeah, that's what I thought. Huh."

"Looks like we've got ourselves a bona fide cat burglar."

"That's new." She hadn't actually had one of those. Oh sure, there had been tons of the ham-handed smash-and-grab jobs. All boom and no finesse. But a real professional? Not in all the years she'd been patrolling. She had actually come to think of them as a myth, her own personal white whale. Not anymore.

"You getting this, Big Brother?" she asked, as she zoomed in with her camera.

"Roger that. Nice suit." Mariska nodded.

Leather vest, pants, and knee-high boots. It was like looking in the mirror. Except in red, and the full, black mask was veiling the face of the criminal. She hadn't been able to deal with the full mask when she wore one. It obstructed her view too much and she couldn't breathe.

And it chafed like hell.

Mariska turned from the rooftop and headed for the opposite side before facing the museum once more.

"Am I good to go?" she asked, tugging her hood into place.

"Wind currents are strong and in your favour. You're clear."

"Rock, rock on." Mariska took strong steps forward and picked up speed as she headed for the edge of the building. Her foot met the ledge at full sprint and she launched herself forward, body slicing through the air as she flew away from the building. She arched her back and maintained position as she quickly pulled the rip cord to release her parachute.

Mariska's canopy filled with air and she tugged on her toggles to double-check for control as she steered her body towards the museum, expertly navigating the buildings as her canopy cut through the air. She landed short of the rooftop, nearly a block from her intended target. Considering the distance, she hadn't expected to do much better. She shucked her rig for later pickup, unholstered her grappling gun, and dived off the roof ledge towards the museum's fire escape.

The grapple clamped easily onto the metal railing. She swung in a wide arc and kicked her feet up to land over the rail, then skidded to a stop on the fourth level down. She released the grapple and headed for the roof at a sprint. Time to work off her bad mood.

A LIGHT SNOW drifted lazily downward as Alana climbed the fire escape, heading towards the top of the roof. Red leather gloves gripped the cold metal rung tightly. She had already had a near miss when her boots slipped on the second rung. She hated working in the winter, and Canada certainly had enough of it. If she were back home in L.A., she wouldn't need anything more than a light sweater at most. Instead, here she was, seriously contemplating thermal underwear beneath her gear.

"Why I thought this was a good idea, I'll never know," she murmured, watching her breath cloud in front of her.

Alana swung her legs over the edge of the fire escape and onto the roof of the Royal Ontario Museum. Her boots crunched noisily in the gravel atop the cement. She headed for the triple set of skylights. They would be the easiest way to access the third floor where the urn was being kept as part of the new Egyptian exhibit.

Alana placed a large, handheld suction device on the edge of the skylight, pulled her new laser cutter from her belt, and marked a hole large enough for her body to fit through. The glass fizzled quietly as it melted. She shivered as flakes of snow slid between her skin and her jacket. Icy feathers landed on her lips, the only portion of her face the black leather mask left exposed. The slightly stylized balaclava kept her conspicuous red hair tucked out of sight and the red goggles prevented any chance of identifying her by eye color or retinal identification.

The laser cut through the remaining glass. Alana pulled it out of place, then released the suction device. Nonchalantly, she kicked the cut glass out of her way and strolled towards a vent. She unclipped the front of her belt buckle to reveal a small carabiner and fifty feet of thin, high tensile wire. She wrapped the wire around the vent and connected it to itself with the carabiner.

Alana sat on the edge of the skylight, her feet dangling in the open air, then nodded and pushed off. She hit ground level—her knees buckling and taking the brunt of the impact. She stood quickly, one hand on the throwing daggers strapped to her chest. There weren't supposed to be any guards on this level for another ten minutes, but she wasn't about to take any chances.

Coast clear. Alana unclipped the line from her belt and dangled it as she looked around. Down the steps on either side of her was a second-level balcony that looked out onto the vast first floor. The high-domed ceiling was a painted mosaic of rich golds and reds, reminiscent of some of the art she had stolen in India. On the first floor, a large meditating Buddha sat, uncaring, next to the skeleton of a large dinosaur, who seemed to guard the large hall and steps that led to Alana's current level. She turned her attention to the room where the urn was kept.

The David & Eaton Court.

There it was, in a medium-sized circular room where glass walls allowed the casual observer to see inside without entering. It was good to know she wouldn't have to kill her source for giving her bad information. The urn was housed inside a glass case that butted up against the nearest glass wall.

She pulled her laser cutter from her belt and took another look around to be sure no one had come to check on the display early.

Of course, it would have been easier to kill the guards, deactivate the alarms, and smash her way in, but it wouldn't have been half as fun. She cut a hole large enough for the urn in the glass wall, unfolded the suction device and pulled the glass from its place. She put it gently on the floor, then did the same with the glass from the case.

Once she was out, she didn't care who knew how she got in. The urn would be out of her hands by morning, and there would be no way to trace it back to her. She just didn't feel like beating back a dozen guards to make a measly fifty grand.

She wasn't even sure why the urn was worth so much. She pulled it from its case, inspected it, and shrugged. It didn't feel all that heavy, so the metal in it couldn't be worth that much. It was also downright ugly.

"One man's junk . . ." she said quietly, pulling off her backpack and stowing the urn inside.

She tightened the straps to ensure its protection and made sure it was resting comfortably in the thick padding before zipping the bag up. She reseated the bag, hooked herself back onto her line, tightened the clamps, and pulled herself up towards the ceiling. She heard footsteps far below her just as she reached the top of the skylight.

Suckers.

Alana pulled herself out of the skylight and her boots landed quietly on the gravel. She walked to where her line was tied off, shivering as the snow slid down the back of her neck. She unclipped her carabiner from the line, leaving the high tensile wire in place.

She double-checked the straps on her backpack to ensure it was well seated and looked around for any evidence she would mind leaving behind. She adjusted her gloves and walked back towards the fire escape. That had been easy enough.

Relatively speaking.

In her first days as a thief, things had gone wrong on a regular basis. Her ability to improvise and her lack of remorse with regard to killing kept her out of a jail cell. Many of her thieving peers had morals, codes of operation, that prevented them from acting lethally when going after the goods.

Alana had never had those qualms.

Her spandex shirt was chafing against her neck. She scratched at the base of it. Snow-soaked spandex was nobody's friend. She checked her watch. Only midnight.

If she hurried, she could catch Mariska on the phone before she fell asleep. Their non-fight from earlier was bothering her. It wasn't so much that she'd said anything bad, just that what she had said hadn't come out in quite the way it was supposed to.

The feeling of unsettlement in her gut was something she was unfamiliar with. It was distinctly unpleasant and she wanted it to go away. She had no problem admitting she was emotionally dense. Still, she was fairly certain that resolving whatever issues were under the surface of Mariska's vexation was the only way to relieve the jittery feeling in her stomach.

"I don't think that belongs to you."

Alana turned around to find Guardian with fists on her hips. She had on her usual turquoise leather getup, form fitting pants and a top that fit snugly around what looked like a tailored Kevlar vest. Rather than the bare arms Alana had seen earlier in the fall, the woman had a navy blue, long-sleeved spandex shirt to ward off the cold. She knew first hand the spandex wasn't worth much more than bare skin.

"Didn't your mother ever teach you about taking other people's toys?" the slightly shivering Guardian asked.

"Didn't you ever hear of finders keepers?" Alana said, her voice lowering in automatic disguise as she tossed out two smoke bombs. The smoke screens went up quickly and she headed for the edge of the roof. She was in no mood to duke it out with the do-gooder tonight. She had an important phone call to make.

She made it to the fire escape. A surprising kick to her shoulder came from the side and knocked her off her feet to the roof with a crunch. She growled low in her throat and tucked her legs under her butt and used her hands to flip to a standing position. She put her guard up, scanning the rooftop for her opponent.

"If you wanted to play hide and seek, you should have reminded me to count."

Alana turned to see Guardian resting easily on the roof's edge, head canted to the side. The deep hood of her vest hid her identity, as did whatever she was using on her throat to alter her voice to something bordering on masculine. Clever girl.

"I've never played well with others," Alana said, a cocky grin firmly in place.

The Guardian nodded as though she found this to be of no surprise. "You can make this really easy."

Alana wasn't certain but something in the woman's tone made her sound as though she hoped that wouldn't be the case.

"Sorry, not today." Alana lowered her shoulder and charged Guardian.

Guardian ducked down and took the tackle full on. Alana grunted as she felt strong arms encircle her waist and use her momentum to throw her over Guardian's hip and onto the roof.

She cursed under her breath and kicked upwards as Guardian approached and got her solidly in her sternum, drawing a grunt. Guardian grabbed Alana's ankle and flipped her onto her stomach.

Alana quickly unsheathed a throwing dagger from her belt and flung it towards Guardian's face. The hood hid if Alana had managed to hit her mark but Guardian turned to the side and abandoned her grip to roll away. Alana stood, smirking as she watched Guardian put her hand to her face and inspect her gloved fingers.

"Nice shot."

"Not nice enough," Alana said as she grabbed a second dagger.

Guardian shook a finger at Alana as she rested her hand on a shurikan on her belt. "Bad idea." She tightened her fingers on the shurikan.

"Look, it's snowing, I'm soaked, you're soaked, why don't we call this a night and go home, huh?" Alana asked, searching for an exit, any exit. She had a feeling this woman wasn't about to let it go and that she was in for a good fight. She had seen the tape from the fight club. Guardian had skill.

"Sounds like you're in a rush, got someone waiting on that?" Guardian pointed towards the container on Alana's back.

"Maybe, or maybe I just have better things to do than hang around in the snow with someone who uses Xena episodes as a fashion consultation."

"I have no words to describe the irony of that statement," Guardian said, with a shake of her head. "One last chance, come in quietly and I won't have to hurt you." She firmly grasped the shurikan, the turquoise metal flashing against the navy blue gloves.

"Just not going to let this go are you?" Alana asked, resigning herself to a full-out fight. And to not talk to Mariska. That thought irritated her, and she focused her irritation on the tall annoyance in front of her as she calculated the distance between them.

Alana ducked the first shurikan as she released her dagger, but the second embedded in her shoulder just beneath the protection of her leather vest. Grunting in pain, she threw herself in the opposite direction as she fired off a second and third dagger at Guardian.

She heard at least one connect and Guardian went down on one knee as Alana landed and rolled back onto her feet. She tore the shurikan from her shoulder and tossed it aside as she watched Guardian inspect a long cut along her thigh.

Alana crossed her arms to block Guardian's jump kick that threatened to take her head off. She landed a solid blow to Guardian's solar plexus as she dropped. Guardian barely flinched and flung a long leg into Alana's kidney.

Alana stumbled back. Guardian caught her temple with a right hook. Tired of being outdistanced by the arrogant upstart, Alana shot forward, wrapped strong arms around Guardian's lean torso, and threw her over her hip. She pushed down hard as Guardian fell, making sure she hit the roof hard.

Guardian threw her legs around and took Alana out at the knees. Alana rolled as she fell and came to standing position but she had lost the advantage. Guardian was ready to rock.

"You just don't give up do you?" Alana asked in exasperation.

"It's one of my more charming traits," Guardian said as she circled Alana.

Alana rolled her eyes and waited for the next move. Guardian threw out a front kick. Alana took a step back so Guardian would overextend her swinging leg.

Guardian landed hard on her kicking leg, then bled off the excess momentum by pushing up and launching a hook kick at Alana's head. Alana ducked, avoiding the blow, only to catch a side kick in her gut. She doubled over in pain, head rocking back as an uppercut connected with her jaw.

Guardian was good. She was also starting to get on Alana's nerves.

"All right. That's. Enough. Of that." Alana blocked the oncoming punch and wrapped a strong hand around Guardian's fist. She twisted Guardian's wrist, and blocked the next punch with her forearm before shooting forward and landing square in the center of Guardian's face. She heard the rather distinctive pop of cartilage breaking and sneered beneath her mask as Guardian stumbled back, hands coming to her nose.

"Son of a bitch," Guardian muttered.

"You want to play with the big girls? You may want to learn how to take a punch," Alana said.

Guardian let out an animalistic yell, startling Alana.

The glass of the skylight gave way beneath them.

Alana could have slapped herself. *So much for a nice clean get away*.

She grabbed the rappel line and let out a yell of pain as the thin line cut through her gloves and into her hands. She clamped the heels of her boots tightly together around the wire to slow herself down. Guardian fell on top of her and pushed her off the line.

The crash of breaking glass sounded an alarm. Alana landed hard land on the unforgiving marble floor, Guardian thumping down next to her. Alana groaned, rolled onto her side, and eased to her feet. She looked down at Guardian, who seemed was struggling to stand.

Served the do-gooder right for trifling in her affairs.

Heavy boot steps echoed around them. Alana grabbed the clamps and pulled herself up. She ignored the searing pain that was shooting through her shoulder and hands as she climbed.

She spared a quick look down to see Guardian on her feet, cradling her ribs as she pulled for some sort of weapon from her leg. Alana ducked to the side as a grapple and rope shot past and landed neatly next to hers. Huh. So she wasn't the only one with nice toys.

As she climbed, Alana heard the mechanical whir as the retractor worked to pull Guardian off the floor and towards the ceiling. She hit the rooftop while Guardian was still midway and debated kicking the grapple free to let the pain in the ass drop to her death. She took a step towards the grapple and grasped her shoulder in mind-numbing pain.

Guardian would have to wait.

Alana secured her package on her back and tucked her left arm into her vest, then headed for the fire escape. She trotted down the escape, dropped into the alley, and looked up to see Guardian on the top step.

Victorious, she let out a satisfied laugh at the frustrated yell that echoed from the rooftop.

Amateur.

CHAPTER 8
Guilt, Table For Two

"I WANT TO know who the fuck that was!" Mariska screamed as she kicked open the door to the basement. She carelessly tossed her parachute to the side and stalked up to Lucas's computer. "That bitch nearly killed me."

"So I saw." Lucas waited for Mariska to drop her lightly tinted sunglasses into his hands. "Are you all right?"

"Broke my fucking nose, nearly recracked my goddamn ribs." Mariska tugged her gloves from her hands and roughly pulled her hood back.

"Uh huh," Lucas said, his concentration on the data downloading from her glasses.

"Are you listening to me?" Mariska asked. "We went through a skylight!"

"I believe that was your doing," Lucas said.

Mariska reached towards his neck. Her cell phone rang as it skipped along the desk.

"Find her." She picked up her phone and stalked to the far corner of the room. She clicked the button on. "Hey."

"Hey, babe, are you all right?" Alana asked. "You sound . . . angry."

"I'm fine, what's up?"

"I just wanted to call and make sure you were okay. You rushed out this morning."

Mariska sighed. "I'm really okay, you just hit a couple of hot buttons with our conversation this morning and I didn't want to snap at you." She rubbed under her nose and grimaced as she dislodged dried blood from her upper lip.

"I'm sorry if I offended you. It wasn't my intention."

"I know, really, it's okay. I've just had a rough day."

"Okay, I hate to do this now but I have to fly back home for a few weeks and deal with some business. My meeting didn't go well."

Mariska didn't know whether to be happy or not. On the one hand, it meant not seeing her girlfriend. On the other, it meant not having to lie about looking like a raccoon. "That sucks. When do you leave?"

"In about two hours, I'm catching the red-eye."

"Do you need a ride or anything?" Mariska asked, hoping she wouldn't be taken up on the offer.

"No, I've got a driver coming. I think he might actually be at the door."

Mariska could make out the muffled conversation.

"Sorry about that," Alana said.

"No need." Mariska leaned her back against the wall, wincing as her side twinged. Nothing broken, thank Christ. Lucas was right, her ribs were her weak spot. She needed to find a better way to protect them. Kevlar was great for stopping bullets but she seemed to be getting tossed into walls and down from heights a lot recently.

"I need to get going. He'll be up shortly. You're certain we're okay?"

"We're okay, I'm sure. Call me when you get in?"

"It'll only be six o'clock," Alana said. "You're a late riser."

"It's okay. Wake me anyway."

"All right. Get some sleep. You sound like you're starting to get sick."

Mariska put her hand on her nose. She did sound pretty stuffed up, but mostly because dried blood was clogging her nostrils. "I'll be hitting the sack pretty quick. Have a safe flight."

"Thanks, babe, I'll talk to you later."

"Bye." Mariska clicked off the phone, tossed it onto the table, and stripped out of her battle gear. No point in getting it any bloodier.

"Do you want me to call Acco?" Lucas asked.

"No. There's no sense in waking him up for this. We still have some local in the cabinet." Mariska left her gear splayed across the basement table as she went up to the training level to get the medical supplies, an oddly quiet Lucas following after her.

She kicked off her boots, sat down on the medical table and picked up the mirror.

"Damn it. I look like I ran into a parked car," she said, turning her face to the side and looking out of the corner of her eye to survey the damage. She could see the distinctive disparity between the upper part of her nose and the lower, which had shifted slightly to the right. Fucking bitch. "I'm gonna kill her."

Lucas looked at her over the rims of his reading glasses and raised an eyebrow.

"Of course, by kill, I mean bring her in for prosecution under the proper judicial system," Mariska amended as she gently touched the swelling area.

Pain shot through her skull, and she pulled her hand away with a wince. She hadn't even started on the deep gash across her eyebrow. Damn thing had only stopped bleeding because dried blood had sealed it shut.

The red-hooded freak would do well to either get out of town or get caught by the cops. If Mariska got a hold of her, she was determined to even their score. She smiled slightly as she remembered watching the woman get to her feet in the museum. She was favouring her shoulder pretty heavily.

"Could you come over here and set this please? I look like Owen Wilson."

Lucas pushed himself up from his stool and readjusted his glasses as he walked to her. He bent down to inspect her nose and "hmmed" at Mariska as he took her chin and turned it left and right. "She certainly did a number on you." He touched her brow.

She jerked back. She could feel the wound reopen and leaked blood down her temple. "Um . . . ow!" She glared at him.

"Don't be such a baby." He pulled the medical tray and his stool over and sat down.

Acco had given them all some rudimentary medic training over the years. Neither Mariska nor Lucas wanted to call on the doctor for every scraped knee and busted lip they encountered in the field.

"I can't do much with your nose until the swelling goes down in a couple of days. I think I can get that eye sewn up and patch up the rest of you."

"A couple of days? Hell no, you're setting this bitch tonight," she said, pointing at her disfigured face.

"Mariska." Her name came out almost as a sigh. "Chances are it won't even set right if I do it now." Lucas took her chin to take a second look.

"I don't care. Every time I breathe I can feel the cartilage scraping together. Fix it."

He sighed again. He placed the heels of his hands at each side of her nose, ignoring Mariska's sharp intake of breath. "Ready?"

She nodded minutely and closed her eyes. The sound and feel alone would be enough. She didn't need to see the snap of his wrists that would bring her nose back into alignment.

"Here we go." He pressed on her nose and turned his wrists.

Mariska felt nauseated and fought blacking out from the flash of intense pain as the cartilage rubbed against itself and slid back into place. She looked down at the metal medical table to see her fingers wrapped around it with a white-knuckle grip.

"Better?"

Mariska forcibly breathed out of her nose and sent flakes of dried blood into her lap along with a small trickle of fresh red liquid.

"Much."

"Good." Lucas cleared her eyebrow of blood with baby wipes. "You know why this happened, right?" he asked as he brushed at the blood.

She fought the urge to jerk away from his hands, his touch rougher than normal. "Because the top of her skull and my face got into an argument?" She looked up as Lucas pressed on the wound to clear it of any detritus.

"Because you got sloppy," Lucas said, turning away from Mariska to thread the needle. He pulled out a syringe of local anesthetic to numb the wound.

She slapped his hand away as he moved towards her. "Pardon fucking *moi*? I got sloppy?" She glared at him. "You're the one who didn't tell me Bizarro was running around poaching fucking artifacts. She wasn't on your radar either, jackass. How the hell was I supposed to know she was a goddamn ninja?"

"You think normal women run around on rooftops breaking into museums? You should have assumed she'd have been above par when it came to combat."

Above par when it came to combat? Who the hell was this pretentious ass and where was Lucas?

"Do I look like a fucking psychic? Where the hell were you on your recognition programs? With that new upgrade you were whining about, you should be able to take a cell phone picture of a toenail and be able to techno geek your way to an ID. I'm the one who's out there in the field. I'm the one doing the legwork. I'm the one constantly putting my ass on the line and all I get from you lately is shit."

"If you stopped patrolling like shit, you wouldn't get shit. You're getting complacent. You're used to the same old criminals. Stupid assholes who don't think beyond the heist. We got into this business fighting a mafia don, or don't you remember? Ever since we took him down, you've been getting sloppy. Last year, you wouldn't have ever let that woman get the best of you." Lucas tossed the medical instruments back onto the tray and pulled off his latex gloves. "Get your head out of your ass, Mariska. We have a new bad to fight and we won't make it through if the one doing the legwork doesn't start taking her job seriously again and stop fucking around."

"I don't take my job seriously?" she slid off the table and towered over a seated Lucas.

"Ever since you began to see Alana, you've missed patrols and cut out early. You're letting her cloud your judgement and it's starting to show when you're out on the streets."

Mariska glowered at him, clamping down on the urge to take a step forward and crack him on the jaw. "Leave Alana out of this."

"I would, if you'd leave her bed long enough to do your job. Or have you forgotten we're supposed to be protecting this city?"

Mariska stared at Lucas as though seeing him for the first time. "Not that it's any of your goddamn business, you priggish ass, but I haven't slept with Alana yet."

"You've been dating someone for three months and you haven't slept with her?" he asked in disbelief.

"Excuse me." She turned to him. "At what point in our friendship did I give you the impression that I was some kind of bed-hopping tramp?"

"I know for a fact you and Lisa didn't wait that long, and, let's be honest, you weren't exactly a saint before you and my sister hooked up."

Mariska was taken aback by the venom in his voice. Where the hell was it coming from? "Okay, first of all. You bringing up my sex life with your sister is creepy to the max. Second, it was different with Lisa, so drop it."

"I won't drop it. You've been out of whack for months now. You're letting whatever this is with Alana get in the way of our work."

Something in the way he said "Alana" made her bristle. She wasn't sure whether he was jealous that he was no longer her sole confidant or that, despite his earlier protests, he did feel she was betraying Lisa by moving on. Whatever the case, it was quite obvious he wasn't as happy with her relationship as he had let on.

She shook her head. As if moving on from Lisa wasn't hard enough without him flip flopping between cheering her on or cutting her down.

"Why are you busting my balls? What the fuck is wrong with you tonight? Need I remind you, you're the one who told me to get out there and move on? I'm just doing what you told me to do, big brother. Never mind that you could take a page out of your own book and try and actually live your life for a change. We survived, Lucas. You're going to start having to live with that fact sooner or later instead of hiding down here trying to find a way to make it right. Lisa's gone, your little sister is gone, and nothing we've done since her death will ever make that change." Mariska headed for the stairs. She would sew herself up at home like a normal person. It would give Lucas time to cool off and pull out whatever stick had been shoved up his ass.

"If you'd been on your game that night, protecting Lisa like you were supposed to, we wouldn't be having this conversation."

Mariska sucked in a breath, willing herself to maintain some semblance of calm when all she wanted was to scream at him.

So this was the crux of the matter.

She'd wondered if he held her responsible for Lisa's death. She had okayed the plan, insisted Lisa was ready, and he blamed her for it. He'd always denied that vehemently. Seemed he was a better liar than she'd given him credit for. She was torn between hanging her head in shame for what she felt was Luke's justified rage and lashing out to defend herself.

"You want to know why I'm busting your balls, Mariska? Because I remember the last time you let your concentration slip, let your emotions get in the way of the job." He paused. "You got my sister killed."

Mariska tightened her hand on the stair railing. She ran Lucas's words through her mind one more time to make sure she had heard them right.

She calmly turned and tackled hit him full on. They crashed to the floor and rolled across the dented hardwood.

He threw punches into her ribs, and she cried out as he caught a tender spot. He managed to muscle her down and straddled her stomach.

Mariska wriggled in his grip and snorted as he took solid hold of her wrists and tried to pin her hands above her head.

Moron.

He had never learned or, at least, never broken that habit. She wasn't sure if it was his own ego or the general thoughts of the male half of the species but getting her on the ground wasn't a sign of victory.

"What is it about that night that bothers you more? The fact that it was us that made it out and not Lisa? Or that it was you, our defacto leader, who ended up too crippled and useless to go back out there and do the job that you love so much?"

He yelled and tightened his grip on her wrists. She could feel her skin bruising beneath his fingertips. That was what she wanted, a nice tight grip. She pulled her feet under her butt, swung her hands down to her hips and used her legs to push her pelvis up. Lucas shot face first towards the ground and let go of her to stop from breaking his nose on the hardwood.

His chin still skimmed across the floor as he rolled feet over shoulders and back into a fighting stance. Mariska swung around and kicked her feet out at the ankles and brought him back to the floor. He lay there, winded, as Mariska pushed herself to her feet.

"Maybe, if you had been on your game, protected your sister like you were supposed to, we wouldn't have had to do this," she said, spitting out a mouthful of blood. "Or have you forgotten that I was the one saving your sorry ass while you bled out on that shitty warehouse floor?"

She walked down the steps, leaving a crying Lucas to wallow in their mutual guilt.

MARISKA LOOKED AT her reflection in the steamed-up mirror and debated if she could get away without actually sewing up the gash on her forehead. The gash ran the length of her brow—a painful reminder of the head butt that had gotten past her guard.

She had taken a shower and washed away the dried blood and afterward had tied an ice pack to her ribs. Her black eyes were developing nicely, as was the bruise along her cheekbone where one of the punches had clipped her. A neat slice ran along her jawline and on her left thigh where the throwing daggers had skimmed by her.

Mariska touched her finger to her eyebrow and let out a sigh as the cut seeped blood once more. The swelling around it had forced the wound to reopen and it was liable to leave a nasty scar if she didn't do some damage control.

"Fuck." She couldn't bother Acco with this, not at this hour. The man had a life, and they'd imposed on him a lot recently. She could deal with it herself. Hopefully.

She picked up the lidocaine and rubbed it along her brow, then looked for her medical kit while the area numbed somewhat. Had she thought she could sew a straight line whilst drunk, she would have shotgunned the bottle of whiskey in her cabinet.

She stood in front of the mirror, threaded the needle, and reached up towards her eye. She let out a mild curse as she tried to maneuver herself properly. Spatial awareness had never really been her thing. Finally getting the hang of it, she pushed the needle through the skin and sucked in a breath as she tugged on the thread to pull it tight.

It had been a while since she had to sew herself up.

Her last attempt at self repair had been in the spring before last when Lisa and Lucas had gone on a family vacation and she had been left to her own devices for two weeks. She'd promised not to patrol on her own. Lisa had convinced her of the stupidity of going out totally solo.

It was a promise she fully intended to keep until she saw the armoured truck robbery and a security guard facing down the barrel of a sawed-off shotgun. She ended up with a couple of buckshot pellets to pull out of her leg, and the pesky little pellets left wounds that required stitching.

Acco had been inconveniently out of town as well. Unwilling to show up at the hospital with such an obvious wound, she had sat down with a bottle of JD and a medical kit and put in six stitches on her leg.

Neither of the siblings had been pleased.

Mariska sighed at the memory and inspected the stitches in the mirror to ensure they were straight. They weren't, but damned if she was going to take them out and do them again. She clipped off the suture, tied the end, and threw the spent medical kit into the garbage. The wound to her thigh, though long, wasn't quite deep enough to warrant stitches. A sterile bandage held down by a healthy dose of medical tape worked, and she limped to the kitchen for more ice.

She grabbed a glass and a Ziploc bag and filled both from the ice dispenser before heading to her cabinet for the whiskey. She knelt down to grab the bottle in the back of the cabinet and her hand skimmed across a smooth leather-bound book. She took out the bottle, poured herself a stiff drink, and capped the bottle, then grabbed the book.

She hadn't looked at the scrapbook in a while. Once upon a time, it had been her souvenir of their accomplishments as the Guardian team. Now it was just a painful reminder of what they had once been. She sat at her coffee table, placed the glass beside her, and flipped through the scrapbook. The first page was an article from nearly four years ago, their first, when she and Lucas had foiled a mugging.

She looked at the next page, an article dated only slightly after the first. It described two masked persons who had stopped a fight outside a bar from escalating to an all-out riot. And again, a month later, when they had foiled a robbery attempt at a deli.

Mariska sipped her drink and smiled as she read the headline crediting the police with taking down one of the most powerful mafia dons on the east coast. There was no mention of the Guardians, though they were the ones who had raided the docks and found the evidence needed to put the man and nearly three quarters of his organization away. It had been one of their greatest achievements and the beginning of the end.

Mariska snapped the album closed, finished her drink with a zealous gulp, and left the glass on the table as she headed for her bedroom. She lay on the bed, gray eyes watching the bright red numbers of her alarm clock as they cycled through. Slowly, she felt her lids grow heavy, the alcohol taking effect, and allowed herself to drift into sleep.

CHAPTER 9
Bad Dreams

MARISKA PUT HER hand to her shoulder and turned to check on Lisa. She yelled as she saw Lisa slide down the crate, a trail of blood in her wake. Mariska's and Lisa's cries of grief were drowned out only by the sound of two quick shotgun blasts. Mariska watched in horror as Lucas fell, yelling out in pain. She had no time to help him as a third and fourth shot connected with her vest, forcing her to the ground with barely a whimper. She couldn't breathe deeply enough to manage anything more.

Her vision began to darken as someone with sharp shoes launched kicks into her ribs.

She tried to turtle to protect her head and grunted as she felt something in her midsection crack. She had never broken a rib before. So that's what it felt like. It didn't matter, she was done. They were done. It was over. Mariska had known this would probably be the way things ended. She just hadn't expected it to be so soon. They still had so much to do. So many people to help.

People to help.

Lucas groaned in the background as Mariska felt her way up Lisa's body, willing her eyes to clear so she could see her.

"Lisa?" She shook her. "Lis? C'mon, baby, talk to me." She searched Lisa's neck for a pulse. She found none. She tugged her glove off with her teeth in frustration to check again.

Nothing.

"Rish?" She turned at the sound of Lucas's pained and weak voice. "She okay?"

The disparate howl that tore from her throat would haunt her dreams for years to come.

"Noo!" Mariska shot up in bed, sucking in deep breaths to try to bring her heart rate under control. She ripped the covers from her sweat-soaked body and stumbled out of bed to her bathroom where she threw up everything her stomach had to offer.

God fucking damn it.

It had been a while since her nightmares had been that intense, that crisp. Her mind went into rewind, intent on retracing the dream. Something was niggling at her. Something new. She shook it off and rinsed her mouth out before wiping a cold cloth across her face. She ignored the dull ache that seemed to permeate every part of her body, then tossed the cloth into the bathtub, eyes falling on the frosted glass shower door.

Her mind sent up a flag. She turned to her makeup drawer and pulled out an old tube of lipstick. She uncapped it and closed her eyes as she concentrated on what her subconscious was trying to tell her. A symbol from her dream came to her mind's eye and she drew on the glass door. She opened her eyes and took a deep angered breath at the symbol before her.

"Fuck. Me."

STELLA.

CHAPTER TEN
Surrender

"STELLA, IT'S GOOD to see you back in LA," Adam said as Alana clapped him on the shoulder after she exited the car.

He closed the door and followed her into the warehouse. He had been one of her lieutenants for years and was running the operations in the City of Angels. There had been some trouble with the local politicians of late. Some newbies had been elected and hadn't learned the way things worked around her city. It would take finesse and some subtle threatening to get the wheels greased again and operations back into full swing.

Alana walked into her office. Nothing had changed from when she had turned over direct control of LA nearly three years ago to set up operations in Toronto. Of course, to maintain discipline, she passed through on occasion, usually in surprise, to make sure all was well. She picked through the file folders on her desk, each of them a profile of the upstarts who needed to be taken care of.

Some could be ignored. They wouldn't make it beyond their first term. There was no point wasting good money when the next election would take care of her problem for her. Two or three looked to be the right type to take a bribe and seemed to have the political maneuvering to maintain their new seats for some time to come. The other two required a more direct approach.

"Get me an appointment with these two," she said, handing Adam the files. "No rush. Grab them on the way home from work. I don't want to start running into houses and pulling them out just yet."

Adam nodded.

Alana sat down. "Do let them know that's a possibility, if they give you trouble on the pick up tomorrow."

"Will do, boss."

She nodded at him in dismissal, and he disappeared.

Alana sat back in her chair, breathing deeply of the old leather. She had rousted an old opponent from the warehouse, a smart-mouthed businessman who thought he had the stomach for crime. She had left him to his own devices until he got the wrong idea about parts of her territory and moved his men into her streets. The consequences had been swift, undeniable, and by the time the blood had stopped filling the streets, she had annexed his men, his territory, and his contacts.

That had been nearly ten years ago. At the tender age of twenty-two she had moved from being a solo thief to leading her own men. Her descent into a life of crime had started early on. Her father had abandoned her mother when Alana was four. Her mother did the best she could by Alana, but there were few well-paying jobs for those who had no education, no experience, and a toddler at home.

By the age of eight, Alana had been left to her own devices while her mother worked to keep them housed in a one bedroom apartment. It was easy enough to fall in with the youth gangs in her school. They recruited early, practically right off the playground. Tired of being bullied and pushed around, she had excitedly accepted when the older sister of a classmate had invited her to a local hangout. They had taken her in, making her feel truly wanted.

When she looked back on it, with the wisdom of years of manipulating others behind her, she knew that had been the plan. Rope her in, ply her with promises of a life of luxuries and the safety of her new family. It had worked. She had done whatever they wanted, without question.

She had cut her criminal teeth picking pockets at the mall. Then had come the home invasions. Small enough to fit through the dog door and smart enough to know what was valuable, she had been a practical prodigy in her circle.

Boosting cars had been the next logical step, and soon she was driving stolen vehicles, barely able to see over the steering wheel. From there, she had moved into the weapons- and drug-running aspect of the business. One of the men, a big brother of sorts, had warned her if she intended to make it big, she would do well not to use the drugs they pushed.

While Alana had been tutored in the art of criminality, her mother had gradually succumbed to the hardships of her life. When Alana was fifteen, her mother had drunk herself to death, unable to cope with the hand life had dealt her. At that point, Alana had felt almost nothing over the loss, save for a twinge of nostalgia.

Gang life had taught her not to grow attached to anyone. People came and went daily, recruited to the family only to die in drive-by shootings or drug deals gone bad. The lucky ones ended up in jail. Some died inside, some made it out into the legitimate world, most went right back to the neighborhood to pick up where they'd left off.

At sixteen, a police roundup had swept the streets, courtesy of a fresh-faced politician. She had been one of the few to escape. Left alone, Alana had fallen back on her oldest tool, thievery. She had survived well enough on the usual house robberies, but her intelligence and daring had demanded more of her. She honed her skills, taking on increasingly difficult jobs and using whatever means were necessary to get them done. Eventually, people sought her out for her skills. Unwilling to reveal herself to buyers who would not do the same, she had adopted the mask as a means of protection. It wasn't unheard of for thieves to get bumped off after they had completed their job.

As her skills matured, so had the outfit. What was once a means of anonymity was now an integral part of her identity.

By twenty, Alana had tired of stealing riches for the rich. She wanted her own piece of the proverbial pie and she was willing to do what it took to get a slice. She returned to her old haunts, long since abandoned, to recruit for her new gang. Members hadn't been hard to find. She had used the techniques that had brought her in, promising safety to the frightened and riches to the greedy.

No longer the freckle-faced baby of the group, she was the masked leader of an organized unit. They hadn't been much more than street thugs at the time, comprised of a hodgepodge of old gang members, newcomers, and the occasional cop.

A few good deals and her unwillingness to go gently into the night ensured that STELLA would make its way to the top. It had taken time and patience, as all things worth having were wont to need. By the time she had turned day-to-day operations over to Adam, they had stakes in most of the docks in LA and had branched out all over the West Coast.

Not bad for a runty pickpocket from the wrong side of town.

Alana checked her watch. Eight a.m. eastern time. She picked up her phone and punched in the number from memory. She had waited a couple of hours to call Mariska. Despite Mariska's request, Alana knew she needed her sleep. She was surprised when it was picked up on the second ring.

Hey," Mariska said in a subdued voice.

"Morning. You feeling okay? You sound down."

"I've had better days," Mariska answered.

Alana frowned, Mariska's day had barely begun. That couldn't be good.

"How was your flight?"

"Long and boring. I wish I was there to help you feel better," Alana said, surprised by her own candor. She'd been eager to get back to her old stomping grounds and out of range of that pain in the ass, Guardian. But now that she was actually in Los Angeles, she found whatever attachments she'd been holding onto about the city didn't seem to compare to a certain someone back home.

"I wish you were here too," Mariska said quietly.

Alana narrowed her eyes at a noise in the background. It sounded suspiciously like a sniffle. She sat forward, pushing the phone closer to her ear. "Are you all right?"

"Yeah, just a really bad night. Lucas and I got into a fight. It was pretty bad. He said some things . . ." Mariska trailed off. "Anyway, I don't think we're really friends anymore."

"I'm sorry, Rish, is there something I can do?" If Alana worked quickly, she could fly back home and be there for her. She tamped down sharply on that idea. She had a job to do that didn't include flying across the continent to hold Mariska's hand.

Mariska was a grown woman and could handle herself well enough until she got back. Right? *Of course*, she told herself firmly, ignoring the feeling of discomfort in the pit of her stomach. She couldn't go back. Going back was admitting that she'd let Mariska far enough into her life to do some serious damage. Strong affection was one thing. The very idea of abandoning her business for her girlfriend meant something deeper was brewing.

"I'm okay," Mariska said.

"Are you sure?"

"I'm sure. I'm going to see my mom this morning. She's the ultimate cheer-upper."

Alana admired Mariska. She was ever the trooper, soldiering

on with her life, even while she was hurting. She respected her for that. "Yeah? What kind of trouble are you two planning on getting into?"

"The kind that happens in a church," Mariska said. "My mom goes with a bunch of her girlfriends. They make pierogi and do some pickling. That kind of stuff. I promised her I'd go."

"Sounds . . . exciting."

"Best pierogi outside of Roncesvailles." Knowing Mariska's love of food and her skill in the kitchen, Alana had no doubt of it.

"I'll bring you some when you get back."

"You'd better."

"Scout's honour," Mariska said. "I need to get going. I'm supposed to be in Scarborough in an hour, which means I'm already late."

"Okay. I'll call you later in the week when things have settled a little."

"Sounds good."

Alana hung up and sat back in her chair. That went well. She hadn't done anything foolish like suggest she could come back to Toronto. She wouldn't fly home straight away. She had work to do.

But . . . that didn't mean she couldn't push things along a little faster. It would no doubt cost more but what was the point of having riches if not to make yourself happy with them? And she knew, even as she tried to deny it, that her happiness lay with a young woman half a continent away.

MARISKA ARRIVED AT the church nearly twenty minutes late, which was a good ten minutes early for her. She'd used all of her makeup application skills to hide the dark bruises and the small cut on her face. She left her hair down in hopes of covering the angry gash over her eyebrow, though she doubted how well it would work.

She looked up at her childhood church, taking comfort in its familiarity. It was a place of warmth and love, made all the more so by her family. It wasn't much of a building. Yellow brick and brown shingles. A small sign above wooden front doors declared it a place of worship. It was unassuming and tucked away into her parents' blue collar neighborhood.

The inside was equally Spartan with simple hardwood floors and basketball nets at either end. It also doubled as the local community center. Fold-up chairs were set up and taken down on a weekly basis for the sermon when the pastor spoke from a podium that was rolled out from the corner. None of that mattered. Between the Sunday sermons, the potlucks, the fundraising, and any other number of events from her childhood, she thought of this place as a second home.

Mariska stepped inside and closed her eyes, the familiar sight pushing old memories to the surface. Lisa and Lucas had come with her to many of the events here. Everything from teenage sock hops, family weddings, potlucks, and basketball games. Her mother had even attempted to teach Lucas how to cook. The exercise had failed miserably but the entire family had enjoyed watching him try.

Mr. and Mrs. Forsythe hadn't been as hands-on with their parenting as Mariska's parents had been. Concerned that the siblings weren't getting as much guidance as they needed, the Coopers had welcomed them into the family. By the time they hit their teens, Lisa and Lucas were as much a part of the Cooper clan as Mariska was.

When Lucas lost a fight at school, it was Mariska's father who drove down to pick him up from the nurse's office. And it was Mariska's mother who Lisa went to for advice when she had floundered in making her university choices. Mariska choked up a little. Her mother had been so attached to Lisa. When Lisa died, Mariska knew her mom's heart had broken right along with hers.

Mariska shook off the negative thoughts. They had all shared nothing but good memories inside these walls. This wasn't the time or the place to bring sadness. Plastering as wide a smile as she thought she could get away with, she headed to her family.

The women were already at work at the tables, chattering away in Ukrainian or Russian, sometimes in an odd mix of the two. Mariska had a handle on the Ukrainian. Her parents were both first generation immigrants, but the Russian was beyond her ken. She understood a smattering of the language here and there but it was mostly the Russian derived slang words that had made their way into her parents' dialect.

Her mother was easy to spot, flanked by her two sisters and a group of women they regularly went to tea with. Mariska walked up to the table and accepted the kisses of her mother and aunts along with gentle chides that she was, as ever, far too thin.

"You don't come to see your mother enough," her mom was quick to say as Mariska stood at one end of the table and began to knead dough. Her knuckles, sore from the fight the night before, ached in protest. She nodded placidly, knowing it was only the first of many times she would hear it from the women around the table. Her aunts would be next.

It was good-natured ribbing though, and as much as Mariska made a fuss, she was happy to listen to it, if only because it showed how much they cared. She felt a moment of sadness for Alana. Mariska knew she had lost her mother at a young age. Alana hadn't been clear on the details. With no siblings and no other family to speak of, it seemed Alana had been on her own for some time.

In the early afternoon, her mother called for a break for tea after three hours of animated conversation, with Mariska's aunts telling more than one joke that had her blushing. Twenty-two years in and they could still surprise her. Hanging out with her family left her feeling more lighthearted than she had felt in days.

Her hands were stiff from kneading endless batches of dough, and she was fairly certain she never wanted to peel another potato. Luckily, she had to work so she wouldn't be staying for the second round. She collected two bags of pierogi—payment for her work—and stood to go.

"And how is this woman, Alana?" her mother asked as Mariska pulled her coat on.

Mariska was surprised Alana hadn't come up earlier. Her two aunts seemed to be immersed in their own conversation, but she was fairly certain either of them would be able to repeat the conversation verbatim should her mother need the backup.

"She's good, Mom."

"You need to bring her home. Lisa was always here making food. We knew her. We don't know this girl."

Mariska smiled slightly as her aunts, no longer pretending to ignore the conversation, voiced their agreement. It was true. Lisa had been attached to her hip even before they had begun dating. She swallowed, trying to push down the sudden lump in her throat.

"I'll bring her, Mom," Mariska said, realizing she meant it. She wanted her mother to know Alana, wanted Alana to be a part of this life. To be a part of the family. Her family. *Aww crap*, she thought with a slight bit of panic. She had gone and fallen in love with Alana.

"You have a picture?"

Mariska precariously balanced her pierogi in one hand as she pulled her wallet out to show her mother a photo of Alana. It was quick to make the rounds of the table, her aunts making sounds at the photo booth shots Mariska had managed to wrangle Alana into. She had rarely seen Alana quite so carefree as they made goofy poses at the camera.

"She's pretty but too thin," her mother said, drawing Mariska out of her thoughts before her arms were loaded with an extra package of pierogi.

"You must take care of her, Mariska," one aunt chided.

"We didn't teach you to cook just so you could starve this poor woman," her other aunt chimed in.

Debating between rolling her eyes and holding up her hands in surrender to her family, she simply stood mute. Her mother handed her a large paper bag to put her pierogi in and signaled to her sisters. Mariska stood in place as her aunts loaded her down with keilbasa, cheese, and a large loaf of bread they had evidently bought at the Uki deli.

"There, Kisa, you cook for her." Her aunts gave her twin kisses on the cheek before returning to their table to stuff the never-ending pile of perogies.

Mariska's mother walked her to the door as she shifted the over-stuffed bag to the side to give her a hug.

"Thanks, Mom, this was great. It was . . . just what I needed." To be reminded that there were people who cared about her. No matter how important Lucas was in her life, she could get by without him if she had to.

"Then you'll come back sooner and see us."

Mariska nodded, pushed open the door, and walked out into cold air.

"And you bring the girl home to meet your mother!" her mother called from across the parking lot as Mariska headed for the bus.

FOUR DAYS LATER, Mariska was mind-numbingly bored as she sat in the warehouse basement and scrolled through recent police reports to determine where she would be patrolling for the week. She'd been working the downtown core pretty regularly for the past while. Maybe it was time to move towards the west end.

Lucas was nowhere to be found. Barring any crazy criminal catastrophes, he would be at work for some hours to come. Mariska was glad for it. She was able to keep a lid on her anger so long as she wasn't thinking about him or the fight the past weekend. She had a bad feeling that if they were forced into close confines with each other, they were liable to have a repeat of their throw down.

Mariska looked up from the computer as the alarm system beeped a proximity alert. It wasn't uncommon. The sewer systems were maintained by the city and the occasional worker strayed close enough to the warehouse to trip the motion sensor. Even a disturbingly large rat had managed to set off the alarm.

Mariska scrolled through the various video feeds until she landed on the sewer camera. She could make out a thin form as it walked down the tunnel, a small flashlight in hand. She sighed as recognition dawned. Brooke, the girl from the arena two months ago. She had found her way back.

"Well, shit." Mariska sat back, hands clasped behind her head. "Clever girl, I'll give you that."

She hadn't heard from or of the girls since Acco had delivered them into Perkins's care. She could only guess why Brooke was trying to find her or how long she'd been searching the tunnels for the warehouse entrance. It crossed her mind that maybe Brooke needed help. If that was the case, she couldn't turn her away.

"I already know this is a bad idea," she said as she walked over to her gear, pulled her vest over her shirt, and tugged her mask into place.

She flicked the switch to activate the door and leaned against the threshold as she waited for Brooke to make her way towards her.

"If you're looking for a shortcut to the beach, you missed the turnoff two pipes back," she said to the grime-covered young woman.

"I can't believe I found this place again."

"Yeah, you and me both." Mariska stood up straight, uncrossed her arms, and walked back into the computer room. "Well, c'mon if you're coming. You're letting in the smell."

Brooke followed her in, intelligent brown eyes surveying the room before they met Mariska's.

They stood, studying each other.

"You hungry?" Mariska asked.

"Starved," Brooke said.

"Come on." Mariska led her to the elevator. "I hope you like pierogi."

One large plate of pierogi and some stilted small talk later, Mariska thought it was time to get to the point. "So, you plan on telling me what you're doing here, or am I supposed to guess?"

"I want you to train me. I want to be like you."

Mariska was unable to contain her sharp bark of laughter.

"No," she said with a shake of her masked head. "You most certainly do not—"

"Yes, I do."

Mariska massaged her temples. "Look, you don't want this life, okay? I'm twenty-two. I've been shot, stabbed, thrown off a building, watched one of my best friends nearly bleed to death while the other died in my arms. Believe me, kid, you don't want this life."

"You need help."

"I do, do I?"

"Yeah. When you got hurt helping us, you didn't have anyone to watch your back." Brooke's face was the picture of stern resolve. "I can be that, I can watch your back."

"I admire your courage, really. But please believe me when I say that the last thing I need or want right now is to teach another young woman how to get herself killed. Go home, Brooke."

"I don't have a home. I live on the streets, and they're not safe. I have to do something. I'm going to sit here until you agree to let me help." Brooke sat back in her seat and crossed her arms defiantly.

"No, you will not. You're going to march your bony ass back out into that sewer and forget you ever found this place. I'm not in the market for a sidekick."

"What am I supposed to do? I ran away from home, I didn't finish high school. What else can I be? A waitress? A hooker? Maybe, if I'm really lucky and I try real hard, I can be a stripper."

"You're being melodramatic," Mariska said, taking the plate from the table and putting it in the sink.

"This life can't be worse than what I came from."

"Okay. Say I teach you. What about Alexis? Who protects her when you get yourself killed on the streets?"

Brook stared at her, silent.

"That's what I thought. Believe me, when you're my age and you have intact ear drums and feeling in both your calves, you'll thank me."

"You're really not going to take me?"

Mariska knew that look, that tone. It was the voice of someone who thought if she argued hard enough, stood her ground, made a case, she would get what she wanted. Lisa had looked at her and Lucas the same way. She felt a little bad for bursting Brooke's bubble but damned if she was going to bring another person in to die.

"I'm really not," Mariska said. "Come on, I'll drive you home or whatever."

"I'll find my own way back."

Mariska sighed. What was one more person being pissed at her?

Brooke stomped down the stairs. Mariska followed sedately after her. A quick flick of a switch on the basement level and the sewer door opened. Brooke disappeared into the tunnels.

"What a week."

ALANA TUGGED HER purse higher onto her shoulder, one hand wrapped around a bag of Mariska's favourite takeout, the other scratching absently at her arm. Her physician had removed the stitches two days ago and handed her Vitamin E to reduce the scar. Until then, she would have to rely on long sleeves and make-up to hide the discoloration.

It took some finesse and a little more money than she would have preferred but she'd made it back to Toronto in half the time she had anticipated. The twelve days away from Mariska had been . . . illuminating. She'd dealt with the issues posed by the politicians quickly enough and settled a dispute with a rival gang. Well, only if "settled" meant wiping out one's opponents.

That had all been run of the mill. Her own soul-searching

proved to be the most interesting. She had gone out with the top executives of her company to a posh sushi restaurant, and the waitress, a lithe Asian woman with midnight hair, had flirted with her mercilessly. Having gone three months without bed games of any kind, Alana had been sorely tempted. She had even been at the point of giving the waitress the address of the apartment she kept in Pasadena when something held her back.

She had an uneasy feeling in the pit of her stomach, a concern for Mariska's feelings. What if she found out? She had worked so hard to establish trust between them, was she willing to risk that on a one-night stand? She found she wasn't. No matter how small the probability that Mariska would find out, no matter how attractive the waitress was, she couldn't bring herself to do it.

She—who had killed countless people, run slaves, bedded women without regard—was now unable to commit a simple act of sexual indiscretion. The discovery had been nothing short of intensely disturbing. She certainly hadn't intended to develop these feelings when she had first thought of approaching Mariska in that seedy bar three months ago. She'd hoped for a bit of fun—the conquest of a younger woman and maybe a decent conversation if she was lucky. Apparently, she had bitten off a little more than she could chew.

Alana knocked on Mariska's door.

Mariska opened it and stared at her in wide-eyed surprise. "You're back early."

Alana stared back in shock. "Oh my God, your face."

Mariska looked at her in confusion before she touched the stitches in her eyebrow. "I could have sworn I told you. Lucas and I got into a fight." She stepped aside to allow Alana in.

Alana put the food and her purse on the floor, and tugged Mariska into the light to take a better look. Mariska closed her eyes as Alana brushed gentle hands over damaged skin.

"Okay. I think there was a miscommunication. When you said fight I assumed it was a shouting match not Fists of Fury. Lucas did this to you?"

"I gave as good as I got," Mariska said with a small shrug. "I hit my head at some point. It's a little fuzzy."

"Did they let a first year med student sew you up? The stitches are completely uneven." Alana thought she saw a flash of distress in Mariska's eyes and cursed herself. "I'm sure it'll heal just fine though. It doesn't look bad enough to leave much of a scar." She waved her hand. "Are you hungry?"

"Not really," Mariska said. "But that's sweet. Thank you."

"I'll put this in the fridge for later. How about we just sit and relax?"

The grateful look Mariska threw her bordered on heartbreaking. Food stowed, Alana sat on the couch next to Mariska, who had a blanket pooled at her feet, the TV quietly on in the background. Mariska settled her head into her lap and pulled the blanket up tightly to her shoulders.

Alana had been surprised to learn that Mariska's habit of cuddling didn't bother her much. Not at all actually, if she was being honest. If she were being totally honest, she'd even admit she enjoyed the closeness. She'd never been able to enjoy such innocent connections with other people and it was a pleasant change.

"I thought you weren't coming back for another week."

"Well, that was the plan."

"What changed?"

"You had that fight with Lucas and you haven't sounded right since. I've been worried."

"I'm okay, I'm dealing. You didn't have to come back early," Mariska said, her fingers tracing patterns on Alana's denim clad knees.

Alana kissed Mariska's tanned temple. She could have fought the feelings that were developing, the ones that were settling down somewhere so deep inside her she hadn't even known the spot existed. With this one gesture, she admitted, if only to herself, that Mariska was becoming an important part of her life.

Given the circumstances, Alana said all she could think to say as she ran her hands through soft brown tresses. "Yes. I did."

"Alana?"

"Hmm?"

"Let's go to bed."

CHAPTER 11
Mom, Money, and the Mafia

ALANA WOKE SLOWLY, her mind sluggish to register where she was. The bed was considerably smaller than her king size at home. There was also a wall of warmth plastered to her chest, and she felt the rhythmic exhalation against her collarbone. She took in a slow, contented breath before brushing a kiss against Mariska's forehead and adjusting her hold on her.

She had no idea what time it was. The heavy blackout curtains prevented her from judging by the sun, and Mariska was blocking the alarm clock. It didn't matter. She didn't particularly care as the only thing on her agenda for the day was staying close to Mariska. Maybe they could rent a movie and just spend some time together. Their time apart had left her craving Mariska's presence.

Mariska shifted in her sleep and burrowed more tightly into Alana's shoulder. She tugged the covers higher around them, knowing Mariska tended to get cold at night. Why she insisted on setting the heat to a temperature akin to that of an icebox, Alana would never know.

"I don't have to get up, do I?" Mariska asked, her voice muffled against Alana's bare chest.

Alana shook her head, as she ran her hands through Mariska's hair and gave her scalp a scratch. She could almost swear Mariska purred.

"Nope, we can stay in bed all day if you want."

"Mmm, that would be nice. Too bad I have to work tonight," Mariska said, pulling away slightly so she could push Alana from her side to on her back. She then draped herself over Alana, head resting comfortably on her naked chest.

Alana continued her gentle scalp massage, enjoying the weight of Mariska's body on top of her. She checked the clock. Nearly ten. Odd. She rarely slept in so late. "I'm calling in sick for you."

"You can't. I need the hours," Mariska said, tightening her arms around Alana's midsection before yawning widely.

Alana looked down at her, mentally wincing at the set of stitches and the faint outlines of bruises on Mariska's cheeks. Dark circles lined Mariska's eyes. She was exhausted.

"You're tired. You need the rest. Play hooky with me," Alana said.

"Some of us can't actually afford to blow off work," Mariska said.

"I don't want you to blow off work," Alana said, drawing her nails up Mariska's back. "I want you to quit."

Mariska chuckled. "Funny. That'll happen. You gonna come sleep over when I live in a cardboard box?" She pushed up to look at Alana, her playful expression changing as she caught Alana's look. "You're serious? Alana, we're not all wealthy executives. I have enough in savings to float me through maybe a month. I can't afford to throw away a perfectly good job."

"I'm not telling you to throw away your job," Alana said.

Mariska gave her a confused stare.

"I want you to open your bar."

"With the thousand dollars I have in my account?" Mariska asked with a snort, which quickly turned to a wince. "Last I checked, it was a little more expensive."

"I'll invest in it and I know enough bankers to swing a loan for the rest," Alana said.

"Alana . . ." Mariska shook her head, and she pinched the bridge of her nose as though to ward off a headache.

"Listen, I've wanted to invest in something new. I already have a number of holdings on the West Coast," Alana said. It wasn't quite a lie. "I looked over the proposal you gave me. It's sound."

"This is insane." Mariska tried to roll off her, but Alana held her tightly in place.

"Why? I have the contacts to make this happen. If there was ever a time to try, it's now."

"I don't have a location, a construction crew. The business proposal was a school project, for Christ's sake."

"With real-world applicability, it'll work."

"Even if I did accept, and that's a big if, I'd still need to work. Rent doesn't pay itself and it'll be months before I could open."

"Take it out of the investment. That's how everyone else does it."

Mariska gazed steadily at her. "I'm not the type to be a kept woman."

Alana pinched the bridge of her nose. "Who's talking about being a kept woman? You'll be paying the bank back with interest, and I'll be earning profits comparable to my percentage of investment. Once you're on your feet, you can buy me out or we'll leave it as is."

"That's a big risk for you," Mariska said.

Alana shrugged. It wasn't really. Not if she burned down a couple of bars and paid the right cops.

"I wouldn't invest the money if I couldn't afford to lose it. There's always some risk with new business. But you've worked in this type of thing long enough to know the market and what will or won't work. I trust you, Mariska. You need to start trusting you."

"It's always a little harder when it's someone else's money I'm risking," Mariska said. "I wouldn't want this to go bad and have it ruin us."

"It won't go bad and even if it did, it won't ruin us. You're a hard worker and you've got a good head for business. If it tanks, it won't be because of you."

"Why are you doing this?"

"Simple answer?" That was easy. "To make money."

"Honest answer," Mariska said.

Alana grinned. Clever girl. She sighed, tapping her fingers on the small of Mariska's back. "I care about you and I worry. I want to see you succeed and I don't want to watch you kill yourself to do it. I had to climb my way over everyone and his dog to get to where I am. I don't want that for you."

"Can I think about it? It's a big decision."

Alana didn't really think so. It was a bit of a no brainer. It was a golden deal really. "Of course. Take as long as you want. I, on the other hand, am going to go out and grab us some breakfast."

"You don't have to do that," Mariska said. "I can make us something."

"Nope." Alana kissed Mariska's forehead, careful to avoid the small bandage that covered the bridge of her nose. "Stay in bed and rest up. I'm going for caffeine and sustenance." She threw her long legs out of the bed, grabbed Mariska's sweat pants and U of T hoodie.

Mariska laughed quietly.

Alana turned to her. "What?"

"You look adorable," Mariska said, motioning to the slightly oversized shirt and the pants pooling at her feet.

"Adorable?" Adorable was for puppies and small children. Not women who were hard-hitting executives by day and world-feared criminals by night. "I am not adorable."

Mariska held out a hand, and Alana went to the bed.

Mariska pulled her forward and wrapped her arms around Alana's neck. "Believe me, you look adorable."

Alana nodded, willing to agree to damn near anything when Mariska's lips were two inches from hers. She straddled Mariska and pulled back. "Breakfast . . ."

"Can wait."

MARISKA WALKED UP the steps to her childhood home, noting the fresh set of shingles on the roof. Seemed her dad and cousins had finally gotten it finished. She didn't knock, merely pushed open the door and deeply inhaled the smell of her mother's baking.

"Wow, that smells great," Alana said, taking a breath of the sweet, warm air.

"You think this is good? Wait until Christmas rolls around. Mom!"

"In here."

Mariska followed her mother's voice into the kitchen where she and Mariska's aunts were busily mixing batter. Alana was at Mariska's side, quiet, but seemingly happy to go through the gauntlet.

"Church bake sale?" Mariska asked, as she reached for a cookie.

"Kisa, don't touch," her aunt said, holding up a batter-covered spatula in warning.

Mariska debated if she was fast enough to get the cookie into her mouth before she was assaulted with muffin mix. Judging by the look in her aunt's eyes, she wasn't. She abandoned the attempt and kissed the flour-covered women on the cheeks.

"So, you finally bring her home to meet your mothers," her aunt, Olenka, said. "She's still too thin."

"Did she cook for you?" her aunt, Kalyna, asked.

"Yes, I damn well did. We had pierogi for a month."

Her mother and aunts emitted disappointed guffaws at her language. Mariska grimaced.

"Alana Pierce, this is my mom, Janina, and my aunts, Kalyna and Olenka."

Alana didn't seem to notice or care if she got flour on her smart-looking suit, she smiled as Mariska's mother and aunts kissed her cheeks and gave her a firm hug.

"Come sit, talk, you want some bread? Fresh baked." Mariska's mother guided Alana to a chair at the dinner table.

"If Kisa had told us you were coming, we would have made food," Kalyna said. "She's too thin. Why always so thin?" She asked in Ukrainian.

"Kisa?" Alana asked, looking at Mariska.

"Childhood pet name," Mariska answered. "It's Russian, means kitten."

"Aww, that's cute."

Mariska shook her head and stepped aside as Aunt Olenka cleared the table.

"There's leftovers," her mother said, as she pulled plates of food out of the fridge.

"There's no need . . ." Alana started to say.

Mariska touched her hand. "You're going to weigh an extra five pounds when you leave here, whether you want to or not. Just go with it."

Alana's eyes widened at the plates Mariska's mom put on the table. "Uh . . ."

"Take, eat," Aunt Kalyna said.

Mariska was unsurprised as Alana loaded her plate with a heaping helping of the kielbasa.

"Ah, see Kisa," Aunt Kalyna said in Ukrainian. "This is how you fatten her up."

Alana added some cabbage rolls. "What did she say?" She stopped her fork midway to her mouth.

Mariska leaned over, happily dropping a kiss on Alana's cheek. "She said *bon appétit*."

Two hours and many calories later, Mariska's family sent them off with hugs, kisses, and a large bag of leftovers.

"That was fun," Alana said, as she steered the sleek Mercedes down Bloor Street.

Mariska was glad Alana had a good time. It surprised her a little. She'd been concerned she might feel out of place amongst her blue collar family. Even when her father returned from his shift at the auto plant, Alana shook his hand and was welcomed by a hearty back slap.

"I'm glad you liked them. They're important to me," Mariska said, rubbing her hand along Alana's arm.

"They're very . . . open."

"You mean about my being gay?"

Alana nodded.

"Yeah, I know. It made it so much easier to come out when I was younger," Mariska said. "My family went through a lot in the Second World War, on both sides. I guess my grandparents grew up seeing what intolerance can do to people, and they taught their kids accordingly. Don't get me wrong. There was still some disappointment, but it was mostly centered around having kids and being able to get married in my parents' church."

"Well, there's a way around any problem," Alana said. "Let me know, and I can make it happen."

Mariska's eyes widened.

"Um, not that I'm asking you know . . . I wasn't saying . . ."

Alana seemed near a panic. "I meant . . ." She took a deep breath. "I want to be someone you can always count on, Mariska. No matter what. I . . . love you." She looked at Mariska. "I want you to be happy and if that means getting married in your parents' church, whenever it happens, I'll make sure you get there."

Mariska gently kissed Alana on the cheek.

"You're a good woman, Alana Pierce, even if you are a dirty oil executive."

Alana grinned.

"And I love you, too." Mariska didn't think she had ever seen Alana smile so brightly. She could relate. It had felt great to say. After all the back and forth, it was nice to know where she stood.

"All right, I have a question," Alana said.

"Shoot."

"Cooper? How the hell does that happen?"

Mariska laughed. "I should let my didi tell this story. He does it better. Long and short is, my paternal family's name was actually Kosakowski. When my grandfather went through immigration, the guy couldn't spell it so he asked Didi what his trade was. Didi didn't have much English so all he managed to get out was chickens. Chickens are raised in a coop, ergo Cooper."

"Did they actually put that much thought into it?"

"Didi says they did. Personally, I think the guy heard the hard 'k' of our name and went with what came to mind."

"Typical government."

"So when you came across the border, did they change your name?"

"Wouldn't you like to know?"

TWO WEEKS LATER, Mariska looked around a dilapidated retail space, trying to see beyond the filth that littered the floor.

"What's that smell?" Alana asked, her nose screwed up as she kicked away a disintegrating pizza box with the pointed toe of her boot.

"I choose not to dwell on the negatives," Mariska said, using the sleeve of her hoodie to wipe the grime off the countertop. It was dented wood, the varnish peeling underneath the layer of dust. But it wasn't split, and with the right decor, the distressed bar top would give the place character.

"If you would let me loan you a little money, I could get you a location better than this," Alana said. Her incredulity at Mariska taking on the lease of the small space was evident in her voice.

"We talked about this. You've already done enough." Enough had been everything in Mariska's opinion. She'd turned down Alana's offer a month ago, unwilling to gamble someone else's money on her own venture. Or perhaps it was her pride. At any rate, she had thanked Alana for her generosity but had insisted on standing on her own feet. Seeming to accept, or at least understand her hesitation, Alana had instead offered to put her in contact with the proper people at the bank. That offer she had accepted.

Despite Alana's influence, Mariska had been turned down for her loan. Mired in student debt with too little collateral for the bank to collect if she went belly up, she had barely gotten in the front door. She then spent two frustrated weeks trying to come up with collateral to no avail. Had she been on speaking terms with

Lucas, she could have asked him for help, but that avenue was closed.

She'd been at the point of giving up until Alana had volunteered to cosign. Her condo alone was worth more than the loan Mariska was requesting.

Mariska had balked at the suggestion, almost as much as Alana personally investing. It meant risk on her part. Thankfully, Alana was no slouch at digging in her heels. She merely waited Mariska out.

There had been a few heated conversations, most revolving around Mariska being too mulish for her own good. She had gone to her mother to ask for advice. Her aunts had been home—no surprise—and she'd been treated to three cuffs to the back of the head for being too proud.

Who was she to turn down help from Alana? Were they not partners? Would her mother or aunts turn down help from their husbands? Surely not. Oh the insult. Hadn't they raised her properly?

Feeling duly chastised, she had gone to Alana's condo and asked if the offer was still open.

"Of course. Don't worry, Rish, I won't hold your hesitation against you," Alana said with a wink.

Alana then dragged her to the bank the next day, evidently worried she would change her mind. With Alana's powerful signature behind her, the ink had barely dried on the application before the approval had come through.

As Mariska held the piece of paper, the exuberant expression on Alana's face was awe-inspiring. The kiss Mariska laid on her in thanks left the loan officer nothing short of scandalized.

Unwilling to lose momentum, Alana had contacted her realtor and, within a week, they'd viewed fifteen properties in Mariska's price range. She finally settled on the smallish unit on Bloor Street in the west end.

"Twenty grand," Alana said.

"Eh?"

"Twenty grand. Hell, I'll give you the money for Christmas." Alana took in the suspiciously stained corners of the room. "At least then I could sleep at night knowing you won't get knifed in your own bar."

Mariska let out a guffaw. "It's not that bad. And there's an apartment over me. When my lease comes due, I can move in here. It's going to be perfect."

"You want an apartment over a bar? I'll find you another one." Alana already had her cell phone out.

Mariska tsked and took the cell phone away. "It's going to be fine. Besides, this neighborhood will never get clean unless reputable businesses move in. There are two art galleries going in. Give the area five years, and it'll be a little more gentrified."

"You don't have to save the world, Mariska."

"I know that, but I like the area. It's cheap, and I'm just starting. If I move any closer to downtown, the rent will kill me before I can even get off the ground. Trust me on this. I know what I'm doing."

"All right, but don't think I'm not going to worry."

"Duly noted, but you don't have to. I did a year at York University. If I can make it out of there, I'm untouchable," Mariska said.

She'd chosen the location for its business potential, but there were other reasons as well. There was a sewer access at the rear of the building that would allow her to move from the warehouse and back with impunity. She had free reign with the apartment and she would build in a gear closet and medical supply chest.

It would also allow her to keep an eye on the Parkdale area, one of the areas worst hit by STELLA's organization.

"So have you spoken to Lucas?" Alana asked.

Mariska flipped a chair over to give herself something to sit on while they waited for the contractor. Her cousin Andryko would be running the job. Most of the renovations would be done by her family. She felt bad dragging them from Scarborough, but Aunt Kalyna assured her it was no problem.

"No, he hasn't called. No e-mails either." Mariska sighed. He hadn't even spoken to her on the radio while she was on patrol. She only knew he was on the other end because he occasionally left himself logged in to the computer.

"Maybe you should try to speak to him. He's been your friend for, what, fifteen years?"

"Yeah, well, even Clark Kent and Lex Luthor were best friends once," Mariska said, her tone petulant.

"Look, I'm not exactly his biggest fan. But he's important to you. This bar, it's been your dream. Don't you want to share that with your best friend?"

Mariska took Alana's hand. "I am."

"I'M NOT TRAINING you," Mariska said into the microphone. She could see Brooke in the camera as she leaned against the sewer tunnel wall, arms crossed, staring at the closed door.

Mariska leaned back in her chair and scrubbed her face with her hands in exasperation. The girl had shown up over an hour ago and had simply stood there, waiting for acknowledgment. Mariska ignored it for as long as she could but . . .

"This is ridiculous." She pressed the intercom button. "Brooke, go home. You're going to freeze down here." Brook didn't move. "Fine, be stubborn."

She returned her attention to the screen and searched for any pattern in STELLA's movements. It was no good. This was Lucas's bailiwick, but she refused to ask him for anything.

It didn't matter how much she agreed with Alana or how much she wanted Lucas to share her dream with her. She had yet to forgive him for the things he had said to her.

"Not like I did any better," she muttered. But that wasn't the point. If Lucas Forsythe thought he could silent treatment her into submission, he had another thing coming.

That being said, she now had a computer geek problem and no computer geek to solve it. Unless . . .

"Brooke, I'm leaving. You can't stare down the security cameras so go home and thaw out." Mariska pulled the information disc from the computer, shut the unit down, grabbed her freshly loaded utility belt, and headed for the stairs.

Not being able to be in the warehouse with Lucas had forced her to get back to basics. No ATV, no remote unlocking of computerized doors, no alarm shutdowns. It was like in the beginning, where she'd relied on her low-tech gear and her wits. Of course, back then, she had a partner in the field with her, but that was neither here nor there.

Mariska left the warehouse, tugging her coat tightly around her body to ward off the crisp air. She headed for Virtuos Technology and arrived just as the clock hit four. She saw Lucas walk out of the building and head for the subway, his limp making odd tracks in the fresh snow. She felt a small pang of sympathy for him. The cold weather was hard on his damaged body.

She waited until she was certain Lucas was gone before she headed for his office. She stood at the door, breath coming out in cold puffy clouds. Her target—head down, hands buried in a *Star Trek* jacket—walked past her.

"Crash," she called out.

He turned to her, his face on automatic blush, tinging red.

"How about I buy you an orange juice?"

"Okay," he whispered.

She motioned for him to follow her to a small restaurant half a block away.

"How have you been?" she asked as they sat.

"O-Okay," he replied, his head down.

"Crash, dude, relax. I'm gay. This isn't a date. There's no reason to be nervous. You're a geek, Luke's a geek, it's safe to assume I like geeks. You're not going to get beat up, and I'm not going to steal your milk money." He nodded, finally looking up at her. He had gotten better with her when she'd been bringing him lunch, but she hadn't been by in nearly two months.

"You and Luke got into a fight, eh?"

"Yeah, we did," she said. "Sorry I haven't brought you anything to eat. I promise I'll make it up to you. My mom's still got cookies left from Christmas."

He grinned, the topic of food seeming to get them into more comfortable territory.

Their waitress took their orders—orange juice and a piece of pie for Crash and a tall glass of milk for Mariska.

"I need a favour, Crash."

He looked at her and waited.

She pulled the disc from her pocket and handed it to him. "There's a map on this disc. It's a list of crimes, dates, types, addresses that kind of stuff."

"Okay . . ." He took the disc from her and adjusted his glasses to look at it.

"I need you to see if there's a pattern, however obscure. I want to know where they're going to hit next," Mariska said. "I can't see anything but I'm not a mega math genius."

"It's really simple actually, you just have to assign contingents to each factor and then . . ."

Mariska could practically feel her eyes glaze over.

"Um, I can take a look for you, no problem."

Mariska smiled. "Thanks, Crash, and if you wouldn't mind, could we just keep this—?"

"Between us?"

She nodded.

"Of course, it'll cost you some of your mom's pierogi though."

Mariska laughed and sat back to accommodate the waitress as she brought their orders. "You drive a hard bargain, my friend. Tell you what. You put a rush on it and you'll never have to worry about your pierogi supply again."

"Awesome." He dug zealously into his plate of pie. "So, why do you need this anyway?"

She could tell the truth, but there was no sense revealing herself if she didn't have to.

"I'm opening a bar. I need to know if I should be expecting trouble in my area." Mariska took a long pull from her glass of milk. She was determined never to break another rib, even if it meant buying stocks in a dairy farm.

"Okay. Well, I should be able to do that."

"Perfect."

MARISKA SCANNED THE alley from a rooftop, shivering a little in the cold. She had layers of thermal underwear on under her leather gear but nothing would come close to a nice mug of hot chocolate and cuddling with Alana. She yawned. She'd been up early with her cousin Andryko to discuss quotes and design ideas. There had been a rushed supper with Alana, who barely finished her food before heading up the elevator of her office tower to get back to work.

Mariska had decided to make the most of her night. She would wait to see if one of Crash's predictions panned out and then head south, further into the Parkdale area to patrol. She was surprised to see her new geek in residence walking down the main street towards her building.

"Now why the hell would you be doing down here?" she muttered.

He was quite obviously out of place, clad in his *Star Trek* jacket and walking down Queen Street West in the middle of the night. She could see shadows moving in the alleys. Crash was too big a target for the local lowlifes to resist.

"Damn it."

She caught sight of a van in an alley across the street and narrowed her eyes. She couldn't be certain but it looked like it was the van that the two wise guys had been driving when they met with Beregic in the fall. She kept one eye on Crash and one on the van. She stared as the van doors opened to reveal a large cache of weapons.

"Son of a bitch." So they'd moved on from dealing kids to dealing weapons out of a van. "Classy, real classy."

She hated STELLA.

Mariska heard movement in the alley directly below her and looked down to see two men walking with purpose towards an unsuspecting Crash, who had stopped to tie his shoe. In Parkdale. At one-thirty in the morning. Was he freaking crazy?

Mariska looked between the two alleys. One was her ticket to finding STELLA, the organization that had murdered Lisa. The other . . .

" . . . is the reason you got into this gig. Innocents first, criminals second. Always." She hooked her grapple to a fire escape, jumped, and held tight as the line descended to the ground. Her boots touched cement just as the men left the alley to pounce on Crash.

She shot forward and grabbed Thug One by the back of his shoulders, then swung him around into a lamppost. She turned to Thug Two and landed her shin in his soft belly. It drew a pained "oof" from him as he doubled over, holding his stomach. She swung a right hook into his jaw and he hit the cement, spitting out teeth as he fell.

Mariska grunted from a solid punch to the back of her thigh that nearly sent her muscles into spasm.

"That was dirty." She shot out an elbow and broke Thug One's nose.

He didn't even flinch as he stared at her, wild-eyed, blood running down his face.

"Junkies," she said. "Wonderful."

There were few people as dangerous as cracked-out junkies looking for another fix.

"I know this probably isn't even registering but you're going to feel that in the morning. Quit while you're behind."

He charged, and she dropped to one knee, bracing herself. She put her arm between his legs and used his momentum to flip him over her shoulder. He landed with a hollow thud, then rolled on the ground, gasping for air.

"Uh, is he okay?" Crash asked, his eyes wide.

Mariska gave Thug One an absent glance and waved it off. "He's fine, just got the wind knocked out of him." She looked at the alley where the van had been. Long gone. Perfect. She turned to Crash then gripped of the front of his jacket. "You want to tell me what the hell you're doing here?"

"I wanted to see."

"See what?" she asked, giving him a shake.

"You, in action. I mean, it is you, right? Mariska?"

She slapped a hand over his mouth and pulled him into the alley, away from prying eyes.

"I knew it," he said, as she took her gloved hand from his mouth. Crash looked ready to clap his hands in geeky elation. "You're a superhero."

Mariska rolled her eyes skyward. "Superheroes fly around in red capes and sling webs. I'm a vigilante. How did you know it was me?"

"Well, some of the locations you gave me . . ."

"Wait." She held up a hand. "I'm not having this conversation here. Give me your hand."

"Huh?"

Mariska pursed her lips, wrapped an arm around his slight frame, pulled him into her as she grabbed her grapple gun and activated the retractor. Their feet left the ground, and he let out a startled "whoa" as they headed for the roof and landed.

"Now, speak," she said, holstering the grapple gun.

He looked down at the alley with a broad grin. "That was so cool."

"Focus, Crash," she said, snapping her fingers.

"Oh. It was easy. Some of the crime spots you gave me weren't in the police records but I cross-referenced them with neighborhood newspapers that reported the incidents. They spanned enough area for it to be unlikely you had heard about each of them. It stood to reason that either you were there at the scene or you were in contact with someone who was." He gave a self-deprecating shrug. "I actually thought it might be Lucas, you know. Like maybe his limp was a Kevin Spacey kind of thing."

"A what?"

"You know, Kevin Spacey in *The Usual Suspects* where he's hiding as a guy with a bum leg but he's actually the mastermind." He looked at her expectantly. "I had to know which one of you it was."

Mariska sighed.

"So you thought you'd drop by a potential crime scene and try to ID me? You ever hear a story about a cat and a bad case of curiosity?"

"I thought, maybe I could help."

Mariska pinched the bridge of her nose. Not another one. As if Brooke wasn't enough.

"Look . . . I appreciate the work you've done but you're not a field guy, okay? Being out here like this . . . What if you'd been wrong? What if I'd been late? Do you know what those guys could have done to you?"

He hadn't seemed to consider the possibility.

"This isn't a movie or a comic book, Crash. You don't get a second chance. Do you know what you did?" She stared into his eyes. He shook his head.

"I was going to take down a weapons dealer. There are going to be more guns on the streets tonight because I had to help you. Because you were curious."

He hung his head, his small shoulders dropping forward, hands tucked into his pockets. She was being harsh, but he had to understand this wasn't a game.

"I know it was an honest mistake, I get that. But I can't afford to make mistakes, Crash. It gets people killed."

Crash looked at the empty alley across the street. "I . . . I didn't think." He seemed to be on the verge of crying. "I'll fix it." He turned to Mariska. "What can I do?"

"Just . . ." She let out a breath, bringing herself under control. "Just tell me what's next on the list."

He pulled a piece of paper from his pants pocket and unfolded it. "They've been targeting some of the bars on College Street.

They're rumored to be mafia run. The pattern indicates they'll hit another one tonight."

"Where?"

"Near College and Ossington."

Practically in her backyard. Great. She idly wondered how long it would be before someone from her local mob would arrive to shake her bar down.

"Did you drive?"

He nodded.

"All right, let's move. I'm too tired to haul my ass over there."

His eyes sparkled.

"Don't get any ideas. You're dropping me off and going home, got me?"

He nodded.

"Good."

Ten minutes later, she was on top of yet another roof, trying to figure out which of the bars was going to be a target. It was just past two, and the occupants of the clubs were beginning to fill the streets as they headed home. She hoped STELLA would at least have the decency to hit the bar after they closed to not risk lives unnecessarily.

"Why am I not surprised?" she muttered, as a black car careened around a corner at top speed.

She couldn't tell if it was STELLA or just a random drunken moron but they were going to kill someone regardless. She had no way to stop them. She touched her grapple gun. What was the tensile hold of the wire? Lucas had told her once. Was it enough to hold a speeding car?

"No time."

She pulled the gun out, took aim at the rear tire of the car, and fired. She jammed the gun between two rungs on the fire escape, hoping it would hold fast. If it or the fire escape buckled, there was going to be a problem.

The line pulled taut as the grapple wrapped itself around the wheel of the car. For one moment, Mariska worried the line would snap. The car came to a jarring halt and Mariska grinned as the driver's head bounced off the steering wheel.

"Karma's a bitch." Mariska unclipped her utility belt, looped it over the grapple line, and jumped off the fire escape. She slid down the line towards the car, her feet touching the asphalt just as a crowd began to gather. She clipped her belt back on, walked to the car, and knocked on the window. The dazed driver looked at her, his bleary eyes nearly closed.

Someone in the car locked the doors as Mariska reached for the handle. She sighed and put her fist through the glass, the hardened plastic knuckles of her gloves taking the worst of the impact. She reached in, manually popped the lock, and opened the door. The smell of booze accosted her, and she fought the urge to lash out at the driver. Instead she grabbed hold of his shirt and pulled him from the car. He came out easily enough and she threw him against the car.

"Do you have any idea what you could have done?" she yelled, shoving him harder against the car, hoping to get him to at least open his eyes.

He was concussed, no doubt about it. Blood was pouring from his temple. Mariska couldn't have cared less. His selfish actions could have cost any number of people their lives.

She threw him to the ground, pulled out a set of riot cuffs, and attached him to the undercarriage of his car.

"Call an ambulance," she said to the person nearest her.

The young woman complied as Mariska looked at her taut grapple line still attached to the wheelbase of the vehicle. She needed to put some slack in it before she detached the line.

Now what?

She sighed and reached in to turn off the car engine, slightly surprised to see the woman in the passenger seat shy away from her.

"You going to drink and drive again?" she asked, looking at the occupants of the sports car.

They shook their heads.

Mariska put the car into neutral. "Good, 'cause if I catch you at it after this, I won't be as polite as I was to him." She nodded at the driver who was moaning on the ground.

Car secured, she went to the front end and pushed against it, hoping to roll it back enough to put some slack in her grapple line. If she released it while it was taut, the snap would put everyone on the street in danger. She grunted as her boots slid along the asphalt. She couldn't get the traction she needed to push.

She was surprised as two of the club goers, twenty-something-year-old men in expensive shoes and silk shirts, came up beside her and pushed. Someone else took the open door and between the four of them it was easy to roll the car backwards enough to put the needed slack in her line.

"Thanks," she said, shaking hands with each of them.

"You help us, we help you. Right?"

Mariska nodded in appreciation. "Right."

She unhooked her grapple, leaving the wire. It was too tightly wrapped around the axle to bother with and after the test she'd put it through, she wasn't certain she would trust it again. She moved towards the fire escape to collect the gun. An explosion rocked a bar half a block down. A number of people hit the ground as glass and fire shot out from the windows and into the street.

She ran for the building. Two men were calmly letting themselves into their car. She recognized the bigger of the two as the man from the arena, the only one who had escaped. She ran for them with her hands up to shield her face from the heat as she passed the burning bar. Her gloved hand skimmed the back of the tailgate as they accelerated into the street. Missed.

To follow or not to follow? She could run them down. Between the stop-and-go streetcars, the taxis and drunken pedestrians they wouldn't be able to make much of a quick getaway. She could catch them.

Mariska turned to see a street full of people, some moving, others not. She took a deep breath, calming herself. STELLA could have tonight. She would catch them later. No matter her vendetta against the criminals, her responsibility was to the people who had been hurt. She jogged up to a couple, a man on the ground, a woman leaning heavily on his leg as it pumped blood around a large shard of glass.

"Here." Mariska pulled a field bandage from her utility belt. "Wrap it around his leg and keep the pressure on. Help is on the way." She patted the woman's shoulder and moved to the next downed person, checking for a pulse. Nothing.

Mariska tamped down on the emotions that threatened to choke her. She couldn't help. She had to prioritize and move on. Sirens screamed in the distance, moving steadily closer. Guardian couldn't be here when the police showed up but Mariska could.

She ducked into an alley, pulled her hood back, and unbuckled the vest. She tossed the leather and Kevlar vests behind a dumpster and pulled her mask down to her neck to act as a scarf. She stripped out of the leather pants. Clad in black Lycra pants and a long sleeved undershirt, she tucked her sunglasses in with her vests. She stared balefully at a pair of old sneakers hanging off the edge of the dumpster and looked down at her footwear.

Knee high blue leather boots after a Guardian sighting? She may as well walk up to the first patrolman she saw and ask him to slap a set of cuffs on her.

"Thick socks, hot shower," she repeated to herself as she unbuckled her boots and tugged the sneakers on to her feet. They smelled. "Thick socks, hot shower." She looked more like a jogger than a vigilante now. Odd for two-thirty in the morning but it would have to do. She walked back into the street and headed for a woman who was trying to get to her feet.

"Whoa there, easy," Mariska said, wrapping a strong arm around the small woman's waist. Given the odd angle of the lower part of her leg, she would bet her ATV that the leg was broken. The woman was obviously in shock. "C'mon. Let's get you out of the street."

Mariska worked the street, along with other good Samaritans and the ever-increasing presence of police and paramedics. She paused in her work and wiped her forehead. She felt an odd cross between sweating and a bone-deep chill that was nearly sending her into full-body shivers.

"You should get inside. You're not dressed for this."

Mariska turned in surprise to come face to face with Detective Perkins.

"I . . . uh, I'm all right," Mariska said, crossing her arms to keep her body heat as contained as possible. She felt naked in front of Perkins, and it certainly had nothing to do with a lack of clothing. She wasn't wearing a mask, a vest, or a motorcycle helmet—nothing to protect her identity from the woman in front of her. It was disconcerting, even if Perkins didn't show any signs of recognizing her as Guardian.

"Uh huh. You're about ready to fall over. It's been over an hour, come on Miss . . ."

"Cooper," Mariska said.

Perkins pulled off her coat and draped it over Mariska's shoulders. The tall woman dwarfed Mariska and her coat hung loosely on her body.

"Miss Cooper." Perkins smiled encouragingly.

It was an odd look for the detective. In all the time Mariska had known her, she'd never seen her crack a smile.

"That coffee shop is open and it's taking in strays. Let's get you something to drink."

Mariska nodded, she couldn't very well fight Perkins when she was wearing her coat. And she did need a break. Her hands were nearly numb.

"Little late to be jogging, isn't it?" Perkins asked, as she motioned for Mariska to sit down.

"We all have our quirks," Mariska said, echoing the words Alana had once told her. "I function better at night."

Perkins looked into Mariska's eyes as if searching for some sign of dishonesty. Mariska felt somewhat akin to a bug under a microscope at the steady gaze.

"Lucky for those people out there," Perkins said, evidently done with her search as she sat back in her chair.

Mariska looked out at the streets where the last of the victims were being loaded into ambulances. She hadn't made it in time. People had died. STELLA had won again. She was sick with the knowledge of it.

"Yeah," she said with a sigh, "lucky."

CHAPTER 12
The Months In Between

"LUCKY," ALANA CALLED out as she looked down at the newspaper reporting the explosion on College Street. She hadn't meant for quite that much of a to-do. Apparently she'd given too much of a free hand to her explosives guy.

"Yeah, boss?" Lucky asked as he walked into her office and crossed muscled arms over a barrel chest.

"What the hell is this?" She held up the paper for him to see. She'd asked him to quietly dispose of a few bars in the area. The word "quiet" apparently hadn't been properly emphasized.

"You wanted them out of the way."

Alana rubbed her forehead, tempted to let out an aggrieved sigh. "Granted, but did you happen to think that maybe, blowing up a bar with people still inside might generate a little more heat than we wanted to bring down on ourselves?" She had wanted to eliminate a little bit of Mariska's competition, not start a mob war.

"Sorry, boss. Franco made the bomb. He just told me to put it inside."

Alana sighed. "Franco." The name was almost a curse. She had used him for the subway train debacle back in August. The bomb on the train was meant to be a decoy, a fake, something to keep the cops busy and out of the way while her men worked the real target, the banks downtown. When she had heard there had been an actual explosion, she had been less than pleased. She hadn't been particularly concerned with the victims. It was just bad business.

If a subway station of people had been killed, there would have been no end to the hunt for STELLA. She would have been forced to abandon Toronto and her operations there. Franco had been lucky. Guardian had managed to keep the damage minimal, so Alana had left him alive with the strict warning that he was walking on very thin ice. Now, with this . . . It was a complete disregard for her leadership. He was obviously a sociopath.

The same thing had been said about Alana. More than once. At least, she had the sense to temper her behaviour. Franco was a loose cannon with the ability to do serious damage.

"Boss?"

"Kill him. Make it quick and clean. Make sure the cops find him. I want it to look like he was acting independently." He nodded and headed for the door. "And Lucky?" She stared at him with hard eyes. "Don't fuck this up, or you'll be joining him."

He nodded curtly and left the office, the door swinging closed behind him.

"All right. On to other business." Orson, another STELLA goon, cautiously moved up to her desk. "I want the guns moved out of this region." She pointed at an area on the map of Toronto. Mariska's bar sat in the middle of the section she had outlined.

"Why, boss? Sales are up. We're making a killing."

"Exactly," Alana said. She didn't need that many gang bangers with guns running around in Mariska's backyard. "Eventually some moron is going to end up killing a kid and people are going to start asking where the guns came from. I don't need that kind of heat, especially not after this bullshit." She pointed at the paper. "We're doing well. I want to get a good run out of this city so let's not get stupid."

"Okay, boss."

Alana looked at the map. It wasn't good enough. She needed to do more than move the guns. She needed to secure the area so Mariska wouldn't run up against any of the local mafia. And she needed to do it with as little collateral damage as possible.

"While we're at it, pull out of that area completely," Alana said.

"But, boss, if we do that, Carrero's men'll move in."

"Exactly. Contact our men in the police department. I want to force a crackdown on the area. The police will pick up Carrero's men, and we can have the neighborhood without having to go to the mats." She would not tolerate a gang war anywhere near Mariska.

"Where should we off-load the guns? I know a guy in Scarborough."

Alana's thought about Mariska's family, earnest people who didn't deserve the evils she inflicted on a city. Mariska had already lost too much. Alana wouldn't risk it. Better the collateral damage she didn't know.

"Send them to North York. Let them deal with it." It wasn't much. She couldn't save an entire section of the city from itself, but at least she could control the criminals roaming Mariska's streets. It would give her business a head start and Alana could have some peace of mind. She knew Mariska would succeed. All she needed was a chance.

"NOT A CHANCE," Mariska muttered as she looked at the map of potential crime sites.

Even if had it been the original Guardian team, they would have been hard pressed to stake out all the sites. Brooke was right. She needed someone in the field with her. She just couldn't stand the idea of training someone else, only to lose them to the streets.

Speaking of her resident statue, Mariska looked up at the screen. Brooke was at her usual post, leaning against the sewer wall, staring balefully at the door as though she could open it with the powers of her mind.

Mariska had left a knapsack full of food hanging on a hook for her. She didn't want to encourage the kid, but Brooke was looking progressively thinner. She hadn't been all that big to start with.

She heard the descent of the elevator. That was curious. Lucas wasn't off work for another three hours, and she hadn't heard anything on the scanner that would prompt him to leave early.

He stepped off the elevator. "You used Crash to determine crime patterns?"

Oh. That. So he had been playing Big Brother when she had saved Crash.

"Why hello, Lucas, how have you been? Anything new and exciting in the past three months?" She turned nonchalantly in her chair to look at him. She was unashamed to admit she enjoyed seeing him in such a rage. He was so red, even the tips of his ears were pink.

"Where the hell do you get off telling Crash who we are? You completely compromised—"

"Unclench a little, big bro," she said. "I didn't mention your name. Besides, that guy practically worships the ground you walk on. Even if he knew, he'd never tell."

"Not the point, Mariska, and you know it. This wasn't your decision to make."

She gazed up at him. "I assume this is the point where I'm supposed to pretend I care. Aren't you tired of lying to people?"

Lucas seemed to deflate slightly before his eyes flicked to the computer screen. "What the hell is she doing here?" He pointed at the screen where Brooke could be seen leaning against the sewer door.

Mariska took a cursory glance at the screen and shrugged. "Selling Girl Scout cookies. I'd let her in but she says she doesn't have the chocolate mint ones."

"We lie to keep people like her safe," he said, tapping the screen.

Mariska snorted. "No. You lie to keep you safe. You sit here in your subterranean Ivory Tower, giving out orders and saving the world from a distance. Lisa died and now you're too afraid to let anyone in." She knew what it was like. How hard it was to leave that place of sorrow.

"You're not being fair. This isn't just your secret to tell, Mariska."

She shrugged.

"I guess since you're feeling so free, you'll tell Alana. Assuming you haven't already."

"I haven't, actually," Mariska said.

It wasn't that she didn't trust her, but Guardian's first encounter with Alana had been less than encouraging. She needed to gently guide Alana towards the idea.

"I do intend to tell her eventually. I'm tired of living a double life. I lie to my family, my coworkers. I lied to Lisa for the longest time. I need someone I can lean on, and that obviously isn't you anymore." Mariska pushed herself out of her chair. She pulled the disc with the map from the computer and logged herself out.

"So she buys you a bar and all of sudden I'm the pariah?"

"She didn't buy the bar, she cosigned my loan for it. You're not a pariah, Lucas, you're an ass with a martyr complex." Time to leave. The warehouse was obviously too small for the both of them.

"You know what, Mariska, fuck you."

Mariska sighed. So this was what a decade and a half of

friendship had come to. What an asinine attempt at reconciliation. Typical Lucas.

"You know what, Lucas? Fuck you back."

UNSETTLED BY YET another fight with Lucas, Mariska headed for Alana's, hoping she could cheer her up. She made her way into the large condo suite at near dusk, the dying rays of the evening sun washing through the floor-to-ceiling windows.

Mariska loved the view of the city from Alana's windows. The light from the setting sun painted the distant buildings in a golden hue. She always thought it odd to see the city with its near angelic halo—a stark contrast to the darkness she so regularly encountered in the streets below. From this height, it could be so easy to forget why Guardian existed.

In this light, even the sleek furniture that decorated Alana's living room seemed to take on a softer tone. It was comforting, considering Alana's place wasn't a particularly cozy apartment.

No plants. No pets. The few personal pictures lining the shelves were those that had been taken since she and Alana had gotten together. Nothing much that Alana could get attached to. It seemed the opposite to Mariska's apartment, which was an odd mishmash of hand-me-down furniture, pictures everywhere, and books shoved into every cranny she could find.

Mariska dropped her backpack by the door and was surprised to hear sounds of a heated telephone call coming from Alana's bedroom. She checked her watch. Nearly four thirty on a Saturday. Odd. Alana rarely worked weekends. Judging by Alana's voice, the conversation wasn't going well.

Mariska moved closer to the door of Alana's bedroom, her natural curiosity warring with the fact that it was none of her damn business who Alana was yelling at.

"Listen to me, you little granola cruncher. I'm trying to save you the trouble of collapsing your pissant lobby group by miring it in legal fees so deep, they'll need a bulldozer to get you out."

There was silence as Alana presumably listened to the person on the other end.

"I don't care what drunken excuse for a scientist you pulled out of your ass to file that report." A momentary pause. "If you think it carries that much weight, I may have to come down there and beat you with it." The person on the other end was so agitated now that Mariska could hear their voice, though she couldn't make out the words.

"Listen to me." Mariska was taken aback by the ice in Alana's voice. "If you don't let this drop and grant me access to those wetlands, I'll have every lobby control group crawling so far up your ass you'll be able to list them as your proctologist."

She hadn't heard Alana speak that way since the night they had met. She was reminded that in most circles, Alana could be labelled as something akin to a pit viper. It was hard to remember she was a ruthless executive at the office. It never seemed to bleed into their relationship. She was amazed at how people could compartmentalize aspects of their life so well.

"You do not want to go to court with me, Hurst. I guarantee you that. Give me what I want, or I'll crucify you and take it anyway." A pause. "Just do as I say or I'll fucking bury you." There was the tight snap of a phone being closed and then the soft footfalls of Alana walking across her bedroom. Mariska stepped away from the door, not wanting to give Alana the impression that she'd been eavesdropping.

"Mariska?" Alana seemed surprised to see her.

Mariska could understand why. It had only been a week since Alana had presented her with a key, and she had yet to show up unannounced.

"Hey." Mariska kissed Alana hello. "Rough night?"

"You heard that?"

Mariska remained silent.

"I need those wetlands to close an account. My career is riding on this, so yes, rough night." Alana ran her hands through her hair, green eyes more flustered than Mariska recalled ever seeing. Her normally unflappable lover seemed quite put out. No wonder she'd been so snappish with the person on the phone.

"Anything I can do?" Mariska asked, wrapping her arms around Alana's waist.

Alana stayed tight a moment, then relaxed and rested her head on Mariska's shoulder.

"No, thank you though." Alana lifted her head. "It's Saturday night, I don't even want to think about those goddamn rigs until Monday."

"I know a good way to relieve some stress," Mariska said, a leer firmly in place.

Alana smiled. "How about a nice hot soak in the Jacuzzi with a bottle of wine and we watch the sunset? I think we both deserve a little R & R."

Needing no further encouragement than soft lips against hers, Mariska followed Alana to the bedroom.

THREE DAYS LATER, Mariska sat in the warehouse, feet on the desk as she scrolled through the various crime scene reports from the night before. There hadn't been much action on the STELLA front lately, just the usual run-of-the-mill street fights and muggings. It was a nice change of pace and it allowed her to spend more time with Alana. Always a plus.

The phone beside her rang and Mariska looked at it curiously. That was weird. She didn't realize it could receive calls. She thought it was solely an outgoing line. She put on her throat mic and picked up the receiver.

"Hello?"

"Big Brother?"

"Negative. This is Guardian. How can I help you, Detective Perkins?"

"I've got someone on my six. I need a license plate check."

"I can't do that, Perkins. I'm afraid Big Brother is the computer geek of this dynamic duo."

"I thought this was his number?"

"I'm guessing he forwarded his number to our operations center. He must have forgotten to change it back," Mariska said. "How long have you been followed?"

"I answered a tip at Jane and Finch twenty minutes ago. They were on me as soon as I pulled out of the Driftwood apartments."

"All right, give me the plate. I'll see what I can do," Mariska said.

Perkins listed off a hodgepodge of numbers and letters.

"Hold them off, I'm going to see if I can get a hold of Big Brother." She absolutely, positively, did not want to call him, but if it was Perkins's safety at stake, she was willing to swallow at least a bit of her pride.

She patched her personal cell into the headset and dialed

Lucas's line at work. She let the phone ring until the machine picked up, then slammed the phone down in frustration. It was lunch. Even if she found him, he wouldn't be near a computer. She sighed and dialed Crash's office number.

Crash picked up the phone. "Virtuos Technology, Mark speaking."

"Crash, I need you to do something for me. Can you hack the DMV database?"

"Mariska?"

"Yes, can you run plates for me or not? Faster is better."

"They're pulling up closer," Perkins said in Mariska's other ear.

"I'm working on it, Detective. Keep moving." Mariska switched to her other conversation. "Crash?"

"I'm almost in. What am I looking for?"

Mariska was impressed. That was fast. She listed off the plate number. "Car is registered to the metro police, looks like it's one of their motor pool cars."

"Stay on the line, I may need you again," she told Crash. "Perkins, the car is one of yours. Do you know why you would have a tail?"

"It starts with a 'B' and ends in 'eregic.' I'm going to guess those are his friends, probably worried he ratted them out before he ended up in the lake."

"Call it in," Mariska said. There was little she could do from here.

"I tried that before I called you," Perkins said, her tone indicating she thought that would have been obvious. "My radio is fragged and dispatch at the desk isn't picking up."

Oh. That wasn't good, that spoke of conspiracy deeper than whoever was in the patrol car.

"All right, I'm on my way." Mariska pulled on the wireless headset as she walked to her gear and tugged her leather vest onto her shoulders. "Just keep moving, I'll find—" There was a loud crash and the sound of metal meeting metal. She could have sworn she heard a rather colourful curse involving someone's mother and a horse. "Perkins? Can you hear me? I'm on my way. Nina?" The line went dead in her ear.

She allowed a moment of panic of losing another ally of their team to wash over her before containing it and moving into what she did best. Performing under pressure.

"Crash?"

"Still here."

"They lowjack every police vehicle with a GPS transponder. I need you to locate the car with the license plate I just gave you," Mariska said as she sprinted up the stairwell.

She slid in through the open window of Lucas's old Mustang and turned over the powerful engine. The garage door barely opened enough and she sped out of the warehouse, kicking up snow and gravel as she went.

She headed west on Lakeshore and turned up Jane Street, the rear end of the car inches from connecting with an oncoming truck as she slid around the corner. She ignored the blasting horns and shouted obscenities and accelerated between two cars, intent on finding Perkins before she ended up as road kill.

"They're turning west on Sheppard," Crash said.

"I see them." Mariska pulled sharply on the wheel, slid through the icy intersection, and narrowly avoided being t-boned by a delivery truck. She accelerated, her rear end fishtailing, the car taking a stuttering step forward before it found traction and picked up speed. She pulled up behind the cars. Perkins's back end had been severely damaged, the bumper leaving sparks as it dragged along behind the rest of the car.

"Mariska?"

"Don't use my name over a nonsecure line. And don't harass me while I'm driving." She accelerated and drove her vehicle into the back end of the enemy cop car, trying to give Perkins some breathing room. They needed to get off the populated streets before someone got killed.

Perkins evidently had the same idea. Using the extra bit of room, she swerved into an alley and off the street. Mariska and the other car followed, skidding along the snow and pavement as they tried to make the tight corner. She was surprised to see Perkins's car stopped just ahead and she quickly slammed on her brakes. The enemy car did the same.

They all piled into the back of Perkins car and shoved it forward before they came to a jarring halt.

Mariska pushed open the door of the Mustang and tackled the

officer on the driver's side as he tried to get from the car. She bounced his head off the frame of the car. She climbed over the roof and delivered a swift kick to his partner's head, putting him down for the count. Satisfied they wouldn't be going anywhere soon, she went to Perkins, who had pushed open her car door and was dazedly trying to get her seat belt unbuckled.

"Easy, Perkins. I've got you." Mariska undid the belt and pushed Perkins back against the seat to check for injury. "You've got a nasty bump on your head. I think you're concussed."

Perkins didn't fight as Mariska felt along her body for broken bones. Nothing wrong so far as she could tell.

"The last thing I need is to bring Acco a half-dead cop," Mariska muttered as she checked Perkins's eyes for dilation. "I think you're okay. Mind telling me what the hell you were doing? A rear end at that speed? You could have died."

"Just trying to keep people from getting killed," Perkins said, brushing dark hair back from her face.

Mariska gently squeezed her chin. "Yeah, well, you just be careful you don't get yourself killed, Nina. I'd hate to have to train another cop."

Perkins let out a quiet laugh.

"I'm going to go check on our friends. You stay here."

Perkins gave a small nod.

Mariska headed to the driver of the other car. She grabbed him by the ankle and dragged him under the open door, deeper into the alley.

He was coming to, albeit slowly.

"We're going to have a talk, you and I," she said, pulling out a shurikan and flashing it at him. "It's going to involve a certain level of pain. How well you behave will be a direct indicator of whether or not you'll be capable of walking out of this alley."

He looked at the shurikan with wide and frightened eyes.

"Do we understand each other?"

"You won't hurt me. I'm a cop," he said, his voice betraying that he wasn't certain of his own logic. "You'll have the whole force come down on you."

"Cops already hate me, and I'm pretty good at staying low. Besides, once it hits the streets that you're a dirty cop, I think people will feel a little less sympathetic to your cause."

"What do you want?"

"I want to know who set you against Perkins."

"STELLA."

She shook him fiercely. He wasn't about to get away that easily. "I know that. I want a name, a person, an address. Something."

"I don't have a name. We just get a phone call when they want something done," he said, reaching into his pocket and pulling out a red cell phone.

Mariska dropped him to the ground and put a heavy boot on his chest to keep him down.

She tucked the cellphone into her vest and took out a set of riot cuffs. She dragged him back and chained him to his car and did the same for his partner who was still out cold.

"Um, not sure if this matters, but the tracking program shows a bunch of cars headed for your location," Crash said.

Mariska started at hearing his voice. She'd forgotten he was still on the line.

"Thanks. I'll call you later." She disconnected and hurried to Perkins to make sure she was still conscious.

"Didja get anything from them?" Perkins asked, her voice tired.

"Aside from a nasty case of whiplash? Just this." She handed Perkins the cell phone. "I'm betting it rings soon and whoever is on the other end of the line is the one who set you up."

"You keep it," Perkins said, handing the phone back. "There isn't a cop in this city who can go up against STELLA single-handedly. You might have a chance. I'm trusting you to get this done."

Mariska nodded, giving Perkins's arm a squeeze of reassurance.

"Thanks for coming for me."

"Thanks for trusting us enough to call for help when you needed it." Mariska went to her car. "I'll be in touch." She climbed in and peeled out of the alley, punching in Crash's number as she drove.

"It's me," she said before he greeted her. "Is Lucas there yet?" She needed him to hack the phone company so they could trace the call. This was their hottest lead on STELLA so far. They couldn't let it go. Even if she wanted to beat him over the head with a stick, this was too big of an opportunity to ignore.

"No, he hasn't been here all day," Crash said. "He's taking a sick day."

"A sick day?" Mariska asked incredulously. He hadn't taken a sick day in all the time he'd worked at Virtuos Tech.

"Yeah, he's been taking a lot of those lately. He . . ." Crash sighed. "He hasn't really been the same since you guys—"

"Fought." Aww, hell. Just . . . hell. "All right." She would deal with that later. "I need you to be outside waiting for me in five minutes."

"But it's only twelve thirty. I can't leave now," he said. "The boss'll kill me."

"You want to help, Crash? This is the life. We have to make sacrifices, yes or no?" She could almost hear the gears working in his head.

"Yes. I'll be there."

CRASH WAS WAITING for her when she arrived, looking guilty, as though he were skipping school and was worried his parents would find out.

"Get in," she said, barely stopping the car long enough to allow him to open the door and get in.

"I have to stay late on Friday now," he said, his tone the closest thing to an audible pout that Mariska had ever heard. "I'm going to miss my Battlestar Galactica RPG with the guys now."

"I'll make you supper." Mariska headed for the warehouse, the bright sunshine of the day belying the dark feelings that were settling in on her. STELLA had gone after a cop, not just any cop, her cop. Perkins had been put in the line of fire because of the work she'd been doing to help Guardian. She had to put the organization down before they took another shot at her allies.

She pulled into the warehouse. She turned off the engine and pulled the mask from her face, openly revealing herself to Crash. Knowing and seeing weren't the same. It appeared he felt the same way as he looked at her as though for the first time.

"Come on, we don't have much time," she said, closing the dented car door. The front end had been heavily damaged in the collision. It would take weeks to make the car fit for the road. Crash followed her down the steps to the operations center, eyes becoming saucers as he took in the array of computer equipment.

It looked like her geek-in-training was on the verge of having a religious experience as he took in the computer hardware Lucas was running. "I need you to trace a phone call. Can you do that?"

"With all this?" he asked, his arms sweeping the room. "I could hack NASA with this gear."

"Good." Mariska logged him into the computer. "Get to work. The call should be coming in any minute, and I won't lose this guy." She handed him the red cell phone and let him do his thing.

She massaged at her neck to rub out the stiffness from the crash. She hadn't taken any real damage. She just had an overall sore body. She took a quick peek down the front of her shirt and sent up a silent thank you that her seat belt hadn't left a bruise across her shoulder. No way of explaining that to Alana.

"Call's coming in," Crash said. "I'm ready with the trace."

"How long does he have to be on for?" she asked.

"It's a cell signal. I can triangulate based on the towers he's using and have a general area as soon as he picks up. I can narrow it down more the longer you talk. I'll need thirty seconds to get an address."

Mariska secured her throat mic and picked up the phone. "Cop Killers Anonymous, how may I direct your call?"

No answer.

"Oh come on, that was funny. You can laugh a little. I am. I just got home from kicking the collective asses of your little buddies. I bet you're wondering where they are. I'll let you in on a secret, one of them is probably sleeping off his concussion in the back of an ambulance. I'd bet the other is down at the police station spilling his guts as we speak. Well, as I speak anyway." She paused, waiting for the person on the other end to break the silence.

"Still nothing? How about this? You and your bosses are going down. No one touches my people and gets away with it. When I'm done with you, there won't be enough left of STELLA to sell a dime bag to a junkie." She heard a click and the line went dead. "I think I hurt his feelings. Tell me you got something."

"Apartment buildings at the edge of Parkdale," he said, swiveling his chair to look at her with a boyish grin.

"Good boy. Give me the address. I'm about ready to kung fu some ass."

Twenty minutes later, she pulled up her ATV under the address and climbed the access ladder to get to the surface. She hated using the sewers in winter—the damn covers had a habit of freezing solid. She shouldered it once, twice. The metal, shrieking in protest, gave way grudgingly on the third time.

Mariska looked up, way up, at the towering apartment complex. She wondered how she was going to find which apartment STELLA's man was in. Calling the number as she walked by the doors, hoping to hear a ring, didn't seem like the best method. The phone number itself had been a dead end. Literally. It was registered to a guy in Etobicoke whose current address was six feet under.

Mariska tapped her thigh. She'd been hoping a plan would come to her as she made her way over. No such luck. She heard the sounds of a scuffle. It wasn't tracking down her guy but it would keep her busy while she figured out what to do. She headed deeper into the alley and jerked back as something hit the dumpster in front of her.

"That sounded like it hurt." Someone getting rolled in a back alley in Toronto. Who knew.

Mariska walked up to the scuffle, eyes narrowing as she recognized one of the three combatants. She shook her head as Brooke tried to divide her attention between her two opponents only succeeding in making herself more vulnerable.

"I'd watch the one on the left," Mariska said as she leaned against the dumpster. "He looks like a hair puller."

Brooke turned to her. Mariska pointed at the two men, silently telling her to keep her focus on the task at hand. The men, seeing Mariska, froze.

"Don't let me scare you gentlemen. I'm just here to catch the show. Continue."

Whether they believed her or not, they pounced on Brooke.

Brooke dodged the blows better than Mariska had anticipated, which, though interesting, really didn't mean squat. As her Sensei told her as a child, fighting was like hockey. It didn't matter how good of a goalie you were, the more shots people took at you, the greater the likelihood one would sneak through. With Brooke's smaller size and the power the men were putting behind their punches, one hit, one goal, and it would be game over.

Mariska sighed and snapped out her baton. She walked calmly

behind one of the men and gave a quick swipe to the back of his knees. He went down. Brooke turned and landed a solid punch in his jaw.

Mariska raised an eyebrow when the man didn't go down. She looked at Brooke expectantly. Brooke stared at the man as if surprised he was still conscious.

"Not everyone in this city has a glass jaw," Mariska said. "Behind you."

Brooke turned and ducked to the side as a vicious punch headed for her nose. Mariska tugged on the back of Brooke's coat to pull her out of the way and cracked the guy on the fist with her baton.

Mariska backed about ten feet away from the men, pulling Brooke with her. "Look, this is ridiculous. Why don't you guys go home and we call this a night?" She had better things to do.

The men exchanged a glance and then barrelled towards Mariska and Brooke.

"Any other bright ideas?" Mariska asked.

Brooke shrugged and charged the men.

"Points for guts, penalty for stupidity. Don't lead a tackle with your," Mariska winced as Brooke took a hit to her temple, "head."

Brooke dropped to the ground, stunned.

Mariska blocked the man's kick to Brooke's head with her shin and shot out her baton into the other man's groin. He went down, body tucked into a tight ball as he rocked back and forth.

Mariska swiveled and brought her elbow up to meet his face with a satisfying crunch. As he backed away, she grabbed Brooke by the front of her jacket and pulled her to her feet. She flung her towards the man, determined to teach her a lesson.

"His nose is already broken, the hard part's over," Mariska said.

Brooke put up her arms too low to protect her head and the man whacked her across the cheek.

Mariska sighed. Lots of guts, not a lick of natural talent.

Brooke finally found an opening and landed a kick in his kidney. The man caught her foot, swung her around, and tossed her into the brick wall.

"Okay, lesson's over."

The goon stood over Brooke and pulled back his fist. Mariska hooked her elbow around his and drove her boot into the back of his leg. As he went down, she pushed him head first into the brick wall, knocking him out.

Brooke gave her a gaze of gratitude, with a good dose of wounded pride.

"I could have handled him," she said, the perfect picture of teenage petulance.

"He outweighs you by a hundred pounds. You telegraph your kicks a mile away and you punch like a girl. He would have taken your head off," Mariska said, pulling the man's wallet out of his pocket. She checked his address. Not far from where they were, a local scumbag then.

"Then teach me. Show me how."

Mariska shook her head. Brooke had nearly had her ass handed to her in a measly two-to-one fight and she still wanted to live the life. She was either very brave or very dumb. "We've been through this before, *ad nauseam*. It's not going to happen. Let it go." She turned away from Brooke and headed for the front of the alley. She needed to find STELLA's man.

"I'm not going to let it go. I'm going to do this whether you help me or not. If you don't help me, I'm probably going to get myself killed out here."

"Yup, guess so," Mariska said, with a shrug. She refused to be baited by that trick again. Lisa had used a very similar argument, threatening to go off on her own if Lucas and Mariska didn't take her in. She wasn't going to make the same mistake twice.

She was not.

"Haven't you ever wanted to be more? Wanted to show people that you could be more than what they thought?"

Despite herself, Mariska's mind strayed to Alana. Hadn't Mariska pushed so hard to get her own bar so she could make herself better? Make herself feel more worthy of her wealthy, successful lover? She didn't want Alana to ever be ashamed of her or what she did.

"I'm not teaching you to be a vigilante," she said, her tone adamant. "But if you insist on getting into fights, I will show you how to defend yourself."

"Yes," Brooke said, pumping her fist into the air.

"On two conditions."

"Name them."

"One, you will do as you're told, no matter what. I've been in this a long time and I know what I'm doing."

"And two?"

"Two, we'll discuss tomorrow." Mariska pulled out her wallet and handed Brooke three crisp hundred dollar bills. She had meant it to be for a dresser for her new apartment above the bar but the money would be better served to go to the girls. "Get yourself and Alexis some new clothes and backpacks. Both of you meet me at Bloor and Landsdowne at eight a.m."

Brooke looked at the money as though debating whether or not to take it. "I can't pay this back."

"I know. You don't have to. Just be there tomorrow morning."

Brooke nodded, then turned to go back into the alley to head off to wherever she called home.

"Brooke?"

Brooke turned.

"Please try to stay out of trouble until then."

Brooke gave her a small nod and trotted off into the alley. Mariska headed back towards the building to try to find STELLA's thug.

She let out a frustrated huff as her phone rang. She just wanted to kick someone's ass. Was that really so much to ask? She looked at her caller ID and tugged off her throat mic before she pressed connect.

"Hey, babe. What's up?"

"Where are you?" Alana asked.

Mariska looked around the dingy alley. "Running errands." She hated to lie.

"Okay, you need to get to the bar. There's a problem with one of the designs. Sounds like Andryko is about to get into a fist fight with your flooring guy."

Mariska massaged at her temples, trying to ward off the headache she felt coming on. Figured. One of the few subcontractors she wasn't related to and her cousin had to go all Neanderthal. Men.

"How did you . . . ?"

"Your cousin called your aunt, your aunt called your mother, your mother called me. If someone in your family sneezes, I'm guessing you all catch cold."

Mariska pinched the bridge of her nose. She didn't want to

even hazard a guess as to how her mother had managed to track down Alana's work number.

"Why didn't someone just call me?" Mariska asked.

"They did, but your phone's been busy." Of course it had been. Between Perkins and Crash, she was going to have to give her cell phone company a kidney in penance for going over her minutes.

"Shit, sorry. I've been trying to get deliveries organized and—"

"It's all right. You're opening a business. It's bound to get hectic and it's not always going to go smoothly. Do you want me to go down there and—"

"No!" Mariska said, albeit a little too forcefully. "You go down there, and I'll be short a flooring guy and I don't have a backup for one of those."

Alana laughed lightly. "What if I promised to be nice?"

"I'd say your version of nice and mine are a little bit different. I'll go down and ask them to stop spraying my bar down with testosterone. How's work?"

"Shit, but moving along. I was hoping I could steal you away for a late supper."

"That sounds great. Pick me up at eight thirty?"

"I'll see you then."

Mariska punched in the number to Crash's cell phone.

"Uh, hi, Guardian. Did you find what you were looking for?"

"Negative. I got to the apartment towers and screamed for STELLA's boy to come out and play but obviously he's a pansy. Any way to narrow it down to a specific apartment?"

"No. At this point, the signals are all on top of each other. Maybe I can do something though." Crash worked his magic. "There, I think that should do it."

"Do what?"

"Whenever he makes a call, he should come up on your screen. You can track wherever he goes. Maybe you can catch him when he's not somewhere so . . ."

Mariska looked around at the towering apartment buildings. "Needle in a haystackish?"

"Yeah."

"That'll do. I'm going to ask you for one more favour, then I think we're good for the day. Do you mind?"

"No, of course not."

"All right, patch me through to a guy named Merrick. His number should be in the database."

"Yeah, got it."

"Lock up when you leave and I promise you, supper on Friday will be awe inspiring. I owe you big, little brother."

"I'm older than you," he said.

"Yeah, but you're smaller than I am. When you start wearing big boy pants, we'll talk about changing your name." She heard a chuckle followed shortly by the connecting pips of the phone.

"What?" was Merrick's greeting.

"I need papers and ID for two girls. Make them both seventeen. While you're at it, I'll need transcripts from a high school. Somewhere out west."

"When do you need them by?"

"Tomorrow morning. Seven a.m."

"Christ. Not giving me a whole lot of time."

"You've done more with less," Mariska said. He'd been the one to make and remake her various identities through the years. Fake ID, false social insurance numbers, whatever she'd needed to stay one step ahead of the people who would try to find her. She had met him in high school. He'd been small time back then, handing out IDs to kids who wanted to get drunk. She supposed all of their talents had matured over the years.

"I do like a challenge. Usual drop?"

"Yeah. I'll leave a tip for you if you can get me transfer papers to that high school near Dufferin and Bloor."

"Piece of cake."

Mariska hung up and gave one last baleful glance at the apartment towers, knowing her enemy was somewhere within. "Catch you later."

SEVENTEEN HOURS, ONE fistfight, a rushed dinner, and a languid night in bed later, Mariska met up with Brooke and Alexis at the corner. The girls were easy to spot, huddled together, fresh backpacks on top of what looked to be second-hand clothes.

"So you buy new book bags but you don't buy new clothes. Some might consider that odd," Mariska said.

The girls turned to her, eyes widening to take in Mariska's unmasked, five-foot-nine frame. She had traded her dark blue boots for soft, brown leather knee high boots and her turquoise vest for a full-length black duster that hugged her athletic body.

"What? You didn't actually think I was going to walk you to school with my utility belt on, did you?"

"School?" Alexis said, looking between Mariska and Brooke as if to gauge her seriousness.

"Yup." Mariska pulled two envelopes from her satchel and handed them to each girl. "We'll deal with getting you your health cards and driver's licenses later. This is enough to get you started. You're transfers in from Calgary. I suggest you do some research on what it's like out there so you don't sound like complete asses."

The girls opened their envelopes and shook the contents into their hands.

"What are these?" Brooke asked, holding up a set of keys and a bank card.

"There's money in the account. The information for accessing it is all in there. It isn't much." Mariska had used a decent piece of her savings just to get the IDs and to keep her lease on her old apartment. "It'll get you through a month or so but you're going to need to get a job. Both of you. The keys are to my old place. Most of my stuff is still there. I was going to sell it but you're welcome to it. I'll pick you up after school and take you there." She began to walk. "Now come on, you don't want to be late on your first day." They walked along Bloor in silence.

"This is stupid," Brooke said as they stopped outside the school.

Mariska looked up at the high school and back at the girls.

"You want to live in my world, you play by my rules. Remember?" She waited for Brooke's grudging nod. "You want me to teach you to fight? The first rule of a fight is not to get into one. So, until I'm satisfied that you won't use what I teach you to go out looking for trouble, you're going to cool your heels here."

Brooke looked ready to object.

"Second rule is to use your brain. You won't be much use to me if there's nothing up there." Mariska tapped Alexis's head. "You really want to know how I do what I do?" She dropped a textbook into Brooke's hands. "First, you're going to learn to think. Don't come back to the warehouse until you've got something to teach me." She turned on her heel and walked towards her bar, hoping to keep her cousin from coming to blows with her new floor installer.

"Why are you doing this?" Brooke asked.

Mariska stopped walking. Why was she doing this? Inviting these young women into what was already a complicated life? Part of her hoped that pushing the girls towards an education would dampen Brooke's desire to roam the streets as a crime fighter. That maybe, if Brooke found she could be something great without having to put on a mask, she'd give up on pursuing a life of danger.

It hadn't stopped Lisa.

Maybe Brooke would be different. Maybe this opportunity to think about her choices would show her all the potential her life had. Then she could choose the life she really wanted, not just follow in Mariska's footsteps because she thought that was all she had open to her.

"I'm doing this because you were right. You deserve a chance to be better and this is the first step. I want you to see that the life I lead . . . It's not all there is for you. I want you to have a chance to be the normal kid that I was."

"This isn't going to stop me. I know what I want," Brooke said.

"Good, then you won't mind working for it. This is your chance to be more than what everyone thought you could be, Brooke. Don't waste it standing around in sewers and picking fights you can't win in back alleys." Mariska looked into deep brown eyes, trying to convey that all she wanted for both Brooke and Alexis was for them to be sure of the choices they made.

Brooke finally broke eye contact and nodded. "Fine. But I'm not doing any of that pep squad crap and I refuse to eat any cafeteria mystery meat."

"Then after today, I suggest you brown bag it. No matter what they try to tell you, every meat they put on the menu is a mystery."

CHAPTER 13
Biting Back

MARISKA TUGGED HER coat closer around her body, trying to ward off the biting wind as she headed for the subway. Her phone rang deep within her pockets. She cursed as she searched for it, hands nearly numb as her fingers finally wrapped around it.

"Hey, sweetheart, I'm almost at your place."

"Great, dinner's on its way. Just wanted to make sure it'd be warm when you got here," Alana said.

"I'll be there in ten."

"Okay, see you then." Mariska closed the phone and was about to tuck it into her pocket when it rang again.

"Did you need me to pick something up?" Mariska asked, as she debated whether to try beating the crosswalk light.

"Mariska."

She stopped in the middle of the sidewalk, ignoring the irritated glares from her fellow pedestrians. "Lucas?" They hadn't spoken, really spoken, in nearly four months. They were both stubborn to the point of stupidity but she was determined not to be the first to break the silence.

"Yeah. I . . . I wanted to tell you . . ." Mariska held the phone closer. " . . . I mean, I wanted to say . . ." He sighed. "I think I've found STELLA's headquarters, or at least a base of operations."

Mariska perked up. "How?"

"Actually, one of the leads you had. Got a hit off the phone tap on STELLA's guy. His signal has stalled at the same place a few times. I'm guessing it's a hangout for our favourite thugs."

Ah, so he had noticed she'd been keeping an eye on STELLA's man. "Where is it?"

"Oddly enough, it's a warehouse on Lakeshore. They're not more than a few clicks from us."

"Shit." That close the entire time. Figured.

"I know we're not exactly buddies at the moment . . ." Lucas's voice trailed off.

She debated staying silent, making him find the words to ask her to come in and help.

"I'll come in tomorrow and take a look," she said. "This is the job, Lucas, whatever is going on between us . . . we have a responsibility. I . . . I won't let this get in the way if you won't."

"I'll . . ." He sighed. "I'll do my best. I'll see you tomorrow."

"Goodnight." She closed the phone. Well, it certainly hadn't been Lucas on his hands and knees begging for forgiveness, but it was something. Maybe they could build from there.

Mariska arrived at Alana's apartment building and let herself in. Alana was in the kitchen, working on a glass of wine.

"Hey, you." She kissed Alana before pulling her coat off and draping it on the back of the chair.

Alana smiled, handed her a glass of wine, and then motioned her to sit at the table.

"Smells great," Mariska said, filling her plate with roast beef and potatoes.

"Courtesy of the steak place across the street," Alana said, cheerfully. "So, how's it coming? Any more throw downs between Andry and his subcontractors?"

Mariska laughed, rubbing her temple at the mention of her cousin's fistfight the week before. "No, not so far. They're starting to put the baseboards in tomorrow. Andry has the lights coming in on Monday. We're on time and on budget so far."

"Fantastic."

Mariska relaxed and drew a deep breath. It was their six-month anniversary. She was happy they had lasted as long as they had but could also sense a melancholy mood sitting at the edge of her consciousness. She and Lisa had been a few days shy of the landmark when everything had gone wrong.

"You okay?" Alana asked.

"Fine. Just thinking."

"Thinking about something that makes you sad?" Alana asked, taking Mariska's hand across the table.

"Lucas called," Mariska said, trying to throw Alana off the track.

Explaining the true circumstances of Lisa's death meant explaining about Guardian. Mariska wasn't certain she was emotionally up to that at the moment. Soon though. She and Alana were getting to the point in their relationship where it wasn't right to hide such a big part of herself.

"Did you two sort things out?"

"No, not really. We just kind of ignored the giant pink elephant in the room," Mariska said.

"Then why did he call?"

"I think it was his way of apologizing without actually apologizing. He wants to meet tomorrow night."

"You're kidding."

Mariska shook her head. "No."

"Are you going to go?"

"Yeah. Maybe it'll give us a chance to talk and get back on stable ground." She truly hoped that was the case. Four months without her best friend was hard, especially when she was on patrol. She had no one to banter with on the radio or take out cameras.

She wasn't truly alone. She knew Lucas was in the basement, watching through her glasses as she patrolled. Ever the big brother. This last week, he had even begun to make short suggestions for patrol. She had even gotten a clipped "well done" after a particularly harrowing gang fight a few nights ago.

"Just make sure you talk with your mouth and not your fists this time," Alana said, squeezing her hand.

Mariska pulled out of her thoughts and went back to concentrating on her meal.

"I don't want to see you hurt again."

"I owe it to him to go. For a while, we were all the other had," Mariska said, with a shrug. "Life's too short to carry hatred."

She thought her words were fairly ironic considering it was the desire for vengeance that was pulling her and Lucas back together. At least, it was on her part.

Mariska hadn't yet told Lucas that STELLA was responsible for the warehouse. His temper tended to run pretty hot, and he would have done something stupid.

"You're right," Alana said. "I guess I'm just not built that way."

Mariska shook her head. "You're one of the most caring people I know." She settled herself in Alana's lap. The fact that Alana was so giving had surprised her in the beginning, given how they had met. But the Alana that Guardian had encountered had never really shown herself to her.

"You bring it out in me," Alana said, wrapping her arms round Mariska's waist. "I've never had this kind of relationship with anyone."

"I'm glad. That makes me special," Mariska said, running her hands through Alana's soft, auburn hair. "But I wish you'd had someone around for you, before me."

Alana shook her head and rested it on Mariska's chest. "I'm glad it was you."

MARISKA THREW HER duffel bag onto the countertop and looked around the basement for any sign of Lucas. She shrugged and pulled out her gear. He could hold a grudge as well as she could, but even he wasn't enough of an ass to ditch her when it was this important. Especially after he had swallowed enough of his pride to call her.

She heard his familiar steps, the left one slightly heavier than the right, as he came down the stairs. She paused in unpacking her gear to look at him. He was thin, even for him. She would bet he spent all of his free time underground staring at computer screens.

"Hey."

"Hey." He gave an almost helpless shrug that she returned. "How are you?"

"I'm good. Haven't taken much damage lately. I'm ready for this," she said, keeping things superficial. The next step was his.

"I didn't mean . . ." He paused and sighed. "Good, I'm glad you're ready."

Or not. She fought the urge to sigh. If Lisa had been here, she would have locked them in the basement until they sorted themselves out. She took a deep breath. Tonight, she would get the chance to make STELLA pay for what had been taken from them. That was what was important. They had a job to do.

"So, what are we dealing with?" she asked.

Lucas limped to his bag, retrieved a large schematic, and unfurled it on the table.

Without thinking, Mariska grabbed his cane from the shelf behind her and passed it across the table, her attention already focused on the blueprint.

The cold always made him achy. Their first winter after, when she had moved into his apartment upon his return from rehab, she had spent her nights alternately freshening hot water bottles or rubbing ointment into his knees. They had been so close then.

"All right," Lucas said. "Looks like there are three main entrances—one through the front where the trucks offload, one in the back on the lakeside, and one sewer entrance. The front entrance will be heavily guarded, the sewer is partially collapsed and the water is going to be effing cold."

"Lovely. Suggestions?" Mariska asked.

Lucas's blue eyes fell on the freshly serviced Scuba gear.

Mariska nodded. "Water it is."

MARISKA PULLED HERSELF along the bottom of the lake bed, using the odd seaweed and rocks to move herself rather than expending all her energy kicking.

"Your GPS shows you're heading off course. Turn right ten degrees."

Mariska switched position and adjusted the waterproof audio transmitter that was sealed into her ear canal.

She moved her body like a serpent, minimizing how much effort she was putting out. She needed her energy to keep her body warm in the frigid waters for the nearly two-kilometre swim. Why she had chosen this over duking it out with a few dime-a-dozen thugs, she still wasn't certain.

Her patrol gear was strapped to her back and sealed to keep it dry. She also had some surveillance equipment to set in place. They would get hard evidence and form an educated battle plan before making their strike. As much as she wanted to go in and tear the place down, she remembered how it had ended the last time. They would take their time, wait for their enemy to make a mistake. One way or another, STELLA would find itself at the end of Guardian's justice.

"Almost there, one more klick."

A sharp retort was on her numbing lips—Lucas should be glad she was underwater and couldn't talk. In what world was a kilometre in frigid water with thirty pounds of gear strapped to her body considered almost there? She still had to try and haul herself onto the docks afterward. And swim back.

Almost there, my well sculpted ass. She grimaced as she neared the dock where the weeds became thick and unmanageable. They wrapped around her arm or leg or the fins of her boots with each stroke she took.

"You've still got a hundred meters. Why have you stopped?"

Mariska tugged harshly with her arm, trying to either break or uproot the weed that had wrapped solidly around her wrist. She couldn't afford to move too violently or she risked wrapping her entire body in a tangle of weeds. She'd tire herself out trying to get free and not have anything left for the swim home or to get beyond the last of the weeds to the docks.

She let her body go still then pulled out the knife that was strapped to her leg and hacked at the weed. It gave way and floated out to the darkness. She wished she could turn on the flashlight on her shoulder. But she couldn't risk it this close in. It certainly didn't help that the weeds were blocking the moonlight from reaching the bottom of the shallowing water.

"Keep moving. You shouldn't be far from the entrance now."

She nodded, knowing he couldn't see her. They hadn't figured out a way to waterproof the video camera on her glasses. She parted the weeds in front of her and saw a clearing near the sandy bottom.

The clearing was more of a bald spot, barely big enough for her if she stood upright, but she paused there anyway. She had to get into the docks themselves before she could use the snake camera to find an exit point. From there, she had to start mounting the surveillance equipment. One camera at every door and audio transmitters in any phone she could find. She had no more than twenty minutes. Then off to grab her gear, get back in the water, and be back with Lucas in the operations center before sunrise.

"You stopped moving. You all right?"

A small panic button was sewn into her neoprene suit in case of emergency. She hadn't pressed it and she wasn't about to. Lucas would realize she was good to go when she started moving again.

Mariska took a deep breath through the regulator. Facing down STELLA was different now that she knew who they were. What they had done. The idea was positively nerve wracking, if she was being honest with herself. These were the people who had ended the Guardians as they had been known and reshaped what was left of the team into something new. Something darker. It was about time she and Lucas repaid them the favour.

Mariska swam, staying low to the bottom where there seemed to be some distinction between sets of weeds. She felt something against her leg that was unplant-like, looked back, and tried to discern in the darkness what had slithered past her. Fucking creepy. Diving in the tropics she could understand. Pretty fish, clear warm water. What jackass would willingly scuba the Great Lakes?

She continued on. She could see some light above her that shone off something silver in the water. Something silver and moving. That couldn't be good.

Mariska dove a little deeper and her chest skimmed the sand. Whatever the hell it was, she intended to stay away from it. Knowing her luck and the state of Lake Ontario, it was some radioactive three-eyed goldfish with a taste for human flesh waiting for an unsuspecting diver to devour whole.

Or, she thought as something moved towards her, *it could just be a really fucking big eel.*

Mariska jerked back as the eel headed for her, nearly hitting her shoulder as it swam over her back. She turned to watch it go, hand resting on the sandy floor of the lake. She felt that feeling again— something other than weeds wrapping around her arm. She looked down as another eel came up from the sand and wound around her arm. She shook her arm and it moved harmlessly across her chest. Her upper body was entangled in the weeds again.

Her uncontrolled thrashing wasn't doing anything but kicking up more sand and wildlife, further entangling her in the weeds. But it was hard to let her mind do the talking when she was underwater, in the dark, wrapped in weeds and live things.

"Guardian? Your GPS signal stalled again. Are you all right?" Mariska grunted as the regulator tore from her mouth. The end of it tangled in the weeds as she moved her head around. Her panic threatened to overwhelm her and she forced herself to be still in the water.

She kept her mouth closed and searched with her free hand. Her fingers found the regulator. Her lungs burned from lack of oxygen as she shoved it back into her mouth and inhaled deeply. She pulled her knife out and cut away the weeds. She freed her arm and torso first, then relieved her legs of the seaweed.

She could definitely do without the wildlife on the way back.

Mariska kept to the lake bed as she swam, being more careful about where she put her hands. The eels were more afraid of her than she of them, but that didn't mean she wanted them swimming all over her again. The lights overhead were getting brighter now and the lake bottom seemed much closer to the surface. She was right near the docks.

Game time.

She came up to the dock entrance. STELLA was smart. They had gated the water entrance to the warehouse. It looked like it operated on some sort of mechanical pulley that swung the gates inward and allowed the boats to enter. Judging from the lack of animal and plant life around it, she had a feeling it was probably hooked up to some juice as well.

Great.

She swam along the length of the gate looking for a way—any way—to get herself beyond the gates. Damned if she had swum all this way, just to turn back. It would have been nice to search with a light but she had to rely on what was coming from above and her own sense of touch to find some means to get herself through.

The gates didn't rest on the sand floor, but they didn't allow enough room for her to swim under them either. There certainly wasn't enough room to swim over the top. Not without turning into a human glow stick. *Fuck. Fuck. Fuck.*

She touched the rock on the other side and pushed along it, trying to find anything that might give. A rock actually moved under the pressure and fell with a muted thud to the sandy floor. She reached inside the small hole and pulled on the rocks, careful not to touch the gate.

Something had a bit of give, and she braced herself against the rock wall and tugged as hard as she could. A large rock fell to the floor, kicking up sand around her, clouding the water. When it cleared, she could make out the outline of a hole large enough to get through. Not with her scuba gear though.

Figured.

She unstrapped her weight belt and grabbed onto the rock to keep herself from floating upward as she shimmied out of her tanks. She wrapped the weights around them, then hooked the shoulder straps around a rock outcropping to keep them settled near the bottom.

She put her backpack full of camera equipment on, prepped the snake camera, and searched for the small personal respirator—a handheld tank with mouthpiece attached that held a few minutes of oxygen. She would have to find a way into the warehouse quickly or end up having to choose between drowning and death by thug.

Bag settled and respirator functioning, Mariska took one last deep pull from the large tank and maneuvered herself through the hole. She sucked in her stomach and ran her body along the rock as she pulled herself through.

Her legs cleared just as an eel swam beside her, its long body waving back in forth through the water. The tip of its tail skimmed the bars of the gate and Mariska jerked back as the whole body of the eel seemed to freeze before it started to convulse. She watched, wide eyed, as the eel floated upward to the muted sounds of laughter filtering through the water.

So much for the docks being deserted.

She continued to pull herself along the wooden struts that supported the docks, then headed for the warehouse. Finally, she came to the edge and fished the snake camera up through the water to have a look around. Lucas would guide her from there.

There were two guards at the edge of the docks about twenty metres away and a second set of guards near the warehouse edge where she was positioned. She took another breath from the respirator, then looked at the gauge. She was already halfway empty. She had, at best, five minutes left and these guys didn't look to be going anywhere soon.

She could swim back and try to sneak around the back end of the property, but the place was obviously well guarded. It likely wouldn't make a difference. She pulled a waterproof surveillance mic from her belt. She allowed herself to float upwards and placed the mic just above water level, her gloved hand nearly invisible among the shadows of the dock.

"Guardian? The first mic just went active. I'm getting a signal and readable audio." She wouldn't be able to answer him until she surfaced, and that was too risky, even under the shadow of the docks. She was one flashlight or water reflection away from becoming Swiss cheese. She looked at the gauge. She had one or two breaths left. Then she was screwed.

"They're not moving," Lucas said as she moved the snake

camera around to get a proper visual. "Tap your emergency signal if you need a way in."

Mariska looked at her gauge, sucked in a deep breath, the last one, and tapped her badge.

"I'm going to black out the block. They'll lose main power but they may have emergency generators," Lucas said. "I'm already in the city grid but it'll take a few seconds to put the power down."

Mariska looked at her watch, barely able to make out the digital reading. She had never gone over a minute without oxygen. She hoped Lucas didn't run into any roadblocks. Already, her lungs were on fire.

"I'm in. Just looking for the right grid area, I have to take it all down to avoid suspicion. I'll lose power as well, and the spike might kill our comms. You'll be solo for up to three minutes until the generator kicks in and I can reboot. Tap if you understand."

Forty-five seconds.

Mariska held tightly to the wooden strut, trying to keep herself from thrashing around as her lungs screamed in protest at the lack of oxygen. She tapped her badge twice, trying to convey the urgency of the situation to her partner.

"Going silent in five, four, three, two, one."

Mariska was officially alone, underwater, with no oxygen. Without the help of the lights, she wouldn't even be able to find her way back to the scuba tank, not before she drowned. She focused on the sounds of the men above her, trying to gauge where they were.

The ones at the edge of the dock were sweeping the dock with their flashlights. Luckily, if she could judge by their receding voices, the ones inside had moved further away. She had no choice but to risk surfacing. Her lungs were threatening to explode in her chest if she didn't get some oxygen. She swam upwards, hiding herself behind a strut. She sucked in as deep a breath as she could in silence.

She checked her watch. Two minutes and forty seconds until Lucas would reboot and reopen the comms channel. She searched for the bottoms of boots between the slats of the dock. Finding none, she pulled herself up and rolled behind a set of crates.

She quickly climbed the crates and squatted as low as possible at the top of the highest stack. She didn't have time to peel the neoprene suit from her body, so she was forced to shiver as she searched for good places to hide the cameras. A number of men were milling around in the darkness, their flashlights the only source of light.

So much for emergency generators.

"Or not," she muttered, as lights in the corner came on. The whir of a generator firing up could be heard over the shouts of the guards beneath her. No matter. There was still ample shadow and Lucas could likely keep the grid down for a few minutes at least. Her best bet was to find STELLA's office and bug that first. No doubt if the woman, Stella, had a place of work in her last warehouse, she would have one here as well.

Mariska looked upward. The I-beam overhead was too high, and she couldn't risk the noise a grapple would make. She sighed and looked across the room. The I-beams lowered another three metres where there was a hoist in the center of the room. She could make those if she took a run at them.

Hopefully.

She kept low as she sprinted across the tops of the crates and launched herself off the edge, fists first, towards the lower I-beam. She caught it with strong hands and allowed her momentum to launch her legs upwards and catch the crossbeam. She held on tightly with her legs as she performed a midair sit-up and pulled up her body by her abs.

Mariska moved through the beams, pausing only to place a camera in the crevice and attaching an audio mic to it. She dropped onto her stomach and wrapped her arms around the beam as a flashlight passed her position. It kept going, and she breathed a small sigh of relief. Now began the search for an office or anything with STELLA's insignia.

She found the damnable symbol on a glass door and, just for a moment, her mind transported her back to where she had lain in wait for Lisa to arrive. She felt panic tighten her chest and fought to keep her perch as her mind recoiled at the memory.

Mariska pushed the feelings out of her mind. She had time to freak out later. She couldn't afford to make any mistakes tonight, not when she knew the price of failure. She crawled along the beam, constantly scanning for any errant lights that could expose her.

She checked her watch quickly. Forty-seven seconds until Lucas was back online. He would be able to keep a better eye on the guards, then she could work faster. For now, she had to get into the office.

There.

It looked as though it had been put in as an afterthought. The roof was exposed, simple two by fours holding the T-bar for the tiles aloft. It would be easy enough to break in the top, assuming she didn't fall on her ass through the tiles.

Mariska lowered herself as far as she could from the I-beam, arms stretched taut as she tried to judge where she would land. Sending up a quick prayer to Lisa for a hand, she let go and landed on a single two by four. Her arms pinwheeled as she tried to maintain her balance, her bare feet searching for a grip. She fell backwards, turned, and braced against another two by four with her hands.

"Christ. It's never easy."

She pushed herself up, crawled to a corner, and lifted up an edge of one of the tiles. The lights were off. No emergency lights in the office itself. It appeared to be empty. She popped the tile and dropped down. A small jump and a bat of her hand knocked the tile back into place. She would have to risk a small light now. As long as she kept it low, off the floor and glass door, it wouldn't alert any of the guards who were running around trying to restore power.

Speaking of power.

"Guardian, I'm back online. You have thirty seconds before the city restores power."

She pulled a mic from her bag, unscrewed the telephone receiver, and tucked it in. She planted bugs over the entire area, having a feeling what they needed would be in the office, before anywhere else.

She could hear the men getting closer. One of them was shouting orders about checking the boss's office. She cursed, then ducked beneath the desk. She heard the door open. Heavy steps signaled the entrance of one of the henchmen. The light swept along the floor. She held her breath as it came perilously close to her feet.

"He's coming around the desk," Lucas said.

She moved her hand to the baton resting on her thigh, ready to take him down. The lights came back on, washing the room in bright light. She could see the man's boots at the edge of the desk near the chair and thought they seemed familiar. The dull brown leather reminded her of something. A previous bad guy? A movie maybe?

Gladiator. That was it. Maybe. His boots moved away before she could figure it out.

"He's leaving. You should be clear in a second."

The thug didn't turn off the light as he left. Mariska grunted quietly as she unfolded herself from the desk, then looked around to ensure he was actually gone.

"Did you recognize him?" Mariska asked quietly as she planted a bug under the desk.

"He's the beefcake who broke your ribs in August," Lucas said.

Motherfucker. *Gladiator* indeed. He also had his hands in the bar bombing the month before.

"Why didn't you say something? I'm gonna—" She began to move towards the door.

"Do what you need to do and get out of there," Lucas said. "This is reconnaissance, not the time to start evening scores. Mind on the mission."

Mariska blew out a frustrated breath before moving out fully from behind the desk. She supposed it didn't matter. Now that she knew where to find him, she could come back and sort him out soon enough. She crawled low along the ground towards the corner she had dropped in from.

Mariska flattened against the wall as she stood up and clipped the handle of a built-in wall unit with her arm. She stifled a curse as her funny bone stung.

She hated doing that.

Curious by nature and wondering what a criminal mastermind could want with a fairly ornate cabinet, she pulled on the door. An alarm blared and shouts went up around the warehouse. She stared at what was behind the heavy wooden doors.

"Oh. Shit."

"What is it, Guardian? I can hear alarms, are you all right?"

"That fucking bitch." Mariska glared at the red costume that hung in the cabinet. "Stella is the thief who shit kicked me at the museum."

"What? Are you certain?"

"Pretty fucking much." Mariska inspected the left arm of the red suit—the neat slice had been sewn with even stitches. No doubt about it, it was the mark from her shurikan.

"They're at the office door. Get down!"

Mariska dropped to the floor, covering her head as automatic gunshots ripped easily through the drywall and glass, sending sprays of wood and dust everywhere. When the barrage stopped, she jumped up the wall and pulled herself through the ceiling. There was no hope for it now. They knew she was there. Might as well make the best of it.

"Big brother, put through a call to the PD and route them here." They were taking Stella down. Tonight.

"Are you sure? Response times are pretty good on this end of the city. You may not have time to get—"

"Do it!" She threw herself to the side as the thugs sighted her on the roof of the office. She landed hard on a crate, pulled a flash bang from her belt, and tossed it over the edge.

It exploded in a chorus of screams of surprise. She jumped down next to a guard who had stumbled away from the pack, grabbed him by the shoulders, and threw him into a crate head first, knocking him out. His gun clattered to the concrete floor. The others turned on her with guns firing. She pulled herself onto another crate, out of range.

She dropped a piece of rope down on a lone searcher, looped it around his neck, and pulled him off his feet. He kicked his legs as she hauled him up, slammed his head against the wood, then dropped him back to the ground.

The others had headed for the front. That was fine. In about thirty seconds they would run headlong into a squadron of cop cars with a bunch of illegal weapons in their hands.

Amateurs.

Mariska used the crates to get as close as possible to the docks. There was no point in taking foolish chances. She dropped down quietly and took a quick look around before walking to the water's edge.

"Police have arrived and engaged with STELLA's men. You should have more than enough time to . . ."

A strong hand came out of the water, wrapped around Mariska's ankle, and pulled her off her feet.

Her head landed solidly on the wooden dock, dislodging her earpiece, stars exploding in front of her. She kicked a bare foot at the surfacing face of her attacker.

He made a splash as he fell back into the water.

Mariska stood up, searching for him. It was the gladiator, had to be.

He pulled himself out of the water at the dock's edge. She could see the feral sneer on his face as the moonlight illuminated his towering form.

"There's no one to save you this time," he said, wild eyes focusing on her as he took a step forward.

Mariska put her hand on her belt. "Yeah, the boys in black and whites are just here for the bachelor party."

She could hear a police siren from a boat in the distance. Lucas was right; they were getting better. There was a time she would still be sitting on hold with the operator.

"We both know how this is going to end," he said, cracking large knuckles.

Mariska cocked an eyebrow as they walked towards each other. "With you in cuffs or at the bottom of the lake?"

He snorted, then shook his head. "Don't think so. You've been a thorn in my boss's side for a while now. Time to pull you out."

"You know, it's too bad I'm gonna break your jaw. Otherwise, you could tell your boss just how badly I'm going to kick her ass."

They charged as one. Mariska with a shurikan upraised, her opponent with two meaty fists. She let fly with her weapon, aiming high on his massive body.

She clipped his right cheek, just under his eye. He turned his face slightly to the side as the weapon hit. She hit the deck, shot out a leg, and took him out at the knees. He Superman-ed towards the wood, hit chin first, and slid to a halt. He moaned quietly and attempted to push himself to his feet. Mariska pulled a flagpole from its holder and advanced on him.

"There's no voice in my head to save you this time, asshole." She brought the staff down hard across his shoulders. He landed on all fours, and she bent down low enough to drive her knee into his face. She would have kicked him if she'd had her boots on, but she had no intention of breaking her feet on his worthless mug.

He flipped over onto his back. She brought the staff down

hard across his stomach, then raised it to put the end into his face. The staff wasn't pointed but she knew the right places to strike. It wouldn't be hard to end it. She had no doubt if he were in her place there would be no debate. She'd be dead.

He certainly deserved it. No telling how many innocent kids he'd killed in that ring, or other people he had hurt at the behest of his boss. She brought the staff down hard. His head dropped and lolled to the side. She knelt down, checked his pulse, and nodded as she felt it going like a freight train beneath her fingers.

As much as she wanted him to suffer, they had decided long ago they couldn't be executioners. Killing a man in battle was one thing. Killing him in cold blood was a horse of a different colour. They might all be on the wrong side of the law, but that made their code all the more important. She and Lucas had to have some rules. Otherwise, they were the same as the criminals on the streets. Another dangerous gang.

Mariska pulled his wallet from his pocket. There was no ID, only some cash, which she pocketed. A women's shelter not far from her apartment had been looking for donations. His other pocket yielded a shorted-out cell phone, red. So he had been the thug on the other end of the line when the dirty cops had chased Nina down. She drove her heel into his ribcage.

"Perkins says hello."

She caught the tattoo on his left hand, STELLA's symbol. On the right, the word Lucky was tattooed across his fingers.

"Not tonight you're not," she said, handcuffing him to the rails of the docks.

The lights of the marine unit were scanning up the dock now. Mariska let a shurikan fly, knocking out the power to the electric gate. She ran for the edge and dove in. She hit the water with barely a ripple and swam for her gear and found it easily thanks to the police lights that lit up the water.

A police raid on her main storehouse. That would get Stella's attention. Mariska couldn't help the grin, nor the warmth in the pit of her stomach that fought the frigid waters as she began the long swim home.

CHAPTER 14
Chaos

"YOU'VE GOT TO be fucking kidding me!" Alana very nearly threw her coffee cup through the TV as the six a.m. news blared the story of a large arms warehouse being raided by police overnight. "Son of a bitch." That shipment was meant for one of the larger Peruvian cartels. They weren't going to be pleased.

God damn it!

Cold rage simmered in her guts as she headed for her room. She would need to deal with Lucky. The others didn't know enough to cause her any trouble. They weren't anything more than dime-a-dozen thugs. Lucky. He knew a little more about the operation.

She couldn't afford to keep him around. Alana picked up the phone and dialed the appropriate number.

"Forget the others. Lucky doesn't make it to breakfast," she said and hung up. It was unfortunate. He was a good soldier, and she liked him, but not enough to risk him rolling over on her. He didn't know enough to identify her, but he could definitely slow her local operations down.

Alana would have to start making plans to leave the city. It would be near impossible for anything to be traced back to her but she couldn't take the chance. She had thought she could get another year of out Toronto before moving down to Miami. Nothing down there had been set up properly yet. She would just have to move plans along a little faster than usual.

She walked to her nightstand and picked up her earrings, the new pair Mariska had gotten her. They weren't much. Alana could have bought ones of far better quality, and Mariska knew as much. It was the fact that Mariska had saved up to get them for her, putting in extra hours at the restaurant while also keeping everything sorted with the bar she was opening. It had been touching, as had been the silver-framed picture of the two of them sitting in High Park near the Zen ponds.

Alana sat on the bed and picked up the picture. Mariska had one arm tucked around her waist, the other wrapped loosely around her free hand. Her own hand was near Mariska's cheek. Alana had been pulling her in for a kiss when the shutter had gone off.

After seeing her face in the picture, Alana had physical proof that she was in love. She had never experienced it before. It was such an odd feeling in the beginning, putting her in a constant state of unease. Now, it was a warm blanket. The thought of it was as much a comfort to her as the physical presence of the woman who evoked the feelings.

Shit.

Now what?

She couldn't try to pull Mariska out of Toronto, not after just having gotten a business started. Nor could she simply take off. Not yet, not when there was such little risk of being caught and so much worth staying for. She could still get her Toronto operations back up and running. The main storehouse had been taken but she had little weapons caches all over the place.

She could dip into it to keep from pissing off the Peruvians and then figure out what to do from there. If it got too hot, she would leave the city, but she would tell Mariska and let her make her own decision about staying or leaving with her. For now, she would remain within the city. If she had to leave the best thing she'd ever found, she wasn't about to do it without a fight.

Alana knew her main problem. The damned Guardian. The police and politicians were paid well to keep their noses out of her business. The only one dumb enough to attack her openly, then bring the cops down on her, was that little upstart. She was going to have to do something about that now. She'd been willing to let it go when the woman was just beating on a couple of thugs, but this was becoming unacceptable. Now Guardian was endangering her entire operation and threatening her everyday life.

If she was going to stay in Toronto and make a try at a life with Mariska, Guardian was going to have to die.

"HEY." ALANA KISSED Mariska on the cheek, sat down, and put the coffee on the table in front of her.

"Thanks, you're a lifesaver," Mariska said, then took a deep pull from the cup before dropping her gaze to the invoice in front of her. "These invoices are completely out to lunch. The dry waller went from charging me fifty cents to seventy five a square foot."

Alana watched as Mariska worked out the problem on paper, entranced by the movement of her lean hands. She captured Mariska's fingers with her own.

"I'm sorry. I shouldn't be working at breakfast." Mariska pushed the papers to edge of the table and turned her attention to Alana.

"You look tired." Alana used her thumb to brush at the dark circles under Mariska's eyes. "Long night?"

"Yeah, Lucas and I hung out pretty late. Then Crash and I were working until God knows when on the computer program for the cash register. Did I mention the electrician soaked me for an extra two grand?"

Alana gave her a curious look. She really didn't want to have to kill an electrician.

"Don't worry, he already got an earful. He's only soaked me for an extra two fifty now. You okay? You seem . . . off?"

"I'm all right, just had a long night myself," Alana said. "I've got a new account at work, and it looks like it's going to be eating up a lot of my time."

"Aww, what's up? More granola-crunching hippies chaining themselves to trees and making trouble?" Mariska stuck her tongue out to show Alana she was teasing.

Alana knew full well that Mariska was more liable to be chained to a tree with the rest of the granola crunchers than anything else. Always trying to save the world.

"Yeah, something like that." Alana took a sip of her coffee. "I'm going to be putting in some pretty late nights for the next little while . . . not for too long. I'm going to push hard to finish it quickly." Alana watched for Mariska's reaction.

Mariska reached across the table and brushed an errant strand of soft hair from Alana's face. "It's your job, Lana, it's okay. It was around before I was. I knew coming in that it wasn't always going to be a nine to fiver."

Alana took Mariska's hand and kissed lean fingers. It was selfish she knew, but she wasn't leaving this. Not even if it meant bringing the city down around Guardian's ears.

"Besides, it's not like I don't have a million things to keep me occupied." Mariska motioned with her head to the chaos around them.

Sawdust coated the floor as the baseboards were stapled to the wall. Wires hung from the ceiling, boxes of lights were piled high in the corner, and she hadn't even started to wade her way through the shipment of liquor that had come a week early.

"After all this is done and you're all set up here, how about we go away some place warm, you and me?" Alana said.

"Sun, sand, and you? Just try and keep me off that plane." Mariska ran her hand along Alana's chin and gave her one last kiss before she went to meet with the lighting subcontractor who had walked in. "Thanks for the coffee, now go save the world from the crazy hippies."

Alana wouldn't save *the* world. She was going to save her world. That was all that mattered.

"WHAT DO YOU want boss?" one of the men asked, as they stood in a semicircle around her.

Alana studied the man who had spoken. "Chaos."

ALANA WATCHED IN satisfaction as the city seemed to erupt around her. It was the third night of her push to flush out Guardian. The little do-gooder had been running around the city with nary a pause, thwarting muggings, only to have to deal with a bank holdup or a carjacking or a convenience store robbery. Lockups were starting to overflow as Guardian put down one criminal after another. They only stayed in long enough for the ink to dry on their bail requests. After that, Alana had them back on the streets.

It was expensive, keeping a revolving door of thugs, but it was worth it to see Guardian stretching herself to the absolute limit. Soon, there would be no doubt in Guardian's mind as to exactly who had set all of the chaos into motion. No one, but no one, got in her way. The hero was going to learn that fact as all would-be heroes had learned before her.

Alana turned to her new head guy, Buck, and motioned with her head. He nodded back, signaling to the men in the truck, who backed the vehicle into the glass of the Porsche dealership. They were out of the truck in seconds, unlocking the safe to the keys and then driving the cars off the lot. Beside her, she could hear the screams of a convenience store clerk as he was held at gunpoint. If Guardian wanted to create chaos in her life, Alana would create chaos in hers.

MARISKA GRUNTED AS the fist caught her across the chin. She ducked, then drove her fist into the solar plexus of the man and wrapped a cuff around his wrist as he fell, then linked him to the dumpster. She swung her leg and took out his partner at the back of the knees. His shotgun clattered to the ground and let out a loud boom as it fired. Shards of brick sprayed out from the wall and she hoped none had made it through the stone. These were residential buildings.

She slammed the thug's head into the cement, knocking him out before she cuffed him to the wrist of his partner and called it in to Lucas.

"I've got another on Indian Road and Bloor," she said as she aimed her grappling gun at the roof of the building and allowed herself to be pulled up to the top. This was insane. It had been nearly two weeks of constant bombardment. She had been running from one end of the city to the other, trying to stem the tide of crime that had broken out across the city.

STELLA and its leader had made no qualms about alerting Mariska as to who was responsible. Seemed the woman had taken personal offence about the whole raid on her storehouse. Mariska smirked as she jogged across the building rooftops. She had hit a nerve that night. Finally gotten a strike in on the bitch responsible for Lisa's death. That alone was worth every bruise and hour of missed sleep.

The good news was, the wave of crime had helped Lucas establish patterns of the attack. Using Crash's super geek algorithm, he had been getting increasingly better at forecasting where the next hits would be. The predictions were sometimes a few blocks off but she was usually in the right area of the city when the shit started to hit the fan. Sooner or later, she would swoop in on a party when Stella herself was there. Then all bets were off. No more kid gloves, no more ideas of heroism. When she finally got a hold of Stella that would be the end of her and her organization.

"Alarm going off at a Polish bank three blocks away near Dufferin and Bloor," Lucas said.

Mariska acknowledged him, leapt from the building, and swung herself down to the street. She hit the ground at a run and sprinted along the road, unconcerned about the possibility of being spotted by the cops. They were all occupied with keeping the peace in North York. Violence beyond all reason had erupted in the Jane and Finch area, and the local division had called in all free units for backup.

"Witnesses report seeing a woman in red leather," Lucas said.

Mariska increased her speed, dead set on catching Stella. There'd been enough violence, enough chaos. She wasn't about to spend the rest of her life running pell-mell across the city to amuse the bitch.

It was going to end. Tonight.

Mariska reached the community bank quickly. It wasn't more than a small savings place. They wouldn't have much in the way of hard cash. Stella knew that. Mariska was equally certain Stella knew she was in range to answer the alarm. The red-leather freak was calling her out.

"Gentleman, I'm afraid the bank is closed. I'm certain they'd be willing to open an account for you during normal business hours," Mariska said to the four men who were tossing the place.

She stepped in through the broken window, heavy boots crushing the glass under her. The men pulled out and Mariska let her shurikans fly before they got a shot off. The first connected with one man's hand, sending the gun to the floor. The second hit the other man in the head, snapped it to the side, then drove him to the ground.

"You're going to die tonight, hero."

Mariska turned in time to see a red boot coming directly for her head. She took a step back, but caught the heel of a sturdy boot. She tackled the woman at the waist and pushed them through the remaining intact window with a splintering crash.

They rolled along the cement and off the curb. Mariska threw rabbit punches into Stella's side, trying to get her to release her grip. She managed to get a knee between them and pushed hard, sending Stella across the pavement. Mariska scrambled to her feet. Stella brushed shards of glass from her shoulder as she calmly got up and walked towards Mariska.

"What is it with you and glass anyway? Seen one too many action movies?" Stella asked.

Mariska reached into her vest and pulled out a shard that had managed to sneak beneath the Kevlar. She tossed it aside and faced her opponent in silence.

"What? No more offers to take me in nicely?" Stella put her wrists together as if to offer them to Mariska.

Mariska reached for a shurikan.

Stella laughed lightly. "No, I didn't think so."

"You're not just some thief stealing insured goods anymore. You're a weapons dealer. You killed innocent kids in those clubs you run," Mariska said, watching Stella's hands for any throwing knives. Once bitten and all that.

"Please," Stella said, with a scoff. "Useless little panhandlers, streets are cleaner without them. So you see, we're peers of a sort. You keep the streets safe, so do I. I just go about it in another way."

"Watch yourself. She's dangerous," Lucas said.

"I'm aware," Mariska said quietly as she and Stella circled each other in the street.

"You know what happened the last time you went up against me, and the time before that, and, oh yes, the time before that. You really don't have a good record where my organization is concerned," Stella said. Mariska straightened. "Didn't think I'd remember, did you? How I put you and your partner down. Whatever happened to him anyway? Last I saw on the cameras, he was bleeding out on my warehouse floor with Gerrero's little courier girl."

"What's she talking about?" Lucas asked.

"Nothing, shut up. I'm handling this."

Stella canted her head and raised a finger. "Oh ho, gone but not forgotten. Who's the voice in your head, little hero? Is it him? Or is it the other one, the girl? I didn't scare her away when I started playing grown-up games did I? Your team seems to be a couple of people light this time around."

"What did she mean about the warehouse?" Lucas asked.

In that moment, Mariska could have killed Stella. This wasn't how she'd wanted to tell him about Lisa and STELLA.

"It was her, Big Brother. STELLA was in charge of Tuchi.

They were the ones who wanted to spark the war," Mariska said. She swore she could see the bitch smirk beneath her mask.

"Think he holds any hard feelings?" Stella asked.

"I know I do," Mariska said, her voice low and angry.

"I just bet you do," Stella said. "Come on then. Come teach me my lesson, hero."

Needing no further goading, Mariska flung a shurikan at Stella.

Stella flashed up a pair of knives and deflected the shurikan back at her. "Gonna have to do better than that."

Mariska jumped forward and swung her leg around for a hook kick. Stella moved to the side and punched Mariska in the kidney as she landed. Mariska winced as she dropped down to take Stella out at the knees. Stella jumped over her leg, planted both feet on the side of Mariska's head, and pushed off into a back flip. Mariska hit the ground hard and rolled with the momentum to try and put some distance between her and Stella.

The bitch was good.

"Guardian? I've lost visual. Your camera is down. What's your status?" Lucas asked anxiously.

"I'm all right."

"No, you're not," Stella countered, releasing a barrage of throwing knives.

Mariska put up her arm to block and cried out as one dagger landed deeply in her forearm, the other skipping along the top of her arm then stuck in her shoulder. Stella swung her leg and drove the blade further into her shoulder and forced her to the ground.

"Guardian?" Lucas's voice faded as a fist rocketed into her jaw, threatening to send her into the black.

Mariska held up her hands to block the unending strikes, barely managing to deflect some of the energy. She howled as the knife in her shoulder was twisted and ripped from her flesh. Her mind barely registered the distant clink as it was tossed to the side.

"End of the line, hero." Mariska heard Stella say as the second knife was pulled from her arm and held to her throat. She wasn't certain whether she was grateful for it or not, but Mariska's grip of consciousness slipped completely.

"Guardian!"

ALANA HELD THE knife to Guardian's throat. Guardian had gone limp in her arms. Whether it was from blood loss or the storm of punches she'd landed on her head, she wasn't sure. Two weeks of constant fighting had taken their toll. Guardian hadn't performed half as well as she had at the museum. It was almost unfortunate.

Alana had hoped this last fight would be something to remember, something worthy of all the trouble Guardian had caused. Now she was just one more broken hero under Stella's belt.

Pathetic.

She dropped Guardian roughly to the ground, letting her land with a dull thud.

"Let's see the woman under the mask."

She used the knife to cut up the center of the leather vest, pulled her up by the Kevlar to tug the hood and mask from her head. She stared, stunned at the large, lightly tinted glasses that covered the eyes of the hero. They weren't enough to disguise her, not from someone who knew her.

"Oh, Christ. You can't be serious," Alana said with a shake of her head. She looked at her again, hoping the street lamps overhead or perhaps her own mind were playing tricks on her.

Mariska.

"Boss, what's up? The bitch dead yet?" Alana looked up at her approaching men. She couldn't deal with them yet.

"Get back! Get out of here. I'll deal with her when I'm good and ready." She kept her body between Mariska and the men. She needed a minute to think.

"You sure you're okay, boss? We can load her in the truck if ya—"

"I said, Go!"

The men blinked at her surprised and walked off with collective shrugs towards the large truck they had used to back into the bank. She waited until they drove off before looking down at Mariska.

"God damn it, Mariska."

She still had to kill the woman. Guardian couldn't be allowed to live. Not when her men knew she had her dead to rights. It would look weak to let her live or claim she'd escaped. She still had to kill her.

Didn't she?

She touched her gloved hand to the bleeding face and the faintly scarred eyebrow. She could remember so clearly the rage she had felt towards Lucas when she had thought he'd been the one who had injured Mariska.

Damn it.

She couldn't kill Mariska. It was out of the question. The woman she loved? The woman she had torn the city apart for, just so she could stay with her? She was beginning to remember why she'd spent all those years alone. Problems like this never would have cropped up in LA.

Alana couldn't just leave. Well, that was a lie. She could. But her abrupt departure would likely clue Mariska in that something was awry. She doubted Guardian would ever stop searching for Stella, especially after the taunting she had given her.

She hung her head as another realization came to mind. The lover Mariska had lost, Lisa. She hadn't been killed in a mugging gone wrong. She was the third member of the Guardian team, the kid her guys had killed in the warehouse that night. Alana had been the one to put the haunted look in Mariska's eyes.

God damn it.

Guardian would never stop looking for her or STELLA. Sooner or later Mariska would figure it out, would come for her. Alana kissed Mariska's forehead lightly. She wouldn't spend her life living in fear of Guardian's vengeance and she wouldn't break Mariska's heart by leaving without telling her why.

It would end soon, one way or another. But not like this. She wouldn't kill Mariska in the middle of the street while cowards too frightened to help the hero watched from their windows. She picked Mariska up, walked towards her car, and slipped her into the passenger seat.

She pulled the sunglasses from Mariska's face and tossed them into the road. Logic dictated she kill Mariska and have done with it, then move on. Her heart was telling her a different story and she knew that denying it at this point had the potential to make the rest of her life miserable.

If she was truly honest with herself, she respected Guardian. Respected that someone willingly went into the streets to protect the pathetic little plebes who were too weak to fend for themselves. It was a noble idea, made more so now that she knew the woman behind the cause. It no longer seemed like an attempt to assuage some hero complex. Mariska never did anything simply to get attention or bolster someone's opinion of her. She did what she did because it needed to be done and she had the ability to do it.

Alana was now certain the same was true of Guardian. She wasn't a hero for the sake of fame or applause but for the sake of the innocent people that needed help. It didn't make her any less a pain in the ass and certainly didn't change the overall shape of things, but it did make her feel a little more . . . uneasy about killing her. That was also without factoring in the fact that Guardian was also her lover.

MARISKA AWOKE TO an intense pain in her shoulder. She frowned, surprised she was alive to experience the pain. That wasn't right. Her last clear memory was of having her ass kicked all over the street. No way she actually managed to pull that one out. Lucas, maybe? He seemed to be in progressively better shape lately, if a little thin.

She opened her eyes, turned her head, and tried to figure out where she was. There were no bright fluorescent lights or hum of computers so the warehouse was out. She forced her arm to move if only to prove that she wasn't shackled in. Being tortured to death wasn't her ideal way to go.

Mariska looked down at the heavy blanket that covered her to her shoulders, a sharp contrast to the hard metal table she was resting on. Slowly, she pushed herself into a seated position, holding the blanket to her body when she realized she was bare chested. She looked down at her shoulder and touched her hand to the bandage that had been taped to it. Her forearm had been tended to as well, gauze wrapped neatly around the wound.

Where the hell was she? Had some citizen of the neighborhood swooped in and saved her? Unlikely, but all things considered, not completely far-fetched.

She slid off the table and wrapped the blanket around her shoulders. She found one of her sweatshirts lying on the table next to her Kevlar vest. She sighed. There was no doubt then that Stella knew who she was. The shirt was probably meant to be a gesture to show how easily Stella could work her way into her life. How easily she could destroy everything Mariska had built.

Fucking bitch.

Mariska tugged the shirt on and grabbed the Kevlar vest. There was no way she would be able to get it on and get the straps done up with her shoulder the way it was.

She tried the door, mildly surprised when it gave way without trouble and let her out into a small warehouse. Windows were broken and the cold night air blew through the building. She debated going back for the blanket. She put the thought from her mind as she caught the light at the far end of the warehouse. It shone from a small makeshift office, STELLA's symbol stenciled across the glass door.

"You've got to fucking be kidding me," she said as she walked towards the office. It smelled like a trap but what choice did she have? She was injured, alone, and, she checked her ear, likely untraceable by GPS. Pretty fucked as far as choices went.

"It's all about the lemonade," she muttered as she walked to the office.

She opened the door, half expecting a set of thugs to crack her over the head or at least attempt to rough her up a bit. The office was empty save for the desk and a pot of coffee in the corner. She touched her hand to the glass. Still hot.

Whoever had tended to her or was supposed to be looking after her couldn't have been gone too long. She debated only for a moment before the chill in her bones demanded she pour herself a cup. She didn't understand what exactly was going on but she doubted Stella patched her up just to poison her with a cup of coffee. She took a deep sip, the hot liquid hitting her throat and traveling to her stomach, warming all the way down. God, nothing solved the world's problems quite like a good cup of coffee.

She frowned at the familiar taste. She sniffed at it, recognizing it from somewhere. She picked up the coffee bag. It was Alana's favourite, the exact brand. That was weird.

Mariska narrowed her eyes. Something was seriously amiss. The blanket and pillow on the table showed concern. As did the careful ministrations of her wounds. Stella was a calculating, murdering criminal. The Florence Nightingale thing wasn't exactly in her repertoire.

She looked around the room and put the coffee on the desk, her mind in overdrive as she opened drawers and tossed papers.

There had to be a clue. Some reason for why she was here and not lying dead in the street. Light from overhead reflected against something at the foot of the desk. Mariska knelt down and picked up a diamond stud with steady hands. She rolled the small earring along the pads of her fingers, her jaw clenched as she shook her head.

"Can't be."

CHAPTER 15
The Lies We Tell

MARISKA STUMBLED INTO the operations center, shivering from the cold. It had started to rain, of all things, as she had walked from Dundas to Lakeshore. The warehouse wasn't all that far from the operations center—thank God. She would have taken the subway, half dressed and all, if the damn thing had still been running. Oh well. It was really the least of her worries.

"Mariska, Jesus, I've been trying to contact you for hours. I found your earpiece and glasses in front of the bank. I—"

"Thought the worst," Mariska said, as Lucas wrapped a towel around her shoulders. "So did I."

"You escaped?" Lucas asked, as he led her to a seat.

She shook her head, hoping Lucas could actually see the motion through the severe shivers her body was wracked with.

"She let me go," Mariska said.

He picked up the electric teapot, turned to her, and raised an eyebrow.

"She . . . let you go?" he asked, confused.

Mariska could understand. She was still confused about it herself.

"I don't think I get it. This is Stella. She's the worst criminal Toronto has ever seen."

"I know."

"She's killed dozens of people, possibly hundreds. She's responsible for Lisa's death." His tone indicated he was still angry she hadn't shared that piece of information but was concentrating on the big picture.

"I know," Mariska said, as she pulled the diamond earring from her pocket.

She held it out for Lucas.

He limped over and took it from her. "What's this?" He eyed it for a moment before handing it back.

"An earring that looks exactly like the pair I gave Alana. It was in the warehouse when I came to, along with a pot of coffee. It was the hazelnut stuff from Costa Rica that Alana likes. I've never seen anyone else drink it," she said, looking meaningfully into eyes that were as familiar as her own.

Lucas's eyes widened as he shook his head. "No. This is your girlfriend we're talking about. You would have known if she was running around the city as a super criminal."

"You mean the way she would know if I was running around the city as a vigilante?"

"Are you certain?"

"Of course not," Mariska said, rubbing her eyes to alleviate the stress headache she felt building. "I mean, coffee and an earring? It's not exactly a smoking gun."

It was odd, yes. Suspicious? Most probably. Outright damning? Not quite.

"I was out for almost five hours. With Stella's resources, it wouldn't be hard to figure out who I am. Finding Alana would have been just as easy. She's not exactly low key. A set up like this, Stella's counting on it throwing me off my game. Making me question myself. It all makes sense, except . . ."

"Except, why did she let you go?"

"Yeah, that very big except." Mariska held the small earring in a calloused hand, willing it to speak the truth to her. Was she actually that foolish? How could she have been so blind? "I trust her, Luke. I love her."

"Hey." He touched her arm. "This is all circumstantial, you said it yourself. Stella's psychotic, okay? She gets her jollies from fucking with people. Maybe she let you go so she can push us around some more."

"Like a cat playing with a mouse before she kills it?" Mariska asked, not enjoying the imagery.

Lucas grimaced. "Yeah, something like that."

Lucas was being diplomatic for her sake but she knew he didn't believe his own argument. Things didn't work like that in their world. There were no abstract plots or conspiracies. The simplest explanation was usually the right one. The only thing Stella should have done was kill her and she didn't. Something had held her back. That didn't make sense. Unless, Stella was someone who was familiar with the woman under Guardian's mask.

Still, the stubborn part of Mariska refused to believe Alana was capable of Stella's atrocities. She had held doggedly to the hope that Lisa might someday return. Now, she found herself clinging desperately to the idea that her lover was innocent or, at worst, an unwitting pawn in Stella's game.

"If Stella's playing with us, Alana could be in danger. My parents too." Mariska tamped down on her panic.

This was it. Her nightmares realized. Her strongest opponent had found the chink in her armour. Mariska had potentially put the people she loved most in the crosshairs of a dangerous killer. She had to protect them.

"Mariska."

"No. Wait. Just let me think for a second. My parents will be okay. There are about a million Coopers to go through before Stella will get them. Alana's apartment has enough security to withstand a siege."

"What about Acco and Perkins?"

"They'll be fine. There's no reason for Acco to be on Stella's radar and Perkins is sharp enough not to be caught off guard. Not after the hell of the last two weeks. We'll just go into lockdown until we can figure out . . ." Mariska froze. "Oh my God."

"What?"

"My apartment."

"What about it?"

"The girls."

Lucas looked at her as though she were in danger of having a mental breakdown. He probably wasn't far off the mark. "Dammit, they're at my old apartment. My name is still on the lease. It'll be registered."

"What girls? What the hell are you talking about?"

"Brooke and Alexis."

"Wait? What? Why the hell are they at your apartment?"

"Long story. Move now, chastise later." Mariska stood and strode to the wall safe. She keyed in the code, opened the door, and pulled out a metal lock box.

"Mariska."

"Don't argue with me about this." She lifted the pistol out of its place and loaded a clip.

"This isn't who we are. We don't kill in cold blood."

Mariska looked at the silver-plated Glock, taking note of its flawless body. It had never seen combat. She had only fired it on the range. She'd bought it for Lucas after the accident, when Lucas had been at his most vulnerable. She wanted to be certain he could defend himself if the warehouse were ever compromised.

The solid weight of the gun was a comfort to her. She rubbed her thumb over the rough grip of the handle, and her gaze rested on the trigger. The gun had the potential to solve so many of their problems. It was easy to shoot someone. To kill from a distance. That was why they had made a conscious decision not to use firearms.

They realized they needed a projectile weapon of some kind. They weren't always in close-range combat and they needed long-range weapons to take out guns.

Lucas had taken quickly to throwing daggers, a weapon Mariska never had much taste or skill for.

She'd been introduced to shurikans by her childhood martial arts instructor. She had gone to the dojo to take in a class and a young student had mentioned the Guardians' use of throwing knives. He had evidently seen their most recent fight on the news where Lucas had disarmed a gunman with a well-placed shot to the wrist. The conversation led Sensei Matsuto to give a brief lecture on the various throwing weapons available to a skilled warrior. He touted the shurikan as a particularly useful tool.

Mariska looked at the gun in her hands, remembering the admiration and pride in Matsuto's voice as he spoke about the Guardians' decision not to use firearms. They were drawing a clear line, they would not become like those they fought against.

The solid weight of the gun felt right. But it wasn't the right weapon. Not for her. It never had been. She had a choice not to use it. Her body was still in good enough shape to defend herself. Lucas's wasn't.

"I'm sorry, Sensei," she murmured quietly, "but our world has changed. I can't let our choices endanger the lives of innocent people. Here." She held the gun out to Lucas.

Lucas looked at the gun as if it were a snake threatening to bite him. He hadn't had the stomach for them after Lisa's death. Neither of them did. Mariska had been more forgiving about firearms before Lisa was shot. Now she gave no quarter. The moment she saw the flash of a gun, her sense of diplomacy quickly took a nosedive.

"God damn it, Luke. If Stella makes a move on those girls, this is the only chance you have. Take the gun."

He pulled it reluctantly from her hands. She hadn't seen him so nervous about handling a weapon since they were children.

"Good, let's go." Mariska pulled her utility belt from the table and draped it over her shoulder as she headed for the elevator.

"What's our game plan here?" Lucas asked, after they had made their way out of the warehouse and into his BMW.

"Quick extraction. If it gets hairy, get the girls and get out. I'll hold Stella off as long as I can."

"What if . . . ?" He looked at her helplessly. "If it's Alana?"

Mariska closed her eyes, willing that possibility from her mind. Alana wasn't Stella. Mariska needed to believe she was innocent. That way, there would be no hesitation, no second guesses. She had already made too many mistakes. She couldn't afford another.

"We have to take care of those girls, Luke. If Stella makes a move for them, it can't matter who's behind the mask. Put her down."

They spent the remainder of the drive lost in their own thoughts. Lucas was presumably going over every possible scenario. It was his ritual before battle. Mariska was content to sit in quiet, repeating "it's not Alana" as a silent mantra, willing it to be true.

They came to a stop outside Mariska's old apartment, and she pushed open the car door as she called Brooke's cell phone.

"Hello?" a sleepy voice asked.

"Alexis?"

"Yeah. Mariska?"

Mariska wondered for a split second why Alexis was answering Brooke's phone. "I'm outside. Get Brooke up and get a bag packed. I'm coming upstairs. Be ready when I get there." She clicked the phone off. "Why isn't Stella here?"

"You wanted there to be a psychopath holding two young women hostage?"

Mariska leveled a glare at Lucas. "Of course not, but it would have made some sense. If Stella let me go to play the emotional torture card, why wouldn't she hit the easiest target?"

"I don't know, Rish. I say we count our blessings on this one."

Mariska couldn't do that. Stella was crazy, not sloppy. Something was wrong.

"Stay with the car," she said, heading for the lobby door.

Ten minutes later, two cranky teenagers were dozing in the back seat as Lucas drove through early morning traffic. He took random turns, pointedly ignoring the area of the city where the warehouse was located.

"I don't see anyone," Lucas said, after they had driven aimlessly for nearly an hour. Mariska turned in her seat and surveyed the empty road behind them for anything out of place.

"Me either. So it wasn't a ploy to trace us back to the warehouse from the girls' place. What the hell is Stella playing at?"

"I wish I knew."

Mariska leaned back against the seat, closed her eyes, and thought. The entire night didn't make sense. Stella beating her down, learning the face behind the mask and not capitalizing on it? She was at her most vulnerable, her most exposed. Why was she still alive?

Nothing about Stella suggested she was one to take unnecessary risks. Mariska didn't believe Lucas's theory about Stella just wanting to play with them for a bit before the final strike. Stella was an efficient criminal. The only reason to leave Mariska alive would be to use her to trace back to Lucas. That way, Stella could finish the entire Guardian team, for good. Except, Stella hadn't made a move. She hadn't leapt out with her army of thugs to run Mariska and Lucas down. It was all wrong.

There had to be something in Stella's reasoning she was missing. Something to explain the odd behaviour. Something that didn't involve Alana and the cold lump of betrayal that sat in Mariska's throat, threatening to choke the life from her.

"What are you thinking?"

Mariska opened her eyes, taking in the bright lights of the city. Her city. Did she have the conviction to do what was required to protect the people she loved? Could she live with asking the questions if the answers weren't what she wanted to hear?

"I think . . . I need to see Alana."

Four hours later, Mariska checked her watch as she rode the elevator up to Alana's place. Alana would be out for her morning run. She let herself into the apartment and closed the door quietly behind herself. She looked around the living room, wondering if there was a major clue she had somehow missed in the past six months.

It wasn't as though there was a giant "I'm A Supervillain" sign hanging off the balcony. But surely there was something she'd missed. No one was that good at hiding themselves. Not even Mariska. There had been more than one heart-stopping moment when she had seen a shurikan peeking out from her purse or a mask draped over the back of a chair.

Mariska headed for Alana's bedroom, noting how neat it was in comparison to her own—one of the many differences between them. In the beginning, she had often wondered how they'd made it as far as they had. They didn't share the same taste in music, in movies, they rarely even agreed on where to eat. Why had it worked so well? How had she gotten so attached to a woman who was so innately different? And how had she missed the signs that all was not as it appeared to be?

Mariska shook her head. She couldn't afford to allow her mind to trail down that path. She had a job to do. She walked into Alana's closet, eyes set on the jewelry shelf in the back. She sniffed at the air, something was . . . familiar. She pulled one of her hooded sweatshirts from the hanger and breathed in deeply. She clenched her jaw as she recognized the smell. The same scent that was on the clothing at the warehouse.

"It's laundry detergent. Alana and about a million other people use the exact same brand," she told herself, willing her racing mind to calm.

Hands trembling, she picked up the jewelry box and ran her fingers along the glossy black surface. Steeling herself, she opened it.

Empty.

Well, not quite empty. The jewelry Alana kept could put a sizeable down payment on a house. But the box was devoid of the earrings she had bought for Alana. She wasn't quite sure how to measure the wave of relief that seemed to wash over her at the discovery. She didn't have much time to evaluate the emotions running through her mind. The quiet *snick* of the outer door opening alerted her that Alana was home. She closed the jewelry box and walked into the bedroom, pulling the sweatshirt over her shoulders.

"Hey you," she said as Alana walked into the bedroom.

She saw a quick flash of surprise in Alana's green eyes before she gave her a subdued smile.

"Hi." Alana kissed her lightly on the lips. "What are you doing here so early?" She went past Mariska to strip out of her jogging gear.

"I thought I could interest you in some breakfast. What do you say? The greasy spoon by my place? Undo all the hard work you just did?"

Alana looked at her, searching her eyes for . . . something. "Sure. Just let me get changed."

Mariska watched as Alana undressed, taking in pale, freckled skin. There were few scars marring her, unlike Mariska, whose body was a road map of the fights she'd won and lost. Alana turned to the side, exposing her arm to the sunlight and, for a split second, Mariska could swear she saw the faint outline of a thin scar along her bicep.

She turned away at Alana's questioning gaze.

"Something wrong?" Alana asked.

"No." Mariska walked to Alana and cupped her jaw with a gentle hand. "I just . . . I forget how beautiful you are sometimes. I see you almost every day, but sometimes I forget to really look, you know?"

"I know the feeling. We were lucky to find each other."

Mariska nodded, kissed Alana's cheek before stepping away and allowing her to finish getting dressed. Twenty minutes later, they were seated across from each other, nursing large cups of coffee. Mariska shifted under Alana's inscrutable gaze. She had been giving her odd looks since they had left the apartment.

"What's up?" Mariska finally asked, when one stare had gone well past the point of innocent curiosity.

"It's what you said from earlier. I look at you all the time but you have so many facets. I'm never really sure what I'm looking at. Is it the slightly scattered university student? The mature business owner? The playful kid who makes me laugh?"

"Well, I don't think I have the lockdown on the dual identity thing in this relationship. What about you?"

Alana looked like she was in danger of inhaling her coffee.

"I mean, you run an oil company right? Generally speaking,

that's not exactly a moral business, and I've heard you get down and dirty over the phone. But you're never that way with me."

"No." Alana seemed to consider Mariska's words. "I guess I'm not."

"So, what did you get up to last night? I called but I got your voicemail."

Alana looked over the rim of her cup with a curious expression. "The new client is proving to be more . . . complicated than I first thought. I was at the office all night."

Mariska flinched inwardly. That was a lie. Lucas had hacked the surveillance cameras at Alana's company. There had been no mistaking the sun-touched hair and confident stride of Alana as she left the building just before five p.m. the previous day. Strike one.

"I'm sorry to hear they're being difficult."

"It's to be expected," Alana said. "I don't think they really know who they're dealing with. I'm hoping things will settle down when they realize I mean business."

"You know," Mariska said thoughtfully. "Not everyone runs scared just because someone starts throwing their weight around."

Alana let out a light chuckle. "Sweetheart, I think that depends on how much weight you have to throw."

"Don't you worry that someone will take a shot at you? I mean, I'd be concerned that someone would come after me, or worse, my family."

"Rish." Alana sighed. "Your family are the nicest people in the world. I can't imagine anyone wanting to hurt them." She seemed tired of the topic. "How about you? What did you get up to last night?"

Mariska winced as a passing waitress clipped her injured shoulder.

"You okay?" Alana asked.

"Yeah, fine. I think I pulled something at the bar last night. I was just doing the liquor count, cleaning up the mess that's kind of been piling up."

"You pulled a muscle doing the liquor count?"

Mariska could admit that wasn't the best excuse in her repertoire. Given the circumstances, any excuse would have sounded hollow to her ears. She had a horrible feeling Alana knew how she had injured her shoulder at any rate.

"Yeah, I've been working pretty hard. I guess I wasn't paying attention to what was going on."

"I've been working hard too, and you don't see me pulling any muscles."

Was that a quiet jab at Mariska's poor performance last night?

Alana had warned of the extra hours she would be working just before Stella had put the hammer down on the city. A light bulb seemed to go off as Mariska remembered the odd lull in crime when Alana was in Los Angeles. Strike two.

"We don't all get to sit on top of Mount Olympus, commanding the peons from the heavens." Stella had an army of thugs at her disposal. Mariska had two teenagers, two computer geeks, an old doctor, and an overtaxed cop. "Some of us still have to get our hands dirty."

"Mariska, you don't get to where I am without getting down in the dirt first." Alana seemed to sense the shift in conversation. They weren't just trading bad cover stories anymore. They were talking openly and honestly, perhaps for the first time—even if it was in a weird code.

"Have you? I mean have you ever had to do something you really didn't want to do?"

"Like you said, I work in the oil industry. My life is full of things I don't want to do."

"But you do them."

"It's my responsibility, to my company, to the people I employ. If I don't do my job, I'm not the only one who loses."

Mariska fought the urge to raise an incredulous eyebrow. Was Alana actually extolling her criminal activity as a legitimate form of employment? She had to admit, Alana had chutzpah.

"You could do something else. Your life doesn't have to be about . . . oil."

"Maybe, once upon a time, it didn't have to be. But our lives are the choices we make. There's no denying that. I've worked too hard and too long to give up now."

That was it? As far as excuses went, that sucked. Alana had worked too hard at being the bad guy to want anything else?

Mariska had hoped for some traumatizing backstory or a need for money for some giant world domination scheme. A grandiose end goal that would somehow justify the means. Not this unapologetic excuse, that trafficking people, drugs, and guns were business as usual.

Alana hadn't even had the decency to drum up some false regret. Who the hell had she been sleeping next to for the past six months?

"I've worked hard too," Mariska said.

"I know you have, sweetheart, and I respect that." Alana put her cup down. "What if I asked you to leave all this behind? You and I could just go away? Someplace far from here."

Mariska thought about it, it would be so easy. Make a new life, forget about this one. Forget about past failings and a future that promised only more pain.

"I would say that, as much as I want to, I can't. My life is here. My . . . responsibilities are here."

Alana took Mariska's hand across the table. Calm green eyes met hers. Mariska thought she could see a hint of pleading in her steady gaze.

"It's not your job to save the world, Mariska."

"Maybe it's not," Mariska said, staring confidently back. "But if we all said that, this world would be a horrible place to be. Someone has to stay and fight."

"Even though you want to be somewhere else?"

"Even though I would rather be anywhere else," Mariska said, tracing the lines of Alana's face with her finger. Reluctantly, she let her hand drop, sat back, and pulled her hand out of Alana's. "Besides, we both know you couldn't leave either. You've got your difficult client to deal with. You're not the type of person to leave a problem unsolved."

"You're right." The admission seemed to pain Alana. "I wish I could walk away but I have a bad feeling this is a problem that would follow me." She focused an intense stare on Mariska.

"Problems do have a way of doing that. If you don't deal with them, they have a tendency to come back when you least expect it."

The waitress placed the cheque between them. They reached for it, but Alana was faster to pull the slip away.

"I'll handle it," she said, pushing twin stray locks of hair behind her ears.

Mariska studied the face of the woman she had come to love.

She was truly stunning—a clean jaw framed by soft tresses that were alternately scarlet and crimson, depending on sunlight. Said sun shone brightly behind Alana, giving her delicate ears the appearance of glowing. The diamond stud refracted in the sunshine, a beam of light catching Mariska in the eyes. She followed the gentle curve of Alana's other ear.

Strike three.

The earrings she had bought Alana were small. She couldn't afford anything larger. They'd been meant to be more a token of her love than a measure of it. They were small enough that it would be easy to miss that one had dropped off. Between kicking Mariska's ass, patching her up, and any other ensuing STELLA chaos, Alana hadn't realized she'd lost one. So, Stella was capable of making a mistake.

Mariska closed her eyes, fighting against the burning tears. She had wanted a smoking gun. This was about as good as it got. Any hope she had that everything so far had been random coincidence was now gone. Denial was no longer an option.

Anger it was.

Her rage against Stella warred with her love for Alana, threatening to send her stomach into an uproar.

She couldn't deal with this.

She couldn't do this.

"Mariska?"

"You're always taking care of me."

"As much as I can," Alana said, staring into Mariska's eyes, seeming to sense that something had fallen into place. That the conversation had slid firmly into treacherous territory. "As much as you'll let me."

Mariska bit down on the urge to bark out a frustrated laugh. This was absurd. Here she was having a polite conversation, full of doublespeak, with the woman who had masterminded Lisa's murder.

Alana wouldn't give up her life of crime, and Mariska couldn't let her walk. She also couldn't engage her now. Not in such a fragile mental state. Not when she wasn't fully committed to the fight. Alana would trounce her. She had to come to terms with what came next. She needed distance. Time. A very large drink wouldn't be out of the question either.

"So, what are your plans?" She pulled the earring of the pocket of her cargo pants. She rolled it across her fingertips, feeling the sharp edges, the smooth surfaces.

"I thought we could meet up tonight."

Mariska nodded. It would be better not to drag this out. She was questioning herself enough as it was. If she gave herself too much time to think, she was fairly certain she would find a way to talk herself out of what needed to be done.

"Sounds good." Mariska stood from the table, begging herself not to break down. She opened her hand and put the earring on the tabletop.

Alana looked down and gave a minute nod. There were no questions now. No doublespeak. No masks to hide behind. They both knew where they stood.

Alana looked up at her, regret warring with pride in forest green eyes. Mariska didn't think it was regret for her crimes, rather it was regret that her crimes had led them to this. She pressed her lips firmly to Alana's, knowing it would be the last time.

"I love you, Alana."

"I love you too, Mariska."

Mariska made her way from the table towards the door. She turned back to see Alana gazing at her steadily.

"I'll see you tonight."

"Yeah. I'll catch you later." Mariska walked from the cafe, a confidence in her gait that she didn't feel. Christ, she needed a drink.

"SO, DID YOU get anything?" Lucas asked, as Mariska walked into the warehouse apartment. "Does she know who Stella is?"

"She is Stella," Mariska said, walking past Lucas to the cupboard. She pulled out a bottle of vodka.

She had found the first open bar after her conversation with Alana and made fast friends with Jack Daniels. Having been thrown out after a small tussle with a guy who grabbed her ass, she elected to make her way to the warehouse. She had debated going to her bar, but she didn't think she could take it, sitting there, alone, in the business Alana had helped her build. She didn't even want to think about how Alana may have gotten the money that allowed her to cosign for her.

"Are you sure?"

"Uh huh." Mariska put the bottle to her lips and took a long pull from it.

"But . . . if you knew that . . . you had her in the cafe, you could have taken her in."

"First of all," Mariska said, "I like that cafe and I'm not about to start busting up a small business. Second, have you ever tried to have a throw down in heels? I'm a vigilante, not some kind of super stripper."

"Mariska," he said, frustrated. She was amazed at how fast he could go from consoling best friend to pure mind on the mission. "That's not why it happened and you know it. She could rabbit on us. If Alana is Stella, she has limitless resources. She could just disappear."

"She could, but she won't."

"How can you be sure?"

"'Cause if she does, she has to worry about me showing up on her doorstep six months from now with an ass kick-o-gram." Mariska leaned towards the wall, misjudged, stumbled, and nearly ended up flat on her ass.

Lucas looked at her crossways, eyes focused hers as she took another swig from the bottle. "You're drunk already."

She shrugged.

"Maybe a little."

"Damn it, Mariska. Why are you being so glib about this?"

"C'mon, Lucas. What's the point of being a superhero if I can't make poorly timed jokes in the face of imminent death?"

"Are you okay?"

Mariska took the bottle from her lips and leveled a stare at him. "My current lover, the woman who helped me get over my dead lover, happens to be the person responsible for said dead lover's demise. I'm just fucking ducky, Lucas."

He seemed to do a momentary double take at her venomous sarcasm. "Look, I know this is hard for you. It's a shock. But we have to do damage control. She knows who you are. Brooke and Alexis are safe but your parents . . ."

" . . . are fine," Mariska said with an absent wave of the bottle. "Alana won't hurt them."

"You can't know that."

"Sure I do. She told me as much when we had our little heart to heart. She's made it clear it's between us." She motioned with the bottle to show she meant herself and Lucas. "Now that I think about it, the whole conversation was kind of funny in an ironic, crush your soul kind of way." She let out a humorless snort and took another drink.

"How much did you have to drink before you got here?" he asked.

"I'm still standing, so obviously not enough," she said, wiping her mouth with the back of her hand.

"This isn't a joke."

"I beg to differ. I'd put money that some higher being is text messaging LOL to his buddies right now."

"Damn it. Mariska. You know you can't trust her."

"She wouldn't lie to me. Okay, maybe she would but not about this."

"Are you listening to yourself? She's a sociopath, she doesn't give a shit about you or your parents."

"Yes, she does, Lucas," Mariska said, her voice tired. "If she didn't give a shit, we wouldn't be having this conversation. You would be sitting with my parents, waiting for my body to show up in the morgue."

"She's trying to get into your head."

"She doesn't have to try, she's already in there. And she's in here." Mariska tapped her chest. "She's the woman I love, Lucas, and I have to take her down. Could you try, for just one minute, not to be an insensitive prick?"

"Look, I'm sorry. This is a shitty situation, no doubt about it. You have to remember, you have a responsibility to the people around you."

"I know." Something about the word responsibility threatened to send Mariska into violence. She hated her responsibility. She hated that she couldn't look the other way. Hated how Guardian and her god-damned morals kept getting in the way of her happiness.

"Mariska, she knows who we are. There isn't time to think. God damn it. We have to stop her."

Mariska tightened her hand around the neck of the bottle, her mind going blank for a moment of anguished rage. "I know!"

She heaved the bottle and smiled grimly as it hit the wall with a satisfying crack and shattered against the brick. Her false composure shattered with it. She felt the anger drain from her body into sorrow. She sank to her knees, head in her hands, willing herself not to cry out her grief.

Soft footfalls broke the heavy silence and a light hand rubbed her back in slow, gentle circles. She looked up through watery eyes at a worried Alexis. Sweet young Alexis, who had become an unwitting player in Alana's bid to gain control of Toronto's underworld. Alexis hadn't been given a choice. STELLA's world had been thrust upon her.

Alexis hadn't been given a choice but Mariska had. She had chosen to be the hero. In the beginning it had been optional, a mask she could take on and off at her convenience. No longer. Whatever choices had led her down this road, whatever exits she may have taken, they were all inconsequential. She was who she was now. Guardian.

Alana had made her choices too. She knew the potential consequences of the life she'd made for herself. Alana could no more turn away from STELLA than Mariska could turn away from the innocent people she vowed to protect.

"Is everything okay?"

Mariska turned at the sound of Brooke's voice. She was staring at them with an unreadable expression. Her thin body radiated tension as her gaze moved between Mariska and Lucas, trying to determine what was going on. Mariska squeezed Alexis's hand in thanks and forced herself to her feet.

These girls were her responsibility. No matter how much she hated the word itself or the concept of it, it still remained her burden to bear. She couldn't walk away from it, couldn't shirk it, couldn't pass it to someone else. However, that didn't mean she couldn't put up a solid wall of denial.

"Everything's fine," Mariska said, putting her emotional walls in place.

She needed a mental shield against the depressing reality that would come crashing down on her all too soon. She headed for the elevator, sparing only a short glance at Lucas, who seemed intent on having a staring contest with the table top.

"Where you going?" he asked, not looking up at her.

"Home. I need a shower, a nap, and a ginormous bottle of aspirin."

"What about Alana?"

Mariska rubbed at her eyes tiredly. "I'm meeting her tonight."

"What? Where? Why?"

"For the requisite good-guy-bad-guy duel to the death, I assume. That or she's going to break up with me."

"You're not taking this seriously."

"I just put back a two-six of vodka. How much more serious do I need to be?"

Lucas looked anywhere but at her. "I'll drive you," he said finally, his tone subdued.

"Brooke can drive me. At least she knows when to keep her mouth shut."

The muscles in Lucas's jaw worked as if he was deciding to lash out at her petulance or give her latitude because of the situation. He held out his car keys to Brooke. She was quick to take them and follow Mariska into the elevator. Alexis squeezed herself in beside them, and they rode the elevator down. The walk to Lucas's BMW was quiet, and Mariska slid into the passenger side, and closed her eyes against the bright afternoon sun.

"What are you going to do?" Brooke asked quietly.

"My job," Mariska said. "You want to be a hero, Brooke? Take a good look. This is what it looks like at the end of the day. There's no glory in what we do. Cops chase you. Crooks chase you. In the end you have to give up the things you want most."

"But you still do it."

"I do it because there's nothing else left for me. I've lost too much, given too much to this life to abandon it and have it all be for nothing. This is who I am now. I protect people. The only way to do that is to bring Stella down."

Brooke pulled up in front of Mariska's bar.

"But this isn't who you have to be. Our decisions shape who we become. There's a point you'll reach where you can't go back. Where you'll have to surrender yourself to the consequences of the choices you make."

Brooke was silent, no doubt contemplating Mariska's words.

Mariska sighed, pushed the car door open, and stumbled out. She leaned against the doorframe, wishing she could make Brooke understand that this life came with a price. She found she had no words of wisdom, no pearls of knowledge that would make the world clear. In the absence of philosophy, she settled instead for practicality.

"Don't go straight back to the warehouse, drive around a bit. If you see anything suspicious, call Luke and he'll talk you through it."

She made her way slowly to her apartment above the bar.

She reached her door, looking at the scarred wood, willing it to give her answers and rammed her hand into it before registering that her hand had even moved. Pain blossomed across her knuckles. She knew pain. She understood pain. She threw her fist into the door again, feeling the skin split and blood drip between her fingers.

This was familiar. This was good. She launched her fists at the door, mercilessly pounding it, almost deaf to the hollow thuds. Finally, the aged lock gave way and the door swung open. She dropped her fists and looked down past the bloody knuckles to the envelope that lay just beyond the threshold.

She knelt to pick it up, letting out a surprised "whoof" as her balance failed and she landed ass first on the hardwood floor. She dropped her keys, the metallic clang ringing out through the mostly empty apartment. The envelope was addressed to her in Alana's tight, neat scrawl.

She noted the quality of the paper, the heavy threads. She used a blunted fingernail to open it and pulled out a photo with a sticky note attached. The photo was Alana's favourite. A random snapshot from one the many amateur photographers who were running around the park. They had been so happy that day. So carefree. Mariska peeled the sticky note from the picture and read the note with as much sorrow as she assumed it had been penned with.

I'm sorry.

"Yeah." Mariska leaned back against the doorframe, letting out a soul deep sigh. "Me too." Cradling her head in blood-stained hands, she wept out her grief.

Long moments later, she took a deep breath, focusing her mind.

She had to cast it all aside. Her sorrow. Her confusion. Her hopes for a future with Alana. There could be no confusion. No hesitation. There could be only the ultimate truth.

She was the hero. Alana was the villain. This was the job.

CHAPTER 16
Go Time

SOMETIME LATER, AS the sun set along the towering buildings of the downtown core, Mariska made her way back to the warehouse. Her hands hurt, her shoulder throbbed, and her head was screaming bloody murder as she keyed in her passcode and let herself inside. She took a large swallow of her two-litre bottle of water and walked down to the computer room. Lucas was at his monitors, busily trying to access some program or other, likely trying to track down Alana's exact whereabouts.

"How are you feeling?" he asked, without turning around.

"Like a cat shat in my mouth. If this headache doesn't go away, I may just ask Alana to kill me and have done with it."

"Not funny."

"Not joking."

He sighed and swiveled his chair to face her. "I want to take Alana down." He pinned Mariska with ice blue eyes.

She fought the urge to bark out a laugh. Judging by the stony glare he leveled at her, that wasn't the best reaction.

"Lisa was my sister. I deserve a shot at the person who's responsible for her murder."

"And how do you plan on taking her down exactly? You wouldn't last one round with your knees, Luke. Just because you can walk without a cane now doesn't mean you're ready to put the mask back on."

"I can do it," Lucas said, his resolve firm. "I've seen the way she fights. I can beat her."

"You can't and you know it," she said. "Either you're being a douche bag because you're out for revenge or you're trying to save me from doing what needs to be done. Cold-blooded killer doesn't suit you and it's been a long time since I've needed someone to protect me from the choices I make."

"You're too close to this."

"And you're too close to me." She stared at him, daring him to refute her. "You're not thinking clearly. You're trying to make a stupid choice because you don't want me to get hurt. It's too late for that, Lucas. I'm hurt. I'm not going to make it worse by letting you sacrifice yourself for the mistakes I made."

"Mariska."

"No!" She sliced her hand through the air. "I've already messed up badly enough. First Lisa, now this." She gave him a pleading look. "I've got a chance to fix this mistake."

Lucas stood, walked to her, and took her hands. He didn't question the bruised knuckles or broken skin. He knew her well enough not to have to ask.

"Lisa wasn't your fault," he said firmly. "I was an asshole for saying it. More than an asshole. You're right. I was jealous that you were moving on, that I wasn't the only person you confided in anymore. I didn't mean it. And this . . . Neither of us could have seen this."

Mariska looked into his eyes, seeing that he meant it. She nodded and rested her head against his chest for a moment. "It wasn't your fault either, Luke." She needed him to know she didn't blame him either. In case . . . well, just in case. "I have a chance to set this right. I can't let it pass."

"If you asked her, maybe she'd leave town . . ."

Mariska knew even suggesting the idea pained him. She could hear it in his strained voice. Offering to let his sister's killer go free. She shook her head, then pushed off his chest. "I do that, I just put the burden of STELLA on someone else. I can't, this is my responsibility."

"Then I'll come with you."

"No, I've got to do this on my own." She couldn't risk him. Couldn't risk losing a brother.

"This woman has kicked your ass twice. Four times, if you count the arena and the warehouse. You need backup."

Mariska zipped up her leather vest, foregoing the Kevlar. She wouldn't be able to get the damn thing on, and Alana wouldn't use a gun on her anyway. "No. I need to know that if this goes wrong, you'll still be here to keep going." She loaded her utility belt to the nines, hoping in spite of herself that maybe she could bring Alana in alive.

"What do I do without you?" He followed her as she walked to the sunglasses, pulled out a fresh pair, then settled a new ear piece in her ear.

She could tell he was asking about more than the job. What would he do without his best friend, his last link to his sister and the life they had all shared? She couldn't answer that. She couldn't think of the broken man she would leave behind if this all went wrong. She wouldn't have the strength to leave him if she did.

"You train Brooke. She's made of strong stuff. She's got the heart for it," Mariska said. "Just don't let her quit school. Don't let her make this her whole life. She has to know that there's something beyond wearing the mask." She turned to him and pulled up her hood.

"I don't know if I've got it in me to do this on my own," Lucas said as Mariska walked up to him and clasped his arms. "I would never have gotten this far without you. You're my rock. These last four months, they almost killed me. I can't do this by myself."

"Yes, you can," she said, looking confidently into his eyes. "We've made it this far, Lucas. We can't quit now. This is who we are. This is what we do."

"You're the one who's talking about not coming back," Lucas said, his eyes watering.

Mariska smiled slightly, under her hood. "Like you said, she's kicked my ass twice. Hope for the best, prepare for the worst." She tugged him into a hug. He was her brother in all things, and it hurt to leave him.

Resolved, she stepped away and offered him her hand. He shook it firmly, sealing the deal. The mission wouldn't stop with her.

"If I don't come back . . . you'll tell my parents?"

He nodded.

"And I'll say hi to Lisa for you."

Lucas nodded again, and Mariska could see he was struggling to keep the tears from falling.

"This is the job, Luke. This is who we are. No matter what happens, I'm glad we did this. I'm glad I had the chance to be someone people could look up to. You gave me that, Lucas. Don't ever forget it."

He coughed, wiped his eyes, and straightened his back. "I won't."

They nodded at each other in unison.

"Time to go to work."

ALANA STOOD AT the top of her building, binoculars out, searching for any sign of Mariska. She had managed to hold herself back from calling her. Barely. She wanted to be certain Mariska was all right, that the revelations at breakfast hadn't sent her into a downward spiral. It had been hard not to give in to her instinct to try to comfort Mariska. To check on her would be to acknowledge how much she meant to her. Tonight would be hard enough as it was.

It didn't help her mood any that it had started pissing rain. They weren't the fat warm drops of a summer shower either. They were liquid daggers pelting at her constantly. She hoped Mariska dressed for the weather.

"Stop," she said. She couldn't think like that anymore. She tucked her binoculars into her vest and stepped away from the ledge. She wouldn't fight Mariska here, not where they had shared so many good moments. She needed somewhere more neutral. She wanted to give Mariska an even chance.

At least, part of her did. The other part was still frustrated that she hadn't already killed Mariska and moved on to the next problem.

No matter. What was done was done. She had left a clue to how to find her. Now, she was waiting only long enough to ensure Mariska would actually show. She would. There was simply too much unfinished business between them.

Alana looked into the distance, vision slightly obscured by the heavy rain that fell. There. Two blocks away, Guardian was jogging towards her building. This was it. She made her way to the ground below, then took off into the alley. Mariska was smart. It wouldn't take her long to figure it out.

It was almost time.

MARISKA PAUSED OUTSIDE Alana's building, waiting until the security guard, Max, stepped out into the rain for a smoke. She slid behind him, slipped quietly inside, and went quickly for the elevator. She would have preferred the stairs. A grapple would make short work of the eleven flights. Unfortunately, with her shoulder and bicep as damaged as they were, she wasn't certain she'd be able to keep a grip. Instead, she was forced to endure the mind-numbing elevator music as the car headed upwards. She fidgeted uncomfortably in her gear, distinctly aware of how out of place she was.

The elevator dinged Alana's floor, and she stepped out. Finding no one in the hallway, she continued on to Alana's door and debated whether to kick it in just for the dramatics or to use her key. She used the key. No point in disturbing the neighbors. Mrs. Trotsky's dog would bark to no freaking end.

Any dramatic entrance would have been wasted. The apartment was empty. Very empty. As in never seen an occupant kind of empty.

"Huh, neat trick. Where was that when my lease was up?" she asked as she walked through the large apartment for any hint as to where Alana would have gone.

Surely Stella hadn't just left. Too much lay unsettled between them. She narrowed her eyes at the lone book sitting on the counter in the kitchen. She picked it up. *Why I Am So Wise* by Nietzche.

"What's that?" Lucas asked, his familiar voice a comfort in her ear.

Mariska allowed her mind to travel back to when she first met Alana. "I know where she's going."

WIND WHIPPED OFF the lake, sending buckets of sleet nearly horizontal as they pounded against the brick buildings around her. Alana's fingers were damn near numb from the cold of it. It would have been nicer if it had snowed instead. Snow was so peaceful, so calming. This just had her feeling like a drenched rat.

The moon had disappeared beneath gunmetal gray clouds. Beyond the lights of the bar, there was only darkness. Occasionally, a car passed by, beams from the headlights quickly swallowed up by the dark depths of the water in front of her.

Alana closed her eyes, taking it all in. The feel of icy water droplets as they dribbled down her neck. The smell of wet concrete mixing with car exhaust. The sound of bar conversation warring with the pounding of strong waves against the shore. The sight of Mariska walking confidently towards her from down the street.

A full-length vest of turquoise leather grazed the tops of Mariska's knee-high, navy blue boots. Beneath the vest, Alana could see the utility belt, hanging low on well-rounded hips. Her gloves, extending well past the elbow, were of the same dark blue as her boots and fit snugly on lean arms. Around her neck was dark blue spandex, presumably Mariska's mask. Her trademark sunglasses sat atop a slightly crooked nose, dark hair pulled tightly back into a ponytail.

Guardian in all her glory.

Alana found it slightly ironic that she had never seen her look sexier. She stood beneath the awning of the bar, mask tucked in her hand, and waited for Mariska.

MARISKA CAUGHT SIGHT of Alana beneath the awning and took a deep sigh.

"You okay?" Lucas asked.

"Yeah. Listen, big bro. This is as far as you go."

"What? I don't understand . . ."

Mariska tugged the sunglasses from her face and turned them so she could face the camera. "I'm not going to let you watch me die, Lucas. Be good. Be happy."

She dropped the glasses and ground them beneath a sturdy boot heel. He had gone through enough. If it all went bad, she didn't want him to see it. He would punish himself enough as it was.

"Alana," Mariska called out as Alana stepped forward, the rain plastering fiery hair to her skull.

"Clever girl," Alana said. "I knew you'd find me."

"Nietzche is an interesting choice for a Friday night," Mariska said, recalling the words she had said to Alana a lifetime ago.

"We all have our quirks," Alana said with a shrug and self-deprecating smile.

"Why? Why all this?" Mariska asked, needing something, anything, a piece of a scrap of logic to justify Alana's behaviour. Absolve her somehow.

Alana merely shrugged and took a step forward. "It doesn't really matter does it? Not now. I could say I wish it wasn't this way. And it would be true. Just like it was true when I said 'I love you.' I still do. But . . . this," Alana motioned between them, "this is who we are." She raised her voice to be heard over the pounding rain. "I'll never be anything but the bad guy, and you're too much of a good guy to look the other way. It's one of the things I love about you. Your passion, your conviction."

Mariska snorted. "You love me, just not enough to stop this?" She stepped towards her.

"Oh, sweetheart," Alana said, her voice was regretful, "that's the point. This is what I am, and I don't love anything more than myself. I wish I could. I just don't have it in me."

"So this is it, then?" Mariska asked, her hand resting on a shurikan on her belt.

"Unless you want to walk away. You'll never see STELLA again." She looked Mariska in the eye to convey her honesty.

"Will you stop or will you just move your crimes to another city?" Mariska asked.

Alana's silence gave her all the answer she needed.

Mariska wished she could let her go. Believe that Stella would melt away, never to hurt anyone again.

God, how she wanted to fool herself.

But she couldn't.

They couldn't.

Alana was right, this was who they were. This moment had been coming for two years.

"Lisa, Lucas, all those innocent kids. You have to answer for what you've done, I can't let you walk," Mariska said, trying to convince herself as much as Alana as she pulled a shurikan from her belt.

"I know." Alana pulled her mask from her vest and tugged it onto her face.

Mariska pulled her hood up, concealing herself in the deep shadow of the leather.

It would be easier that way.

She knew they both could pretend the other wasn't behind the mask. It was someone else. Someone they hadn't loved. Hadn't wanted to have a future with.

Alana pulled a knife from her vest and twirled it in her hand. "Okay?"

"Okay."

They nodded at each other and charged as one. Mariska launched a shurikan and Alana threw a knife. The weapons collided and clattered on the pier as Alana and Mariska met in a tackle.

Alana grunted as Mariska rammed her shoulder into her stomach and drove her backwards. She grabbed Mariska about the waist as she headed for the ground and twisted around so she broke her fall. They landed roughly on the wooden slats of the pier, Mariska grunting loudly as Alana landed on top of her.

Mariska felt a dull pain in her midsection and Alana reared back and punched her in the ribs. Mariska curled up, dropped her hands to protect her damaged ribs. Alana threw a punch at Mariska's exposed temple just as Mariska bucked her hips and sent Alana forward threatening to send her chin skidding along the wooden slats. Alana rolled along her shoulder, then got back onto her feet.

Mariska swung a long leg out and connected with the back of Alana's knee, dropping her to the ground. She drove her fist downward. Alana rolled to the side, and Mariska's hand cracked on the solid wood. She winced as she shook her hand. She got to her feet, fists up.

Alana threw a back kick at Mariska, nearly catching her in the chest. Using her momentum, she continued through with a roundhouse.

Alana cursed as Mariska took hold of her kicking leg, swept her other leg from beneath her, and dumped her on her ass.

"About damn time," Alana said as she got back to her feet. "Stop holding back, Mariska. I'm not going to."

Mariska nodded, knowing she had to take the advice to heart. She couldn't give anything less than her best. She dove forward, pulled Alana's legs out from under her, and dropped an ax kick to her shoulder, causing her to cry out. Mariska jerked back as a dagger skimmed past her throat to land in the back of her hood.

She stepped back and Alana rolled to the side and onto her feet. Alana swung her elbow and Mariska lifted an arm to block it. She grunted at the impact on her forearm as she blocked Alana's other elbow with her other arm. Mariska slammed the top of her skull into Alana's nose.

Alana stumbled back and put her hand to her nose. Mariska remembered she had pulled the same move in the museum.

"*Touché*," Alana said, as she snapped the cartilage in her nose back into place.

"Okay, that was just wrong." Mariska shivered in discomfort. Or it could have been the cold. This goddamn rain could knock it off anytime now.

Alana feigned a punch and Mariska brought her guard up to meet it. Alana drove a kick into Mariska's stomach, forcing her back.

Mariska doubled over, sucked in a breath, and tried to block out the pain as she brought her hands down to meet the next strike. She was behind the eight ball again as Alana switched gears and landed a blow to her head that knocked her into the railing that edged the pier. Mariska blinked away the stars dancing in front of her eyes. Alana grabbed Mariska's hair and slammed her head into the railing. Mariska grunted as she fell to the pier, dazed.

Mariska was losing steam. She swung a leg out and knocked Alana off her feet. She rolled over, drove her fist into Alana's temple, then tried to push herself to her feet.

Alana growled as Mariska got to all fours and dived for Mariska's midsection, crashing them both into the railing. Mariska grabbed the shoulders of Alana's vest and launched a knee into her stomach.

Mariska lunged at Alana, who swiped her knife from inside Guardian's hood. She drew it along Mariska's neck.

"Fuck," Mariska muttered, wincing in pain.

Alana came at her again in a blur. Mariska threw up her forearm and cried out as it sliced deeply into her already injured arm. She landed her other palm in Alana's damaged nose.

Alana's head snapped back, then she grabbed around Mariska's neck, driving her backwards. Mariska felt her feet slip on the slick boards, her back connected with the railing, and she toppled over it.

Mariska did a full flip in midair and managed to shoot out her hands to grab the lower level of the pier. She held fast to keep from plunging into the icy water below. Panic overtook her as her numbing hands threatened to slip.

She was in trouble.

She looked up and saw Alana peering at her. Alana leaned over, and Mariska swung a fist up and crunched it into Alana's jaw.

Mariska let out a yell as she pulled herself over the railing. She was thrown backwards with a jump kick to the sternum, nearly taking her off her feet.

THE HOOD FELL from Mariska's face and Alana could see the blood that poured from a gash across her cheek. The haunted look Alana so wanted to remove from Mariska's eyes was more intense than she'd ever seen it.

And she had been the one to put that look in her eyes.

She had increased the suffering of the one person she truly loved and wanted to protect.

A fierce cry tore through the night air. Alana grunted as Mariska tackled her full on. Mariska wrapped strong arms around her midsection as they scudded backwards. Alana slammed into the railing, the wood giving way. Suddenly, they were airborne.

Christ, here we go again.

Alana tried to pull free of Mariska's grasp as they fell. Mariska held on as if she was determined to take Alana with her if this meant the end of both of them.

Alana felt a grudging respect for that, even as they crashed into the icy water and the world went black around her.

THEY HIT THE water, the force of the impact breaking Mariska's grip on Alana. She spun around, her sense of spatial awareness shot to hell as she tried to figure out which way was up. The inky black water blended seamlessly into the dark night sky. She blinked around in a panic that she didn't know where Alana was either.

Lisa, if you're watching, I could use a hand here.

Mariska kicked without direction, hoping she was headed to the surface. She broke through the water and took a deep breath, only to be submersed as a tall wave washed over her. She could see the shore, not far off, but far enough. She looked around, treading water, trying to ignore the dull ache in her legs as her heavy boots threatened to drag her down.

Where was Alana? Did she survive the impact? Alana's body had been the first to break the water and take the brunt of their landing.

"Alana?" she called out, her voice a hoarse whisper as the cold water pressed against her chest. She cleared her throat. "Alana!"

Nothing but the sound of the waves crashing against her. Mariska clicked on the flashlight in her belt and dove under the surface.

She found nothing on the first dive or the second. She became frantic with her need to find Alana. She had to know. Frigid waves crashed down on her as she swam the length of the pier, hoping to find something, anything, even as her body protested. Her brain knew she had to get out of the water. She was nearly numb, hypothermia was settling in. But her thoughts pushed her onward. She couldn't leave without knowing.

A large wave crashed and pitched her nearly limp body towards shore. She slipped under the water and swallowed sea water. This was bad. She summoned the last of her strength and pushed her head above the surface.

She coughed to expel the water in her lungs and sucked in more in her struggle to keep her head above the surface. She wasn't more than thirty feet from the water's edge.

Mariska could feel the hypothermia play with her consciousness. Spots danced in her vision, and the darkness itself seemed to be moving. And she could have sworn the waves themselves were saying her name, calling to her.

She would close her eyes for a moment's rest, then start back up again. She just needed a minute. She stopped kicking, stopped struggling against the water that kept calling her name as it enveloped her in its icy embrace. She felt her body slip under the surface, powerless to stop it, and not certain she would have if she could. Lisa was gone. Alana was gone. It was so easy to let go. And she was so very tired.

"Oh no you don't." A strong voice penetrated the water. Firm hands were around her biceps, pulling her to the surface. "Mariska! Mariska, open your eyes, stay with me."

"The waves . . ." Mariska mumbled. They were talking to her, holding her . . . shaking her?

"Mariska! Look at me, dammit. C'mon, don't you dare die on me."

Mariska opened her eyes. Her vision was blurred as she looked at her saviour, blond hair framing blue eyes. Eyes that she knew almost better than her own. Eyes that were so like his sister's that, for one brief wonderful moment, she could swear Lisa was staring at her.

"Luke?"

"Yeah, it's me," he said as he held her in one arm and used the other keep them afloat. "I figured it was about time I saved you for a change." He held her close to his chest as he swam on his back towards shore.

"'Lana . . . she wen . . . went in . . .'" Mariska's mouth and brain fumbled to find words. "Hav . . . have to f-find her." She felt a pause in Lucas's kicks before he continued on.

"She's gone, Mariska. I saw you both go into the water from the highway. She never surfaced. She's gone."

Mariska let out a choked sob as she held tightly on Lucas's strong arm. She had known it was a possibility and for a few raged-filled moments, she had wanted it to end this way. Lisa, Lucas, all those other people avenged. Stella dead and Guardian the victor.

She didn't feel very victorious.

Mariska slumped against Lucas as he dragged them towards the water's edge. They made it just beyond the water and Lucas's legs gave out, unable to support them both any longer. Mariska hit the sand with a groan, her body shivering as it tried to create heat.

"H-how . . . you f-find me?" she asked as he pulled her to him and rubbed her arms to bring the blood back into them. It wasn't helping much, they were both soaked and the sand was leeching whatever warmth they had left.

"I had a lock on your GPS when you cut communications. I couldn't let you face her alone, I couldn't lose another sister to that . . . woman," he said, his blue eyes blazing. "Sorry, I'm late."

Mariska saw the conflicting emotions in his eyes, the worry, the guilt, and something bordering on satisfaction as he looked out at the churning dark water.

"You . . . You're r-right on t-time."

EPILOGUE
Identity

" . . . WAS A VICTIM of the gang violence that swept across the city last winter. Rumours of a vigilante patrolling the streets during the crime wave have been continuously denied by the police, despite numerous eyewitness accounts. Anyone with information . . ." Mariska picked up the remote, changed the channel, and settled it on the football game before turning back to the stack of glasses her bus boy had left on the counter.

Two months.

Two months since Guardian had brought down STELLA.

Two months since she and Alana had gone off the pier and into the icy waters below.

Mariska put the glass down and braced herself against the bar, trying to fend off the sting of tears. She took in a deep breath and exhaled, repeating the process until she found her center. She'd been doing a lot of that lately. She wished she could convince herself that she had done the right thing. That the only way that night could have ended was with one of them dead, and she should be grateful she came out on top. Her mind wouldn't allow it. She constantly found herself replaying the battle through her mind, looking for some split second that would have allowed her to bring Alana in alive.

This was the hardest part. She knew that eventually the replays would slow and then stop altogether. It had been the same with Lisa in the warehouse. That didn't make it any easier. Not with the pain so fresh in her mind. Not when she still reached out for Alana at night.

"Breathe, Rish, just breathe," she murmured, trying to compose herself.

"You all right?"

Mariska looked up at Nina sitting on the stool across from her. She nodded, giving her a small smile of reassurance. It had been disconcerting when Nina first showed up at her bar. Mariska worried that she had somehow discovered her identity, knew that she was Guardian. But no, Nina lived in the neighborhood and just stopped in for a beer after a hard shift.

Mariska found she liked Nina. The somewhat gruff persona Nina wore with her badge seemed to peel away when she sat conversing with Mariska or the other patrons. She'd become a regular during the last month. She often engaged Mariska in conversation or simply sat at the corner of the bar, reading through the newspaper, subtly glancing at Mariska as she worked on her drink.

Mariska knew enough to recognize the signs of a crush when she saw one. Lucas had commented on as much when he had come in to keep her company. Seeing Nina's interest, he'd been quietly hinting that maybe Mariska should try to dip her feet back in the dating pool. Mariska quickly vetoed the idea.

That was the last thing she needed. Going from dating a criminal mastermind to dating an officer on the police force that was salivating to get a chance at bringing her in. She didn't think Nina would trade Guardian for a promotion, but she also hadn't thought her last girlfriend was some kind of mistress of mayhem either. Besides, a cop and a vigilante? The drama attached to that would be enough to fill a book.

"You sure you're okay?" Nina asked again. "You look like you've got something heavy on your mind."

"I'm all right, really," Mariska said, refilling Nina's beer. "Thanks for asking, though."

Nina nodded and returned to her paper as Mariska resumed drying the glasses. Mariska's phone rang in her back pocket, and she gave a small sigh of relief for being pulled from her morose thoughts.

"Ray, could you finish this?" Mariska asked the bar back, already on her way out from behind the bar. She slung her dish towel over her shoulder and clicked on the phone as she headed for the back door. Her regulars were seated at the bar, nursing their beers as they chatted about the game, all of them acknowledging her as she passed. She touched a friendly hand to their shoulders as she walked past them into the kitchen.

"What's up?" she asked as she hip checked the back door open.

"Big drug deal in a bar on Dufferin tonight. I'd send Brooke in for a recon field test, but it looks like they may have connections to the remnants of STELLA."

"I thought most of them were already in jail," Mariska said, searching her memory for anyone who may have escaped arrest. The cops had been sweeping most of them up over the last couple of months.

Without Alana to lead and protect them, they had gotten sloppy. No one had stepped into the power vacuum. As far as Mariska or Lucas knew, what was left of the group was slowly dying.

"Most of them are, but it seems there was a decent little warehouse that was missed and they're trying to offload the product," Lucas said. "How are your ribs?"

Mariska touched her hand to her rib cage and pressed firmly to test them. They were fine. They'd been fine for nearly a month now. It hadn't been her body keeping her off the streets and Lucas knew it. After that night at the pier, Mariska nearly let her grief, her guilt overtake her again. Lucas pulled her through as he always had and together they put the pieces of her life back in place. All except this one.

Mariska hadn't been able to go back to the streets. Hadn't been able to put enough trust in herself to keep others safe. She had debated not going back to the streets at all. Simply let Guardian die in the dark depths with Alana. She couldn't. Too much had been lost and there was still so much more to do before she could hang up her mask for good.

"Rish, you still there?"

"I'm on it. I'll come in and gear up. Call Brooke in. I'll take her with me, as long as she's finished her English paper."

"It's done. I read hers and Alexis's over last night while they ran laps."

The girls had become part of their family. A vigilante's slightly twisted version of family. They would never have a house with a white picket fence and a dog named Rover but they took care of each other and it worked.

Shy little Alexis had become Lucas's shadow at the computers, eager to learn whatever Lucas had to teach. Even Brooke, the typical stormy teenager, had mellowed somewhat, settling in nicely once she realized the rug wasn't about to be pulled out from under her.

"You sure you're ready for this? I could just tip Nina to the deal and let the cops handle it."

"No, it's okay," Mariska said. She had to get back on the horse sometime and cleaning up what was left of STELLA's mess was as good a place as any. "I'll be over as soon as Delia comes in to take her shift."

Mariska said goodbye to Lucas and left the quiet alley for the din of the bar. Her bar. She had been surprised when a registered letter showed up at her apartment the day after Alana's disappearance. It had been signed and dated the night before and within it was a receipt from the bank for her business loan. Paid in full by Alana Pierce.

Alana had paid off Mariska's debts—all of them—and signed the bar over to her. Mariska wasn't certain how Alana had set so much in place so quickly. Her condo had been sold. She had resigned from her company. Even her accounts had been closed, the money transferred to an account of which Mariska was the sole executor. It seemed that, even if Alana had won on that dark night, she had planned to leave Toronto for destinations unknown. It was odd. As Alana had been plotting to kill her, she had been just as careful in planning for Mariska's well-being, should Mariska be the victor. It was these two sides of her had that made it so hard to reconcile the Alana she loved with the criminal who had so terrorized Mariska and her city.

Mariska wondered if such a dichotomy existed within herself. She didn't think so. Perhaps it had once, when being Guardian had been a choice. But now, with so many sacrifices behind her—Lisa, Alana—she could no more put the mask down than she could stop breathing.

No matter what else came, her duty to the city, to the innocent people in it, would come above all else. This was the job. This was who she was. The Guardian.

About the Author

Born in Montreal, Quebec and having had her fill of infant poutine, Terias MvKlay moved to various locations in Alberta where she tipped cows, joined the army, and learned to drink beer. In an attempt at higher education, Terias headed back east to Toronto, Ontario to attain her bachelor's degree in Sociology Honours. When working a research job didn't produce the expected results of creating a league of super villains, Terias moved on to more physical ventures. She currently holds a personal training certificate and spends her days moulding her clients to be her personal super soldiers.

Enjoying the adventures in her mind more than attending class, Terias caught the writing bug in high school and never seemed to shake that monkey from her back. After a few failed starts, she's now ready to unleash her first novel, *The Surrender*, on an unsuspecting world. Terias' non-writing time is divided between playing rugby for the Yeomen Lions, playing Batman: Arkham Asylum, or regenerating in her sleep pod.